# SHAYLA'S DOUBLE

## BROWN BABY BLUES

Lori Aurelia Williams

*Simon & Schuster*

*New York  London  Toronto  Sydney  Singapore*

ALSO BY LORI AURELIA WILLIAMS
*When Kambia Elaine Flew in from Neptune*

SIMON & SCHUSTER BOOKS FOR YOUNG READERS
An imprint of Simon & Schuster Children's Publishing Division
1230 Avenue of the Americas, New York, New York 10020
Copyright © 2001 by Lori Aurelia Williams
All rights reserved including the right of reproduction
in whole or in part in any form.
SIMON & SCHUSTER BOOKS FOR YOUNG READERS
is a trademark of Simon & Schuster.
Book design by Paul Zakris
The text for this book is set in 11.5-point Goudy.
Printed in the United States of America
10 9 8 7 6 5 4 3 2 1

Library of Congress Cataloging-in-Publication Data

Williams, Lori Aurelia.
Shayla's double brown baby blues / by Lori Aurelia Williams.
p. cm.
Summary: Thirteen-year-old Shayla is upset when her estranged father's
new baby is born on her birthday, but she learns that her problems are
nothing compared to those faced by her friends Kambia and Lemm.
ISBN 0-689-82469-6
[1. Family life—Fiction. 2. African Americans—Fiction. 3. Emotional
problems—Fiction. 4. Alcoholism—Fiction.] I. Title.
PZ7.W66685 Sh 2001
[Fic]—dc21                                                    00-052221

This book is dedicated to the memory of my best friend, Manuel, who taught me how to see a spring shower in the middle of a hurricane.

It is also for my friend Robert, who is both kind and brave enough to be the first reader of all my work; my sister Lydia, who often pulls me over those hills and mountains that get in my way; my brother, John, who offered to set up a stand at his job and sell my first book (if nobody bought it); and finally, my sister Lisa, who spends her leisure time crocheting hats for cancer patients, never realizing that our greatness is often achieved through the smallest things we do.

Many, many thanks and much praise to my editor, David Gale, who helps me buff out all the rough spots; my agent, Barbara Ryan; and all of the readers who purchased and loved *When Kambia Elaine Flew in from Neptune*.

# Chapter 1

A daughter was born last Saturday night to Mr. Anderson Fox, my so-called father, and his new wife, Jada. She came into this world at 11:35 P.M. on the exact day that I was born thirteen years ago. Her mother named her Gift, Gift Marie. It was a name that popped into her head the day after she took a bad tumble down Peachtree Hill. She was on her way to Bobby's New Fish Shack to get his all-you-can-eat catfish platter. It was raining, and the heel of her leather pump just slipped right out from underneath her. Before she knew it, she had rolled headfirst down the slick hill and landed on her belly in a patch of soggy bluebonnets. She was pretty messed up. Two of the brothers that worked down at the shack had to pick her up. They drove her to the emergency room with Gift cramping something terrible in her stomach. In fact, Gift continued to cause her a lot of pain long after she was admitted to the hospital. The doctors said that Gift wasn't doing too well inside her stomach. All kinds of things were torn loose. Gift had to come out.

They took her out four weeks early. She was quiet and sickly, and refused to take her mother's breast. The doctors and nurses didn't expect her to make it through the night. They were pretty sure that before dawn broke the next morning, the Shadow of Death would be walking across her face.

But things didn't happen the way anyone expected. The next morning little Gift was lively and well. She had fought and kicked her way through the night with a determination that the hospital staff said they had never seen in a baby as beat up as she was.

"It's a miracle," one of the nurses told Jada. "She truly is a gift from God." Apparently Jada thought so too—that's why she named her Gift, but I don't think that she's a present.

This morning when Grandma made me go with her to visit Gift at the hospital, all I saw was a tiny bundle of wrinkled tan skin, short, curly black hair, and deep brown doe eyes. It was those eyes that made me shudder. Even from birth I could tell that they were special eyes. They were dissecting eyes, eyes that could take all the pieces of you apart, examine them, and put them back together to tell a story, your story. They were the eyes of a writer, my eyes.

As I stood there staring at them behind the nursery viewing window it occurred to me that Mr. Anderson Fox had found yet another slick-as-okra way to get over. He couldn't find a way to play me like he had played Mama, so he had just tossed me aside and created a new model. He wouldn't rebuild the fences that he had torn down with me. He would just put up new ones with Gift. I didn't want to, but I felt angrier than I had ever felt in my life watching him with his big toothy grin, sitting in an oversize rocker, holding her up high for all the world to see. He held her tenderly, his huge hands cradling the back of her head gently, as if she were as fragile as a baby sparrow. His searchlight eyes were beaming with pride, something that they had never beamed with for me. It was more than I could stand, and even though I knew that it would make Grandma madder than a bull in a rodeo, I backed away from the window and started to leave.

But as soon as I walked away from her side, Mr. Anderson Fox handed Gift to a friendly-looking nurse and raced out of the side door to meet me, still wearing his paper nursery-room gown. I sped up, but he caught up to me as I reached the double doors of the elevator. As usual, I didn't want him to know that he had any power over my feelings at all. I took a deep breath and pulled my mouth into my fake daughter smile.

"Did you see her?" he asked excitedly. "Did you see her?"

I nodded my head. "Yes, Daddy, I saw her," I replied softly. "I saw her."

"She something else, ain't she?" he asked, his big toothy grin spreading wide across his smooth face in an earnest smile for maybe the first time in his life. "Ain't she special? Don't you think she the cutest baby you ever seen?"

"Aw, I don't know, Daddy. I guess she's all right for a baby. You know, at that age they all kinda look alike. It's not that much to see."

"You don't think so, really?" he asked. His smile fell for just a moment, but a second later it was right back up. He glanced back at the nursery. "Naw, she's special. She different from all them other babies in there. You can tell. Just look at her. They ain't got nothing on her." He turned back to me. "You'll see. Your sister gonna be something great. Before you know, she gonna rule the world, have everybody doing what she say."

"I guess, Daddy," I said, desperately reaching for the elevator button. "I guess."

"Yeah, she gonna rule the world," he repeated. "I tell you it's something. I was hoping for a boy, but I'm pretty glad I got me another baby girl. Ain't that nice? You having another sister, a little sister. Now you gonna be able to teach her stuff just like your sister, Tia, taught you." He broke into a fit of laughter. "You know what? You can even teach her about that writing stuff. Your mama say you real good at that. Maybe you can teach her about that. It'll be good, you and her doing the same thing."

"It would be great," I lied. I looked away for a moment and

stared up at the glowing red light over the double elevator doors. I swallowed hard again. The elevator wasn't the only thing with buttons that were lighting up red. My buttons were lighting up too. I could feel Mr. Anger making his way into my eyes in his anger suit. "I gotta go, Daddy. I got some stuff I need to do today. I told Mama that I would help her out with some things."

"Are you sure?" he asked, actually looking disappointed. "The baby is doing real well. They not gonna hook her up to anything else. Maybe I can see if they'll let you hold her."

*No, I don't want to hold her, not now or ever!* I heard Mr. Anger shout, but I just looked away again.

I glanced down the hall past Grandma and several goofy-acting adults lined up in front of the glass windows waving and making funny faces at the mostly sleeping infants. I saw Jada, wearing a gown similar to Mr. Anderson Fox's, being wheeled toward the nursery by a heavyset nurse with a dingy white uniform that looked like it could use a dip or two in bleach. I felt like rolling my eyes and screaming at Jada that she had no right to create Gift, but there was no way that I would actually do it.

Even though I was still up against a rock on how I felt about Mr. Anderson Fox, I was pretty sure that I liked Jada. She was young, really young, barely twenty-four. She was a smart, petite sister with looks that any chick would be seriously envious of, but she wasn't stuck on herself or anything. She didn't dis other girls or act like she was better than them. She wasn't like that. She was really down-to-earth, kind to everyone. She even helped out twice a month at a new homeless food bank in her hood. She cooked vegetables, washed pans, and even mopped up after everyone else was gone. Everything about her was really cool. The few times that Grandma had dragged me over to her house to see Mr. Anderson Fox, she had been very polite and friendly. She had even asked me about myself and listened while I told her, something Mr. Anderson Fox had never done. "Anderson didn't tell me that you liked to write. He told me that he thought you wanted to be a nurse or something. Good for you. It's always great to have a dream. I'd love to hear some of your stories sometime," she said in a voice that sounded so sincere it immediately won both me and Grandma over. In fact, Jada has pretty much won all of us over, even Mama, who's still put out with Mr. Anderson Fox for playing her and pretending that he wanted to get back together with her.

"She's a good girl," Mama said the first time that she met her. "She's much better than your daddy deserves, and that's a fact, but according to your grandma, the Bible says that God smiles on the bad and the good alike."

I couldn't be mad at Jada. It wasn't her fault that she fell in love with Mr. Anderson Fox. I'm not sure whose fault it was. I pushed the elevator button again. A loud *ding* sounded and the door whooshed open. A serious-looking doctor with a coarse beard and stern, dark eyes stepped off. He muttered a low hello and pushed past me. I returned the greeting and stepped through the open doors.

"Good-bye, Daddy," I said. "I'll see ya later."

Mr. Anderson Fox opened his mouth to say something more, but Grandma hollered and cut him off. "Wait up, Shayla," she yelled, coming up the hall in her flowered duster, shaking her cane. "Don't you go nowhere without me." I placed my hand in the door to keep it from closing and waited for her to join me. She hobbled up shortly. "Anderson, your wife is asking for you," she said to Mr. Anderson Fox. "You better go see what she want."

"Okay," Mr. Anderson Fox said. "I'll be right there. How you doing?"

"Oh, I guess I ain't about to slip away. Ain't nothing on me completely broke down. So I figure I'm doing all right." She pointed her finger at him. "That's a fine baby your wife done give you. You treat her well. You treat her like a child ought to be treated."

"Don't you worry about that. Don't you worry about that at all. She'll be well looked after. I'll see y'all later. And don't forget, y'all come by and see the baby as much as you want." He took a few quick steps down the hallway and turned back. "Ain't it great? You and your little sister having the same birthday. Ain't that funny? Who woulda seen something like that coming. Life sure is strange sometimes." He winked one of his searchlight eyes at me. "Yeah, it's great," he said happily, starting to walk off down the hallway again. "Yeah, it really is great."

Grandma Augustine stepped into the elevator and the door slid closed. I pushed a button that said GROUND and the car started to descend.

"Yeah, it's freaking great," I said under my breath. "It's just freaking great."

"You be careful," Grandma said sternly. "I seen the way that you were looking at that baby. You ain't being right. That child is your sister, and I know that you don't like it, but she ain't going nowhere. It may not be fair, but she got as much right to life as you do. Don't let your feelings for your daddy get in the way of you having feelings for her. Do you understand me?"

I bit my tongue and looked down at my feet. Of course I understood her. I knew that Gift had a right to life. I just didn't think that she had a right to mine. She had no right to my birthday, no right to my eyes, and no right to the father that I wasn't even sure I wanted. I just couldn't believe it. I had never seen Mr. Anderson Fox so happy. Grandma was right. It wasn't fair. Gift should have been born into her own life, not mine. Because of Gift misery was spreading through me like a virus.

"Grandma, I don't want to talk about it," I mumbled. "Just leave it alone, okay? She may be his daughter, but she's no sister of mine."

Grandma shook her head. The elevator slowly eased to a stop on a street-level floor located beneath the hospital. The doors started to slide open, but she reached over and pushed the green Close Door button and they slid back together again. She placed her callused hand on my arm. I continued to stare at my feet.

"Baby, this is only a little rain," she whispered soothingly. "That's all it is. It's just a little rain, no more. Don't you turn it into a storm. Don't you let them dark clouds hover over you and block out all of the good in you. You knew this was coming. You had eight months to know that that child was gonna be here. Now she's here."

"On my birthday," I mumbled. "Why couldn't she have been born on her own day?"

Grandma started to rub my arm lightly. "I'm sorry, sugar," she said. "Like I said, I know this ain't fair. But trust me, baby. There ain't too much that is."

"Grandma, I said that I didn't want to talk about it," I repeated. I pushed the Open Door button. The doors slid aside to reveal a packed doctors' parking lot filled with shiny, new-looking cars. Nailed to a concrete pillar in the center of the lot was a metal sign with the words THIS WAY TO BUS STOP. I stepped out of the elevator and started toward it, but Grandma caught me by the shoulder.

"You know," she said, starting one of her childhood stories, "when I was a little girl growing up back there in Deer County, Texas, I had the same kinds of dreams as other little girls. I wanted just what they wanted."

"Grandma," I whined loudly.

"I wanted just what the other girls wanted," she continued. "Even though I was a shy little thing, and not much interested in boys, I dreamed of growing up, getting me a fine man, and having me a big, beautiful wedding, like most of the girls in my town. On the day of my wedding I would be something really special, something great, like a princess or a queen."

"Grandma, what does this have to do with anything?" I snapped. "We're going to miss the bus."

"Wait just one minute, missy. You just let me say what I got to say first. Anyhow," she continued, "things went just like I wanted. I fell in love with your grandfather. He was a good man, and not too long after we starting courting, he asked me to go down the aisle with him. I couldn't wait. It was just what I wanted. I planned and planned and planned. I had it all—a lovely gown made from cloth taken from my own grandma's wedding dress, six pretty bridesmaids, a nice big three-layer cake, plenty of homemade decorations, and several beautiful flower arrangements. I was ready to be a wife. I had everything set, but then things fell apart."

"What happened?" I asked, trying to hurry things along.

"Well, there wasn't but one colored church in Deer County," she said. "It was the only place where black folks could exchange vows. It was a fine church, but it was tiny and hand-me-down poor, with just one room and an old outhouse in the back. It was barely big enough to turn around in, and because of it we couldn't get no steady preacher. There just wasn't enough money to pay him, and no place for him to sleep. Even a man of God got to eat and have some place to live. Only John the Baptist could get away with eating locusts and sleeping under the stars."

"Grandma," I whined again. "Hurry up."

"I'm getting there, baby. Well, since we didn't have no coins to toss at his feet, all we could get was a little preacher with hair about as gray as mine. He lived in another town miles away. He came every other month and stayed just as long as it took to make sure that folks knew what path they were supposed to be taking. He was a good man, a kind old fellow who did everything from marrying to burying to settling squabbles between folks, and he did it for absolutely nothing."

"That's good, Grandma. Thanks for the story, but I'm going."

She tightened her grip on my arm. "No, you ain't. You just let me finish. I'll pull things together for you directly," she said. "It was three days before my wedding when the tomatoes started to rot. Old Mr. Murdy, who lived down by Bluefish Creek, was on his way home from a coon hunt when he had a heart attack and fell plumb dead right out in the woods, in the middle of one of the worst floods we had ever had in Deer County. It was two long days before anybody could get to him, and by then he looked pretty bad. He had to be put in the ground, and soon. It just wasn't no two or three ways about it. His funeral had to be the next day. My wedding day."

"I'm sorry, Grandma," I said softly, and I genuinely started to feel sorry for her.

"You," she said, shaking her head. "Lord, I cried and cried and cried. I swear I cried more tears than the water that fell from that storm. Things went from perfect to just a big ole mess in such a short while—and it was too late too call it off. Mama and her sisters had cooked up a ton of wedding food, and Christian kinfolk had come from all over Texas to see a church wedding. Good grief, I called old Murdy everything that I could think of. I even wished that he would end up in hell, instead of heaven, but it didn't make no difference. On the day of my wedding your granddaddy and I stood in the center of the aisle and said our 'I do's' with Mr. Murdy's casket just a baby step away. I was pure broke down by the whole thing. I really wished that I was the one that was going into the ground instead of him.

"But here's the thing. On the way out of the church my mama took me aside and told me just what I'm about to tell you. 'No day belongs to you. They all belong to the Almighty. He decides what happens and what don't happen on his day, you don't. Now, you just remember that and be glad for what you got, 'cause you didn't have to have nothing.' Ain't nothing promised to you, baby," she said, rubbing my arm again. "I know that you still ain't got much for God and all, so let me just repeat: This is only a little rain in your life. Don't you make it into a storm. You deal with this like you deal with everything else—with a level head and common sense. You can get through this, sugar. It ain't the end of the world. It ain't the end of anything. Don't worry about the things that you can't change."

"All right, it's okay, Grandma," I lied, not wanting to hurt her after she had shared such a sad tale. "I see your point. Like you said, it's not the end of the world. I won't worry," I said, starting off through the parking lot. "I promise I won't."

But I did worry; in fact, on the humid, un-air-conditioned bus ride back to the neighborhood, worry is all I did. I sat quietly in my vinyl seat staring through the foggy bus windows at the blistering summer sun and thinking about Gift. Grandma didn't understand. It wasn't just that I was upset with Gift's birth. Gift had stirred up too many questions in me. What did it really mean that she was born on the same day as me? Who was I supposed to be now? I didn't know. Grandma hadn't thought about bringing it up, but yes, there had been other daughters born to Mr. Anderson Fox before Gift. I personally knew of at least three, all with Mr. Anderson Fox's smooth brown skin, sculpted cheekbones, and big toothy grin. They were the daughters that he had had with other unlucky women who had been foolish enough to fall for his baby-I'm-all-you-need charm, like Mama. But they weren't true Shaylas. They were all imitations—until now, until Gift, born with my eyes, on my day, to take my place. She was different from the others. Mr. Anderson Fox had never really claimed any of them, hardly even knew their names, but he knew Gift's. He was proud of her. She was his new Shayla, the one that he could shape and mold into anything that he wanted, the one that would be happy to call him Daddy.

I pulled up the tail of my cotton T-shirt and fanned it back and forth. For a moment I imagined myself burning up from the heat, my flesh melting, sliding from me like candle wax, my bones turning into ash and blowing away like Kambia used to say she could do when she had on her magic purple bracelet. Would I still be me afterward? Would there still be a Shayla? Up until this morning I would have said no, but I couldn't anymore. I wiped my sweaty brow with the back of my hand and tried to project myself to a nicer place; lately it would have been school. I had volunteered for a special summer-school program for smart kids, and I really liked it, but things were kind of a mess there, too.

The mess was Lemm Turley, the new boy in the Bottom, our hood. He was from a small town somewhere in Texas. He was my homeroom buddy, assigned by my teacher, Mrs. Luna, who thought that it would be a nice idea for me to show him around, since I was one of the best scholars at our school.

He was the same age as me, okay looking with a cleft chin, a small overbite, and intense chestnut eyes. He was totally smart, and he would have been cool, but he was an "always kid": always on time for school, always knew all the right answers to questions, always volunteering to help hand out materials, always eager to share his school supplies. He also had kind of a charm rap like Mr. Anderson Fox that he used on everyone, but it mostly worked on the girls and the female teachers, especially the older ones. He was forever complimenting them on their hair, makeup, and clothes, telling them how attractive they were, using really proper speech. "Oh, you look darling today, Ms. Sanders," he would say to our elderly music teacher. "Your gray hair reminds me of silvery moonlight." Or "Aren't you a dear," he would say to Ms. Edwards, our aging librarian. "Your face is more beautiful than a love poem." He laid it on as often and as thick as he could when he saw the senior ladies, sometimes even telling them that he just didn't understand why they had settled for being teachers when they could have been models, actresses, or even movie stars. My stomach hurt every time I heard one of the fake statements come out of his mouth. Sometimes I made gagging noises behind his back, but I would never have considered making them to his face.

The truth of the matter is I felt a little sorry for Lemm. According to the neighborhood, he had had a pretty crappy life. He was the only surviving child of three children, the other two kids having been a pair of younger twin girls. Lemm's mother ran off two years ago when the twins were born. Folks say that for some strange reason she just went stone crazy after their birth. She didn't want to breast-feed either one of them, refused to pick them up, and turned a deaf ear when they cried. She said that she just couldn't handle being a wife and a mother anymore, said she felt all tied up inside, like there was something holding her down, and no matter how hard she struggled, she couldn't get free. So she just up and left one Monday morning while Lemm was at school. She walked right out of the door, leaving her babies in their bassinets, wet and screaming.

After she left, Lemm's father took to drinking. He was messed up over his wife leaving, so Lemm got stuck taking care of the twins. He dropped them off at day care before he went to school, and picked them up when he got home. He was both father and mother, the only one that they could count on to bring them a bottle during the night.

But one afternoon things went from bad to worse. One of the babies at the twins' day care came down with something really nasty, and the rest of the kids had to be picked up immediately. Lemm's class was away on a field trip, so the school called his dad instead. Although he was smashed, Lemm's dad made it to the school just fine that afternoon, and the teachers were in such a hurry to get all of the kids out that they either just didn't notice the state that he was in or simply ignored it because he was only walking home a few blocks with the twins. However it went down, they thought that his taking the twins would be okay. They were wrong. One block from the school Lemm's dad thought that he saw his wife standing in front of a butcher shop across the street from him and stepped right out into the middle of traffic with the twins. A pickup truck plowed into all three of them. Lemm's dad made it, but the twins didn't.

Folks say that the judge wanted to give Lemm's dad a whole bunch of time, but there would have been nobody left to take care of Lemm, so he just gave him several years of probation and ordered him to get off of the drink. They say that he quit drinking the very afternoon of his sentence, but it didn't make much difference because a part of his mind died with the twins. He couldn't even hold down a job, and he and Lemm have been living off government checks since the day he left the courthouse.

I felt real bad for Lemm when I heard the story. I didn't want to be his friend, but I refused to be his enemy.

I leaned my head back against the seat and tried to come up with some place to be other than school. It didn't work, so instead I just thought up a few lines to jot down in my journal when I got home. *Shaylas are being created like lizard tails*, I would write. *You can cut one off, and another will take her place.*

A few blocks from my house Grandma Augustine decided to stop at a discount fabric store. We got off the bus and spent the next three hours browsing through sewing catalogs. By the time we stepped through my gate, Mr. Anger was strutting around in my eyes like a school-yard bully just waiting for someone to go off on. I didn't want it to be Grandma, so I skirted past her on the porch steps, yanked open the front door, and went straight to my room. Once inside I took my blue notebook out of the drawer and scrawled down my note. After that I took a cool bath, dressed in a fairly nice linen dress that Mama had bought me at the Goodwill, gave my hair a lick or two with one of Tia's Afro combs, and walked back through the house.

I stopped and peeked into the kitchen. Mama and Tia had gotten up late as usual and were now having their regular afternoon brunch. It's a new tradition for them, actually eating together on Saturdays, trying to mend fences that years of quarreling have trampled down. "It's good," Mama said. "Me and your sister having a meal together without setting each other off. It's the way a mother and daughter should be. I'm really glad that we are starting to get along."

I was glad too. Last year when Tia and Mama had a big fight, and Tia ran off with her boyfriend, Doo-witty, I didn't think I would ever see them sitting together at the breakfast table again. Mama was really pissed at Tia for taking up with Doo-witty, and not just because Doo-witty was twenty-three and Tia was only fifteen. The thing that really tied Mama's hair in a knot was the fact that the entire neighborhood thought Doo-witty was just a big, slow dope who wasn't worth any girl's time, especially not Tia's. Tia was like Jada. She had a great body and a great mind. Tia could choose. Why on earth would she have chosen Doo-witty? Nobody knew—except Tia. Tia knew that Doo-witty was special.

It turned out that Doo-witty was actually a promising artist on his way up. He wasn't the brightest street lamp on the block, but he had skills, and those skills got him into a nice college. When Mama found out about it, she had to ease up on Tia and Doo-witty a little. She didn't like doing it much, but she told Tia just to be careful and protect herself, then she stepped back and let Tia be responsible for whatever cards she pulled from the deck.

I watched the two of them. Mama was sitting at the table in her navy blue grocery stocker's uniform. Her huge hands were shoved into a large silver mixing bowl, busily mixing sticky clumps of white biscuit dough. Tia was standing next to Mama, her catlike eyes watching every move of Mama's hands closely, like an apprentice learning cooking tips from a master chef. Tia was dressed in her strapless Hawaiian-print wrap dress. Her long black braids were tied back with a matching kerchief, and a pair of plastic earrings with pineapples on them clung to each ear. She looked like she was going to have brunch on some tropical island, instead of in our tiny kitchen. She was filling Mama in on what she and Doo-witty had done the night before. I caught a bit of the conversation, something about an art show over on the south side of town and a couple of hot dogs at the downtown Coney Island. "We had a really cool time, Mama," I heard her say. She seemed really happy, and so did Mama—but I wasn't. I walked away from the door and left them to their good times.

I stomped down the steps and left the yard. It was around one o'clock, and nearly everyone in the neighborhood was out. Rusty old cars teeming with smiling faces were zipping down the narrow road, filling the air with smelly exhaust, and clusters of slim teenage girls were gathered on the concrete steps of the paintless shacks weaving strands of fake blond and red hair into their own short, kinky black locks. A few of them waved hello as I passed by. I didn't bother returning the greeting.

I was on my way to see the one person who I knew could make me feel better—Kambia. She simply had to be in a much better mood than I was in. She had something to be in a good mood about. She had gone to school this summer too, and today was her graduation from the Girl Help Center, a girls' school located on the outskirts of our hood. It was run by what Grandma called "fallen redeemed saints," street-smart and educated women who had been locked down for doing all sorts of bad things when they were teens, but who had somehow managed to pull it all together when they got to be adults. They did everything from professional counseling to helping the girls find jobs.

Kambia had gone to the Girl Help Center at the suggestion of her social worker, Miss Sayer, and the police about three weeks after she got out of the hospital. They thought that it would be a good place for her. According to Grandma Augustine, the center was a school for girls who had had the innocence snatched right out of them. It was a private school that usually took only girls whose parents had a pretty good amount of cash to sponsor them, but every once in a while it took in a special little girl like Kambia.

The police say that Kambia is indeed a special and *unique* girl. She's a girl who seems to have an ending but no beginning. After several months of searching, the police still don't know where she came from, even though they've gone so far as to put her face on TV.

When I first found out that Kambia was going to the center, I wasn't happy about it at all. It meant that we wouldn't be in school together, and I had promised her that I would always be where she was to protect her, but Grandma Augustine made me see the light.

"That girl been torn up every which way a girl can be torn," she said. "She been hurt inside and out by that trashy Jasmine Joiner woman who called herself her mother, and them no-account men. It ain't gonna be easy, but she got to learn how to sew herself back together. You let her go, and let them ladies at the Girl Help Center show her how to do it. You let them show her how to help herself." And that's exactly what I did. I placed Kambia's hands in their hands, and I hoped for the best.

The best is what I got. The ladies at the Girl Help Center were really great with Kambia. They were patient with her and didn't seem to mind at all when she broke into one of her baby games. They made her go to sessions where they taught her how to say how she was feeling inside, and not hold it in until she couldn't stand it anymore and had to get away from it by creating one of her stories. One of the counselors even made her take a trip back to her old house to gather up her things, after the landlord said that he had held her and Jasmine Joiner's belongings long enough and was going to toss them out on the streets. When Kambia was removed from Jasmine Joiner's, she was way too sick to make the trip back for quite a while, and when she did get better, she was too afraid to go and refused to let me or her parents go either. For her, evil was still marching all over Jasmine's house like red ants, and she wanted to make sure that none of us got bitten. But the counselors at the Girl Help Center said that Kambia had to claim her old life before she could throw it away.

"That's the nature of evil," her lead counselor, Mrs. Dreyfus, a plump, tenderhearted woman with three teen girls of her own, said. "You must first get a firm grasp on it before you can push it away. Kambia has to face her Wallpaper Wolves, the men that hurt her, or she will never be rid of them."

"That's true," Grandma Augustine echoed when I told her about what Mrs. Dreyfus had said. "You have to first let the devil know that he got you by the thighbone before you can shake his hands off."

I guess that's what ran through Kambia's mind the day that me and Mrs. Dreyfus waited for her on the front porch of her former house. I guess she was thinking about getting in her wolves' faces for the first time and letting the devil know that she knew that it was really him that had sent them after her, but when she came out of the house, I just couldn't tell. There was a part of her that looked really beat down, like her Wallpaper Wolves had gotten off the wall and jumped her again, and yet another part of her looked like she had finally gotten the best of them. Tears were jumping out of her olive eyes in all directions, sliding down her flushed cheeks and onto her knit blouse, but her thin pink lips were pulled up into a loose smile, a real smile. It was as if happiness and anguish were going toe-to-toe in her soul and she wasn't sure which one deserved to win out.

"Shayla?" she asked, reaching behind her with her free hand to close the screen door. "Do you know why we cry more bad tears than good ones?"

I shook my head. "I don't know. I guess it's because we usually only cry when we're sad. I guess many of us are pretty happy most of the time," I said, reaching around to catch her hand as it pulled away from the door. It suddenly occurred to me that there was nothing in it. There was nothing in either one of her hands. I guessed there wasn't anything she actually wanted to take from the house. She just wanted to get rid of stuff, like Grandma and Mrs. Dreyfus said.

"That's part of it, Shayla," she said, blinking hard to free her eyes from tears.

"It's okay, Kambia," Mrs. Dreyfus said. "There's no shame in crying your pain away. We've all done it plenty of times." She pulled a crumpled tissue out of her jean-skirt pocket and handed it to Kambia. "Just let it all spill out, Kambia. It's good for you. Don't keep anything bottled up on the inside. Do you hear me?"

Kambia nodded. "Did you know that we are born with all the tears we'll ever cry?" she asked me, softly dabbing at the corners of her eyes. "All the tears that will ever pour from our eyes."

"No, I didn't. I didn't know that at all."

"It's true. There are good tears and bad tears, and we are born with all that we will ever have of both. The good tears live in Good-Tear Land," she said, leading me by the hand down the steps. "It's located way back in your head, deep inside the folds of your brain. It's a beautiful, shady place filled with babbling brooks bubbling over with cool lemonade, and fruit trees weighed down with juicy candy apples and chocolate bananas."

"It sounds delicious."

"It is. It's really a very neat, special place for the good tears. They have a very nice life. They live in tiny little houses made of golden thimbles, lined up neatly in a straight line along a street composed of crystal fairy footprints."

"Wow," I said.

"Really wow!" she said, stopping on the last step. "There's no school or work. The tears just lie around all day under the shade of the trees and eat fruit."

"I could live with that," Mrs. Dreyfus said. "Me and my girls could get along just fine there. But what about the bad tears?" she asked, playing along with Kambia's story. She took another Kleenex from her pocket and handed it to her. Kambia wiped a couple of tears from her nose.

"The bad tears don't have it so nice. They live in a really gross place where trees don't bear fruit at all. They are rotted-out stumps filled with ants and funny-looking termites. The only thing that grows on them is mold, and here and there a cluster of black, poisonous mushrooms. You know why?" she asked. Mrs. Dreyfus and I both shook our head.

"Because there's no sun," she said. "The weather is lousy. There are always thunderstorms that shoot out big bolts of lightning and huge boulders of hail that burn and crush most everything up before it gets a chance to grow."

"That is horrible. Imagine a place where nothing is ever green," I said.

"I know," she said. "And to make matters worse, the bad tears don't have fine houses to live in either. They live in dented thimbles that were once dropped and stepped on by gnomes. Their walkways are made of the termite-eaten wood from the trees, and since there's no fruit to keep them from going hungry, they have to go to Good-Tear Land and pick their fruit every day, all day long."

"Why every day? Why can't they just store some fruit up?"

"They can't," she said. "There's something really strange about Bad-Tear Land. Not only can nothing grow there, but nothing can stay fresh there either. I guess because it stays so damp. As soon as the bad tears bring the fruit back into their land, it turns into a clear powder, clear and tasteless. It can't be used for anything."

"Oh, that's pretty awful too," I said.

"Yes, it is," Kambia said. "It sort of reminds you of the manna that God sent from heaven to the Israelites. They could only keep it a day before it went bad."

"Only, Grandma says that God was really being good to them," I said. "It doesn't sound like anything good ever happens to the bad tears."

"Nothing does," she said. "They work from sunup till sundown each day, and they still have nothing to show for it. Their bitter life never ends. So now do you see why we cry more bad tears?"

I nodded. "Because the bad tears are just dying to get out of the place that they live."

"Exactly," she said. "When the Tear King, who rules both worlds, calls on volunteers to make the long journey to the front of your face and jump from your eyes, only to be wiped away forever, the bad tears always volunteer. They just figure that there can't be any place worse than where they are now. So they raise their tiny little hands first. That's why we cry a lot more when bad things upset us, because the bad tears don't mind coming out."

"I'm sure that's true, Kambia," I said, leading her down the concrete steps, with Mrs. Dreyfus following.

"Kambia, it's a nice story," Mrs. Dreyfus said. "But remember what we said about allowing stories to take the place of our true feelings?"

"I remember," Kambia said. "But I don't have any feelings in me today. I don't feel anything."

"Okay," Mrs. Dreyfus said. "You don't have to talk about anything right now if you don't want to."

"There's nothing to talk about," Kambia said. "I don't feel anything."

We reached her rickety old gate, and she turned back to her house for just a second. "There was nothing in there for me to get," she said. "I kinda thought there might be, but there wasn't. There wasn't one thing that I wanted to bring home with me."

"I figured that out," I said. "I guess I wouldn't want anything out of there either."

Mrs. Dreyfus briefly took Kambia's hand. "That's fine, Kambia. It's all right. You weren't really here to bring anything out. You were here to leave something. You went in and faced your wolves, and that's enough. Small steps," she said. "You just need to take small steps." She caressed Kambia's hand gently. "I was wrong. Today you can be in whatever world you need to be in. We'll try and sort everything out tomorrow."

Kambia blinked at her a few times, like she was processing what was just said, then she took my hand again. "Let's go, Shayla," she said.

We took a couple of steps, but she stopped again. "Do you think that another little girl will come to live here?" she asked. "Do you think that the new family will have a little girl?"

"I don't know," I said. "The landlord can rent it out to anybody. Maybe there will be another girl."

"I hope not," she said. "I really hope not. No little girl should live there. I really hope that another little girl doesn't come."

"So do I, Kambia," I said, reaching for the latch on the gate. "So do I." I opened the gate, and me and Mrs. Dreyfus walked Kambia back to her new place.

But that was months ago, when Kambia was still shaky. Today she is much steadier, stronger. She's aced all of her classes at the Girl Help Center and pretty much pulled herself out of her fantasy world. She hardly ever tells stories now. She's learned how to deal with things, and right now that's what I need. I need to her to tell me how to cope with Mr. Anderson Fox and his new me.

I got to the auditorium of the Girl Help Center before most of the crowd. There was only a skinny, baby-faced teen girl, with a starched white blouse and a new-looking navy skirt, standing in the arched doorway of the small concrete and smoked-glass building. I took a seat on an iron bench across from her and watched as she pulled a plastic Afro comb from her skirt pocket and began raking it through her short 'fro.

I was waiting for Kambia to show up. She had phoned me the night before and told me that she would be there early. She was going to give the welcome at the program today, and she wanted to try it out on me before the rest of the auditorium heard it. She said her mom and dad thought it was really good, but that they would probably say anything she wrote was good, so she wanted to read it in front of someone who would be really honest with her. I told her that I would always tell her the truth.

"I know," she said. "That's why I want you to hear it."

"Okay," I told her. "I'll tell you exactly how I feel about it."

"Great, Shayla," she said, and hung up the phone.

When Kambia finally showed up, the girl was yanking the comb through her 'fro for about the hundredth time, and I was glad to see her, because even though the girl didn't seem to be anywhere near bored with combing out her kinky locks, I was tired of watching her do it. I walked swiftly down the brick walkway to meet Kambia.

Like the girl, Kambia was dressed in white on the top and navy on the bottom in an outfit that I had never seen before—a soft, V-necked blouse with delicate lace around the tail and a full pleated skirt. Her reddish tan hair was parted on the side and pulled up into a ball made of very thin intertwined braids. Her fingernails were sparkling from a fresh coating of pearl polish, and her eyelids were sporting just a hint of light blue eye shadow that made her olive eyes look sea green in the bright sunlight. She was grinning like a prom queen. I suddenly felt very guilty about wanting to dump my troubles off on her on such a special day. I tried to put on the happiest face that I could and stuffed everything inside of me.

"What's up, Kambia?" I asked, throwing my arms around her. I hugged her hard, hoping her good mood would somehow seep into me. "How's it going?"

"Everything's fine, Shayla," she said, hugging me back. "Everything is just perfect and fine."

I let her go, and she pushed away from me a bit and begin posing, placing her hand on her hip and twirling as if she were a model at a big shoot.

"Look at me, Shayla," she said. "Look at me. Do you like my new outfit? My mom got it last night. She said that I needed something extra special to say my speech in today."

"It's pretty," I said excitedly.

She beamed. "It is, isn't it. I picked it out myself." She stuck her nails out. "And look, my mom did my nails, too. Oh, and my hair," she said, reaching up to pat her ball. My mom braided it real fine and then made me a ball."

"I like it," I said.

"You do? Guess what?" she squealed, and started to blink her eyes rapidly. "I got on some shadow, too. It's called Baby Boy Blue. We picked it out at the cosmetics counter in Walgreens."

"You look great, Kambia," I said, feeling some of the rage starting to drain from me. It was funny how just being around Kambia could do that for me, how just being in her presence could make Mr. Anger take off his red anger suit and hang it back up on the rack.

"You really look great!" I repeated, taking her hand and leading her back down the walkway toward the iron bench. "You look fabulous!"

While we sat on the bench waiting for the program to start and her parents to show up, Kambia read me her welcome. It was just how I thought it would be, well written and sweet. She thanked everybody she could think of for coming, even the caterers that were going to be providing food at the end.

As she read I allowed my mind to slip into another place. I imagined that she wasn't Kambia at all. She was Mr. Anderson Fox's Gift at thirteen. I imagined how proud Mr. Anderson Fox would be, sitting out in the audience listening to his favorite daughter give a speech to the entire school. How pretty he would tell everyone that she looked. How great he would say that she sounded. It felt so wonderful to be sitting there listening to his best girl.

Would Mr. Anderson Fox have felt so wonderful sitting and listening to me? I don't know. I never had the pleasure of looking out in the audience and seeing his big toothy grin. Maybe the pride from seeing that grin would have chased my stage fright away, made my words come out crisp and clear, instead of all jumbled up like they always did whenever I had to stand up in front of a crowd. That's what seeing his face might have done. It meant nothing to me now, though. I had learned how to face my onstage fears. I didn't need to see Mr. Anderson Fox's face in the audience. I didn't need to see his face anywhere.

I grinned at Kambia the way that I had once wanted Mr. Anderson Fox to grin at me—honest and sincere. "Your speech is just terrific, Kambia," I said. "It's the best speech that I ever heard."

By the time Kambia's parents showed up, along with Grandma Augustine, both Kambia and I could say her speech without looking at the paper.

"It sounds real good," Kambia's dad said as he walked over to us in a superbly starched pin-striped suit. He was a tall man, slender with a head of cotton and a neatly trimmed mustache to match. He had large deep brown eyes like Mr. Anderson Fox's, but they both went in the right direction. His skin was smooth and wrinkle-free, which made him look a lot younger than his fifty or so years. His real name was Jimmy Major, but folks called him Ten Fingers because he had been a really good piano player during his younger years.

Unlike Ten Fingers, his wife did not have a nickname. Her real name was Honeysuckle Peach, and that's what everybody called her, because they said she was so sweet that if you cut her, nectar would run out of her instead of blood. She was a small, frail woman with tiny bones who sometimes had to get around on a cane like Grandma Augustine, but she got around everywhere. Folks say that you could always find her at neighborhood gatherings helping out wherever she could and passing out some of her smack-your-mama homemade fudge. She had all of the wrinkles that her husband didn't get, but she was still a handsome woman, sienna colored with high cheekbones, shiny black eyes, and coal black hair that hung in ringlets down to her waist. Some people said that she was more Native American than black, and that her great-grandmother was either a Sioux or a Cherokee, a kind healing woman who went from town to town curing poor folks for as little as a cup of meal and a slab of salt pork.

However, none of this matters a pan of biscuits to Kambia. She doesn't care how Ten Fingers and Honeysuckle Peach came to be who and what they are, just that they are. When she goes to bed at night, they sit at her bedside until she falls asleep, and their faces are usually the first things that she sees each morning. They call her "daughter," not "Kambia" or "girl," just "daughter," as if she were a child that had actually been created from their love.

"Yes, it sounds real good, Daughter," Ten Fingers repeated. "It sounds like you got it all covered. Nobody is gonna leave without being thanked today. Everybody is gonna feel appreciated."

"They sure are," Honeysuckle Peach said, coming up and hugging Kambia. She was dressed similar to Kambia in a white and navy suit, except in reverse, with the darker color on the top. "It sounds real nice the way you put your words together, Daughter. I can't wait to hear you read it on the stage."

"Me, too," Ten Fingers said, patting Kambia on the back. "I can't wait to see my little light shine."

"You gonna do real, real good, baby," Grandma Augustine said, hobbling up on her cane with a big smile. "Don't you get even the slightest bit nervous. You gonna do just fine."

"Thank you, ma'am," Kambia said, blushing.

"You welcome, sugar," Grandma Augustine said. Then she turned to me with her usual strict look.

"How come you didn't let me and your mama know that you were leaving the house?" she asked. "When we couldn't find you nowhere, we was worried to death."

I shrugged my shoulders. "I told Mama last night that I was coming early," I mumbled. "Kambia wanted me to listen to her read her speech."

"Well, your mama sure didn't know nothing about it," she said, shaking her finger at me. "She didn't know where you had scrambled off to."

I shrugged my shoulders again. "She just forgot," I said. "I know I told her."

"She didn't forget . . . ," Grandma started out, but she stopped in midsentence, somehow seeing the sadness and anger in my face that I was desperately trying to hide from myself and Kambia. Pity poured into her watery eyes. "Oh, baby, Grandma Augustine's sorry. You know she didn't mean no harm." She pulled me to her huge bosom, burying my face in the folds of her red tent dress. "I'm sorry, baby. I'm so sorry. I know your morning was filled with blisters. I shoulda been cuddling you instead of blessing you out."

I pulled away from her quickly. "It's okay, Grandma. It's all right. I'm just fine," I said, determined not ruin Kambia's big day.

"Naw, no you ain't," she said, pulling me back to her. "You ain't at all, but you just remember what I said earlier today. It's just a little rain. Before you know it, the clouds will be all wrung out, and you won't even remember the drops that fell on your head."

"Okay, okay, Grandma. Everything is just fine," I mumbled into her chest, and pushed myself away from her once more. "I promise. I'm already over it. We don't have to talk about it anymore." I felt the bad tears lining up in the corners of my eyes like Kambia said they would, but I blinked real hard to hold them back. I wasn't much for bawling like a baby, and I sure didn't want to do it in front of Kambia. It wouldn't be right for my tears to stain her day.

"I wish everything were fine," Grandma said, shaking her silvery head. "It burns a hole clean through my soul when you're upset."

"What's she upset about?" Honeysuckle Peach asked Grandma. "What's wrong with the child?" She started to rub my back gently, her bony hands moving up and down my flesh. "Did somebody do you some harm, girl?"

"No. No, ma'am," I said, forcing my mouth into a smile. "I'm fine. There was just something that happened earlier, but I'm over it now."

"Are you sure?" Kambia asked in a troubled voice, placing her hand on my arm. "Shayla, I don't like it when you're sad." I looked at her. Worry was already scrunching her face into knots, caking her Baby Boy Blue shadow.

I forced a gleeful laugh out to go with the smile. "Don't be silly, Kambia. There's nothing wrong with me. I'd tell you if there was, wouldn't I?" I glanced at the doorway of the auditorium. A long line of snappily dressed people with polished shoes and fresh hairdos were filing through the arched doorway. "Look," I said. "It's almost time for things to start. Kambia, you better go in."

Kambia glanced at the auditorium and panicked. "Ooh, you're right," she squealed. "I'm going to be late." She bounded for the door, but her father caught her arm.

"Just one second, Daughter. Me and your mama got you a little something," he said, tapping Honeysuckle Peach on the shoulder.

"Oh, we sure do," Honeysuckle Peach said, smiling at Kambia. She opened a huge leather shoulder bag and took out a small, golden rectangular box. She handed it to Kambia with the biggest grin that I had ever seen, even bigger than Mr. Anderson Fox's. "It ain't much," she said. "It's just something that we thought you would like."

Kambia took the box timidly, mumbling something under her breath about not wanting them to spend good money on her, but they merely waved their hands at the complaint and told her that she deserved the present, and so much more. With that, she stopped fussing and opened the box. Me and Grandma gasped. The box contained a beautiful sterling-silver charm bracelet, made up of tiny puffy little hearts, plump teddy bears, and dancing kittens. It was puppy-dog cute, just the sort of thing that Kambia liked.

"Oh, it's wonderful," she said, grabbing both of her parents and hugging them. "Thank you, thank you, thank you so much."

"It was nothing," they both said, dabbing at the corners of their eyes. "We just thought that you would like it."

"It's really nice," me and Grandma both said. "But I think we better get inside," I added.

We all started for the door, but once again one of Kambia's parents stopped us. "Just one more thing," Honeysuckle Peach said. She opened her bag and produced another box. This one was square, and much larger, about half the size of a shoe box. "I noticed it shoved in the mailbox right before we left home," she said, handing it to Kambia. "It has a tag on it with your school's logo, but no name. I figure the school must have sent one to all of the graduates. I thought you might like to take a peek and see what it is before you give your speech. You might need to thank them for it, too."

"I just might," Kambia said. "It's really nice of them to send me a gift, isn't it, Shayla?" she asked.

I didn't answer. I was too busy looking at the package. The wrapping paper was gorgeous. It was a glittery gold with raised silver roses and carnations. I thought it must be the prettiest package in the world.

"Wow! Open it up, Kambia," I said.

Kambia carefully started peeling away sections of the paper, handing each large piece to Honeysuckle Peach, who folded them up and stuck them back in her purse. Underneath the fine covering was a plain white box with a matching top.

"I wonder what's in it?" Kambia said.

I shrugged my shoulders. "Something really good, I'll bet," I said.

Kambia nodded. She slowly yanked the top of the box off to reveal two or three layers of gold tissue.

"It sure is fancy wrapped," Grandma said.

This time we all nodded.

We leaned in closer to get a better look as Kambia started to tug the tissue back layer by layer, gently pushing each section to the side. Finally the layers were all off, and the four us pressed in even more to get a good look, but before we could see anything, Kambia screamed and dropped the box. She hollered so loud that we all must have jumped a foot in the air.

"What in the world!" Honeysuckle Peach cried, throwing up her hands. "What's wrong, Daughter?"

"I don't want it!" Kambia said, backing away from the present, shaking her head madly. "I don't want it! I don't want it!"

"What is it?!" Honeysuckle Peach cried. "Daughter, what's wrong?"

"I don't want it! I don't want it! Just please, please get them away from me. Take them away, Shayla!" Kambia screamed. "Take them away, please!"

"Take what away?" Honeysuckle Peach asked, frantically trying to grab Kambia's hands. Kambia was waving them around even more than her head, like she was trying to bat away something flying toward her. "What's wrong, Daughter? What is it that you don't want?"

"Them!" Kambia screamed, and started to jump up and down. "I don't want them. Please, please get them away!"

"What is it, Kambia?" I asked, trying to grab her myself. "What don't you want? Just calm down and tell us what's wrong."

"Them!" she cried in a terrified voice. "Please, Shayla, I don't want them! I don't want what's in the box!"

"What!" I said. I bent down to retrieve the box from the walkway, but Ten Fingers leaned over and scooped it up before I even got a chance.

"What in the world is in this thing? What in the world is scaring that child like this? Let me see what this mess is," he said, yanking the tissue paper away.

"It's okay, Daughter," Honeysuckle Peach cooed, still trying to get ahold of Kambia. "Whatever it is, it's gonna be all right. I swear it's gonna be just fine."

"Don't worry, Daughter," Ten Fingers added, tipping the box toward him. "Ain't nobody gonna let nothing happen to you. Everything is going to be all right." He pulled the tissue back, and I peeked under his arm, while Grandma and Honeysuckle Peach finally got ahold of Kambia.

Paper dolls, that's what was in it, just a bunch of half-crumpled paper dolls. They were cutouts from some coloring or tracing book, with thick black outlines. From what I could tell, they were all girls dressed in various outfits—plaid shifts, sailor jumpers, and full skirts. I would have said that they were completely different from one another, except for one thing. Someone had colored all of their hair with a brownish red crayon, and their colorless eyeballs had all been filled in with a green marker. I didn't know what to make of it. It made no sense to me at all. I looked at Ten Fingers, but he just shook his head.

"What in the world?" he cried. "What in the world is this mess?"

"Dear Lord, what is it, Ten Fingers?" Honeysuckle Peach cried also.

"It ain't nothing," Ten Fingers said, bewildered.

"Nothing?"

"Naw, nothing. I don't get it. It ain't nothing, Honey, just some paper dolls. Daughter, it ain't nothing to be afraid of," he said to Kambia. "Ain't nothing in here that can do you harm."

"Yes, it is!" Kambia shrieked, still shaking her head madly. "You don't understand! Please, please just take them away, Shayla! Please take them away from me!"

I looked at her face. She wasn't just frightened. Fear was swarming all over her like flies. It was the same fear she had had the day that we walked down the railroad tracks and I saw the bruises on her thighs, and the day that she hid out from Jasmine Joiner underneath my bed. It was fear that neither her parents nor Grandma Augustine had seen before, and I had hoped that I would never see again. I didn't understand why she was so upset about the dolls, and I didn't care. I grabbed the box from Ten Fingers and threw it as far as it would go. It landed in a clump of hedges on the side of the auditorium.

"It's gone, Kambia. I threw it away, okay? There are no more dolls. Okay?" I said. I caught her face with my hand and forced her to stop shaking her head.

"Did you hear me, Kam? They're gone," I said.

She took a deep breath, let it out, and got real still. Her face got calmer and calmer, until it was almost completely free of fear.

"Okay, okay, Shayla," she said. "I'm all right." She grabbed me and hugged me tight. I could feel her heart pumping away in her chest, like she had just gotten through running up a flight of stairs.

"It's okay, Kambia," I whispered softly. "There's nothing here that can harm you."

"I know," she said. "I knew that you would make it all right." She let me go, and Honeysuckle Peach grabbed her and held her to her breast.

"Are you okay, Daughter?" she asked. "I don't want anything to ever hurt you."

"Me neither," Ten Fingers said, throwing his arm around her shoulder. Kambia let go of her mother and hugged him, too.

"I'm okay," she said. She glanced back at the auditorium. The crowd had disappeared from the door.

"I better go," she said. "I better get in there. It's time to get started."

"Are you sure, baby?" Honeysuckle Peach asked. "You know that Mama don't want you to do anything that you ain't ready to do.

It's okay if you just wanna go home. We'll understand. You won't hurt nobody's feelings."

"I want to do my speech," Kambia said. "I'm okay, I promise."

"All right, then, let's everybody go," Ten Fingers said, patting her back. "Let's go see my daughter steal the show."

Kambia broke into a nervous giggle, and the three of them locked arms and walked into the auditorium, with Grandma Augustine hobbling after them.

I remained where I was until they were out of sight. I ran over to the hedges, reached down in the scratchy bushes, and fished the present out. It was paper dolls, all right, nothing more. Even with the brownish red hair and green eyes I could see nothing that should have set Kambia off the way that it did. I didn't understand her reaction at all. I thought about what Grandma Augustine had said to me earlier about "only a little rain" and wondered if saying that would have worked on Kambia any better than it worked on me. *I don't know why the dolls upset you, Kambia, but I'm sure that it's no big deal,* I might have said. *It's just a little rain. The clouds will go away soon.* I wondered if the words would have calmed her down, but while I tossed it around in my mind, I remembered one of Grandma's African sayings that had to do with rain, and it gave me something else to think about. "To an elephant an afternoon shower may be nothing but a sprinkle," the saying said, "but to a beetle it most certainly will be a flood." I took the dolls out of the box and stuffed them into my skirt pocket. I would try to figure them out before we all got caught in the downpour.

# Chapter 2

This morning I dreamed that I was standing on a snow-covered mountaintop, underneath a cornflower blue sky that was peppered with cottony clouds fluttering throughout the horizon like huge butterflies.

In the middle of the mountaintop was a giant oak tree. The tree's branches were winter bare, and they were filled with what I at first thought were colorful kites waving in the cool breeze, but when I got closer, I realized that they weren't kites at all. They were five beautiful ladies, with cascading braids, soulful dark eyes, and polished skin of ebony. They were dressed in sheer, flowing gowns of gold, mint, rose, turquoise, and lilac—and they were dancing. Round and round the ladies twirled on the branches, moving rhythmically to melodious tunes that floated in from somewhere far away that I couldn't see.

I wanted desperately to join the ladies, to dance to the music while the breezes blew my nylon nightgown and ruffled my short hair. So I scurried up the tree like a raccoon, but as soon as my foot touched the first branch, the ladies up and disappeared. They just vanished, as if they had never been there in the first place. Disappointed, I climbed back down the tree, thinking that I had just imagined the whole thing, but the minute my feet sank into the snow, I looked up and saw that the ladies had reappeared. Well, I didn't know what to make of it, so I started up again, but the second my foot touched the tree trunk, the ladies were nowhere to be seen. I shrugged my shoulders and began to look around for them. I figured that they couldn't just beam in and out with a snap of their fingers, like that blond lady on that TV show *Bewitched*. I looked far up into the horizon, over other snowcapped mountains and other giant oak trees—and there they were. I could see them off in the distance. They were hiding out in the butterfly clouds, their thin arms and muscular dancers' legs sticking out like Tootsie Rolls. I grew angry at the ladies. I shouted at them either to come down or to show me how to come up, but they didn't even bother to stick their heads out and respond. Annoyed, I started for the tree again, but as soon as I got close to it, the buzz of my alarm broke through the melodious music. I found myself lying awake in my bed with Tia snoring noisily beside me, making a sound that reminded me of tearing Styrofoam.

I sighed and stared at the small digital alarm clock on my windowsill. It was a quarter past seven, but when I glanced through the foggy window glass, I could see that the sun was taking its time rising into place. A pale yellow moon was peeping out between a cluster of heavy, dark clouds, and several semibright stars were still happily doing their twinkle dance in the sky. It was morning, but not morning, as if Grandma's and Kambia's God had forgotten to turn on the world.

I grabbed my ratty old robe off a rickety chair next to the bed and hopped out of the covers, mumbling to myself about the lingering darkness. I headed for the dresser, trying to be extra careful and not trip over Tia's sneakers, which were usually just tossed in the middle of the floor. No luck. I got my fuzzy bathroom slipper tangled up in one of her shoestrings, and I went flying. I fell flat on my face in the middle of the shag carpet, and I would have said a few ugly words about Tia and her big feet, but I looked up and saw Grandma standing in the door and thought better of it.

I wasn't surprised to see Grandma. She's been coming over to the house more than usual lately to watch over me, even though she doesn't know that I know it. She's worried that I haven't been myself since Gift was born, that I'm letting Gift's birth rub me way too hard. She says that I ought to be over it by now, that I ought to have moved on. I heard her and Mama talking about it last week in Mama's room while they were working on a new patchwork quilt for me and Tia's bed. "I know that none of us was ready for the way that Anderson fawns over that new baby girl. None of us thought that he would gather that child to him and treat her like she was spun from gold. We never thought that at all," she said, reaching into her sewing kit and picking up her oversize cutting shears. "But you got to give it to him. He really is trying to be some kind of father. He's trying to do all the right things, and I really got to say an amen to that. Now, I'm sorry about Shayla. I wish that he could have done better by her when she was little, but he didn't, and no matter how much we want to, we can't remake that quilt. It's already been sewn and is hanging on the wall. Shayla got to get over this. She's a big girl now. Being all broke down and moody over it ain't gon' change nothing." She trimmed the edges around a heart-shaped piece of cloth with her shears. "It's time she figures out that sometimes life gives you warts, and there ain't nothing you can do but burn 'em off and keep going."

"I know," Mama said, selecting a plastic thimble from Grandma's kit. "I'm not happy with the way that Shayla's been acting either. I've never seen her pull such a fit. I'm really beginning to worry about her. She's usually more levelheaded than this. I've seen her hold it together during a lot worse. Last year when Tia ran off, she spent most of her time trying to find out where Tia was, instead of just sitting in her room bawling her eyes out like some little girls would have. She got sad, but she didn't let it pull her down.

Mu'dear, you know that even from a tiny baby that's always been her way."

"That's true," Grandma said. "I just don't know what's up with her. We ought to take her to another cleansing revival, like we did when Anderson moved in last year. We'll let her bathe in the sand of Jesus' footprints and wash that evil clean out of her before it spreads."

Grandma and Mama are right, of course. Gift's birth is still weighing hard on me. Grandma, Mama, and Tia have gone to see her and Jada at least half a dozen times since she's been home from the hospital, but I've always refused to go. Just the mention of her name makes me either leave the room, pout, or say something really mean that I don't even wish that I could take back. I just can't get over the way that Mr. Anderson Fox boasted about her in the hospital, or the way that he proudly held her up for everyone to see. To me Mr. Anderson Fox has always been like mildew after a shower—just there. He has never been someone that I could depend on and possesses no great qualities that I wish I had. So why is it that when I see him with Gift, I suddenly feel as if he is the most precious jewel in the world and Gift is a robber trying to run off with him?

I waved and forced myself to smile at Grandma in the doorway, to try and fool her into believing that I had gotten up in a better mood than I had been in for the past few weeks, but she didn't buy it.

"What's wrong with you, child?" she whispered.

"Nothing," I answered in my normal voice. I didn't bother with the whisper. It wouldn't have hurt me none to wake Tia out of her peaceful sleep.

"Something's wrong," she whispered back in a voice peppered with worry. "You in here mumbling and fretting something terrible, and a minute ago you were talking up a storm in your sleep. I came to see what demon had hold of you."

"It was nothing, Grandma," I said again with just a hint of annoyance in my voice. "I just had a weird dream. I don't know. It was no big deal. I was in this really strange place."

"What kind of place?" Grandma asked.

"I don't know, Grandma," I said again. "I was just in this really strange place. It was like I was in one of Kambia's dreams or something. It reminded me of one of her tales."

"It did," she said, hobbling over to me. She was still dressed in what she called her good-night housedress, a well-worn sleeveless shift that her church sewing group had sewn for her a couple years ago when she was in the hospital with bad arthritis.

I walked over to the bookshelf and flipped the switch on an old lamp with a cylinder shade and a cast-iron base. Mama had had it since she was a little girl but had now passed it on to me and Tia. It hummed for a minute, then bathed the room in a soft yellow light. I sighed and rolled my eyes.

"Great, I can't believe it's still dark out," I said. "I guess even the stupid world knows better than to get up. What's the point?"

"Ain't no point," Grandma said. "There's no need in you spending your time fretting about what's going on with the world. She knows how to take care of herself. She was doing it long before you was even thinking about coming out of your mama's belly."

I grunted, kicked Tia's shoes under the bed, and headed for the dresser again, completely forgetting about pretending to be in a good mood.

"Well, you gonna chew on it all day or tell me about it," Grandma called after me.

"Like I said, it's nothing, Grandma," I mumbled. "Just let it drop. I don't even want to talk about it. Or anything else, for that matter."

"I do," she snapped. "And since I'm the oldest and the *meanest* here, we both gonna do exactly what I say. Now, what kind of dream was it? The mood you been in lately, I can't imagine too much that would make you holler like a panther. You could scare even the scariest monster off, so it must have been something pretty unpleasant."

"There was nothing unpleasant about it, and I wasn't talking in my sleep," I said. "I know I wasn't, 'cause if I was, Tia would have woken up."

"Tia," Grandma said, shaking her head at the bed. "Your sister could sleep through a twister. A tornado could pull the roof clean off the house, and she would still be playing cards with the sandman."

"Nooo. No, I wouldn't. Trust me, I'm wide awake, Grandma," Tia suddenly burst out. "She woke me up!"

Grandma and I watched as Tia slowly, groggily pulled herself out from underneath the ragged bedspread and sat up. Her thin, curly braids looked like a pit of writhing snakes, and her huge bosom was straining heavily against her crumpled cotton gown, which had gotten a size too small since Mama bought it last year. She stretched, yawned, smacked her lips loudly, and begin wiping crusty patches of sleep out of the corners of her slanted eyes with her hands.

"Good Lord, gal, you sho do sleep bad," Grandma said, shaking her head and laughing. "Look like you start at one end of the bed and end at another. You sleep worse than my cat, Nat King Cole."

"At least he gets to sleep. Shayla, what's this dream all about?" Tia asked. "Why you done woke me up over nothing? Come on, don't give me no funky attitude. What's all this foolishness about?"

Seeing no way to avoid it, I told Tia and Grandma about the dream. They listened carefully, with Grandma nodding thoughtfully after each sentence, and Tia leaning in at every rise and fall of my voice. When I was finished, they both told me what they thought of it.

"It's easy," Tia said. "There was an African-American dance troupe on TV the other night. Remember, you and I were watching it on Mama's black-and-white while she got dressed for work. The dancing probably just slipped back into your head tonight. It's like that sometimes. Things get buried in your mind, then when you've all but forgotten about them, they show up in your dreams. Maybe when you were watching the dancers, you were thinking that it would be great if you could dance too."

"Maybe," I mumbled, and looked away, remembering that what she said was exactly what I had been thinking while I was watching the graceful men and women prance around. I was thinking about how fabulous it would be to be one of the beautiful girls that the men lifted up in the air. But how could Tia know that? Something in my expression must have tipped her off. I didn't like that very much. I didn't like it when people could read my heart by looking at my face.

"Okay," I said quickly. "You're right. I guess I better get dressed." I walked over to the dresser and placed my hand on the wooden handle of the top drawer, but Grandma yanked it back off. I didn't mean to, but I glared at her. She let it pass.

"How many ladies was it?" she asked.

I planned on just shrugging my shoulders, but I noticed that her no-nonsense face had returned. "There were a few," I said. "I don't know—some, not a whole bunch."

"How many?" she asked again. "Now, you take your time and count."

I sighed and formed the image of the ladies in my head. "I think there were five, ma'am," I said obediently.

"And every time you tried to touch 'em, they floated away?" she asked.

"Every time I tried to touch 'em, they disappeared into the clouds," I answered.

"I know what your dream is about," she said. "I know what it's about. That dream is all about you."

"I already told her that, Grandma," Tia said sarcastically. "I told her that it was about her and those dancers."

"It ain't about no dancers, missy," Grandma snapped back. "It's just about her." She took my hands in hers and spoke softly, her face softening just a bit. "Shayla, at some point in their lives all women have this dream, only they don't know it, because there's nobody around to explain it to them."

"Explain what?" Tia asked.

"Grandma, there's nothing to explain," I said.

"There is. Them ladies, they were you," she said. "They were all you—you in the womb, your birth, your childhood, your woman-hood, and your death. That's what they were. They were all part of you, the stages of your life, from your coming out to your going under. They were everything that you will ever be or think about being."

"What?" Tia said. "Grandma, if this is another one of your old-timey interpretations—"

"It ain't old-timey," Grandma snapped. "It's true. And you would be well off to listen to it. Come on, Shayla," she said, grabbing me by the arm.

She dragged me over to the bed, and I sat down next to Tia, who chuckled at me.

"This is a common dream," Grandma said. "Women been having it for years. They been having it since the first woman placed her head on a pillow."

"Wouldn't it be a rock or something?" Tia asked. "I don't think that the first woman had a pillow."

"Never you mind, missy," Grandma said, cutting her eyes at Tia. "It don't matter if she put her head on the ground, you know what I'm saying." She looked back at me and spoke softly. "You see, Shayla, it's almost impossible for most women to ever really get a hold on themselves. Most women spend their entire life trying to figure out who they are, who they want to be, and what they gonna do when they figure the first two things out. They never quite know if they want to wear a dress or a skirt, and where they gonna wear it to after they put it on. It's just nature—the not knowing. That's what your dream is about. You're coming to a point in your life where you gonna have to decide some things for yourself, make up your mind about the kind of woman you want to be. In order to do that, you have to have a firm grip on yourself. You have to be able to take hold of all that you are. Now, you started last year, when you made some decisions about your friend, Kambia. That was your first step in knowing what kind of woman you want to be, but you still got a ways to go. You find out what kind of pot you want to cook in and what you want to put in it, and you'll be able to pull them ladies right out of the clouds. They'll come down and let you do anything that you want with them, 'cause you'll be the one in control."

"Yes, ma'am," I said. As usual I didn't quite believe what she was telling me, but I wasn't in a mood to challenge her about it. Besides, if I believed what she told me, there were now seven Shaylas. I was already having a problem dealing with two.

"Oh, brother," Tia said, rolling her eyes up to the ceiling. "Grandma, you know that I love you, but you sure can come up with 'em."

"I ain't come up with nothing but the truth, missy," Grandma said, wagging her finger at her. "You think real hard, and it'll come to you. You done had the exact same dream. Maybe you was chasing five cats down the street, or trying to jump up and pick five oranges from a tree, but you've had the dream. All women do."

"What about men, Grandma?" Tia snapped. "What you said is only common sense. Lots of folks have problems finding themselves, so to speak, men and women."

"This ain't about finding yourself," Grandma said. "This is about knowing when you done found it. Most women don't," she said. "They keep going through the wrong door their entire life, making the same mistake over and over, like they got no control over how they sheets hang on the clothesline. The dream is about that. It's about knowing that you can use clothespins or just throw them over the line, and about what kind of woman you are when you choose to do them either way."

"A woman that needs a washing machine," Tia said. Grandma cut her eyes at her again.

"It's a female thing," Grandma continued. "I don't know about men. They ain't talkers, women are. We are the talkers of the world. We have to give voice to the things in our lives, deal with troubles with our words. Men don't. Something got to be weighing on them seriously heavy for them to tell you about it. It's just not they way. It's a woman's way to put her heart into words."

"It's a woman's way to get some sleep," Tia said. She slid down underneath the covers and placed the pillow over her head.

Grandma leaned over me. She snatched Tia's pillow off and threw it down again. "Humph, you don't know as much as you think you know, little girl," she said. Tia burst into giggles—and so did someone in the doorway. Me and Grandma looked around. It was Kambia. She was standing in the same spot that Grandma had been standing in. She was wearing a floor-length terry robe and matching terry slippers, and her hair was all done up in foam curlers. Just seeing her made my mood start to get better.

"What's up?" I asked.

"The door was open, so I just came in, Shayla. My mom is sending me to the store to get some breakfast stuff. It's still dark out, so she didn't want me to go alone. I told her that I would come down and get you. Hi, Mrs. Augustine. How are you?" she asked Grandma.

"The Lord put my feet on solid ground this morning, baby," Grandma said. "I got to be doing pretty good."

"You're going to the store. That's cool," I said. "Let's go." I bolted for the doorway, but Grandma grabbed my robe.

"You put some clothes on first, little girl," she said.

"Aw, Grandma, I'm just going down the street a ways," I said. "Everybody does it. I'm not naked or nothing. Besides, you still have your sleep dress on," I reminded her.

"I'm grown," she said. "Besides, you can wear this for day or night. What you got on is for bed, and don't you get too smart with me. You been getting too big for your bloomers lately."

"Aw, Grandma, just let us go. We're only gonna be gone for a bit. I promise we won't go far."

"Okay, okay. Lord knows I ain't gon' get no peace if I don't," Grandma said. "Fine, y'all get on out of here, and come right back."

"Yes, ma'am," I said. I hopped up from the bed and kissed her on the cheek. "Let's be out, Kambia."

Kambia and I didn't waste any time leaving. We ran through the house and out of the front door as quickly as we could. We flung open the front gate and went laughing down the street.

It was fun hearing Kambia laugh again. She hadn't laughed in the past two weeks. After her graduation she started acting kind of strange again. When we got back to her house that day, she refused to go into her room. She said that she knew something or someone was waiting for her behind her bedroom door.

"I can't go in there," she told her parents and me. "It's waiting to hurt me. You can't see it, because it's hiding, but I know it's there."

Her parents and I both told her that it wasn't true and even demonstrated by walking in and out of the room several times, but she wouldn't listen.

"Look, Kambia—see, there's nobody at all," we said, standing in the middle of the room next to her canopy bed. "Look, there's nothing mean or scary in here to get you. It's just us, and you know that we won't hurt you."

"Yes there is something scary in there," she said, trembling in the doorway. "Yes there is, you just can't see it. It'll come out as soon as I step in the room." Finally we all just gave up. Kambia spent her days in the other rooms of her parents' small house and her nights sleeping next to her mother in her mom and dad's bed. For a while it looked like she was going to go completely back to her old scared, story-telling self for good. Then one day she just popped out of it. Her mother and father woke to find her sleeping peacefully in her own bed, curled up next to her favorite toy, Sophie Bear. Apparently she just got over the fear, but none of us are sure why, and we still don't know why she was so freaked out in the first place.

The only thing that Kambia's parents and me could come up with was the paper dolls, which I unfolded and stuck between the pages of my blue notebook. Somehow they made the old Kambia come back out again, but none of us are sure how they did it, and Kambia can't or won't fill us in. Kambia's parents had no choice but to try and get some answers at Kambia's school. They went to see her principal. She was really cool and allowed them to question whomever they wanted, but nobody could tell them a thing about the dolls.

Everybody said that they liked Kambia a lot. The girls at the school said that she was real smart, always helping them out with their lessons, and the teachers said that she was just a joy to have in their classes. They said that they didn't know why anyone from the Girl Help Center would want to hurt her, and yet they all had to admit that the box the dolls came in did come from the school. It was supposed to contain a paperweight, a cute little mouse with a graduation cap, not what Kambia ended up with. The whole thing seems to be one of Kambia's Linda James mysteries. Only right now it's still no big deal. Whatever seeing the dolls did to Kambia, it looks like she's over it. Her counselor, Mrs. Dreyfus, thinks that it's a really good idea to keep an eye on her, but she says that there's no need to put a ladder up against the side of the house if nobody's in danger of falling. "Watch her, but give her her space," she told us all. "We won't worry about it until she gives us something to really worry about."

It was still dark out as Kambia and I strolled down the street. It was a city holiday. Most folks were sleeping in, and many of the stores were closed, but not the one that we were going to—Diamond's.

Diamond's was run by G. G. Diamond, a tall, good-looking

young brother with a well-kept fade, fine threads, and a smooth rap. He was really popular with the ladies, always had some pricey-looking chick hanging on his arm, but to be honest, he was a lot more popular with the men. To the guys he was a you-need-it-I-can-get-it kind of dude. He was really good at helping them out in a jam—furniture, used cars, TVs—he always knew somebody that could get it for them at a good price. If they wanted it, he had it. He made sure that everybody's needs were taken care of, especially his own. Groceries, toys, paints, motor oils, lottery tickets, tires, CDs, fishing and hunting gear; he sold it all. If he could make a profit off of it, he stocked it. In his store you had access to anything and everything that you could possibly use, even some stuff that it wasn't quite legal to buy in a plain old neighborhood store, because G. G. Diamond was good at making sure that the right kinds of folks looked the other way.

It took me and Kambia much longer than it usually would have to walk the twelve blocks to the store. We walked slowly, arm in arm, gossiping about the things that were going on around the hood and sharing personal stuff that had gone on in our lives since the last time that we were together. It was nearly thirty minutes later when we walked into the tiny, lamp-lit parking lot of Diamond's, our house slippers slapping noisily against the warm blacktop.

Except for a few empty beer cans sticking out of brown paper wrappers and some discarded cigarette packages, the normally overflowing lot was empty. There wasn't a soul in sight, not even the shabbily dressed street folks who hung out in front of the store begging for dollars or food as the customers walked in and out. So after commenting to each other on how nice it was not to have to fight a crowd for a change, Kambia and I opened the glass double doors of the large concrete building and went in.

We entered the store and immediately sidestepped to avoid a trio of mean-looking blue crabs with twitching antennae. G. G. Diamond had taken a trip down to Galveston a day or so ago and gotten a great deal on the bug-eyed crustaceans. Barrels overflowing with them could be found throughout the store.

"Wow, they musta gotten out," Kambia said. "I wonder where they're trying to get to?"

"I don't know—back to the ocean, I guess," I said, moving my feet out of the way. "Where else can a crab go?"

"Let's go down another aisle," Kambia said. "We don't want to step on them."

"Naw, we don't have to," I said. "I think that we can just step around them."

We started to walk away. "I'll remove them for you, girls," said a voice behind us. We both turned around. It was Lemm Turley. He was dressed nicer than we were. He was wearing a faded, but neatly pressed, navy shirt, wide-leg jeans, and a pair of oversize no-name basketball sneakers. Except for a bit of early-morning redness in his intense chestnut eyes, he looked really great, not like he had just hopped up out of bed like me and Kambia. We suddenly got self-conscious. Kambia began patting her hair, and I yanked my robe closed.

"What's up?" Lemm asked.

"Not much," I mumbled.

"We just came to the store to get some stuff," Kambia said. "My mom wants some things for breakfast."

"Oh, does she, Lady Kambia," Lemm said. "And how are you this fine morning?"

Kambia got all red faced and broke into giggles, but I just shook my head. Lemm has been calling Kambia "Lady Kambia" since he met her. He first laid eyes on her at a party that her school gave earlier this summer, a costume party, a safe way for the girls to take a night off from the horrible things in their lives, the ladies at the Girl Help Center said.

Kambia had invited me to the party two weeks before the event, and I was really looking forward to it. Mama and Grandma Augustine had even sewn me up a costume, a lamb's outfit, made out of black velvet and really big cotton balls. It was babyish, I know, but they'd spent a lot of time getting it together, making it look as real as possible, and to be honest, I was really kind of proud of it.

I was good to go the day of the party. I was happy all day long, but when I got home from school that Friday afternoon, my mood changed. For some dumb reason Lemm had stopped by my house before going to his own, even though he knew that I wouldn't be there, because I had told him that I had to stay and tutor some kids in English after my last period. I arrived home to find him sitting on the sofa in our living room, drinking Kool-Aid with Mama and Grandma, whom he had somehow already managed to win over. They were busy sewing him up a pirate's costume for the party.

"You ladies are the kindest, most talented people I've ever met," he was telling them.

I was madder than a cat in a tub of water. I had to spend my days with Lemm. I had no intention of spending my nights with him as well. I mumbled a "good evening" to Grandma and Mama. After that I dragged Mama into the kitchen to get her straight on the subject, but she got me straight instead.

"It'll be good for you to spend some time with that little boy, Shayla," she said, leaning against the kitchen cabinet, sewing a string onto Lemm's black eye patch with her heavy hands. "He's a nice boy, kind and respectful. You only have one friend right now—Kambia. What's wrong with making friends with someone else?"

"I don't need anyone else," I said.

"Don't be foolish, girl," she said. "There's nothing better in this world than two or three people that you can count on. I wouldn't ever pass up a chance to make friends with somebody nice that really wanted to be friends with me. If you're smart, you won't either. Now, I don't think that Kambia will mind you bringing him along," she said. "I already spoke to her mother, and she thought that it was a great idea and that Kambia won't have a problem with it."

"That's because she doesn't know him. Everybody in school thinks that he's a first-class geek," I lied.

"And what do they think of you?" she asked.

"Excuse me?" I said, shocked.

"You heard me," she said. "You already told me yourself that the kids in your class sometimes treat you like you forgot to put on deodorant. They treat you like a stepchild, and you're a really great person. If they are wrong about you, can't they also be wrong about Lemm?"

"I-I don't . . . don't know," I stuttered. "I guess they could." I couldn't believe that she was using something that I told her last year against me. When I spoke with her, she didn't seem all that interested in what I had to say about the girls, and even told me that perhaps it was somewhat my fault that the girls didn't want me in their crew, but obviously she had changed her mind. I felt good about that, but not good enough to want to take Lemm to the party.

"Darn right," she continued. "They could be wrong about a lot of things." She grabbed a stainless-steel case knife out of the dish drainer and snipped off the end of the string. The loose piece fell to the floor, and she bent down and retrieved it.

"Now, Shayla," she said, tossing the string into the metal can under the sink. "The one thing that I learned last year with your sister, Tia, is that there are just some things that I can't make you girls do, but this ain't one of them. You're gonna do this. Lemm's a nice boy, and you're a nice girl. It ought to be easy for y'all to find a way to get along. You just treat him like you would want to be treated, and everything will be just fine."

She shook her finger at me. "Now, you go in there and tell him that it would be great if he went to the party with you," she said. "Or you might not be going to the party yourself."

"Yes, ma'am," I muttered.

"Okay," she said, and walked out the door.

I watched Mama leave the kitchen in her grocery store uniform and thought about ditching Lemm the moment she went to work, but I knew better. When Mama said something, she meant it. It wasn't smart to go against what she had to say, and not just because she was as big and as strong as any man. Mama was crazy stubborn. Tia had seen that last summer when she tried to back Mama down about Doo-witty. She did eventually get her way, but she had to run away to do it, and trouble sat on our kitchen table for months because of it. No, it was best to leave Mama alone once her mind was made up. Life was easier that way.

So I had to take Lemm with me to the party, which really bummed me out but didn't bother Kambia at all. She was all done up that night in a princess costume that her mom and dad had rented from some vintage-clothing store. It was a lavender satin gown with a corset waist and a top with puffy sleeves. To accentuate the gown, she wore a beautiful crown of rosettes in her hair that looked like it was made by a fine florist shop. She looked as sweet as a honeydew melon, and everybody kept telling her so, especially

Lemm, who said that she looked like one of those ladies in medieval times, the kind that some knight was always putting his life on the line to save. He started calling her Lady Kambia, and the name quickly caught on and stuck for the night. During the party everybody called her that, even me. But after the night was over, we all went back to just plain old Kambia, except Lemm, who still calls her it every time he sees her. He says that she looks like a lady to him, even in her street clothes.

Lemm pushed his glasses up over his nose and bowed to Kambia. "You look very elegant, Lady Kambia," he said. "You look as beautiful as a field of wildflowers and as lovely as a pond filled with water lilies."

Kambia broke into more giggles, but I just rolled my eyes. "What do you want, Lemm?" I asked, jumping back into my crappy mood for just a few moments. "We're trying to do some shopping here, if you don't mind."

"I don't mind at all," he said. "I was just offering to save you ladies from the beasts."

"Beasts—oh, brother," I said. "What beasts? It's just a few crabs, and we were going to go around them, until you stopped us."

"I wouldn't think of it," he said. "I just couldn't imagine you ladies having to brave the wild for a few groceries."

Now I broke into giggles. "Oh, brother," I laughed. "Get real! Go away, Lemm. It's bad enough that whenever I turn around you're in my face at school. Did you have to follow me here, too?"

I grabbed Kambia by the hand and we started around the crabs, but Lemm ran up and jumped in front of us. Before we could utter a word of caution, he bent down and snatched up one of the crabs. It threw a fit with its legs for a few seconds, then grabbed hold of his pinkie with one of its sharp claws. Lemm hollered and dropped it.

The crab hit the floor, and it and its two friends scurried to safety underneath a cart of metal racks loaded with loaves of raisin and wheat breads. Lemm stuck his finger in his mouth and began to suck it.

"It serves you right for being so foolish," I said. "It's a wonder you didn't get it bitten off."

"I think I did," he whined.

"Oh, good grief, let me see," I said, taking a motherly tone. "It can't be that bad." Lemm took his finger out of his mouth and held it out. Me and Kambia leaned in closely and gave it the once-over. The finger was deep red where the crab had grabbed him, but the skin wasn't broken.

"You'll live," I said, pushing his hand back toward him. "It's only a baby nip. The skin's not even broken. Some protector you are."

"I can't help it if the beast got the best of me," he said. "Men often get wounded in battle."

"Men? What on earth does that have to do with you?" I said, laughing. Then Kambia started laughing too. Lemm looked disappointed for a second, but then it must have struck him as funny too, because he broke into laugher as well. The three of us laughed long and hard, until the sound of heavy footsteps coming our way broke up the amusement.

It was King Red, the store's butcher, a stout, fiftyish, easily irritated brother with a big, bushy red mustache and caterpillar brows, large brown freckles, and processed red hair. He came storming up, his white butcher's apron splattered with fresh animal blood, his hand gripped tightly around a large meat cleaver. It was a sight that probably would have made most kids scatter like Kambia's Three Blind Mice, but we had seen it several times before, so we just played it real cool and put on our most innocent faces.

"What are y'all children up to?" he said, stomping up with a look that would have turned back a swarm of bees. "I can hear y'all whooping and hollering all the way over to the meat counter. A bunch of young'uns making that kind of noise can't be up to no good." He pointed at me. "You, little Miss Thing, what's this all about? What kind of children's mess is y'all up to? And don't try to lie to me. I can smell a lie quicker than a cat can smell a fish head."

"I'm not going to lie," I said defensively. "It's nothing. There's some crabs loose. We were just trying to get away from them."

"Crabs, crabs, where they at? Them damn thangs crawling out of them barrels all over the place. I been chasing 'em all morning. I told G. G. he had bought too many of them damn thangs. It's enough crabs in here to open a Red Lobster."

He began turning around and around in the aisle, checking it out in all directions. "I don't see no crabs. Where they go?" he asked.

I pointed underneath the bread rack. "Down there," I said.

"Down there? Let me take a look." Wheezing heavily, King Red bent down and began looking under the rack; as he did, one of the crabs had the nerve to stick out a claw.

"There they are. I see 'em," he said, chopping at the crab with his meat cleaver, leaving big slits in the linoleum.

Poor Kambia looked horrified, but me and Lemm placed our hands over our mouth to try and stifle our chuckles. For several minutes King Red chopped at the crabs with his cleaver, desperately trying to let them know that he was the one in charge, but he never got the chance. With every whack the crabs retreated farther and farther underneath the bread rack, until they disappeared entirely beneath a large freezer that the rack was standing next to.

"Well, I'll be a hog without slop," King Red said. He stood up, exhausted, wiping his sweaty brow. "Damn, that's just what I needed. Before you know it, this place will be overrun with them thangs. It'll be just what I need for some woman to come in here shopping and have one of 'em crawl up her skirt. It'll be all over the neighborhood. 'Don't come to Diamond's, you'll get a crab in your bloomers.'"

With that Lemm wasn't able to control himself anymore. He broke into laughter again. King Red glared at him. "You think that's funny, young fellow?" he asked. Lemm swallowed hard and stopped laughing.

"No—no, sir," he said quickly. "No, not at all."

"Well, it look like you do. You snickering about it like some little gal." He caught sight of Lemm's pinkie. "What's wrong with your finger there, boy?"

Lemm shrugged his shoulder. "Nothing," he said. "It's nothing. I just hurt it a little."

King Red leaned in closer and got a better look. A big smile spread across his sweaty face. He clapped his heavy hands on Lemm's shoulder, threw his head back, and roared with laughter.

"I see what you did, boy. You was fool enough to pick one of them crabs up, trying to show out for these gals here," he said to Lemm. He shook his head, his gray eyes shining with amusement. "Boy, the next time you want to impress some girls, you buy 'em some ice cream. Ain't you ever heard? You suppose to lose your heart over a gal, not your finger. Lord, I'll tell you. What kind of mess can young folks get into today? Just what kind of mess can they get into?" He howled, walking away.

Kambia and I waited until King Red was well clear of the row before we started up it ourselves, with Lemm on our heels. We left the front of the store and headed toward the produce section in the back, passing barrel after barrel of escaping crabs. As we walked Kambia looked back a couple of times to see what Lemm was doing, but I didn't, even though I was way curious to know what kind of groceries *he* had come out to get.

Kambia and I made it to the produce section in a jiffy and grabbed four huge, bumpy-looking sweet potatoes out of a wooden basket on the floor. We checked them for rotten spots and tossed them in a plastic bag. After that we rushed off to the frozen-juice section and grabbed a can of low-acid orange juice out of a standing freezer with heavy glass doors.

Finally, there was only one thing left to do—fetch a couple pounds of pork sausage from the meat section. We started for the meat counter located in the middle of store, while Lemm left to gather his own groceries.

When we got to the counter, we discovered that we had to wait behind three other ladies. Two of the ladies I had seen around some. They were acquaintances of Grandma's, friendly, gray-haired women that she sometimes played bingo with at her church's game night. They were very polite when they saw us coming. They gave us a very cheerful hello, but the third lady didn't. She just turned and grunted when she saw us. It was pretty nasty of her, but I wasn't shocked. Meanness oozed out of her like toothpaste out of a tube. She just wouldn't be herself if she wasn't giving everybody a hard time. She wouldn't be the one person in the neighborhood most deserving of an ugly nickname like Frog.

To say that Frog was being nasty was definitely only a small piece of the truth. She was being horrible. She was waddling from one end of the glass case to the other in her huge black-and-white-striped robe, stabbing at the stacks of fresh meat with her flabby finger, yelling to King Red that he had better make sure that he gave her the best cuts that he could find. And of course he was none too happy about it. He looked like at any moment he could pounce over the counter like an angry lion and tear her to bits as if she were a plump zebra.

My mind fell on Doo-witty. Frog was his mom, and she might have been mean to other folks, but she was wonderful to him. I decided that for his sake I would at least try to keep her out of harm's way. I took Kambia by the hand and walked up to the counter, foolishly hoping that the sight of two young girls would calm King Red down, though it hadn't made much difference earlier with the crabs. My plan didn't work one bit. As soon as Kambia and I made it to the cold-cuts section, Frog screamed at King Red that he had the fattiest ham hocks that she had ever seen, and he blew like a volcano. Kambia and I stepped away from the counter again to avoid the hot lava.

"What do you mean my hocks is too fat?" King Red yelled, picking up one of the brown hunks of meat and shaking it at Frog. "They suppose to be fat, they pork, ain't they? What do you think they suppose to be—lean?"

"Naw, I don't think they suppose to be lean," Frog yelled back, throwing spit everywhere like she always did. Tiny drops of it landed on the glass case. "I didn't think they was suppose to be lean at all, but they suppose to at least have some meat on them. Look at 'em. Ain't a drop of meat on 'em. They all blubber and bone. I can't put nothing like that in my pot. My doctor told me I gotta keep an eye on my blood pressure and my cholesterol. I gotta watch my figure!"

"Watch it!" King Red yelled. "We all watching it—it's pretty damn hard to miss when you wide as the sea. You so fat, if I cut you, you'd bleed barbecue sauce."

"Excuse me!" Frog yelled back.

Realizing that the argument wasn't going to be stopping anytime soon, Kambia and I decided to just forget about the breakfast meat and leave the store. Kambia said that she thought her mom probably had a little bacon in the back of the freezer. Since we all lived in pretty much the same direction, Kambia thought it would be a nice idea to ask Lemm if he wanted to walk home with us. We headed for the beverage section at the back. It was the last place we saw Lemm. He had told us that he wanted to pick up a couple of bottles of root beer for lunch.

We walked there as fast as we could. It was the best-stocked section in the place—two extra-long rows that carried everything from powdered orange juice to ginger ale to baby formula.

When we reached the section, right off the bat we noticed that Lemm wasn't where he said he would be. He was nowhere near the soda aisle. There was only a shirtless dude, about Mr. Anderson Fox's age, busily tossing six-packs of generic diet cola into his shopping cart. He nodded at us, and we nodded back.

Our plan was still to get out of the store as soon as possible, so we decided that it just made more sense for Kambia to go and pay for her groceries while I went and told Lemm we were about to head out. Kambia walked back up front, and I took off for the second drink aisle. I really didn't want to. Grandma Augustine called it the devil-water aisle, the one where all the liquors and beers were kept—and I do mean *all* the liquors and beers. Devil water, as Grandma put it, was one of the things that G. G. Diamond paid the right folks not to pay too much attention to. He carried any and every form of alcohol that he could get into the store. He had what he called "a little somethin' for every kind of drinker."

I walked into the aisle with no real hope of finding Lemm. I was pretty sure that he had probably already gotten his groceries and left the store. I was just going to take a quick peek and report to Kambia that I couldn't find him, but Lemm was there. He was standing next to a wooden shelf with his back to me, and I could tell by the way his arms were positioned that he was holding something. I figured that it must be a bottle of root beer and started walking over to him, but I had taken only a couple of steps when he hurriedly placed whatever he had in his hand on the shelf and trotted off in the other direction.

I started to call after him, but for some strange reason I didn't. Instead I waited until I couldn't see him anymore, walked over to the shelf where he had been standing, and began looking it over. My eyes fell on something really curious. It was a clear, medium-size rectangular bottle. I picked it up. It was warm to the touch, like someone had been holding it. It was filled with what could have been mistaken for mineral water, if it wasn't for the silver label on the front. STOVALS VODKA was what it read in large, raised letters.

I placed the bottle back on the shelf, glanced around me quickly, then picked it back up. It looked only a tad empty, like someone had taken just a few swigs. I twisted the loose cap off and sniffed the contents. I expected it to have a really strong smell, but it didn't. It had kind of a subtle smell, not loud like the bourbon that Mr. Anderson Fox had sometimes drunk when he was living with us.

I put the bottle back on the shelf and just stood there with my hand still gripping it. Was it what Lemm had had in his hand? I didn't want to believe it, but I was confident that it was. There was certainly no bottle of root beer around to make me think otherwise. I didn't know Lemm all that well, but I did know that he was really smart. He should know better than to be playing around with such foolishness. If what folks said about Lemm's dad getting drunk and accidentally walking out in front of a truck with his own children was true, you would think that Lemm would be the first kid to know that drinking was a seriously messed-up thing to do. You would think that he would be the first kid to give a thumbs-down to alcohol.

I returned the bottle back to the shelf and was pulling my hand away when someone grabbed me roughly by the shoulder. It was a grip that could only belong to Grandma Augustine. I froze.

"What in the world are you doing, little girl?" she asked. "You were supposed to be home a long time ago. You been gone way too long. Kambia's mama been calling the house worried. I had to tell her that I would come down and see about her child. What kind of nonsense have you two been up to?"

"Nothing . . . nothing, Grandma," I stammered. "We weren't doing nothing at all. We were just about to come home."

"Just about!" she cried. "What do you mean, 'just about'? I told you to run down here and run back. That's why I let you go. Otherwise I wouldn't be letting you run around in your nightclothes and such. You know I don't like that."

"I . . . I know," I said. "And we were trying to get back really fast. It just took us a while to get some of the stuff."

"What stuff? Ain't nothing here difficult to find. And what are you doing in this aisle? You ain't got no business over here." She spotted the bottle and yanked my hand away from it, causing it to totter. "What's this?" she asked, grabbing it. "Shayla, what are you doing fooling around with this kind of junk?"

I shrugged my shoulders and looked at the spot where the bottle had been. "Nothing," I said. "I was just passing by and saw it. It looked weird, so I came over and picked it up."

"You know better than to be fooling around with this kind of craziness. You ain't even got no business nowhere near this aisle." She shook the bottle. "It ain't full. Somebody been drinking it," she said. "Lord, I swear people ain't got no shame about doing nothing nowadays." She reached toward the shelf with the bottle, but instead of putting it back, she let out a loud gasp, as if she had just seen a two-headed man coming up the aisle or something.

"Lord, child, don't tell me," she cried. "Lord, Lord, child, don't tell me! I know that you didn't do this, did you, Shayla? I know you know better than to be messing with some junk like this."

"What! Grandma Augustine, you know that I wouldn't," I said, turning away from the shelf to explain, but something took my words away. Grandma wasn't alone. She had someone with her. Someone wrapped in a soft knit blanket. It was Gift. Grandma had Gift. She was holding her tenderly against her shoulder, like she had held me when I was a baby. I couldn't believe what I was seeing. How could she? I felt something welling up inside of me. It was jealousy, a deep, murky, swamp green jealousy that polluted everything in me.

"What are you doing with her?" I asked. "Where's her mom at? Why doesn't Jada have her?"

Grandma set the bottle back on the shelf and shifted Gift upward over her big breasts. "We can talk about that in a minute," she said. "You just tell me what you doing back here messing with this junk."

"I wasn't messing with it," I repeated. "It was just there, that's all. I just took a look."

"A look, what's there to see?" Grandma asked. "You know what this stuff looks like. You done seen it often enough 'round the neighborhood. You didn't need to pick it up, so now you explain to me what's going on."

"Explain what!" I snapped without meaning to. "What do you

need me to explain? You already got all the answers. Nobody ever listens to what I have to say anyway."

"I listen," she said sternly. "Ain't a word ever came out of your mouth that I didn't hear."

"No, you don't, Grandma. You don't even pay attention to me anymore. If you did, you wouldn't have her," I said, pointing to Gift.

"Is that what you back here about? Is all this mess about this here new baby? Honey, if this child is what's making you create problems for yourself, you can stop it right now. You are wrong about this baby. You just wrong."

"No, no, no, I'm not," I said, shaking my head. "I'm not wrong about anything."

"Yes, you are, and I'm sorry. I was gonna tell you this morning when you came back from the store. I talked to Jada and your daddy a couple of days ago. They having a tough time finding somebody to keep her. With the hospital bills and all, they a little tight on money, and the restaurant where Jada work been cutting back on some of her hours. She been out looking for a second job, and you know your daddy still only doing that temp work. It's hard on them right now. There ain't no other relatives that will keep her, and they can't afford to pay for a day care. I told them that I would help out. It's the Christian thing to do. It's right, baby," she said. "You have to know that. Your mama and I raised you to know better. She is, after all, your sister."

"No, she's not! She's Mr. Anderson Fox's daughter. He has to claim her, I don't." I started to walk off, but Grandma jerked me by the arm.

"Don't you walk away from me," she said. "I ain't finished."

"I am!" I snapped again. Then I took a deep breath and calmed myself. "You just don't understand, Grandma," I said. "You just don't get it."

"No, I guess I don't, little girl," she said, pointing to the bottle. "I don't because I ain't never known you to be this foolish."

"I didn't touch any of that stuff, Grandma," I said. "I told you, I just picked it up."

"Then why did you act all nervous when I walked up? Why you act like you were doing more than just taking a look? What's wrong with you, girl?" she asked. "Ever since this baby come in this world, you been acting like you done lost your mind, like you don't know right from wrong. Well, I know. I know if you think any of the mess on this shelf is just gonna up and make this baby go away, you sho is playing on the wrong street corner. Now, do you understand me?"

I just stared at her.

"Answer me, little girl."

My jaw remained locked.

She opened her mouth to say something, but for some reason she just paused for a minute instead. She rubbed her forehead like she was tired, and then compassion settled on her.

"Look, baby," she said with a face full of worry. "I'm just concerned about you. Your grandma Augustine is just concerned about you."

"Grandma . . . ," I started, but I paused as well. The word *concerned* held my voice back. Concerned about me. She was concerned about me. She was so worried that she had the very thing that was making me upset resting on her shoulder. It didn't make sense. For the first time ever she didn't make sense. She knew how I felt about Gift. She knew how much Gift made me hurt.

"Say something, Shayla," Grandma said. "Tell me what's going on with you."

"I don't have anything to say," I mumbled.

Gift stirred, balled her tiny fists up, and started to cry, a loud howl that sounded like Grandma's cat when he's out on the prowl. I looked up.

"It's okay. Hush, hush, sweet child," Grandma said, patting Gift's back gently. The words cut me deeper than the word *concerned*. They tore through me like bullets or King Red's butcher knife. I remembered "Hush, hush, sweet child." I remembered her saying it over my crib before I went to sleep and when I was sick in bed. They were my words. Gift had stolen them, too, like she had stolen my birthday and the father that I didn't want, and now my grandmother.

"Say something to me, Shayla," Grandma said as Gift started to settle down. She picked the bottle up once more. "I know you been upset lately. Just tell me what's going on. I just need to—" The sound of footsteps cut her off.

It was Lemm and Kambia coming up the aisle, and they were both smiling, at least until Lemm spotted the bottle and his smile vanished. He swallowed hard. Panic gripped his face for a second, but it was gone just as quickly. He pulled his mouth into another huge smile, one that could easily have competed with Mr. Anderson Fox's grin.

"Oh, Mrs. Dubois," he said, walking up. "Don't you look lovely as usual. You are the one ray of sunshine on this desperately dark morning." He pulled back Gift's blanket and took a peek. "And what's this? Is this your little girl?"

"My little girl." Grandma laughed, a hint of red coming to her sagging cheeks. "Boy, please. Now, you know this ain't no child of mine."

"It could be," Lemm said. "You're barely out of your youth."

"Go head on, and stop being so silly," Grandma laughed.

"Oh, I see that you guys saw the bottle too," Lemm continued, pointing to it in her hand. Grandma stared at it oddly, as if she had forgotten that it was even there. Lemm took it from her and held it up in front of Kambia.

"See, I told you that someone had been drinking out of it," he said. "I told you that some wino was back here taking a drink when I walked through the aisle."

"Wow, I can't believe that someone would do that right in the store. But don't say 'wino,'" Kambia said. "It's not a nice thing to call somebody. My mom and dad say that some people can't help that they drink too much."

"Some wino—you telling me that you saw a drunk back here drinking out of this?" Grandma Augustine asked Lemm, obviously not heeding what Kambia had said.

He nodded. Embarrassment rushed to Grandma's cheeks, turning them even redder. "There was a drunk back here?" she said with a confused look on her face. "He was the one drinking out of the bottle?"

"I saw him with my own eyes. I was just walking through from the soda aisle, and there he was," he said. "Some bum in a old, raggedy T-shirt and cruddy shoes."

"Some bum," Grandma repeated. She looked at me with regret pouring into her eyes. "Oh, Lord—oh, Lord. I don't know what I could have been thinking. What would make me come up with such a thing?" She patted my hand. "Baby, forgive me. I don't know what got into me. I was just worried about you. You been acting so funny lately. I was just trying to stop you from doing something foolish. Oh, Lord, what was I thinking."

"I don't know," I mumbled. "I don't know anything."

I looked back at Kambia. She had a plastic grocery bag in her hand. "Did you already pay?" I asked.

"Yeah," she said.

"All right, then," Grandma said in a sad voice. "All right, then, let's just get out of here. Your mama looking for you, Kambia. I think it's time for all of us to go back."

"Me, too," I said.

We placed the bottle on the shelf for the final time, and the four us of walked to the front of the store and left. The street was still mostly empty when we got outside, but the real sun had finally decided to start its shift. Its rays were turned all the way up, bathing the skyline in brightness.

"Isn't it pretty?" Kambia asked me. I didn't answer.

"I'm sorry," Grandma whispered, walking behind me. "I wish I had the words, baby. I wish I had the words."

So did I. I felt horrible. I didn't like what had happened between me and Grandma, and I wanted to tell her that it was all right, but I didn't know how. There were no words that could describe how I felt seeing her hold Gift as if she were her grandmother and having her suspect that I was the one drinking the vodka. She had only meant to help, but she had ended up breaking something between us.

I walked silently between Kambia and Lemm, noticing for the first time that Lemm smelled very strongly of peppermint and that he was walking like he wasn't all that sure of his steps, but I don't think anyone else saw him. Grandma was too tied up with guilt, and Kambia never saw anything that she didn't want to see. She was hung up on Lemm. While we walked, he started calling her Lady Kambia once more and telling her silly jokes that made her blush and laugh. She was prom-queen happy again, and Lemm had a lot to do with it. He was maybe the first guy that was nice to her without wanting anything in return. It was for this reason that I decided what Kambia didn't know wouldn't hurt her. It wasn't a secret. It was there for all the world to see; I just wouldn't be the one that made her see it. Kambia had been through a lot lately. I wouldn't pile any more on her. The next time I saw Lemm, we would talk about the bottle, about his lie, and about how he nearly got me into big trouble. For now I just wanted to go home and hide out in my room.

I thought about the crabs in the store. I once saw a nature special on TV where a bunch of crabs had eaten up a man who had had a heart attack and fallen in the water. That's the way I felt, like something had eaten parts of me, the best parts. There would be no journal entry when I got back to the house this time. Like Grandma said, I just didn't have the words.

# Chapter 3

Nell stood in the doorway, drowsily staring at the sleeping infant lying peacefully in the wicker bassinet. It was four in the morning and the child had finally settled down. She had forgotten how intensely tiring nights with newborns could be—the crying, the bottle warming, the floor walking, the feeling of wishing that you could just rest your eyes for a moment or two.

She couldn't believe it. She was doing the baby night shift again, and the child wasn't even hers. She was thirty-eight and already a grandmother, already a grandmother because of a stupid mistake. It was her fault mostly, what had happened to her daughter, Kendra. She was the one who had suggested that Kendra go to the dance, and the one who had bought her the new slinky black dress to wear to it. She had done it out of love, but mostly out of pity. Kendra was a homely child. To be honest, she was downright ugly, but it wasn't her fault. She had inherited her looks from her father, Clinton, a kind, compassionate man who was the best father and husband that any family could ask for, but who unfortunately had a face that pretty much reminded most people of a bulldog.

It was that bulldog face that kept Kendra always an outcast at school. The girls called her a fright queen, and the boys barked whenever she came around. It hurt Nell something fierce. She was an incredibly beautiful woman. She just couldn't believe that none of her good looks had passed on to her fourteen-year-old daughter. That's why she had gone out of her way to help Kendra that night of the dance. It was her idea to buy the high heels that made her look several years older, paint her face up like the beauties of the month in Jet magazine, and ask her neighbor's handsome seventeen-year-old son, William, a star basketball player, to take Kendra to the dance. She only wanted Kendra to be beautiful and happy for just one night.

The plan worked better than she had hoped. She couldn't believe what the outfit and makeup did for Kendra inside and out. She left the house sexy and confident, a total new Kendra, one that any boy would be happy to spend the evening with— and that was the tremendous mistake.

Even though Nell saw the signs early on—the tiredness, nausea, and bloated face—it was four months before she was forced to deal with what had happened to Kendra that night. She found out when the nurse at Kendra's school called her up. She told her to come up to the high school in a hurry. Kendra was pregnant.

When Nell got to the school, she found out that Kendra was as confused as she was pregnant. She didn't understand what had happened the night of the dance. She hadn't really said yes to William, but she hadn't actually said no, either. Doing it with him had just been a part of the evening, like the cheap corsage he bought her and the pancake dinner at IHOP. It was just something that happened when kids went out on dates, he had told her, and since it was her first time on a date, she had believed what he said.

Nell was shattered when she heard her daughter's pitiful tale. Feeling that it was all her fault, she tried to think of something comforting and reassuring to say to Kendra as she sat next to her on the vinyl sofa watching the tears slide down her face, but all she could think of was that it was time to start

*buying diapers again. They would need lots of diapers. She left*
*the nurse's office that afternoon, went to the store, and bought*
*twelve packages of newborn-size Pampers.*

I started this story today while Gift was crying. Grandma Augustine was a little late in getting her a bottle, and she was screaming her head off to let her know that she didn't appreciate it. The noise was so loud it just about uncurled Tia's braids. It was seriously working my nerves, so I took my blue notebook into the bathroom, closed the door, and started writing the story. It was the easiest way that I could think of to drown Gift out.

Gift's over here a lot now, whenever Grandma comes over. When she's here, the house pretty much feels like it belongs to her. She hangs from it like cobwebs. You can feel her essence when you come in, and when you go out, she clings to you like cigarette smoke. Grandma and Mama say that it's a good thing. They say that it's been a long time since there was an infant in the house.

"There's just something about a baby that brings joy to a home," Grandma Augustine said. "They're nicer than a glass of iced tea on a hot summer day."

"Ain't it the truth," Mama said. "I didn't know how much I missed the smell of baby powder."

"Yes, babies are life's present to us," Grandma Augustine quoted from her African book of sayings. "A new birth brings fresh water to a thirsty village."

Mama's reaction to having Gift in the house may be a little strange after what Mr. Anderson Fox did to her, but Grandma's is understandable. Grandma Augustine lost four babies before Mama, and although she says that she has already cried all the tears that she will ever cry over them, I can tell that losing them still hurts.

Sometimes I sneak in the room while she's holding Gift and see her rocking her on her breast. "You're a strong one," she says to her. "I know that you'll make it through anything. That's the way it should be. Children should always go after, never before, never before. A mother should never have to put her own child in the ground."

It was for that reason that I decided that I would at least try with Gift. A couple of days ago, while Grandma, Mama, and Tia were holed up in the kitchen again, picking a bushel of purple hull peas, I walked into our bedroom, where Grandma usually put her down to nap, and stared at her. She was still awake. She was lying there in her snap-up baby overalls, kicking her sockless brown feet and staring up at the ceiling like there was a mobile on it or something, but when she saw me, she started to gurgle and broke into a baby smile. She was all gums and spit bubbles. I have to admit she was pretty cute. She reminded me of a battery-operated baby doll that Grandma bought me once, only her hair was all soft and fuzzy, whereas the doll's hair was just painted on. I stuck my finger out, and she grabbed it and curled her itty-bitty fingers around it. She was soft and warm. For just a second or two I felt a kinship with her. I remembered another one of Grandma's sayings. "Love is like a boomerang—throw it out, and usually it comes right back."

I wanted to throw love out to Gift. I wanted to pick her up and tell her that it wasn't her fault that she was born on my day, but her eyes stopped me. They were focused on me, and I got the exact same feeling that I had had in the hospital, like she was dissecting me. I could feel her pupils separating me into little pieces. She was scanning me, taking in all of the data that made up me. Later, when she could talk, she would be able to spit me back out to anyone that she chose to. She really did have the eyes of a writer. It wouldn't be long before she was writing stories of her own, stories that Mr. Anderson

Fox would be proud of. He wouldn't tell her that she should get a job as a nurse. He would be happy when she said that she had just sent a story off to a magazine or had a poem published in some journal. She was his Gift. It would be fine for her to be a writer.

I pulled my finger out of Gift's grip, turned to leave the room, and found myself facing Tia. She was standing right outside the door, wearing only a thin nylon slip, with her long braids all done up in gold beads. Her toenails were painted gold as well, and her catlike eyes were shimmering with gold eye shadow.

"I thought you were picking peas," I said, startled.

"I was, but Mama and Grandma got to arguing about what kind of freezer bags was best to put them in, and I decided to go hang out somewhere else. Anyway, Doo-witty will be over soon," she said. "We're going to look at a Nigerian art exhibit at the Museum of Fine Arts. You can come with us if you like."

"That will be really cool," I nearly blurted out, but then I remembered how lovey-dovey Tia and Doo-witty could get and changed my mind. The last thing that I wanted to do was spend the entire day watching their faces stuck together. "Naw, I better pass," I said. "I got some school stuff that I need to do."

"All right," she said. "But don't forget that I asked, the next time that you're whining about me spending too much time with Doo-witty and not enough time with you."

"I won't. Have a good time."

"I will," she said. "Doo-witty is taking me to see his new painting down at the multicultural center after we leave the museum. It's only going to be there for a short time. Some big-shot lawyer downtown bought it for his office."

"Wow. Did he pay Doo-witty a lot?"

"Enough for him to buy his mom a new washer and dryer, and

pay for his English tutoring classes down at the College Learning Center."

"Good for him," I said.

"It is," she said. She looked over at Gift, who was still kicking her legs and blowing spit bubbles. "She's really cute when she does that, isn't she?"

I shrugged my shoulders.

"Oh, well. I just thought that I would look in on the baby. I'm gonna go see if Mama and Grandma need some more help before I get dressed." She paused before she left the hall. "Oh, I forgot. That boy is coming over, the one that went to the party with you. He called and said that he was coming by this morning. Grandma took the call. I told her that you might end up hanging out with me and Doo-witty, but she told him to come anyway and take his chances."

"Okay," I said. "Thanks for letting me know."

She nodded and left.

I walked to the doorway and watched Tia swish back to the kitchen, her slip clinging to her round, shapely bottom. She definitely had back, there was no doubt about it. I wondered if my pudgy body would ever look like hers. It was weird. We were sisters, but we didn't look anything alike. I glanced back at Gift. She was still staring at me. It gave me the creeps. I left the room and went outside to the front porch.

I sat down on the concrete porch steps in my jean jumper and checked out the neighborhood. It was about nine thirty. It was warm out, bright and sunny, and folks were already making the best of it. At the house across the street from Kambia's old place, a tall, leggy sister with nylon bike shorts and thong sandals was splashing two giggling little girls in striped bathing suits with a water hose in the tiny front yard, while a group of muscle-shirted guys tossed balls into a netless hoop planted in the center of the gravel driveway. On the corner of the next block up, the children's group of Holy Union Church were setting up a bake sale in the center of the sidewalk. In matching green shorts and shirts, they paraded up and down in front of the small wooden sanctuary carrying large black-and-white signs that read, EVERYTHING UNDER FIVE BUCKS.

For a little bit I thought about what kinds of sweets and treats the children's group might be selling, but slowly my thoughts wandered to Lemm. It's been nearly two weeks since the incident at Diamond's. Grandma and I have made a shaky kind of peace. I haven't actually forgiven her for accusing me of drinking from the vodka bottle, or for telling Mr. Anderson Fox and Jada that she would watch Gift, but we both decided that it was best not to even talk about it for a while. We would just end up saying things that would hurt each other. "I've always said that time heals old wounds, but it's also good for new ones," Grandma said. "We won't talk about it until you got a mind to."

Well, I still don't have a mind to, at least not with Grandma, but Lemm, that's another story. There are some things that we need to get straight, and I know that he knows it, because lately he's been avoiding me worse than a kid avoids cough syrup. In homeroom he takes a seat as far away from mine as he can, when I usually have to scoot my chair over to get away from him. If I happen to come across him in the lunchroom, where he generally makes himself at home at my table, he picks his tray up and sprints from the room like a stink bomb or something just went off. So I was really surprised when Tia said that he was coming over. Maybe he's figured out that it's not much fun running with a heavy load on your back.

By ten thirty Lemm hadn't shown up, but Mr. Heat had. He was roaming from block to block tossing buckets of sweat on everyone that he met, including me. It was blistering out, and I was beginning to feel like a huge bottle of extra-hot picante sauce. I got up to go inside.

"What's up, Miss Shayla?" Lemm's voice rang out as I headed up the steps. I walked back down them.

"Nothing's up. It's hot, I'm hot, and just plain ole 'Shayla' is good enough for me," I said, not at all in the mood for any of his fake charm.

"Of course, Miss Shayla, I'll call you whatever you like," he said. "I'm always willing to please such an interesting and smart girl."

"I'm not that interesting, or that smart, Lemm. And just 'Shayla,' okay? No 'Miss,'" I said once more. "My mom's a Miss."

"As you wish, Miss Shayla," he said, totally ignoring me. "Miss Shayla, you are indeed an interesting and smart girl, especially smart. You are the smartest girl in our program."

"I wish," I said, laughing. "That would really be great, if it were true."

"Oh, but it is. No one is smarter than you," he said, and followed it with a really sweet smile.

I laughed again. "Get real, Lemm," I said.

He wiped his sweaty brow with the back of his hand. Beads of sweat dripped from underneath his fingers and slid into the corners of his eyes. I noticed that his irises were streaked with red again. They looked almost pink in the sun. "Whoo," he said. "It sure is hot. Perhaps we should walk up to the porch."

"Okay," I said.

It was just a tad cooler on the front porch, so we grabbed a couple of metal shell-shaped chairs. I pushed mine up against the side of the house. He positioned his in front of me and threw an even sweeter smile up on his face. I rethought my opinion of his looks. He had nice skin with no blemishes, soft black lashes, and really good cheekbones for a guy. I guess he was just a little bit more than okay looking. He was kind of handsome, except for whatever was going on in those chestnut eyes.

"That's right," he said. "I do think that you are the smartest girl in the program. I am being real. I don't think that anyone is as smart as you. There just couldn't be anyone, not even me."

"Yeah, right," I said with a big grin of my own. "I've seen your papers. You really kick butt on your tests. You always make serious A's."

"Sometimes," he said, "but not nearly as often as you. You're an impressive girl, Miss Shayla. I wish that I was even just a little bit as smart as you are."

"Really?" I asked.

"Really."

"Wow! Thanks," I said. For just one moment I willingly allowed myself to be taken in by his charm. Then I noticed it, just a hint of the scent of something like beer or wine coming from his direction. I checked out his eyes again. They seemed redder than before—red, watery, and sleepy looking. His pupils were huge, like someone was holding a magnifying glass over them.

"You've been drinking, Lemm," I said.

"What?" he said, caught off guard. He pushed his chair away from mine real fast, as if I were a rattler about to strike. The legs made a loud scraping sound against the porch.

"You've been drinking," I repeated. "Your eyes are beet red, and you smell like a wino."

"I don't know what you're talking about," he said nervously, the sweet smile slipping from his face.

"You've been drinking," I said once more. "I don't know what, but something. You look like one of those guys at Perry's 24-and-7 beer joint."

He shook his head, beads of sweat starting to form on his forehead again. "Of . . . of course not, Miss Shayla," he stuttered. "I'm way too young to drink. We both are. Don't be silly."

"I'm not, and you're right. We both are too young, but that's not stopping you from doing it." I pointed my finger at him with one of Mama's best let-me-tell-you-something looks. "You almost got me in trouble with my grandma. She thought that it was me drinking that day at the store, but it was really you taking swigs out of that bottle. You ought to be ashamed of yourself. You ought to know better."

"I don't . . . don't know what you're talking about, Miss Shayla," he stuttered again. "This is totally unacceptable. I can't believe that you would accuse me of such a thing. It's you who . . . who ought to know better. Don't accuse people of things that you can't back up!"

His yelling caught me completely off guard, but I wasn't in a mood to back down. I didn't want to piss him off. I just wanted him to know that what he had done wasn't cool with me.

"I'm not accusing. I'm just letting you know. I thought you wanted to be my friend. Friends don't get other friends in trouble."

"I didn't do anything!" he yelled, his face all twisted up. He looked like something was going to pop loose inside of him, and I braced for the worst, but all of a sudden his face went as calm as mine. It was almost like he just flicked some kind of switch and turned his anger off, like he did with the panic that day in the store. The sweet smile gathered on his lips again. He leaned in real close to me, and this time I smelled the alcohol on his breath. There was no doubt. He was not drinking chocolate milk.

"Yes, you did. You were drinking out of that bottle when I

walked up, then you took off, and I picked it up. Grandma thought that it was me who did it. She didn't even want to hear me out."

"I don't know what you're talking about, Miss Shayla," he said once more. "Are you sure that you actually saw me drink from a bottle?"

I bit my lip and turned the question over in my head. The truth of the matter is no, I didn't actually see him drink from the bottle, but I wasn't stupid. He put something back on the shelf and sprinted away. When I checked out the bottles, the seal on the vodka bottle was the only one that was broken. It was a pretty easy case. I didn't have to be Linda James, girl detective, to figure it out.

"I'm sure, Lemm. Don't try to play me. I know that it was you, and you should know better, especially with what happened to your dad."

The word *dad* erased the calm off his face quicker than a teacher erasing a blackboard. He hopped up out of his chair so quick that you would have thought it was filled with thumbtacks. He stumbled a couple of steps away from it, his feet not quite as steady as they had been just seconds before.

"Leave my dad out of this, Shayla," he said harshly, dropping the *Miss* like I had asked him to do several times. "You don't know anything about him. My dad has nothing to do with what I do. I just told you that I don't know anything about a bottle. Why don't you just change the subject? I don't want to talk about it anymore."

"Then admit it," I said. "Admit it and I'll shut up."

"There is nothing to admit, Shayla," he said, his words starting to slur. "I just came over to see if you wanted to hang out at the library or something. I don't know what your problem is. I'm leaving."

He stumbled a couple of more steps away from his chair. As he did my eyes popped wide open. He was getting more and more tore up as we talked. He was losing his cool, and somehow that was making him lose everything else, too—but why, and how?

My mind drifted back to the day that we first met. Was he drunk that day too? I couldn't remember. He was pretty much like he was today, clever with his words. He used that sugar smile of his and said all the things that he thought I wanted him to say. "I'm really glad that the teacher put us together, Miss Shayla," he said, standing in front of my locker door, beckoning for me to give him the key to my Sergeant lock. "I'm really very happy. Our homeroom teacher says that you are one of the brightest girls in our school. I'm pretty sharp too. Perhaps we can learn from each other. I think it's wonderful that you'll be my guide into my new seventh-grade world."

He had piled it on heavy, so heavy that I got totally absorbed in what he was talking about and nearly missed my gym class. I knew that it was just slop, but I wanted to roll around in it, at least I did on that day. It was the first week of summer school, and I was missing Kambia. I felt like a run-over dog inside, and I needed someone to pay attention to me. Lemm did. But by the end of the day I realized that listening to his fake flattery was a lot worse than missing my best friend. I raced out of the school when the bell rang, running like mad from his words. Looking back on it, though, I couldn't tell you if his eyes were red that day, or if his speech was a little slurred, or what his breath smelled like. His words had somehow blocked everything else out, like they had cast some kind of magic spell over me.

I should have figured out what he was doing that first day. It didn't matter if his words eventually pissed me off; I got so wrapped up in what he was saying, I couldn't see the person that was saying them, and neither could anybody else. He was fooling us all. I felt so stupid. I thought that he was just being slick like Mr. Anderson Fox, but Mr. Anderson Fox only knows how to play lonely women. He tells them what they want to hear, but they aren't really confused. They know what he is. They are just so desperate at the time that it doesn't matter, but Lemm is a different story. With his words he can disguise himself like Superman does when he puts on his regular clothes. He uses his words like an invisible shield to hide what he really is, throwing so much crap at you that you don't have a chance to figure anything out. How long had he been drinking? I couldn't even guess. The truth of the matter is I probably never would have noticed that he was drinking at all if I hadn't seen him do it at Diamond's that day. I would have continued being fooled like everyone else.

I felt even sorrier for Lemm than I had before. He was probably as screwed up as his dad. I had no right making him feel worse than he did, letting him know that I had pulled his cover off. And in fact, I didn't care all that much that he was drinking. I thought it was a dumb thing to do, but I really only wanted him to apologize for not telling Grandma the truth. I didn't want to tear him apart. I swallowed real hard and pushed my pride back down to wherever it had shot up from. I couldn't change what had happened between me and Grandma, but I could change what had just happened between me and him. Maybe Mama was right. I could use another friend.

"Just forget it, Lemm," I said. "It's no big deal. Maybe I'm wrong about the whole thing. Grandma says that even the smartest ant sometimes goes down the wrong trail. I'm sorry. Just forget about it and sit back down."

He stumbled back to his chair, and the minute his butt hit the metal, his face started to go back to its old self. It was amazing, like those shape-shifters in the sci-fi flicks.

"It's okay, Miss Shayla," he said in almost his normal speech. "Anyone can make a mistake."

"Shayla," I said. "I like just plain ole 'Shayla.' My mom is a Miss, remember?"

"I'll remember," he said. "Okay, Shayla, we're still friends, right?" he asked. "You're not mad at me anymore?"

I shook my head. "Of course not, Lemm. It was just a mistake."

"Good," he said, the smile returning to his face. "Let's shake on it."

He reached over and took my hand from my lap before I could extend it on my own. I was shocked at how clammy his palms were. I didn't pull my hand away, though. I waited for him to shake it, but instead he just continued to hold it in his, and I don't know why. It made me feel all funny inside, like there were fireflies or something flittering around inside of me, lighting parts of me up. It was a really weird feeling, something that I never felt when Kambia held my hand, and I wasn't sure if I liked it at all.

I was about to jerk my hand away when Tia poked her head out of the screen door. "Shayla, something's wrong with Kambia," she said. "The folks down at that Girl Help Center want you to come down quick."

"What's wrong?" I asked, snatching my hand away from Lemm's.

"I don't know," she said. "They just asked me if I could tell you to get down there right away."

"Okay," I said. "Tell Mama where I went." I jumped up out of my chair and bounded down the steps, with Lemm bounding after me. I wanted to tell him that he should just go home and take a long nap, but I didn't have time. There was something wrong with Kambia.

*   *   *

Last week in my art class my teacher said that there was no such thing as ugliness. She said that what was unattractive to one person might be completely beautiful to another. Ugly was left up to the interpreter. It wasn't concrete or solid. It was something that changed in each person's eyes. People often called things ugly because they just didn't understand what they were seeing. At the time I thought that she was right, that sometimes things did get misinterpreted, but when I walked into Kambia's classroom, I had to change my mind. What I saw would have been awfully ugly in anybody's eyes, and nobody would have had a problem understanding what they were seeing.

It was Kambia. She was sitting all alone in one of several metal folding chairs that had been arranged in a circle. Her face was drained of color, and her eyes were completely blank. In her hands was something familiar, but not really familiar. It was a dingy white dress, like the one that she had on when I first met her. There was something scribbled on it in red marker, but I couldn't make out the words. The dress was torn in places, but there was no loose thread around the holes, so you could tell that they were freshly made.

I was shocked. I didn't know what to do. I stood there a good long time, staring at the dress and staring at Kambia's pale hands clutching it. Finally I decided to take action. I snatched the dress from her. I held it up and read the words. KAMBIA, THIS IS WHAT A LITTLE GIRL LIKE YOU DESERVES! they read in crooked letters. The words sliced into me deep, even deeper than seeing Grandma with Gift. I flung the dress into a metal trash can behind Kambia's seat.

"Kambia, are you all right? It's me, Shayla. Are you okay?" She didn't answer. "Kambia," I said again. "It's me, Shayla. Are you okay? Answer me, Kambia. Are you okay? Where did the dress come from? Kambia, where did you get that thing from?" Still no answer.

I took both of her hands in mine and started to caress them. They were rigid and cold, and I was pretty sure that the rest of her was too. I pulled her to me and hugged her chilled body to mine. "It's okay, Kambia. You don't have to tell me anything. It's okay. Don't worry. I just want you to be okay." I started caressing her back, like Grandma sometimes did to me when I was upset. "You're going to be just fine, Kam. It's me, Shayla. Nobody here is going to hurt you. I'll find out where that stupid dress came from."

"It was in her locker," I heard Lemm say behind me. I had almost forgotten that he had followed me down. "I just saw one of the young ladies that was at her school's party in the hallway," he said. "She told me that she was supposed to be watching Kambia, but she had to go take her baby to a doctor's appointment. She said that Kambia found the dress in her locker and flipped out. She's been like that for nearly an hour. Her counselor, Mrs. Dreyfus, was trying to call her parents, but nobody answered, so she called you. She figured that you could snap her out of whatever this is."

"I don't know what this is," I said. "I just know that she does it sometimes, but she usually comes right out of it pretty quick. I can't believe that she's been like this for nearly an hour."

"She looks kind of like she's sleeping with her eyes open," he said. "Her eyeballs aren't moving at all."

"No, they aren't," I said. "They don't do anything when she gets like this, but she's not sleeping. Her counselor says that she just doesn't know how to deal with some things."

I let Kambia go and looked at Lemm. His eyes were still a little red, but not drowsy looking like they were before, and I could see pity peeping out through them. "Is she gonna be all right?" he asked.

"I hope so," I said.

"I do too," he said.

He walked over and took the chair on the other side of Kambia. I noticed that he smelled strongly of mint again. I figured that he must have popped a few breath fresheners before he came into the room. "Good morning, Lady Kambia," he said to her. "I trust that you are doing well today." She didn't respond to him, either. He glanced at the dress in the trash can behind her seat and looked back at me, puzzled.

"It's a long story," I said. "I don't know. She used to have a dress like that, but the doctors gave it to the police when she was in the hospital. The police said that if they ever found her old mom, they could use it to help keep her in jail." I started patting Kambia's face gently with the palm of my hand. "Kambia, it's okay. Nobody's going to hurt you. Can you hear me?"

All I got was silence.

"Come on, Kambia," I said, tugging at her elbow. "Lemm's here, and he wants to say hi. We can all walk home together. Maybe Grandma Augustine will make us her lemon sugar cookies, and we can have some cold milk. You better snap out of it, Kambia. If you don't, me and Lemm will eat all the cookies." I tugged her elbow again. She just continued staring, eyes wide open, like there was a movie going on in her head that I couldn't see.

"Should we get somebody?" Lemm asked. "Would you like me to go find her counselor?"

"I'm right here," Mrs. Dreyfus said, coming in the door. Her plump face was filled with concern. "I'm glad you came, Shayla," she said, walking over to me, the heels of her pumps tapping loudly against the wood floor. "I've been trying to get her parents for the past half hour."

"They went out of town for the day," I said. "One of Mr. Major's brothers is having some kind of operation, but they didn't take

Kambia because they didn't want her to miss her Saturday counseling. They're just a little ways away. They left the number with my grandma. You can call her."

"I will. I'll do that later, but right now Kambia is my priority. I didn't want to be away from her for too long. I told one of the other girls to watch her while I made the call, but I guess she just took off."

"She had to go take her baby to the doctor," Lemm said.

"Oh, that's right. With everything that's going on, I forgot about that," Mrs. Dreyfus said. "I really wish that she had reminded me about it before she left, though."

"It's okay," I said. "She doesn't do much when she's like this. She just kind of shuts herself off. I've seen her do it a few times, but it usually doesn't last this long. I think that she's just freaked out because of the dress. Some girl told Lemm that somebody put it in her locker or something."

"That's what we think. I'm glad that she let you take it away from her. I couldn't get her to let go of it, but none of that is important right now." She walked over and squatted in front of Kambia. "Kambia, I know that you're in there. It's okay to come out. Remember what I said about your fantasy world. It's not okay to deal with things like this. Kambia, I know that you can hear me," she said. "We're all right here—me; your best friend, Shayla; and your new friend, Lemm. We all want you to get better, Kambia. You were doing so well lately, really well. None of us wants you to take a step back." Kambia still said nothing.

I caught Kambia's arm. "We better just go home, Kambia. Me and Lemm can walk you," I said, trying to pull her up, but Mrs. Dreyfus stopped me.

"Shayla, I know that you want to help your friend. It's the reason why I called you. However, I can't let you take Kambia out of here like this. She needs to be escorted home by someone responsible."

"I am responsible," I said, feeling a little hurt and annoyed. Everybody knew that I would never let anything happen to Kambia.

"I know that you are, but in the condition that's she's in, I can't let a thirteen-year-old girl take her home. She needs to be released into the custody of someone responsible, like your grandmother," she said.

"My grandmother can't walk all the way down here," I said. "She has a bad leg. Besides, me and Kambia will be just fine. I'm better with her than my grandma Augustine is. I'll take her back to her house. She'll be okay. My grandma can come over there. It's not too far."

Mrs. Dreyfus shook her head. "No, Shayla. If your grandmother can't make it up here, we will have to make other arrangements. My car is parked out back. Let's all go out to it. Kambia, we're going now," she said softly. "We're going to take you home. You know, the place that you came from. We're going to take you back where you came from. Kambia, did you hear what I said?"

Kambia did. She must have heard her loud and clear, and I don't think that she liked what she heard. She jumped out of her chair and bolted. She hit the door and went running out of it like a pack of wild animals was after her.

"Kambia!" I cried. "Stop, wait up!"

I tore after Kambia, with Mrs. Dreyfus and Lemm on my heels. She was running like mad, and I was running like crazy after her. She reached the end of the hall and dashed around the corner. I raced after her, calling her name at the top of my lungs. "Kambia, stop, hold up! Nobody's gonna hurt you!"

"Kambia, wait, please. I think you misunderstood," Mrs. Dreyfus called behind me.

Kambia entered the front hallway and ran to the double glass doors just as I made it around the corner. I yelled to her once more, but she just sped right on through them, banging them loudly behind her. I rushed over to them and looked out, but I didn't see her anywhere, and for just a minute I knew what it feels like when a parent looks around in a busy store and sees that her kid is gone. It wasn't a great feeling. I burst through the doors and went out, with Lemm and Mrs. Dreyfus still calling after me. I guess they weren't as fast on their feet as me and Kambia were. Mrs. Dreyfus didn't look like she was too much of a runner, and I figured that Lemm was still just a little drunk.

I stepped out on the lawn and looked around for Kambia's quilt-print summer dress. I found it easily. She had stopped running and was still on the left side of the lawn next to a statue of a little girl with blowing pigtails and a full skirt. The statue was in a skipping position. It had one hand extended outward and one foot raised high off the ground. It was called the Ashbury Statue because a rich widow, Jane Ashbury, had donated most of the land that the school was on. It was a really weird statue. It was supposed to have the face of Jane Ashbury when she was a little girl, but for some reason the artist decided that he liked her face better as an adult and gave the statue the face of a really old lady. It creeped most folks out when they saw it, but Kambia liked it a lot. She said that it reminded people that no matter how old they got, they should always make time to play. Maybe that's why she was standing next to it with her arm and leg in exactly the same position, looking as if she was about to go skipping off down the freshly mowed grass. I ran over and stood in front of her.

"Kambia, why did you take off like that?" She still wasn't talking. "Kambia, why did you take off?" I asked again, with just a hint of impatience in my voice. Nothing. "Kambia, say something." She just stood there with the same blank expression that she had when she ran from the room. The emptiness in her face made me feel like I had a belly full of rocks. I softened my tone. "Come on, Kambia. Let's just go, please. I promise I won't ever, ever let anyone hurt you. You trust me, don't you, Kambia? You know that I told you I would keep all the bad things away."

"That's it," Mrs. Dreyfus said, walking up with Lemm, who for some reason was walking with a limp. "That's it, Shayla. Just keep talking to her."

"I will, don't worry." I looked at Lemm. "You okay?" I asked. He nodded and slowly sat down on the grass.

"He just took a little fall. He's only a little bruised," Mrs. Dreyfus said.

"Oh," I said.

Mrs. Dreyfus walked over to Kambia. "Kambia, do you remember how we talked about facing our fears and not hiding out? It's okay," she said, reaching out and touching her arm. "It's okay. Everything is going to be just fine. Shayla is here, and she wants to take you home. Please go with her. We're going to take you to your *new* home. We're going to take you to the Majors'."

"Yeah, please come, Kambia," I said. "Your mom and dad will be really worried if they see you like this. Come on," I said, starting to reach for her arm myself. I peered over her shoulder. A couple of girls in extra-short miniskirts and tanks were coming across the lawn toward us. I gulped. The girls were Maya and Debbie from my school. I had known them since elementary school, but now they were members of the D-Girls, a group of homegirls that just about ruled everything in the school. They were great-looking, fly sisters that always had the latest clothes, makeup, jewelry, and albums, which they were able to buy because their moms had figured out that they could trade their food stamps for cash. They could be pretty cruel to girls like me, and last year when Kambia was at our school, they weren't very kind to her, either. According to the neighborhood, a few of the D-Girls' dads had liked to hang out at Kambia's old place. They had been some of Jasmine Joiner's best customers, and the girls didn't like it at all. They were hard on Kambia the times that she actually made it to school. While the other kids pretended to believe her stories and offered to bring her some of their old clothes, these girls called her crazy and said that she was really dirty because she always wore the same dress. "Hey, Shayla, where's your loony friend at?" they would ask me whenever they saw me in the hall without her. "We hope she's somewhere washing that nasty dress."

I didn't want them to see Kambia like she was now. I wanted them to see the Kambia of just a few weeks ago, the one that was doing a whole lot better. That's the Kambia that I wanted them to see.

"Kambia, come on," I pleaded as they got nearer. "Your mom and dad are going to be really upset." She didn't even seem to hear me.

While the girls continued to walk up, I pleaded with Kambia to come with me at least a half a dozen times and even promised her that I would read her one of my stories, but she wouldn't budge no matter what I tempted her with. Not knowing what else to do, I finally decided just to go ahead and grab her by the arm and haul her off. I had a pretty good grip on her wrist when Maya, a light-skinned girl with curly, shoulder-length hair and a body almost as kicking as Tia's, strutted up to me and shouted out a familiar, "Hey, Shayla, what's up with your weird friend?" I glared at her and tried to come up with a really good answer, but before I could, my mind just shot out the easiest one.

"Nothing," I said. "She's just playing a new game."

"What's the name of the game?" she asked sarcastically. "How Dumb and Kooky Can You Act?"

"No," I snapped. "It has a really special name."

"Yeah, right," she said, rolling her eyes. She noticed Lemm sitting on the grass. "Hey, Lemm," she cooed sweetly.

"Hello, Maya," he said. I raised my brows. I didn't even know that he knew any of the D-Girls. None of them were in our program, but I guessed he could have run into Maya someplace in the neighborhood. It *did* surprise me that she would be friendly to him. The D-Girls usually only talked to older guys, guys who could drive and could get things for them, but I guess Lemm was able to charm the D-Girls as well.

"Girls, what do you want here?" Mrs. Dreyfus asked Maya and Debbie. "This doesn't concern you. It would be better if you just went on your way."

"We can go wherever we want," Maya said, placing her hands on her curvy hips. "I heard this part of the school was open to everybody."

"It is," Mrs. Dreyfus said. "But as you can see, we have a situation here, and it would be better if you didn't intrude."

"What kind of situation?" Maya asked. "I thought she was just playing a game. What's it called, Shayla?"

I opened my mouth to speak but realized that I didn't have any idea what I wanted to say. Then I looked and saw that Maya had some kind of cosmetics catalog sticking out from underneath her arm. On the cover was some blond chick with lots of frosty shadow and really even teeth. "The game is called Model," I lied. "You have to strike a pose and see how long you can hold it. You can't blink or nothing, just like those live models they sometimes have in the mall."

"Humph, it still sounds stupid to me. Who the hell would play a stupid game like that? A kook, that's who. She's a major kook," Maya said.

"No, she isn't," Mrs. Dreyfus said in a really stern tone. "And don't use that kind of language around here, young lady."

"I'll use what I want to use," Maya said under her breath. "You're not my teacher. You're not the boss of me."

"That may be true, but you are still intruding. Now, I want you girls to move on," Mrs. Dreyfus said.

"How we intruding?" Debbie, a tall, beautiful girl with silky skin of black lacquer and shapely skyscraper legs, spoke up. "She out here for everyone to see. If she gon' put on a show, we got a right to see it."

"There's no show here. She's just fooling around," I said with a slightly raised voice. I was starting to get warm. I could feel Mr. Anger marching over those crushed rocks in my stomach, heading for his place behind my eyes.

"Is she?" Debbie said, glaring at me with sexy cocoa brown eyes. Debbie was a real looker. Her body was better than both Maya's and Tia's. She was thirteen too, but she was built like Catwoman from the old *Batman* show, so most people thought she was way older.

"I said she was, didn't I?"

"I know what you said," she snapped back. "I just didn't believe you."

"I don't care if you do or don't!" I yelled. "I was just answering your question."

"You know, you got a big mouth, Shayla," she said, pressing close to me. "Why don't you just shut it?"

"I will if you'll shut yours," I said, pressing in myself.

"Okay, that's it, girls," Mrs. Dreyfus interrupted again. "Now, y'all go on. You ain't doing nothing but causing trouble," she said, slipping out of her teacher accent. "Get out of here, right now."

Debbie just rolled her eyes at her. "Just look at her, what planet is she from, anyway?" she said, pointing at Kambia. "Are you sure she's even from Earth? Because that guy on the news said that she just turned up in the street like some stray mutt. He said that trashy Jasmine woman just picked her up, and that she was a prostitute or something. I wonder how much she charged?" she said, laughing.

I heard the sound of the slap before I knew that it was my hand that made it. I slapped her so hard that my whole hand felt like it was on fire.

"You little witch!" she cried out in shock, holding her face. "You hit me." Then she hauled off and slapped me. The force of the blow caught me off balance, and I went tumbling into Kambia. We fell hard, with her hitting the ground and me landing on top of her. After that it was on! I jumped off of Kambia, and before you could cry "by jiminy," I was all over Debbie. I smacked her a good one on the jaw, and this time she went down and I jumped on top of her.

"Shayla!" Mrs. Dreyfus yelled, and tried to pull me off of Debbie, but it was too late. I started pounding her. I hit her every which way I could. I smacked her for what she said about Kambia, for Gift's birth, for Grandma thinking that it was me that was drinking out of the bottle, for every little thing that I could think of. I was livid, and it wasn't all her fault, but it didn't matter. Mr. Anger wanted someone to pay, and it might as well be her.

"I'll knock you into the middle of next week, you stupid cow!" I yelled.

"You little witch!" she screamed back, yanking me hard by the hair.

"Hey! Miss Shayla," I heard Lemm cry. "You had better cut it out before you get really hurt." I just kept right on hitting her.

"Get her, Debbie, don't let her do you like that!" Maya screamed.

With Mrs. Dreyfus trying desperately to grab hold of one of us and pull us apart, Debbie and I took turns beating the crap out of each other. Sometimes I was on top and she was on the bottom, then we would roll over and things would be in reverse. We punched, kicked, pulled hair, and even got in a few bites. I was heavier than she was, but she was stronger and had lots of power in those skyscraper legs. It was those legs that finally separated us. On one of my turns on top I popped her pretty hard in the nose. She hollered like a bear in a trap and kicked me off. I landed next to Mrs. Dreyfus. Then Debbie and I both scrambled to our feet.

"I'm gonna kick your fat ass, Shayla!" she cried, with blood streaming out of her nostrils.

"You're gonna try!" I yelled.

She lunged at me, but Mrs. Dreyfus grabbed her by the arm. "That's enough, little girl," Mrs. Dreyfus said. "You see what happens when you have a hard head. Shayla, leave her alone and let her go away."

"I'm not stopping her!" I yelled.

"Stupid, fat witch!" she yelled back at me. "I hate you and your goofy-ass friend."

"I'm going to kick your butt again!" I screamed.

She lunged at me once more, and I rushed up to meet her, but this time somebody yanked me backward. I thought it was Lemm or Maya, but when I turned around, I was staring right at Kambia.

"Stop it, Shayla! You're gonna get hurt!" she cried, with tears streaming down her face. "Stop it. You're scaring me. I don't like it when people fight!" she sobbed. "Stop it, please, before you get really hurt!" She was trembling something fierce, shaking from head to toe. I felt foolish—foolish and guilty.

"It's okay, Kambia," I said. I gathered her in my arms. "It's okay," I repeated, feeling Mr. Anger make his way back out of my face. "It's all right. I'll stop. I'm fine," I said.

"So am I, Shayla," she said, hugging me back. "I'm okay. I don't want you hitting anybody because of me."

"Okay, Kambia. I won't anymore. I didn't mean to scare you," I said. I let her go, and she sat down cross-legged on the grass. There was life in her again. Her eyes were back to normal, and the color had decided to make it back to her face. She looked fine, just like she said, but she was still trembling, and something told me that it wasn't just from the fight.

"It's over, girls," Mrs. Dreyfus said to Debbie and Maya. "There's going to be no more squabbling here today. You get going, before I call a security guard."

"You don't tell us when we can go," Debbie said, still fuming. I looked around her. Another D-Girl was walking up, Sheila, a pint-size, mocha-colored girl with a knockout body of her own. Like Lemm, she was fairly new in the hood. She had just moved down from California at the beginning of the year to live with her dad and grandma because her mom said that she was too much for her to handle. When she first moved down, she wore a lot of blue-jeans jumpers and didn't dress too much like the rest of the D-Girls. Now she wore skirts shorter than Kambia's so-called mom used to wear— butt showers, Grandma called them. She came up to us in a clingy number that was even shorter than her cheerleading uniform.

"Hey, what's up?" she asked Debbie and Maya. "What's all this craziness about?"

"Nothing!" Debbie snapped.

"Look, whatever," Sheila said. "Anyhow, if it ain't nothing, me, Breed, and David been waiting for y'all down at Breed's house for over forty minutes. Breed say for y'all to get your butts down there, or y'all can forget about them CDs that he was gonna get for y'all tomorrow night. Come on, Debbie, you wanna get some good stuff or you wanna stay here squabbling with boring ole Shayla? Anyway, I thought she used to be your girl. Maya said all y'all used to be cool."

"I told you that was way back in the day. I can hardly even recall it. It wasn't no big deal," Maya said.

I glared at Maya. It was a big deal, and both she and Debbie knew it. There was a time when we were all good friends. It was in the fifth grade. Our classes had combined PE, Mrs. Epps's Alternative Exercise course, a class where we clumsily square-danced to scratchy classic country music. We were homegirls back then, sisters united in the belief that we had no business skipping, bowing, and swinging to music that even our parents didn't like. "Girl, I hate this stuff, don't you?" Debbie would always whisper as we locked arms for the first dance. In those days whisper was pretty much all Debbie would do. She was a quiet little girl who loved to draw the hopscotch board for the other girls at recess, and who was always willing to break you off a hunk of her Snickers bar during third-period lunch. She was sweet natured and giving, nothing at all like she was today. She chose her friends based on loyalty, not on fashion sense—and so did Maya. Maya didn't even think about running with the cool crowd, and she sure didn't hang out in front of her locker teasing the other girls and guys about their whack clothes and shoes. Believe it or not, she was a lot like me, a bookworm. Each day after school she and I would meet up in the school library. Her favorite books were poetry books. On certain days she would have something that she referred to as Poets' Theater. She would invite Debbie to come along, and she'd recite poems to us from thick collections featuring poets like Langston Hughes and

Gwendolyn Brooks. We were close. We jumped rope, played jacks, and made soda bottle dolls together out of leftover yarn and pieces of felt. We even planned on taking all the same courses when we got to middle school. Then puberty hit.

Maya and Debbie blossomed almost overnight. They unfortunately attracted boys quicker than free tickets to a football game, but they found out that nice girls and bookworms didn't get asked to school dances and parties. They discarded their old personalities like used paper plates and started doing and saying only the things that they thought the boys would like. Pretty soon all of the popular guys wanted to walk them home after school, which made every chick want to be their best homegirl.

They had power, and they used it to cut all of the kids that weren't like them out. By the time we got to middle school, our friendship had turned as awkward as our square-dance steps. They stopped speaking to me in classes and cruelly poked fun at me whenever they thought anybody important was around. "It's no big deal," Maya told me one afternoon when nobody was looking. "Can't you take a little teasing? You know how it is, Shayla. We just can't hang around with you no more, that's all. We can't be fooling around in the library or doing any of that other lame stuff we used to do. You'll just have to get over it, homegirl." I didn't just get over it—not then, and not now.

"So, what's up?" Sheila asked. "Y'all coming or what?"

"We coming," Debbie said, dabbing at her nose with the hem of her tank top and walking off. "Shayla, I'm gon' kick your ass the next time I see you, and you can bet on that."

I glanced over at her, but I paid no real attention to the threat. She was just popping and jawing about nothing. The fight was over. We had both gotten some good licks in. Besides, I didn't know

Breed or David, but I had heard of them. They were older than us, tough brothers who were always either doing bad or going for bad. They were the boys that all the young dudes wanted to hang with or be like. She could never let those guys know that me, a nobody, had gotten a few wails in on her. It would make her look weak, and those brothers only dated girls that could hold their own. No, the fight was over. She wouldn't say any more about it, and she would make sure that Maya and Sheila kept quiet about it too.

"Whatever, Debbie," I said. "I'll see you around, *girlfriend*." I looked back at Kambia. "I'm sorry, Kam. I didn't mean to freak you out."

"I'm not freaked out, Shayla. I'm not." I sat down on the grass next to her, and she reached up and wiped away some tears that I hadn't even noticed were in my eyes. Her hand was soft and warm, but still shaky. "You know what, Shayla. I wish that I was that little girl in the statue. If I were her, all I would have to do is stand—birds could land on me, dogs could bark at me, and kids could throw rocks at me, but it wouldn't matter, because I couldn't feel anything. I would just keep standing and thinking about nothing at all."

"But that wouldn't be any fun, Kambia," I said. "You couldn't feel happy, you couldn't feel love, you couldn't feel anything. You would just be a big ole lump. A lump that couldn't do anything but stay in one place."

"I don't think that I would mind it at all, Shayla," she said. "At least I wouldn't know when someone was being mean to me."

"I know, Kambia." I hopped up from the ground and pulled her to her feet. "Mrs. Dreyfus is going to drive us all home."

"Okay, Shayla." She walked over to Mrs. Dreyfus, who smiled at her and put her arm around her shoulder.

"Actually, Kambia, I've changed my mind. I think that it would be better if you sat with me for a while and had a chance to calm down. We'll get you something cool to drink from the break room, then the two of us will go back to the classroom and have a little talk. Don't you think that's a good idea?" Mrs. Dreyfus asked.

Kambia nodded, and the two of them started back toward the school.

"Can Shayla come?" Kambia asked, looking back at me.

"Not just right now," Mrs. Dreyfus said. "We need to talk alone. She'll wait for you. Won't you, Shayla?"

"I'll be right here when you need me, Kambia," I said.

"Okay, I'll come get you in a bit," she said. "I'll get you as soon as we're through."

"I'll be right here," I repeated.

I sighed and walked over to Lemm. I plopped down next to him on the grass. "Are you okay?" I asked, noticing for the first time that his shin was just a tad bit swollen.

"I'm perfectly fine, Shayla," he said. "I think I just need a little ice."

"Can you walk?"

"Sure," he said. "I could run if I had to."

"Okay. I'll see you later. I'm going to just wait here in case Kambia needs me."

"Then I'll wait too. Besides, I may have to protect you if those D-Girls come back and want to fight some more."

"You don't have to, Lemm. I can take care of myself."

"I know," he said, "but since you're looking out for Kambia, I thought it might be nice if I looked out for you."

He reached over and caught my hand again, and I felt that same firefly feeling that I had felt earlier. It was weird, and I wasn't too cool with weird, but I didn't snatch my hand away. Instead I pulled my knees up to my chest and tried to get my head around what was going on with Kambia. I thought of something that had happened a while ago.

Last year, just a month or so before Kambia came tumbling into my life, Grandma Augustine and I were responsible for a confirmation ceremony at her church. It was a ceremony for a group of boys and girls pretty much my age who had gone through months of Christian training and were now ready to turn their lives over to Grandma's God.

Working on the service wasn't really anything that I wanted to do, but Grandma thought that it would be a good way for me to examine my own spiritual beliefs. She said that seeing the kids make their commitment might inspire me to make one of my own. Only there was way too much hard work involved for me even to think of doing it. I never even got the chance to think about God.

First Grandma and I had to hand make certificates and mini scrolls for all of the kids and their parents, write a bulletin that included several hymns and original prayers, organize the order of the ceremony, and approve all of the songs with the choir director. After that we had to make sure that the entire altar was draped in white linen for cleanness, purity, and grace, ensure that the tiny Communion glasses were washed and the silver Communion trays were polished, and plan a reception with homemade cookies and punch. The work for the ceremony was much more than either one of us thought that it would be, but we did it, and on the day of the ceremony our little light shone. Everything was perfect—at least we thought it would be.

As the organist played, seven celestial-faced children came marching up the aisle, ready to become one with their maker, but one of the little boys apparently called another little boy's sister a bad name while they were proceeding. A fight broke out right smack-dab in the middle of the ceremony. Soon the whole group blew up and became one big squabble, just like me and Debbie. Mini scrolls and purple hymnbooks were all over the place. Grandma Augustine was devastated, and I was pretty put out myself. We had done everything right, made sure that everything was taken care of, but something still went wrong. Grandma said that some cast-out angel had slipped out of Hades and done the devil's work. I wasn't sure about that, but what I was sure of was that some things you just can't see coming, like a cold sore or a pop quiz.

I did everything right by Kambia, from telling her secret last year so that she could get help, to encouraging her to go to the Girl Help Center when I really wanted her at school with me. I stuck with her even though she sometimes did things that really scared me. She was my friend, and I thought I had done all that I could to keep her from going back to her fantasy world, but I didn't count on someone sending her packages that would flip her out again. They hit me out of nowhere. They were as unexpected as snow on a summer day. I relaxed my knees and wondered why Lemm's hand on mine felt so much different from Kambia's. Why it made me feel like I had fireflies inside. It was just one more thing that I had to make sense of, but first I still had to make sense out of what was happening to Kambia.

# Chapter 4

Yesterday afternoon Grandma said that she saw Evil peeping in our window. She was in the kitchen cooking up a mess of hot pan sausage when she thought she heard somebody whisper her name. She said she looked all over the room, and even called out to Mama, who she figured might have gotten up a little early to get ready for work, but Mama didn't answer her, so she just turned back around. That's when she saw him. He was standing right outside the glass. She said that he was disguised as a woman, but she knew him for what he was, 'cause the woman just didn't look right. She had deep blue eyes and a youthful face that looked like Beauty had spent quite a bit of time on it, but her hair and skin weren't what they were supposed to be. She had long, flowing hair that Grandma said she at first thought was just a really light blond, but when she studied it a bit, she could see that it was almost pure white, like the hair on an old woman's head, and her skin was newborn-baby soft, but it was sickly looking and cigarette ash gray, like it had been dead for a really long time. Grandma said that she dropped her spatula and started for her Bible sitting on the dining table so she could throw Scripture at it like she did when the devil baby showed up last year after Tia ran off, but before she could hobble over to the table, the woman winked at her and began to retreat from the window. Grandma said that the woman started to sink downward, and kept sinking until the only thing she could see in the window was her own reflection being thrown back at her from the shiny glass.

Grandma was pretty upset by the woman. She was so rattled that she forgot to snap the fire off on the stove, and she turned her sausage patties into briquettes. She said that when Evil himself is standing at your window, you know that he's not out there because he wants to be, he's trying to find a way to get in. She said that we would need something extra special to keep him out, so she took another trip to see Madam Vahilia Racine, the neighborhood's self-styled voodoo priestess, hoping that she could give her some kind of devil-keeping-out potion, but Madam Racine said that she didn't have a potion that would do it. She said that if it was just a little demon, anybody with half a mind for potion making could keep him out, but the devil himself was something entirely different. She said that the only way to keep that strong an evil out was to make a clear decision to choose good instead. She gave Grandma three plastic glow-in-the-dark skeletons and two glass cherubs with halos floating above their tiny heads. She told her to sit them in the place where she thought the devil would be most drawn to. Grandma didn't have any problem deciding that it was any place that I was at. She said that with the way I'd been acting lately, starting fights and getting into all kinds of trouble, I had made myself into a walking magnet for anything popping up out of Hades.

Last night she came and placed the figurines on the bookshelf across from my bed. She told me that Madam Racine said that I had to decide which group I wanted to pick up. The one that I chose would bring either goodness or more evil into the house. It would either let the devil in or tell him to get the heck out. "Choose smart," Grandma told me. "A baby bird only gets one chance to fly after it's kicked out of the nest."

A tiny part of me might have wanted to play along with Grandma, but most of me didn't. I told her that I was very tired and that I really wasn't interested in either group. She rolled her eyes up to the ceiling and turned out the light. After she left the room, and

I lay listening to the sound of Tia snoring, something strange happened. I thought I saw the glowing skeletons beckon to me from the bookshelf, their bony fingers curling and uncurling eerily, begging me to join them. I knew that it was just my imagination, but it scared me about as much as Grandma's woman scared her.

This morning I went to school and during homeroom chewed on what I thought I had seen. Was Grandma right? Had my bad attitude and cutting up placed a welcome mat for Evil on our front step? I thought about the tussle that I had with Debbie and Maya. It had been a long time coming, but I still felt bad about it—and I especially felt bad about the way that I had been treating Gift and Grandma. I made a decision. I attended my classes until the lunch bell rang and then ran back home. When I reached the house, I went straight to my room and snatched the cherubs from the bookshelf. I was fully expecting to go outside to the backyard, where I knew that Grandma would be sitting, and drop them into her lap while she was having her lunch of sardines and Ritz crackers. I was going to tell her that I was sorry about the way I had been acting, and even let her know that I was ready to talk to her about what had happened in the store, but Mr. Anderson Fox showed up out of the blue to check on Gift, and it took about a minute for me to change my mind and wish that I had stayed at school.

I stood at the back door with the cherubs in my hand and watched Mr. Anderson Fox and Grandma Augustine sitting in the shade of the huge pecan tree, rocking back and forth on our old wooden tree swing. Mr. Anderson Fox was holding Gift. I hadn't seen him with her since that day at the hospital. He was cradling her in his arms and humming to her. I couldn't make out the tune over the screech of the rusty swing hinges, but I really didn't care what it was. It was something pleasant, nice. I could hear Gift giggling and see her kicking her feet, her fat brown legs moving up and down excitedly.

She was a happy baby, even happier with him. He was a good father to her, that's what everyone said. To me he was just Mr. Anderson Fox, but to her he was a father, the one with *her* last name. Gift Fox, that was her name, while mine was Shayla Dubois. To everyone who knew me I was connected to my mother and nobody else. "You're Vera Dubois's daughter, ain't you?" the old ladies always asked when they met me on the street. "I knew your mama when she was just a little girl." There was never any mention of Mr. Anderson Fox. Nobody ever told me that I looked like him, walked like him, talked like him, or liked the same kinds of things that he had when he was a little boy. It was always Mama that they compared me with. She was the only parent that I had, but not Gift. She had Jada—and Mr. Anderson Fox.

I felt like someone was jumping up and down on me as I watched Mr. Anderson Fox swinging with Gift, swinging with the only child ever to bear his name. No matter what Grandma said, I still didn't think that it was fair. I walked over to the kitchen counter and slammed the cherubs down next to the dish drainer. They tumbled off the sink and fell into the sudsy water below. I was deciding whether or not to retrieve them when Mama walked up. She touched my shoulder, then reached into the sink and scooped the cherubs out. She handed them back to me dripping.

"Now, you know I don't believe in this kinda nonsense," she said, wiping her hands on the sides of her shorts. It was her day off, and she was going to spend the afternoon at the park with one of her girlfriends. She was wearing a pair of cutoffs and a cotton tank that made her look a lot like Tia with an oversize frame. "I don't believe in this kinda thing at all, but Mu'dear does, and it seems extremely important to her that you believe in it too. She done figured out a long time ago that her backwater beliefs don't set on mine and Tia's shelves too well, so you are her only hope. She says that you are the one in this family that's most like her. It would hurt her to her heart if she knew that you had tossed these things in the sink."

"I didn't," I said. "They just fell. I was only trying to put them on the counter."

"Oh," Mama said. "You just be more careful next time. Besides, you never know, even if you don't believe in something, it may still be able to help you sort something out."

"There's nothing to sort out," I lied. "I don't know why everybody in this house keeps thinking that I have a problem. I just wanted to get Grandma to take that junk off of my bookshelf. Those crazy skeletons kept me awake all night."

"Did they?" Mama asked with an amused look on her normally severe face. "When I was about your age, I got into trouble at school once over a boy. Mu'dear did something like what she's doing to you to me. It was an idea that she came up with herself, a candleholder with Jesus' face on it. She said that it was supposed to guide me back to the true light. That darn thing kept me awake for an entire week. I didn't know whether to ask for forgiveness or run out of the room screaming." She broke into a huge belly laugh, and I couldn't help but join her. It was good sharing a laugh with her. We hardly ever laughed together. I guess we just didn't find the same things funny.

"Anyway," she said after a little while. "I'm not really sure what your grandma meant by putting those things in your room, but the one thing that I do know is that she meant well. She loves you as if she were your mother herself." She walked over to the screen and peered out. I walked over to her. Mr. Anderson Fox was still humming to Gift, and Grandma Augustine was joining in, her silvery head moving from side to side as she hummed along.

"They look like they're having fun," I said.

"I'll bet they are. Go out there, Shayla. Baby, there's room for you. Can't you see that?"

"No, Mama, I can't see that at all." I stuck the cherubs into the pocket of my drawstring shorts. "I gotta get back to school. Lunch is almost over," I told her. "I gotta get back or I won't have time to eat anything."

"No you don't. There's plenty for you to eat here. Me or Mu'dear can whip up something in just a few seconds. There's lots of time for you to stay, and I want you to spend some of it with your father." She grabbed me by the arm and started tugging me toward the door. "Come on, Shayla," she said. "I know that you and I don't always see things the same way, but you're still *my* baby, and I think I have some idea what's right for you. If you got a shoe you want to throw at Anderson, it's time for you to go on and throw it. We're going to go outside and join him under that tree."

"No, Mama, I don't wanna," I whined, jerking my arm away. "I just wanna go back to school. I'm gonna be late."

"Please, Shayla honey, I promise you that there is a way to work all of this out."

I frowned. "Just let me go back to school, Mama."

She paused for a moment, and worry flew in and settled on her face. "Okay, okay," she said. "I won't try to make you do something that you most certainly don't want to do, not this time, but you understand this. I can't make you have feelings for your father that you aren't ready to have. I know that he's hurt you, and I know that you have every reason to not want to throw yourself into his arms, but baby, you gotta believe your mama on this. You ain't hurting

Anderson when you act like you're acting, you're hurting yourself. I know that Mu'dear told you this, but I'm just gonna repeat it. Gift's not going anywhere. No matter how much you want her to go away, it ain't gonna happen. She's tied to you by blood, just like your sister, Tia. Wherever you go, she will always be a part of you and whatever you do, because you and she share the same seed, and I know that I don't have to explain to you what I mean by that. You're not really a baby anymore. Gift's a part of Anderson, and I'm sure that you understand that it makes her a part of you as well."

"She's part of Mr. Andersen Fox," I mumbled. "Only you, Tia, and Grandma are a part of me."

Mama shook her head. "You know that's not true, Shayla," she said. "But I won't argue with you. You go ahead and get back to school. I don't want you to miss your lunch."

"I won't," I said, heading for the door.

"You come straight home when school is out," she called after me. "Tia will be at Doo-witty's. You'll have the room all to yourself. I want you to use the quiet time to think on what was said. You got a wad of cotton in your ears, and it's time for you to take it out."

"Yes, ma'am," I mumbled.

I walked back to my room and carefully placed the glass cherubs back on the shelf next to the skeletons. The sunlight from my open window beamed through them, creating a prism of colors on the wall behind the shelf, a rainbow of purple, blue, and green. I studied it for a few moments, then I turned the cherubs in the opposite direction and watched the prism turn a different set of colors. I wished that life were that easy, that you could change things just by spinning around. Like magic you could make the things in your life a completely different color, replace all the shades of dark with something much brighter. There would be no need to think about things or make a decision. You would just turn, and *poof*, the things you didn't like would be replaced by the things that you loved. I would replace Mr. Anderson Fox and his new me with piles and piles of books—poetry books, novels, collections of short stories, and books of art. After that I would start reading them line by line, page by page, until the rhythm of the text and the beauty of the images played over and over in my head, drowning out any memory of Mr. Anderson Fox and Gift.

In the summer program we got a pretty long lunch period, so I remained at the bookshelf staring at the prism until I just absolutely had to go. It was nearly twelve forty-five, and I would have at least a twenty-minute walk back to my school. I turned the cherubs around one more time to see what kinds of colors would end up on the wall and then walked over to my bedroom door.

I yanked it open and ran headfirst into Mr. Anderson Fox. He grabbed me to keep me from falling. "Hey, baby girl, what's the big hurry?" he asked, steadying me.

"I gotta get back to school, Daddy," I said, releasing myself from his grasp. I backed away from him a bit. The strong musk smell of his aftershave was just too much for me to take. He was back to wearing it again. He hadn't worn it the whole time that Jada was pregnant. She said that it made her queasy. I knew what she was talking about.

"I know," he said. "Your mama told me. She said that you was gonna be real late if you didn't get back soon. I told her that I would take you in the car. I just got the air fixed. It'll be nicer than trying to walk all them blocks in the heat. Don't you think?"

"I . . . I guess."

"Good, let's go," he said, throwing his beefy arm around my shoulder. He was seriously pumped up now. Since the baby's birth he had been working out like crazy. He told Mama that a good father had to be in great shape. He'd put on about twenty-five pounds, mostly in his arms and chest. With his shaved head he looked a lot like a black genie, but without the hoop earring.

I followed Mr. Anderson Fox through the house and down the front steps with curiosity racing through my mind. It wasn't like him to offer to do stuff for me. He had purchased his ride nearly seven months ago and hadn't once offered me a lift to school or anywhere else. If he happened to be driving through the neighborhood and saw me walking to the bus stop, he would wave and keep going. I don't think that he did it to be mean. It was just his way. It never occurred to him that I might need his help to get to some place.

We opened the gate and walked half a block to what Mr. Anderson Fox called his car, a large brown van with a sliding door in the back. He had gotten the van real cheap from the meat-packing plant that he used to work at. It needed a lot of work, and his buddies down at Perry's 24-and-7 told him that they would help him fix it up. They did a fairly good job of working on the inside, but they ran out of cash before the outside could be completed. The van was still covered with huge rust spots on one of the sides, and the other side was still decorated with the words HENRIKSEN'S FAIR-PRICED BEEF spelled out in huge sausage links.

We reached the van, and Mr. Anderson Fox walked around and hopped inside, while I struggled with my door. It was stubborn. I had to yank the hot metal handle like crazy before it finally gave way and let me crawl in. Once inside I eased myself into the huge vinyl seat and fastened the seat belt, while Mr. Anderson Fox leaned over and snapped on the air conditioner. A loud hum burst from three oversize air vents, filling the van cab with cool air. Mr. Anderson Fox turned the key in the ignition, and we sped off down the street.

We drove down the busy road at a sightseer's pace, with Mr. Anderson Fox pointing out places in the neighborhood that he and Mama used to step out to before I was even born, small clubs that were once the nightlife of the community but were now nothing but rotted-out shacks boarded up with rotten boards. He had really fond memories of what he called their "old stomping grounds," memories of Mama in short skirts, fall wigs, and boots, dancing until the sun poked its head through the morning clouds. Those were good times, he told me. Mama was young and alive. She didn't care what anybody thought of her. She and Grandma fought a lot back then, he said, even more than they fight today. Grandma just didn't realize that Mama had something in her that couldn't be bottled up. "Your mama was a bucking bronco," he said. "But your grandma thought that she could just keep her locked up like some ole nag." It felt weird hearing how Mama used to be before I came into the world. It was more than I wanted to know about her personal life. To me she was just Mama, the person who always managed to get the bills paid year after year with no one there to help her out. I didn't need to know much else.

All the way to the school Mr. Anderson Fox filled me in on what he and Mama used to do back in the day. While he talked, I began to wonder again what *he* was actually like as a young man. Some things were up front about him. Except for his searchlight eyes, he was TV-commercial good looking, and everybody knew that he had a way with the chicks, but I wondered about the stuff that everybody didn't know, couldn't see. I knew that Mama's life had turned out the way that it did because she had had Tia when she was just a teen, ended up being married to a guy that Grandma Augustine said wasn't old enough even to know what marriage was, and messed around with way too many Mr. Anderson Foxes, before she finally got tied down completely by having me. She never got to do any of the things that she wanted to do with her life. There was never enough time or money for her to make her dreams come true, but what about Mr. Anderson Fox? Folks around the neighborhood said that he had spent most of his young life bumming from one job to the next and living off his lady friends in between. He said that he didn't have nothing for work. It was just for dudes who couldn't figure out how to pay the rent any other way. It was a run of bad luck that finally made him leave town and take a job at the meatpacking plant. The woman that he was living with skipped town with a younger dude who had a good job up north, and the rest of the women in the neighborhood weren't looking for a new man at the time. He left town and ended up taking the job at the meatpacking company, where he worked longer than he had ever worked at any job, before returning to Houston. He told his friends that it was a good gig for a while, but making hamburger patties just wasn't his thing. What was? What would Mr. Anderson Fox have been if he hadn't spent his entire young life chasing high heels around? Mama said that she didn't know, and Grandma said that she doubted if he would be much more than he is, but I wondered. He was good at selling himself to ladies, there was no doubt about that. Maybe he could have been good at selling other things—maybe houses or insurance. I think that I would have been proud of him then. I wouldn't have minded calling him father right along with Gift.

By the time Mr. Anderson Fox pulled up next to the school, I had learned enough about Mama and "the way it used to be" to write a collection of stories on her and the neighborhood nightlife. I knew all about her old boyfriends, the types of dances that she used to do, and the brand of cigarettes that she used to get out of the machine down at the Cool Groove Lounge. I was happier than a taxi driver with a new cab when Mr. Anderson Fox finally squeezed his van between two compact cars and turned the ignition off. The whole vehicle sputtered and shook for several moments until the motor finally called it quits. I unsnapped the seat belt and reached for the door handle.

"Just a minute, baby girl," Mr. Anderson Fox cried. "Hold up, hold up. I got something that I want to say to you." I sat back in the chair.

"You know me and Jada got the baby now," he said, fingering the hairs of his well-groomed goatee.

"I know," I mumbled.

"Yeah," he said. "We got Gift now, and all three of us is living in Jada's little small place, the same one that she was staying in before I moved in."

"I know," I repeated.

"Anyway, me, Jada, and the baby, we all holed up in Jada's small house. Now, don't get me wrong. It's a nice house, and Jada done paid for it cash money, so ain't nothing owed on it, and that's real, real good. The problem is we all in there together, all on top of each other, like wet clothes in a laundry basket. It's a little too close in there. It's time to make some changes. Don't you think?"

"I guess."

"You right, you doggone right. So, here is what I been working on," he said. "I just got on full-time at Leoni's Vending Machine Company. They gonna give me a pretty good wage and insurance. I'll be making enough money to do something for a change. Me and Jada, we figured that since we had the extra cash coming in, we would go on and move. We found a little place not too far from where we staying now. It ain't all that big, but at least a brother can turn around without bumping into somebody else. You know what I mean?"

"I know."

"Sure you do. Well, anyhow, the point I'm trying to make is that now that we moving, Gift can have her own room. She don't have to be sleeping with me and her mama. She can have her own room with all her own stuff," he said, grinning his regular big toothy grin. "Won't that be good?"

I just stared at him.

"Sure it will," he said. "It'll be great. Anyhow, what I'm getting at is this. We gonna give Gift her own little space, with all new furniture and stuff, and wallpaper that a baby would like. The reason I'm telling you is I thought maybe you would like to help out. Jada ain't gon' have much time with her crazy new work hours. She going back to full time and then some at her old job. She ain't gon' feel like going shopping when she gets off. I thought that maybe you could help her out by picking out some things that would go in a baby girl's room. Jada likes you, and I know that she and your little sister will be happy with whatever you choose. I'll let you know 'round about the time we get ready to move. I'll fill you in so you and me can start picking some stuff out. Is that okay?"

"It's fine, Daddy," I said. "It's just fine." I turned the handle on the door and hopped out. "See ya later!"

"Okay."

I closed the door and watched as he sped down the road, the van getting harder and harder to spot as it wove in and out of traffic. I walked over and leaned against the side of the large, graffiti-covered concrete building. Above my head a bell rang, signaling the end of third-period lunch. All around me teen boys and girls in bright shorts and T-shirts began to make their way toward the front entrance of the school, laughing merrily and trading leftover lunch treats as they tramped through the brown, sunburned grass. I thought about joining the kids, but I was in too much shock even to move away from the wall. Gift was going to have her own room. She was going to have her own space with brand-new furniture and wallpaper that Mr. Anderson Fox wanted me to help pick out. It wasn't just unfair, it was downright wrong. Why should Gift have a room of her own? I didn't have one. I still woke up every morning next to Tia. A rickety old bed and dresser, and a plastic put-together bookshelf were what I called my furniture, and yellowed, peeling tulips were what you would see when you saw my wallpaper. I had never gotten anything new in my room. I didn't have any idea what it was like to go in the store and pick out the things that I liked. No one had ever given me the opportunity to before—until now, until Gift. I would be able to go and pick out some nice new furniture and wallpaper for Gift, something that a baby girl would like. What about what I liked? Did it matter? Not to Mr. Anderson Fox. I wasn't his baby girl anymore, Gift was. He would give her all the things that he never even thought about giving me.

I felt like screaming, like running through the short evergreen shrubs surrounding the West Mall, past the bronze statue of Martin Luther King Jr., past the metal bleachers in the littered baseball field, past everything. I would yell out all the mean things that I felt about Mr. Anderson Fox, tell the entire school what a terrible father he was, tell them about the letters that he never sent me, the movies that he never took me to, the speeches that I gave that he never showed up for. I would let the whole world know what he was, and how he thought that he could replace me with Gift. After that I would go home and write the longest journal entry that I had ever written in my blue notebook. I would keep going for pages and pages, writing down my feelings until my heart was completely empty of Mr. Anderson Fox. It was so much better when I had no feelings for him at all. I pushed away from the wall and headed for class.

I opened the double doors and walked into the main hallway of the school. The smell of hot buttered popcorn hit me as I passed the cracked door of the teachers' lounge. I clutched my stomach, remembering that I hadn't eaten. I strolled over to my locker and slowly opened my new combination lock. I had purchased the lock about two weeks ago mainly because of what was happening to Kambia.

Things still aren't going well for Kambia. Since the dress incident she has received two more packages—a skeleton key with a note attached to it, telling her that it was a key to her old house, where she actually belonged; and a pair of ragged tennis shoes like she used to wear when she was living at Jasmine Joiner's. It was me who found the tennis shoes. They were sitting in a brand-new shoe box on her back porch. I thought that maybe Honeysuckle Peach had bought them for her and forgotten to take them in when she took in the rest of her shopping. I was totally outdone when I saw what they were. I tried to shield them from Kambia before she saw them, but she spotted them anyway. "What are those, Shayla?" she asked me, peeping over my shoulder. When she saw what they were, she flipped out again. In fact, with each gift Kambia has gone into one of her trances for a longer and longer time. Once she stayed frozen for nearly an entire day.

Kambia's parents are afraid to go to the police or tell her social worker what is going on. They're afraid the social worker will take Kambia away. They told Mama and Grandma that Miss Sayer said that Kambia's staying with them and going to the Girl Help Center was just a trial. She said that the state would be monitoring Kambia to see if she got any better, and if she didn't, they might have to take her to a special live-in school where they could give her medicine to try and help her stop shutting herself off, along with other round-the-clock care. "It would be better for her in the long run," Miss Sayer told Honeysuckle Peach and Ten Fingers. "The school would be able to work with her night and day." But Honeysuckle Peach and Ten Fingers don't agree, and neither does Mrs. Dreyfus.

Mrs. Dreyfus thinks that Kambia's new home is the best place for her to be. She says that the best medicine for Kambia is love and support, and she has that already at the Majors'. It wouldn't be fair to make her give up people that she loves and cares for because of somebody else's dirty deeds. She thinks that as long as Kambia can keep bringing herself out of her world, she will be fine, but we all need to work really hard to find out who's sending Kambia the packages before things get any worse.

Two days ago we all got together at Kambia's house and tried to come up with a list of names of people who could be sending the packages. Me, Mama, Tia, Kambia's folks, Mrs. Dreyfus, and even Lemm, who showed up red-eyed and smelling a little too strongly of peppermint, but who threw so many compliments at the grown folks and Tia that they didn't notice. We all sat down at the Majors' table and tried to figure out who would want to hurt Kambia.

The first name that we came up with was Jasmine Joiner's, of course, but we all quickly threw it out. The police said that Jasmine was just a user. It didn't matter to her who she had to take advantage of, as long as her bills were paid. They said that Kambia meant absolutely nothing to her, except for maybe a full belly for a few nights and a new slinky dress. She probably wouldn't bother coming back for Kambia. There were a ton of girls out there just like her—young, vulnerable things just looking for a place to rest their head. As long as she could pick Kambias up off the street like candy wrappers, there would be no need for any of us ever to see her face again. The police kept Kambia's dress and stuff for evidence, but they doubted if Jasmine would ever show up again. When we all thought about it, it just made sense not to place Jasmine on the list. We had to come up with some other folks.

Mama and Grandma tried to come up with a few names from the hood, but they had no luck. After Kambia was admitted to the hospital, folks just clammed up. No man would dare admit, even to his closest friend, that he had gone to Jasmine's, and certainly no woman would say that she had snooped around and found out that her husband or boyfriend had been there. Except for a couple of the D-Girls' dads, who were pimped on by their girlfriends for not paying child support, the entire neighborhood swore that Jasmine's customers had all come from other hoods. Guys from somewhere else were most likely the ones who had hurt Kambia. "We heard it was some dudes out of Fourth Ward," the night crew down at Bobby's Rib Shack Number Three told Grandma when she went to buy some barbecue, their dark, greasy hands clumsily folding the wax paper around her pound of hot links. "They come by here one night to get some pork ribs," they all let her know. "They was dressed kinda fly, but they still looked like some really shady brothers. They looked like they could have been into anything. It had to be them. Nobody in this neighborhood would do the kinds of things that were done to that girl."

"We heard that it was a couple of guys from Third Ward," the lady checkers down at Diamond's told Mama, their nimble fingers nervously pressing the wrong produce keys. "They came in here to buy a six-pack of beer," they informed her. "They looked just like regular folks, but if you looked real close, you could see that there was just something about they eyes. They were shifty, guilty looking. You can bet your life that if anything happened, they done it."

In the end all Mama and Grandma stuck with were the names of the D-Girls' dads, whom the police had already questioned and let go, so that left the rest of us to fill in the dance card. Neither Lemm nor Kambia's parents had been in the picture when things went down with Kambia, so it was easy to dismiss anyone that they could think of. It was also easy to scratch off anyone that Tia could come up with. Tia had run away from home shortly after Kambia came to town.

Mrs. Dreyfus, however, did have a few names that she could put down on the list of people who might want to cause Kambia some harm. The problem was she just didn't think that they would do it. They were girls who had been genuinely friendly with Kambia when she first started at the school, but had grown jealous as time went on because she was doing so well. They were good girls who just felt really bad about themselves, and Kambia's seemingly fast recovery didn't make them feel any better. Mrs. Dreyfus had heard them say a few things about Kambia behind her back, but she didn't think they would go so far as to stuff horrible things in her locker. "They are just a little unhappy with her, but I doubt if anyone would like to see her being hurt again."

With Mrs. Dreyfus not really being sure about the names on her list, that left just me. I tried to come up with a list of everyone that Kambia had come into contact with since we first met. I put down all the people that I could think of, but the more I wrote, the less and less sure I became. I scratched off name after name until I was left with only two—Debbie and Maya. They were the only folks that I could think of who might actually do some harm to Kambia, but unfortunately I ran into a problem with them, too. They both went to Martin Middle with me and Kambia, but neither one of them had attended the Girl Help Center, and as far as I knew, they didn't know a soul in it. There was no way that they could have put the dress in Kambia's locker or sent her the paper dolls in a box that the school had sent out to all of the graduates. But the key and shoes were different. The key had been found taped to Kambia's door in a plain white envelope, and the shoes had just turned up on her back porch. The girls could have placed both of them there, but why would they? They didn't like Kambia, that was clear, but they were usually just pretty nasty to her, not awful. Mrs. Dreyfus said that what someone was doing to Kambia was unusually cruel. It was almost as if there was something that the person thought she should pay for. I couldn't see Debbie and Maya feeling that way. I didn't like them anymore, but I knew them. They were mad about their dads going to Jasmine's, but deep down they had to know that it wasn't Kambia's fault. Saying bad things about her was just their way of making themselves feel better. They were doing the same thing that the girls at the Girl Help Center were doing, only they were doing it in her face.

When it was over, none of us could come up with one single person that we honestly believed would want to make Kambia terrified. It just didn't make any sense for someone to want to hurt her in the way that she was being hurt, and since Kambia still didn't have a clue who would want to see her suffer, there was nothing left for us to do. We all played bingo and ate oatmeal cookies until we felt the sandman calling us, said good night to one another, and went to our beds. None of us could do anything for Kambia that night, and today I guess we still can't.

I continued turning the lock until I heard a loud *click*. After that

I yanked the locker handle open and peeked inside, hoping to find a snack tucked in among my books. There was nothing, only an empty potato chip wrapper with an expired contest ticket glued to the front of it. I slammed the locker closed again and refastened the lock.

I stared down the long corridor that led to my fourth-period writing class. There wasn't a soul in sight. There were just rows and rows of kid-free lockers and closed classroom doors. Behind those doors I could hear muffled voices. Classes had begun.

I ran down the corridor in a hurry until I reached the last door, but I stopped just short of turning the knob. *Why should I go to class?* I asked myself. I was hungry and hurt. I didn't want to spend the next hour listening to my writing teacher fuss at the kids whose essay papers hadn't quite come out to the five hundred words she had asked for. I checked the hallway once more to make sure that no one was there and crept away from the door. I walked back to my locker, opened the lock again, and felt around underneath my smelly gym suit for some loose change. I found a fistful of saved-up milk-money quarters and was about to slam the locker closed again, when a hand reached over my head and slammed it for me.

"Don't close it so loud, Lemm," I said, turning around.

"Why not?" he said, fastening the lock. "What's going on? You're going to be late for our writing class if you don't hurry it along."

I placed the coins in the pocket of my shorts and brushed past him. "Shhh. Don't be so noisy. I gotta go."

"Go where?" he said, catching my arm lightly. "Class is going to start."

"No, it's already started. You better hurry, or you're gonna get into trouble."

"So are you, young lady," he said in an authoritative voice. "You had better come with me before you get yourself into some major trouble."

"Oh, brother, don't worry, I'm not going to get into any trouble. I have an A average, and I've already done the assignments for the rest of the month."

"The whole term?" he said with a shocked look on his face. I checked out his eyes. His pupils looked just like mine, and his irises were as white as a church usher's uniform. He was sober. I don't know why, but my mouth pulled itself into a huge smile.

"What is it?" he asked, staring at me funny.

"Nothing. Nothing at all. I'll see ya later." I shook his hand off my arm and dashed down the hall.

"Hey, Shayla, wait up," he called softly behind me.

I opened the West Mall door slowly, tiptoed down the steps, and waited. A moment later Lemm eased his body out of the door just like I knew he would. He shut it quietly behind him. His eyes darted back and forth nervously as he walked down the steps to where I was.

"I can't believe you're doing this," he said. "I can't believe you're cutting."

"I'm not cutting," I snapped. "I'm just taking a vacation, and I didn't ask you to follow me. You can go back anytime that you like."

"Oh, no," he said. "It's too late now. Besides, someone must be here to protect you from what lies beyond the schoolroom doors."

I broke into laughter. "Lemm, you can't even protect yourself. You must be kidding."

I ran down the walkway and carefully slipped through a thick cluster of pointed hedges that went all the way around the school. When I got out to the street, I didn't even bother waiting. I knew Lemm would be right behind me.

Lemm and I used my quarters to buy a couple of hot dogs and

Little Debbie snack cakes at the five-and-dime store across the street from the school. When we were completely stuffed, we decided to go check out a park in a neighborhood a few blocks over.

Even though it was majorly bright and sunny out, a refreshing sprinkle greeted us as we entered Cortez Park. It was the first rain that we'd had in weeks, and a large group of teens had started a game of tag in it. Bare-chested boys in neon trunks were chasing groups of bikini-clad girls in front of the iron gate that surrounded the small pool, their light brown bodies and dark, shiny hair glistening from the fresh raindrops. Lemm wanted to join the kids, but I told him that I didn't feel like chasing anybody around. We danced around in the rain until the droplets finally figured out that they shouldn't be falling from a clear sky. Then we raced to the back of the park and flopped down on an empty park bench.

"Well, what now, Shayla?" Lemm asked. "We had some hot dogs and got really wet," he said, wringing his T-shirt out all over the cedar bench. "What are we going to do now?"

I shrugged my shoulders. I hadn't thought that far along. I had just wanted to leave school, leave the last place where I had seen Mr. Anderson Fox. I just wanted to be someplace where I didn't have to think about him and Gift. I looked back up at the front of the park. The tag-playing group had stopped chasing one another and made their way back to the pool. They were happily splashing around in the ice blue water. It looked like even more fun than the game of tag, and I did like the pool.

"Hey, let's go swimming," I said.

"We can't," Lemm said quickly. "We don't have swimsuits."

"It doesn't matter. We can go in what we have on."

"I don't know. I'm not much in the mood for wading around, just like you didn't want to be chased."

"Oh," I said with disappointment all over my voice. "I guess we can do something else."

"No, why don't you go anyway. I'll just wait right here while you take a dip."

"Naw, I won't go without you. It won't be much fun if I do it by myself." I glanced back at the pool again. The tag-playing boys and girls were taking turns jumping from the high diving board into the ten-foot section of the pool. There was no one in the shallow end at all. I could wade around without anyone bothering me. "Are you sure you don't want to go?" I asked. "There's nobody in the low end of the pool."

"Yes. But really, you go on. I'll be just fine until you get back." He stretched out on the bench. His oversize sneakers rested against my thigh. "Go on," he said. "I'll just take a nap until you get back."

"Okay," I said. "I'm just gonna wade around for a little. I'll be right back."

I left Lemm lying peacefully on the bench and walked back up to the pool. I opened the gate and hopped down into the shallow end without even feeling the water first. It was pretty cold, but it felt really nice. I waded into it up to my waist and sat down. I let it cover my head until I felt like I had to catch my breath, then I came back up to the surface.

When I got tired of the shallow water, I waded in a bit deeper, where some of the other kids were, and got involved in a game of Nerf ball catch with a skinny, talkative girl who had a huge birthmark on her face that reminded me of an upside-down Christmas tree. She told me that she liked to read a lot, mostly scary books, and I completely forgot about the time while she gave me the 411 on the latest horror book that she was reading. When I finally looked at my Timex, I discovered that I had been in the pool for nearly an hour and a half. I scrambled out of the water and dripped my way back to the bench where Lemm had been sleeping, but he was gone. In his place was a huge black dog with a really sweaty tongue. I sat down on the bench and rubbed the dog on the head.

Thinking that Lemm had just wandered off to another part of the park, I waited for him nearly twenty-five minutes before I decided that it was time for me to go. I felt muddy-water blue again as I rose up off the bench. I just didn't believe that he would take off on me, even though I had left him alone a lot longer than I had expected to. All he had to do was come and tell me that it was time to get out of the pool.

I walked to a nearby water fountain, filled my cupped hands with cool water, and brought a drink back for the dog. He lapped it up. I patted him a few more times and started out of the park. I had made it only as far as the pool when I looked up and saw Lemm running my way. I stopped.

Lemm came tearing up to me like I was a relative he hadn't seen in years. At first I thought he was just really happy that I had waited for him to come back, but then I noticed that his face was eaten up with desperation. "Shayla, Shayla," he said, grabbing me by my arms. "I need you to do me a favor! I need you to help me out!"

"With what?" I asked, startled. "What's wrong?"

"Nothing. It ain't no big thing. You just gotta help me out, Shayla. I need you to cover my back," he said in a very un-Lemm-like voice. "I just need you to help me out."

"Help you out of what?" I asked.

"Nothing!" he said, pressing my arms really hard. "It's nothing. You ain't got to be too concerned about it. Just tell them that I was here with you the whole time. You was at the pool, and I was watching you. Shayla, just do me a favor and tell them that!"

"Ouch!" I cried. "Lemm, you're hurting me. Tell who what?" I asked again.

"Just do it, girl, all right!" he shouted. "Just do me a favor and be cool! Will, you?" he pleaded. "Please, just do me this one little thing?"

"What little thing?" I asked, pulling his hands off my arms. "Lemm, who am I supposed to tell what?"

He looked away from me and stared back at the front entrance. A blue-and-white was rolling through the main gate, its red lanterns flashing on and off as it came up the narrow dirt pathway.

Lemm swallowed hard, really hard. You could actually hear the gulp, as if he had choked something big down.

"What's going on, Lemm?" I asked.

"Shayla, I—I did something really stupid," he said quickly. "I did something really dumb. Just back me up. Please just back me up."

"Lemm, what did you do?"

"Just back me up, Shayla. It'll be fine if you just help me out. I don't have time to explain, Shayla. Just trust me, and help me out." He looked back up at the front gate. "Don't worry, Shayla. It's gonna be just fine."

"What's gonna be just fine?" I asked.

The police car came rolling up just a few feet away from us and jerked to a stop. As soon as it did, Lemm's face went all relaxed again, like I had seen it do several times before.

The police car's engine shut off, and two cops stepped out. They were both young guys, about twenty or so, with trim waists and chests pumped up like Mr. Anderson Fox's. One was a tall white guy with a short, prickly haircut that made him look like he had a mass of porcupine quills on his head. He had green eyes, just a shade or two lighter than Kambia's, and beige skin turned tan from the hot summer sun. The other guy was a brother. He had sharp dark brown eyes, a fade glistening with oil sheen, and a few scraggly hairs jutting out of his chin that were pretending to be a beard. He kept his hand real close to his pistol as he walked, as if he thought that someone would be silly enough to try and grab his gun away from him.

"Hey! You there, little brother," he said to Lemm. "Let me holler at you and ask you a few questions. There's something I need to talk to you about."

"What is it, Officer? What can I do for you today?" Lemm asked in his normal charming, self-assured voice, but when I looked down, I could see that his hands were trembling just a bit at his sides, like his body wasn't quite as confident as his mouth was.

"I'll tell you what you can do for us, young man," the tan officer said. "You can come over here and stand by this car for a minute."

"What for, Officer?" Lemm asked.

"Because I told you to," the officer said in a serious tone.

Lemm and I both walked over to the car.

"What's your name, little man?" the brother policeman asked.

"My name is Lemm Turley, and this is my friend Shayla," Lemm said, pointing to me. "We were just enjoying a day at the park."

"You were?" the tan policeman asked.

"Yes, sir," Lemm said. "It's nice out. There was a brief shower a while ago."

"That was more than two hours ago, son," the brother policeman jumped in. "It ain't rained since then. How long have you been out here?"

"I don't know," Lemm said. "I don't have a watch on."

"Neither do I," the policeman said, holding out an arm covered with tiny, kinky black hairs. "I forgot mine at home this morning, but I still know about what time it rained. It was a really long time ago, not just a little while back. How long have you been out here?"

"I don't know, Officer," Lemm repeated. "Like I said. I'm not in the habit of carrying a watch."

"Oh, you're not, well, what about your little girlfriend, then. Does she carry a watch? How long y'all been out here, little missy?" he asked me.

I shrugged my shoulders. "I don't know, sir. I wasn't paying too much attention," I answered honestly.

"I wasn't either, sir," Lemm said. "We were playing around. Nobody watches the time when they're doing that. We were at the pool. We weren't paying attention."

"You weren't?" the policeman asked.

Lemm shook his head. "No, sir. We were at the pool. It's kind of hard to see a watch underwater."

"So, you were at the pool."

"Yes, sir."

"Naw, I don't know if that's true, Mr. Turley," the tan officer chimed in, pointing back at the gate. "I don't know if that's true at all, young man. You see, me and my partner just came from a store down the street back there. We just came from a grocer's a couple of blocks from here, and the owner said that there was a boy in there that looked just like you. He said that the boy was trying to steal some wine coolers. He said that he caught him drinking out of one bottle and saw him try to stick another one into his pants. He said that he tried to grab hold of him, but the boy pushed him and ran off. How old are you, boy?" he asked.

"I'm thirteen," Lemm said.

"That's about the age that the store owner said the boy was, ain't it, Ryan?" the policeman asked his partner.

"That's about the age," the other cop said. "That means you're just the right age, and he looked just like you."

"There must be a mistake, Officer," Lemm said. "I've been here the whole time. I can't be in two places at once."

"Naw, no you can't," the brother cop said. "So one of y'all is lying."

"Well, it's not me," Lemm said coolly. "I was right here."

"Yeah, you told me that," the policeman said.

The radio in the police car sputtered and spit out something that I mostly couldn't make out. The only thing I heard was "suspect." It was enough to set my hands to trembling worse than Lemm's.

The tan policeman walked over to the car, reached inside, and picked up the radio. He talked into it a second, the whole time looking at Lemm, then he put it back and walked over to us.

"Put your hands on the car, young man," he said to Lemm.

"Excuse me, sir?" Lemm said.

"Go over there and put your hands out on that car right now, young man," he repeated. "We've played around long enough with you."

"I don't know what you're talking about, sir," Lemm said. "I told you there must be some kind of mistake."

"Ain't no mistake, little man," the brother policeman said. "Come on." He grabbed Lemm by the arm and jerked him over to the car.

"I didn't do anything," Lemm said.

"Spread your legs, son," the policeman said, kicking Lemm's legs apart. He began to pat Lemm down. "You got anything on you? Drugs, knives, any kind of weapon?"

"I don't have anything," Lemm said weakly. "I told you I wasn't at any store. I've been here the whole time."

"Well, we got a man down the road that says different," the tan policeman said. "And we gonna take his word until we find out different."

"I didn't do it," Lemm said. "I told you I wasn't anywhere near the store."

"That's not what the man said," the tan policeman told him while his partner finished his search. "That's not what the man said at all. In fact, he said that you been in there at least three times. He said that he tried to catch you the last time you were in there, but you ran out of the door before he could get to you. He described you perfectly. He knows it was you at his store."

"It wasn't me," Lemm said. "I told you that I wasn't there."

"Oh, well, we'll see," the brother officer said. "Come on, boy. When we get down to the station, we'll figure it all out."

"It wasn't me, man!" Lemm said, slipping back into his street slang. "It wasn't me, homey, I'm telling you."

The policeman cuffed Lemm, then he walked him to the car, opened the door, and gently pushed him inside. "Watch your head, son," he said.

"It wasn't me! Just ask her," Lemm said, jerking his head in my direction. "Tell 'em, Shayla," he pleaded. "Tell 'em that I was at the pool with you."

"Is that true?" the brother officer asked.

I started to answer him, but I didn't know what to say. I didn't even know exactly what was going on. I looked around me instead. A crowd had gathered, made up mostly of kids from the pool. Shoulder to shoulder they stood, with their arms folded and giant scowls on their faces. They were scowls caused by Mr. Anger. The kids were mad, and not at the policemen. They were angry at Lemm. He had messed them over big time, brought the law into their normally quiet park. He was a troublemaker, and because of him the next time somebody screwed up in their hood the policemen would be back. They would remember where they had picked up their last teen suspect. Pretty soon it would just be routine for them to stop by and check out the scene. They would treat them like they treated the kids at our park. They would line them all up, pat 'em down, and drag off the couple that they caught with a key-chain blade or a nickel bag of weed. There would be no more freedom in the park. The kids would have to find somewhere else to hang. They would lose something precious to them just because Lemm wanted a drink.

"Tell 'em, Shayla," Lemm pleaded. "Tell 'em, Shayla. Tell 'em that I was right there with you."

I'm sure that one of the other four Shaylas in me wanted to persuade the cops, but all I could do was continue to stare at the faces of the kids. At least one of them had made me feel welcome at the park. I wanted to come back again. It wouldn't be possible now because of Lemm. Once again I was an outsider. Lemm had ruined the park for me, just like Mr. Anderson Fox had ruined things for me at my own house. I liked Lemm, but I was getting pretty tired of people doing stuff in my life that I didn't like.

"Tell 'em, Shayla," I heard him call a third time. In my confusion I weighed those three calls for help against the three times the store owner said he had seen Lemm in his store, and the four things that I was sure I knew about him—he was a slick talker, a drinker, a liar, and a thief. And no matter how much I liked him, I just couldn't shrug off those things about him. Grandma Augustine said that I was coming to the point where I was going to have to decide what kind of woman I wanted to be. I still wasn't too sure about that. What I was sure of was that I was tired of being a girl who had no control over anything, tired of being hurt. I shrugged my shoulders and watched the policemen close Lemm's door and get in the car.

"Come on, Miss Shayla, please!" I saw Lemm mouth through the rolled-up window.

I just folded my arms across my chest and watched as the car slowly drove away. By the time it got to the gate, I was already starting to feel bad about my actions. I didn't know if I had done the right thing. I felt really awful. A new journal entry popped into my head. *Regret is flowing through me like dirty bathwater, and it's already too late to pull out the plug.*

# Chapter 5

After my school let out today, Kambia and I went to the bayou. I think that we were both hoping to find Peace among the cloudy waters, but he refused to show up. For nearly an hour we stood there listening to the waves splash against the bank and watching a swarm of bumblebees gather nectar from a patch of black-eyed Susans growing between the trunks of the shady pine trees. After that we sat down on the edge of the cliff to chat.

I started a conversation about Lemm, even though I really didn't want to be dropping Lemm's problems on Kambia. She hasn't been herself at all lately. She's pale all the time, pale and really tired, like she's hardly sleeping, lying awake all night fretting over who's sending her the packages. She looks deflated, like a tire drained of all its air. When I arrive at her house each afternoon to play, she always tells me that she's too bushed to dress up her dolls or put on a CD and dance, which she usually likes do more than anything. Most of the time she lies in the bed staring up at her lace canopy while I try to entertain her by putting on a puppet show with her stuffed animals or reading a story out of one of her fairy-tale books. "Kambia, let's go outside and play kickball or something," I say to her, but she simply rolls over on her side.

I was only able to get her out this morning by telling her that I was going down to the bayou. She said that she wanted to come because it was the place where she first knew that we would be friends. She said that she could tell because I was really worried when she slid down the cliff toward the water. "I knew you wouldn't let me drown, Shayla," she said. "I knew that if I got too close to the water, you would yell at me to come back up." It was true. I wouldn't let Kambia get hurt that day. I didn't like to see her in pain, but today I was covered with blisters myself. I didn't want to let Kambia know what was going on with Lemm, but I had no choice. I was ripped to pieces over what I had let happen to him, and I needed someone to tell me if and how I could put the pieces back together.

I told Kambia about catching Lemm drinking from the vodka bottle, and that he had probably been drinking for a really long time. I told her that his drinking had gotten the law on him and that he had been arrested, but it was really my fault that he ended up in jail. I told her that I had wanted to back him up that day, tell the policemen that he had been at the pool with me, but I just couldn't. "Kambia, I really like Lemm," I told her. "I don't know why I didn't speak up and help him. I guess I just didn't like him playing me."

While I talked, Kambia sat quietly with her tiny hands resting in her lap. She didn't respond to what I said at all. Her eyes didn't blink and her mouth didn't fly open, but it wasn't because she was out of it again. She was awake and listening. I could tell because she kept bumping the backs of her legs against the cliff, knocking off little clumps of loose dirt. Her relaxed attitude made me realize something that hadn't occurred to me at all. She already knew most of what I was telling her. I could tell by the absence of shock on her face that I wasn't letting her in on something that she wasn't familiar with. After I finished talking, she let me know that my feelings were right on track.

"I know about Lemm, Shayla."

"How?" I asked. "I haven't heard any gossip about it around the hood."

"A girl named China, who went to the party that we all went

to, got arrested on the same day that he did. She told me, Shayla," she said. "She said that she got caught stealing some clothes for her baby."

"That's terrible," I said.

"It is," she said. "She's a really cool girl, but she's only fourteen and she already has two babies to feed."

"Two?"

"Yes, a little boy and a baby girl."

"What did she say about Lemm?"

"She said that she remembered Lemm from the party, and she knew that it was him at the station because of the way he likes to throw out compliments and use a lot of fancy talk. He makes me feel good when he says nice things."

"I don't know," I said. "Sometimes I feel good when he says things, but not always. He fakes a lot. I don't like that too much. What did China tell you?"

"China told me that Lemm didn't stay at the jail too long. She said that he said a lot of really pleasant things to the policemen that arrested him. She said that she didn't remember all of it, but she knows that he told them that he was glad that they were doing their job and cleaning up the streets. He said that it was a job they should be proud of and that he didn't blame them for arresting him, because it was all his fault. He said that lately he had seen so many beer and wine cooler commercials on TV that he just wanted to know what drinking was all about. That's why he was trying to get a few drinks. He wasn't bad, he was just curious. China said that the policemen seemed really happy when he told them that, especially the part about them cleaning up the streets, and it being a proud job. She said that they probably knew that Lemm was just trying to get over on them, but they thanked him for what he had to say anyway, and when he let them know that he was an honor student in a special summer-school program, they started to feel sorry for him. They felt so bad for him that they called the owner of the store and asked him to give Lemm a break if he agreed never to come back in his store. 'What's the big deal over a couple of bottles of drink?' the brother policeman asked. 'I'm sure that when you were his age, you did something really dumb too. He didn't mean to push you. He was just doing the natural thing and trying to get away. If you let him go this time, we can promise he won't be back. Why ruin a kid's life over just a few bucks?'"

"The policeman said that?" I asked.

"That's what China told me," she said. "China said that the store owner must have been a pretty good guy, because the next thing she knew, the policemen were walking Lemm to the door. He's at home, Shayla," she said, still swinging her skinny legs back and forth over the cliff. "He's just been sitting there since the day that he got let go from the station. I guess he's just afraid to go back to school. Maybe he's scared that now everyone will know why his eyes are always so red."

"Maybe they will. Man," I said. "I didn't know that. I haven't called his house or anything. I just thought that he was in juvie hall or somewhere. Man, I'm glad he's not." I got up from the cliff. "Let's go see him. I need to tell him that I'm sorry."

"Okay," she said, scrambling to her feet too. We left the bayou and headed for Lemm's.

Lemm was lucky enough to live in what folks in our hood called a house in a box. It was one of several new charity homes built in our neighborhood for families who normally couldn't afford their own house. Like all of the homes, it was an attractive, small wood-frame house that the charity, along with some neighborhood help, was able to put up in only a few weeks. That's why folks called it a house in a box, because they said that it was made quicker than you could make a box of Hamburger Helper.

When Kambia and I reached Lemm's house, we hesitated before walking up the steps. We didn't know if Lemm's dad was home or not, but if he was, we didn't want to run into him. It wasn't that we were afraid of him or anything. We had met him once before, when we came to pick up Lemm for the party. He wasn't exactly a strange guy, but he wasn't normal, either.

According to Lemm, his dad was only in his thirties, like Mama, but his abnormally saggy face already looked like it could use a pressing out with Grandma Augustine's iron. He was a pretty tall guy, about three okra stalks higher than Lemm, with a perfectly round basketball belly that looked like it was a bit too heavy for his skinny legs. His eyes weren't chestnut like Lemm's. They were common brown and glossy. His dark, kinky hair was streaked with a wide stripe of silver above each ear and had begun to pull away from his forehead. He looked like the old, gray-haired deacons that sat in the back of Grandma's church. There was a sadness about him too, and it was the thing that made me, at least, not want to run into him again. I had seen people blue before, and had been pretty blue myself lately, but he seemed like his whole body was enveloped in unhappiness. It surrounded him like a dust cloud, following him from room to room like Pig Pen's dirt in "Peanuts." He wore his grief like most people wear an overcoat. I had felt miserable for the short time that me and Kambia sat across from him in the living room waiting on Lemm, and I could tell by the way Kambia kept uncomfortably shifting in her seat that she felt the same way too. I had wanted to tell him how sorry I was for his loss, but I knew that no matter what, he would always be screwed up, knowing that he had killed his own daughters. Unlike with Pig Pen's dirt, there was no way that he could wash his sorrow off.

After pacing in front of the house for five minutes, Kambia and I decided that father or no father, it was time to go in. We opened the gate slowly and walked hand in hand up the steps, but when we got to the front door, guilt tugged me back. I waited behind Kambia while she pushed the doorbell.

The bell chimed three times and we heard the sound of footsteps on the hardwood floor. They were heavy steps, and we both braced ourselves for coming face-to-face with Lemm's dad, but when the door finally opened, it was Lemm who stepped out.

I peeked around Kambia, and I didn't like what I saw at all. Lemm's eyes were crimson and drowsy looking, and his fade looked like it hadn't been raked in days. He had on a sweat-stained T-shirt that looked like it had been around for a lot longer than it should have been, and his khaki shorts were wrinkled and grayed from dirt. He was wearing a pair of crappy leather sandals instead of his normal oversize sneakers, and the amount of liquor fumes coming off of his body made me think that we should hurry up and get him out of the sun before he burst into flames. He was nothing like the neat Lemm that we knew, and for a moment I wasn't sure if we had even come to right house, but the minute he opened his mouth, there was no question that the boy in the door was Lemm.

"Good morning, Lady Kambia," he said with a big grin in really good speech. The smell of his breath made Kambia cover her nose with her hand for a moment, but she still broke out in giggles like she always did.

"What brings you over this morning, Lady Kambia?" he asked her. "Do you need rescuing from a horde of barbarians?"

Kambia giggled again. "No, I don't think so. Me and Shayla just came to say hi. Didn't we, Shayla?" she said, stepping aside so that Lemm could see me. I managed to pull my mouth into a nervous smile.

"Aw, Miss Shayla, I haven't seen you in a week," he said with an even bigger grin. "I'm really glad to see you. What has been happening in your life?"

"N-nothing, just school and all," I stuttered, a little taken aback by his smelly breath, but mostly I was startled by his friendly tone. It wasn't what I expected at all. I expected him to be as mad at me as I was with myself, but he didn't seem like he was. I wondered if he was too tipsy to remember what I had done.

"Good for you," he said, leaning against the doorframe. "You're a bright girl, bright girls belong in school. I envy your being able to go there."

"What do you mean by that?" both Kambia and I asked.

"Nothing, it's not even worth talking about," he said with a carefree wave of his hand, but his face looked like he had just dropped something heavy on his toe. He pushed the screen door open.

"Well, come in, ladies," he said. "No real gentleman would keep such thoughtful young ladies standing on the front porch in the hot sun."

When we got inside, it was clear that Lemm had a lot more control over his mouth than he did his legs. His speech might have been pretty clear, but his steps were all jumbled up. He staggered down the narrow hallway, placing his hand against the wall to keep his balance.

"Shayla, I hope he doesn't fall," Kambia whispered to me.

"I'm sorry, ladies, I'm afraid I'm just a bit clumsy today," he said as he nearly stumbled into a wooden coatrack. "I guess that's what happens when everything you know is out of place. I just can't find a way to steady myself."

"What do you mean by that?" I asked.

"Nothing," he said. "Nothing at all."

We followed Lemm down the hallway until we came to a door with a huge black-and-white poster taped to it that read, ONLY SERIOUS POETS AND WRITERS NEED APPLY, spelled out in tiny open books. It was a really cool sign, and I was majorly getting ready to go all green over it when Lemm pulled it down and held it out to me. "I found it a while back at some shop on Main," he said. "I was gonna give it to you last Monday, but things didn't go my way. Here, take it."

I took the poster and looked it over. It was excellent, something that you would give a friend, a true friend, not someone who had let you go to jail. I really wanted it, but I knew if I took it, my guilt would continue to cling to me like chiggers. It would bury itself deep in my flesh, and there would be no way of getting it out. I didn't deserve the poster. I held it back out to him. "I don't want it. I think you should give it to another friend. Maybe Kambia would like it," I said.

He pushed my hand back toward me. "I bought it for you," he said. "I don't want to give it to anyone else. Besides, you're the writer, not Kambia. Kambia has her own special gifts."

I held it out to him again. "I—I can't," I said. "My grandma Augustine says that giving gifts to an unworthy person is like throwing money into a fire. You keep it. I don't have any room on my door for it anyway."

"Yes you do, Shayla," Kambia said. "It's a really pretty poster. Why don't you take it? He wants you to have it. My mom says that it's not polite to refuse to take a gift when someone goes out of their way to buy one for you."

"Take the poster, Shayla. My grandma used to say that even hands and fingers argue sometimes," Lemm said, throwing an African saying back at me. "I don't blame you for what happened in the park. It was just something that happened that day. I want you to have it. Please take it. I bought it for you, Shayla." I didn't see any way of getting out of taking the poster, so I just rolled it up and stuck it under my arm.

Lemm opened the door to his bedroom, which neither me nor Kambia had been in before, and stumbled inside. He collapsed onto a sloppily made twin-size bed and closed his eyes as if he was about to take a nap. Unsure of what to do next, Kambia and I hesitated for a few moments, but finally I took her by the hand and we went into the room too.

Lemm's room didn't stink of alcohol like he did. In fact, the air in it was just fine. It was probably because the room's only window was open and because there were so many plants. The room was filled with them. Pots of them sat in every inch of it. There were clay pots of plump aloe vera plants lined up on every shelf of the oak bookcase in front of what looked like a pretty good collection of spy books, plastic pots of bushy ferns hanging over a black-and-white poster of Louis Armstrong, globe-shaped cacti sticking out of plastic pots on top of a box fan sitting in the middle of the floor, and ceramic pots of ivies crawling up the posts of the bed. I couldn't decide if the room looked more like a flower shop or a jungle, but I liked it. The plants gave the air in the room an outdoorsy smell, and they were spectacular just to look at. I walked over and fingered one of the ivies. The leaves felt smooth and waxy, like someone had polished them with Pledge. "I like your plants, Lemm," I said.

"So do I, but my father doesn't," he said, opening his eyes and sitting up in the bed. "These were all my mother's plants. When she left, he wanted me to throw them out. He said that if she cared about them, she should have taken them with her. I couldn't part with the plants and my mother, too."

"I guess I couldn't either," I said.

"It's okay. My dad hardly ever comes in here anyway," he said, raising his head up. He pointed at the plants on the bookcase. "They get to me sometimes though."

"How?" Kambia asked. She walked over and sat down real close to him on the bed. I guessed she had gotten used to his breath.

"When I forget to water them, some of the plants start to droop," he said. "It almost looks as if they're crying. It makes me think that they're missing my mother."

"I'll bet they are, Lemm," I said, sitting down next to Kambia. "But plants don't cry, people do."

"That's not true, Shayla," Kambia said. "I think plants cry. They're alive just like we are. I'll bet they cry, and even feel stuff."

"How, Kambia?" I asked.

"I'll tell you," she said. "Once, when I was still living with my old mom, I left the house and I went down to a nearby field that was covered with beautiful purple, white, and red flowers. There were tons and tons of them, with bright green stems. They were stretching their necks toward the warm sun, soaking in the light. They were wonderful. I wanted to have one of each kind to press in a memory book that one of the nuns I used to stay with gave me. So I bent down and started picking them. I picked and picked until I had a whole lapful. After that I ran straight home with them so that I could place them in my book while they were still fresh. It was only a couple of blocks, but guess what, Shayla? When I got home, the flowers were all droopy. In just the short time it took me to get from the field they went limp. It was like they were sick or something. I felt real bad about it. I didn't know that picking the flowers would make them ill. So you know what I did?"

"What?" Lemm asked.

"I took them back," she said. "I took them back to the field where I got them. I wanted to put them on their stems again. I wanted to make them all better."

"Kambia, you can't put flowers back once you've yanked them off," I said.

"You're right, Shayla. I couldn't put them back on their stems, so I just sprinkled them between the other flowers and left, but guess what? When I came back the next morning to check on them, they weren't droopy at all. They were stiff and just as fresh as when I picked them. It was like a miracle. That's why I know that plants can cry. Because the flowers were all weepy when I took them away from their families, but when I took them back home, they were happy and snapped back to their old selves."

"Good," Lemm said. "I guess I was right about them sometimes missing my mother."

"Kambia, are you sure that's what really happened?" I asked, worried that she was once again spending too much time in her fantasies.

"It's true, Shayla, I promise. I guess it was one of God's little works. He can do all sorts of things," she said. "The nuns that I used to stay with said that he could wipe the world clean and rebuild it in just a few seconds if he wanted to. If he can do that, I'll bet that he could figure out how to make a few sad flowers happy."

"Amen to that, Lady Kambia," Lemm said. "I have no doubt that your story is true."

"I guess I don't either, Kambia," I said. "Grandma says that miracles do happen."

I got up from the bed and walked over to the window, but there wasn't really anything to see. Lemm's window faced a field, and it wasn't a field full of pretty flowers, like Kambia's. It was a field that some of the companies on the edge of our hood liked to use as a dumping ground, just like folks sometimes did with the bayou. It was littered with rusty barrels, cardboard boxes, and plastic bottles. It wasn't a great thing to see each morning when you woke up. I imagined that it could put even the happiest person in a bad mood. I pulled the blind down and returned to the bed. Lemm was still sitting up, but his eyes were closed again as if he were sleeping. The creak of the bedsprings under my weight woke him up. He pushed himself off the bed with his hands and stood up on wobbly legs. "I hope he doesn't fall, Shayla," Kambia whispered to me again.

"I'll catch him if he does," I said, and stood up too.

Lemm stumbled around the room again, pointing out various items that belonged to his mother. There was a silver-plated vanity set that he kept on top of the bookcase, a string of fake pearls and matching bracelet on the mahogany nightstand next to the bed, and a tin coffee can filled with a collection of old pennies sitting on the floor behind his door. He said that the items were just a few things that he had rescued from his father. He didn't care all that much about any of them, but they were his mom's, and he'd refused to just let his dad toss them out after she left. She might come back to get them one day, he said. Both Kambia and I nodded our head, even though I'm certain that neither one of us thought it was true.

After Lemm got through pointing things out, he stooped down and opened a large metal footlocker at the end of the bed, nearly tumbling over as he unfastened the lock. He fumbled around in the locker for a while, pulling out various items of old clothing and tossing them in a careless heap on the floor. Finally he found what he was looking for and brought it out, a miniature bottle half full of caramel-colored liquid. The black wording on the gold label was small, but I could still make out the words ALEXANDER'S FINE WHISKEY. My eyes jumped out of my head, while Kambia just looked away.

Lemm slammed the trunk shut and sat down beside it. He turned the bottle up to his mouth and boldly took a drink, never once glancing toward me and Kambia. I didn't know if he wasn't looking at us because he was ashamed or because he just didn't care what we thought of him anymore. Either way, the sight of him with that bottle made me wish that we were back on the banks of the bayou.

"You shouldn't do that, Lemm," I blurted out.

He finished downing the contents of the bottle and looked at me. "Why? I'm sure that I'm not shocking you, Shayla," he said. "You've known about my drinking for a long time, ever since you saw me drinking from that bottle at Diamond's."

"You told me that it wasn't you," I said.

"I know," he said. "But I'm sure that a smart girl like you wouldn't believe a lie as shallow as that. You know what I am, Shayla."

"You're my friend," I said. "And you shouldn't drink. My grandma Augustine says that it's bad for you."

"Is it?" he asked, throwing the empty bottle into a plastic trash can next to the door.

"That's what she says," I said.

"Your grandma has something to say about everything, Shayla, doesn't she?" he asked nastily.

"She likes to speak her mind," I said. "She's usually right about most stuff."

"Is she?"

"Yes," I said. "She says that alcohol makes you dumb. Most folks that use it can't control their mouth any more than they can control the weather, that's what she says."

"I'll just bet she does!" he said. "I never met an old lady who didn't have enough tongue to fill fifty butcher shops. Trust me, homegirl, your grams ain't no exception." He was slipping into street slang the way he had on the day that he was arrested. I had heard him use it before, so it didn't send my eyebrows up to the sky, but I could tell by the way confusion was squirming all over Kambia's face that she didn't know what in the world was going on.

"What did he say, Shayla?" she asked.

Lemm looked over at her. "I just told yo' girlfriend that her grams is way too much into other folks' business."

"That's not true!" I protested. "My grandma Augustine never minds anybody else's business. She just likes to tell you the truth. Besides, I read in some magazine that drinking isn't good for people our age. They said that it really plays with our mind and throws us off our game in school."

"Well," Lemm said with a wave of his hand. "I should be just fine, 'cause I don't go to school anymore."

"What are you talking about?" I walked over to him. "How come you can't come to school anymore?"

"I got kicked out," he said. "Some chick down at Kambia's school saw me at the station and blabbed to her girlfriends. One of them goes to our school. She works in the principal's office in the afternoons. She let it slip about me, so the principal called me in."

"What happened?" I asked.

"Nothing much," he said. "She just told me that one of the requirements for the accelerated program was good moral behavior. She said that even though I didn't get put in juvie because of it, stealing was still a reason to kick me out. She gave me a letter to bring home to my dad and told me that she was sure that I was a disappointment to myself, my classmates, and certainly to my family.

'Lemm, you're a great student, and I would like to keep you in,' she said. 'But as you know, this program is very competitive, so more stringent rules have to apply here. I've written down a list of treatment places that I would be happy to discuss with your dad. I'm sorry, but this program just isn't for problem kids, no matter how smart they are.' What a bitch!" he spit. "I hope she falls over dead."

"Ooh, don't say that, Lemm," Kambia pleaded. "I know you're upset, but it's not right to say ugly things about a teacher."

Lemm glared at her. "Kambia, one of these days you're going to find out how to live in the real world, girlfriend," he said. "You let me know when your bus finally makes it up the hill, and I'll let you in on what the real world is about."

"I know what the real world is about," Kambia said defensively, looking like her face would be all wet any moment. "I know what the real world is about, and it's not about saying mean things to people that like you," she said.

"Oh, really. Is that what they teach you down at that Girl Help Center? Is that what your counselor, that nosy-ass Mrs. Dreyfus, told you?"

"I don't know what you mean," Kambia said.

"Oh, you don't—well, let me tell you. Miss Thing came over here the other afternoon offering her help. She said that she could tell from the first time she met me that I was drinking. She said that I was doing a pretty good job of hiding it from most people, but she was trained to recognize certain signs. 'It won't be easy, but we can get through this together, Lemm,' she said, holding my hand like I was some damn little snotty-nose kid. 'Right now I'm very busy with Kambia, but I can see that you're about to fall over the edge. Please let me try and help you, too.'"

"She said that?" I asked.

"Yeah, but I got her straight. I told her to back up off me. I let her know that I didn't need nobody messing around in my affairs. I told her that I wasn't Kambia. My head wasn't floating out there in space."

"That's really mean, Lemm," Kambia cried.

"It's not. It's honest," Lemm said. He yanked open the trunk and fished around in it until he brought up another bottle. It was identical to the first one, except it was full. He unscrewed the cap. And held it out to me and Kambia. "Y'all want a drink?" he asked. Kambia shook her head, and I rolled my eyes.

"No, thanks," I said. "You're going to get into trouble doing that."

"Wow, I thought I was already in trouble. I guess you didn't hear the part where I said that I couldn't go to school no mo'," he said to me. "But then again, Miss Shayla, I guess you don't know what trouble is."

"What do you mean by that?" I yelled.

"I'll tell you," he said. "You think you got problems because your sorry-ass dad got married again and had a new baby. So what, big deal. You still have a mom, a sister, and a grams that really love you and care for you. Some people ain't got that. You're just whining and groaning about nothing. Get over it. Half the kids in the world got a dad that ain't worth the time they mom spent writing his name on the birth certificate. I don't know why you think your pops ought to be any different. He's just a dude. We be like that sometimes."

"Shut up, Lemm," I said. "You're just being cruel for no reason."

"I have reasons for everything that I do," he said. "I'd tell you what they are, but you're probably too stupid to understand them."

"Shayla's not stupid," Kambia said. "You're just being hateful for no reason. I don't like it when you're like this. You're just being mean to us because you've drank too much." She hopped up from the bed. "I wanna go home, Shayla. My mom will be looking for me."

I tossed the poster at Lemm's feet. "Here, take it. I don't want it. You can give it to someone else," I said. "I don't care if you get drunk, but it's not fair to be mean to Kambia." I tugged at Kambia's sundress. "Let's go, Kambia." She walked out the door and I started after her, but Lemm caught my hand.

"Wait, Shayla, please," he said.

"What is it?" I asked.

"I just have something that I want to tell you, that's all."

"What is it?" I asked again. He opened his mouth like he was going to say something, but instead he just stared at Kambia. I turned and stared at her too. "Can you wait for me on the porch, Kam," I said.

"I'll go sit on the steps," she said.

"Okay. I'll be right out."

Kambia left the room, and I stood there staring at Lemm while he held my hand. I got that feeling again from his touch, the one that made me feel like there were fireflies flying around inside me lighting parts of me up. I pulled my hand away and let his drop to the floor.

"What did you want to say, Lemm?" I asked. "Kambia's waiting on me."

He shrugged his shoulder. "I'm . . . I'm sorry," he said. "I didn't mean to say mean things to you and Kambia."

"Well, you did, and it wasn't very nice." I sat down on the other side of the locker. "I'm sorry about your mom," I said. "I don't know what I would do if my mom went off and left me."

"She wouldn't," he said. "My mother was different than other mothers," he said, going back to his proper speech.

"What do you mean?" I asked.

He sighed. "I don't know. Nothing, I guess," he said, placing his head in his heads. He rubbed his forehead for a few moments, then rubbed his eyes with his palms. "I'm getting tired," he said. "I guess I drank too much."

"You shouldn't have been drinking at all," I said. "It makes you say dumb things."

"I know," he said. "I wish I could just stop."

"Can't you? My mom says that if you want to bad enough, you can stop anything. Why don't you talk to Mrs. Dreyfus about it?"

He looked up at me. His eyes were even redder from rubbing, and his face was thick with anguish. He was screaming on the inside, from something. I wished I could guess what it was. I reached my hand across the locker and he took it again.

"What's wrong with you, Lemm?" I asked.

"I can't tell you, Shayla," he said. "If I tell you, you won't like me anymore."

"Yes, I will. I promise. You're my friend. I just want to know what's wrong. It won't matter to me what you say. I'll still be your friend, and so will Kambia."

"Do you swear?" he asked, squeezing my hand.

"I swear."

"I just want to tell you that it was—," he started, but right in midsentence the bedroom door flung open. It was Lemm's dad. I dropped Lemm's hand.

"You're the friend of that little girl on the porch, aren't you?" he asked.

"Yes, sir," I said.

"You better come out here," he said. "I think there's something wrong with her."

I hopped up and ran out of the front door. When I got outside, I found Kambia standing on the porch. She was in a trance again, staring into nothingness. She was rigid with fear, and I didn't have to wonder why. Lying on the porch in front of her feet was a pair of ragged yellow underwear. They were covered with dirt, but I could still make out the horrible brown splotches in the crotch. It was them, the panties that we had buried nearly a year ago.

"Oh, my God!" I cried. "Kambia, are you all right?"

She didn't respond. I ran back into the house to phone Mrs. Dreyfus for help.

# Chapter 6

**For Malissa**

At five we sat on the porch steps
slurping grape snow cones
and watching the bright green lizards
scurrying
in and out of the thick ivy
growing on the chain-link fence

At seven we pressed our faces against
the window at Gilbert's Toy Store and stared
at the long rows of Barbie dolls
until Mr. Gilbert got tired of our sad eyes
and gave us a curly-haired Barbie
with a blue dress and a missing right arm

At eleven we attended the Becoming a Woman
talk in the cafeteria after school and you
whispered in my ear and asked me
what the heck a menstrual cycle was and
I yelled period out loud
and all the girls laughed

At thirteen you started cutting class
and hanging out behind the gym
with girls who wore tight black miniskirts

that looked spray-painted on
and rough-looking boys who sniffed glue
out of empty Coke cans
and Mama told me that I couldn't
hang out with you anymore

I cried for three days

At fifteen you just quit coming to school
and I would see you hanging out
on the corner of Taylor
strutting up and down the block
in black stockings and short shorts
flagging down dudes in old cars
trying to make enough cash
to buy a hit of crack

At seventeen you got caught
in a drive-by shooting
and I held your bloody hand
and stroked your hair while
you died on the filthy gray sidewalk

I love you I said
I'll remember you I said

To me you'll always be eleven

I've been upset for days. I turned this poem in today in my English class, extremely late, not caring at all what kind of grade I would get on it. My teacher, Mrs. Brooklynn, a thin, graceful woman with a love for sonnets, told me that she thought the poem was a pretty good try for a beginner, but it needed some work. She said that I was a natural writer, but writing poetry wasn't the same as spinning a yarn. "There is rhythm in poetry," she said. "The words must twitter in the listener's ear like the chirp of baby birds. Having a gift for verse is the most precious thing you can have," she told me. "There is nothing more horrible in the world than a badly written poem."

I told Mrs. Brooklynn that I did believe that being able to write great poetry was a special gift, but I drew the line on believing that the most horrible thing in the world was a badly written poem. I told her that there were much worse things in the world, things that many a great poet would have a hard time writing a poem about, things that even Langston Hughes wouldn't want to put into verse.

"What do you mean by that?" she asked me.

"I would explain it to you, ma'am, but I have somewhere more important that I need to be," I said, gathering my books. When I got out to the hallway, I was sure I heard her mumble something under her breath about my rude behavior. It didn't bother me though; I was right about what I had said. There *were* things much worse in the world than a badly written poem. I knew that for a fact because I knew Kambia. I knew the things that had happened, and were still happening, to her.

The busload of troubles that's been rolling through Kambia's life finally hit her the day that we were at Lemm's. It rolled right over her, and she hasn't been the same since. She hasn't spoken a word to anyone since she found her underwear on Lemm's porch that day, and even though the Majors are heartbroken over it, Kambia's social worker, Miss Sayer, decided that it was best to take her away from them. Kambia's staying at Mrs. Dreyfus's in one of her extra rooms and she's being visited by a state-appointed child psychiatrist twice a week.

The arrangement for Kambia to stay with Mrs. Dreyfus and not at a home for girls with similar problems, like her social worker wanted, was something that Kambia's parents and Mrs. Dreyfus fought real hard for. They did everything they could to convince Miss Sayer that no matter what, Kambia belonged with at least one of them. "If she can't stay with us, please let her stay with Mrs. Dreyfus," Kambia's mother begged Miss Sayer. "It ain't fair to punish her for being sick by taking away the two folks that love her most in the world. At least we can still see her if you let her stay with her counselor."

"She'll be fine at my home," Mrs. Dreyfus said. "My oldest daughter and the Majors will be there during the day, and in the evenings I can be there as well. It's better that Kambia stays with someone she trusts. She's come a long way with the help of a lot of love. If you take that love away from her now, it's possible that she'll go right back to her old self and have to start all over from scratch. It wouldn't be fair to her or us."

"I guess it wouldn't at that," Miss Sayer said. She went along with the Majors and Mrs. Dreyfus, even though I kind of understand why she didn't want to. All Kambia does now is walk around with her face covered with nothingness. She drags her feet as if they were stuck in cement, her blank eyes focused only on the places in her mind. She won't even look at you when you call her name anymore. It looks like she may finally be in her fantasy land for good.

Yesterday morning I went to see her before I walked to school. She was sitting at a small bistro table eating a bowl of Chocolate Graham Crisps, her unblinking eyes staring straight ahead of her, her hands moving up and down methodically, as if she were a robot or an android. "Kambia, is your cereal good?" I asked, hoping that she would at least give me a nod, but she simply kept spooning the food into her mouth until there was nothing but a pool of brown milk left. She drank the milk and placed the bowl in the sink. After that she left the room without even looking in my direction. I didn't know what else to try, so I just went to the sink, washed the bowl out, and put it away.

Kambia's psychiatrist, Mr. Bond, a sharp, middle-aged guy with feather-duster hair and a taste for wrinkled suits, says that Kambia has finally reached the point where she can't handle both of her worlds. He says that the underwear pushed her off a cliff that she doesn't know how to climb back up. He says that it's going to take a long time to get her back to where she was the day of her graduation, if she can make it at all. "I've seen kids snap right out of this kind of thing with months of therapy," he said. "But I've also seen it take some children years to come out of it."

None of us liked the sound of *years*, especially me, and when I asked Grandma about it, she said that she just didn't know. She said that she thought it was dreadful that somebody was messing with Kambia, and that it was almost like she had been hexed or something, like someone had stuck a doll that looked liked her full of pins, or tied a lock of her hair to an old rag and set it on fire. "I seen folks get mad at other folks and do things like that before," she said.

I don't believe in hexes and I can't imagine anyone getting mad enough at Kambia to put one on her. In fact, I can't even imagine that anyone could hurt Kambia at all, and yet someone has. She isn't herself at all anymore because of the cruel tricks that someone is playing on her. It isn't a voodoo hex or anything, but it probably is some kind of evil, at least that's what the police lady who is working on Kambia's case thinks. She says that she can't see why anyone is sending Kambia the packages, but whoever is doing it means to cause her great harm. They know just what seeing all those things will do to her. "They understand completely the effect these items are having on her," she said, stuffing Kambia's soiled underwear into a plastic bag with gloved hands. "That makes their actions malicious. I promise I'll figure out what's going on," she told Kambia's parents. "Nothing exists in a vacuum. Someone always knows what's going on."

I'm glad that someone does, because all I know is that someone has scared Kambia's mind clean out of her. It ran away from her like folks do from Casper the Friendly Ghost. I don't care about who or why. I just want it to stop. It hurts so much that Kambia won't even talk to me at all. She always speaks to me, even if it is just through one of her stories or when she pretends to be something else. I'm always the one that she spills her heart to. Now it's as if she is hiding deep in a cave that I can't find the mouth to. I want to hear her speak again. I want her words to twitter in my ear, like Mrs. Brooklynn says the words of a good poem should.

I threw my books and the poem into my locker and started out for Mrs. Dreyfus's in a much better mood. I felt almost blessed that I could go there. Mrs. Dreyfus was one of the few teachers at Kambia's school that actually lived in her old neighborhood. She lived in a large black neighborhood just north of the Bottom where the people actually had good jobs and owned their own homes. It was called Aldrich's Harbor because it was started during the 1920s by Mint Julep Divine Aldrich, great-aunt of Morgan Aldrich, the funeral home owner. Mint Julep Divine was a glamorous stage actress who had traveled all over the world when she was young starring in big-time plays. She had been in a ton of them when she was youthful and lively, but old age had finally plopped down on her front porch, and all she wanted was a quiet, friendly place to rest her head in her declining years.

She had plenty of bucks, and at first she chose a neighborhood called Tranquil Serenity to purchase a home in, but the neighborhood was mostly white. Although many of the folks in the neighborhood had heard of her and even attended some of her performances, they didn't want her settling down in their backyard. They held a community meeting and bought the house that she was trying to purchase so that they could freeze her out. "It's nothing personal," they told her realtor. "The world just works better when people own houses next door to their own kind." After seeing how she had been treated, Mint Julep Divine had no problem agreeing with the Tranquil Serenity people. In fact, she decided that it was better if people owned whole neighborhoods filled with their own kind, so that's what she did. She got together with some other performers that she knew who had a few dollars stashed away, bought some land, and built as many houses as she could before the funds ran out. The place was at first called Tranquil Gardens, but later, in the fifties, it was changed to Aldrich's Harbor because people thought that it sounded too much like a final resting place.

It was quicker to get to Aldrich's Harbor on the bus, but unlike Mint Julep Divine, I was low on cash. I had only a dollar that Mama had given me for ironing her uniform last week. I didn't want to spend fifty cents of it just to ride the bus. It was still sort of nice out and the humidity wasn't too bad. I decided to take a shortcut through Hopping Toad Trail. It wasn't as quick as taking the bus, but it would leave me with enough money to buy a freezer pop and a bag of chips on the way back. Besides, Hopping Toad was a pretty neat place to walk through. It was a narrow, winding trail that ran alongside the bayou in our neighborhood, up through Aldrich's Harbor, and back into the downtown area. It was called Hopping Toad Trail because it had once been filled with the brown, bulging-eyed amphibians, until the industrial companies moved into our neighborhood and most of the toads just up and disappeared. You seldom saw a toad hopping down the middle of it anymore. However, there were still lots of squirrels, possums, raccoons, and garter snakes to give you something to look at while you went on your way. I walked briskly for quite a while toward Mrs. Dreyfus's, but after a bit the sun poked its head through the pecan trees along the path. The heat got the best of me, and I slowed down.

I was seriously rethinking my decision of not catching the bus, when I heard what sounded like my name being called from somewhere down the winding path. It was faint, just a little tinkle in my ear. I looked in the direction that I had come from. All I saw was the row of dark green, leafy trees that I had just passed and the shiny black grackles that were flying between them from branch to branch. I shrugged my shoulders and kept going, but I had gone only a few steps when I heard my name again, and I knew who was calling it. It was Lemm. I paused against a tree trunk.

I should have known that somehow Lemm would just turn up on the trail. He had been turning up a great deal lately, popping up out of nowhere, like a bad headache at the end of the day. Last week, while I was in gym class, he showed up so sauced that I couldn't even see how he had made it to the school from his house. He was dressed crappy, like he was the day that me and Kambia went to see him, and he looked like he hadn't been anywhere near any water in days. He staggered over to the bleachers where I was sitting and said something to me in speech so slurred that I couldn't make it out.

"What is it, Lemm?"

He tried to answer me, but there was no way that he could form his words. I stared at his moving mouth until our gym teacher,

Coach Kale, a heavyset man with a huge potbelly and a double chin, came and dragged him out. "You don't belong in this class, young man, or any other class. I know who you are. You're the kid that got kicked out a while back for this kind of stuff. Go home and clean up," he told Lemm as he pushed him out of the door. "You tell your parents to get you some help before it's too late. Do you understand me?" Lemm didn't answer. I don't think that he understood much of what the coach was saying to him. I ran over to the door to try and see if I could help him out, but Coach Kale slammed it shut and told me to go get a basketball and practice shooting. From the gym window I watched Lemm stumble home as I shot two-pointers into the basketball hoop.

Another time he showed up while I was doing a load of laundry at the new Jason's Wash-a-Load. I was putting in a load of whites when I turned and saw him standing in the doorway. He was as drunk as the time before and looked like he was about to fall down. I hurried up and shoved the clothes in the dryer and walked over to him. He was so drunk that he couldn't even raise his head to look at me. I couldn't think of anything else to do, so I just let him lean on me and I walked him back home. On the way he didn't even say one word to me, but I could tell by the way he was dragging his body that something really heavy was weighing him down. "What's wrong, Lemm?" I asked. "Why are you doing this to yourself?" I think he was too boozed up to even know what I was asking him. I walked him home and left him at the gate with his dad, who said that he would put him straight to bed.

When I got home that evening, Mama was mad at me because while I was taking care of Lemm, someone stole her best bras and T-shirts out of the washing machine. She asked me why I had left the clothes unattended. I told her that I had gone across the street to Mother Karen's hamburger joint to use the bathroom, and when I got back, her stuff was gone. I don't think that she believed me, and I expected her to scold me, but she just asked if I wanted to go down to the fire sale with her to see if we could find some clothing to replace the things that were taken. On the way there I wanted so much to talk to her about Lemm and his problem. I wanted to tell her that I didn't like what he was doing at all, but as much as I wanted to, all I could do was ask how much she thought it was going to cost to replace the clothes.

It took Lemm longer than the average kid to walk up the path, but when I saw him, I could tell right away that he wasn't as drunk as the last two times that we had crossed paths. He wasn't very steady on his feet. He kind of wobbled a little as he walked, but he wasn't stumbling like he had been when he showed up at the gym and the washateria.

I didn't know what to make of his appearance though. He still looked like he hadn't been near a tub since Colonel Sanders started making chicken. His ragged striped T-shirt and rumpled khakis were almost gray from dirt, and his fade was filled with lint, but he had replaced his worn sandals with his normal oversize sneakers and an extra-clean pair of superwhite ankle socks. It was as if some part of him knew that he should be cleaned up, but the rest of him didn't have a clue. I leaned against the trunk of the tree and waited for him to reach me.

Lemm walked up to the pecan tree and leaned an arm against the trunk for support, filling the air with the putrid smell of stale alcohol. I didn't cover my nose, though, or back away. I was getting pretty used to the smell, like a farmer gets used to livestock smells. I checked out his eyes. They weren't drowsy looking. They were puffy. His lids were almost swollen closed. He wasn't too torn up, but he had been crying. I was sure of it. His nose was all red, and there were tear scars on both cheeks.

"What's wrong with you?" I asked.

"Nothing," he said. "It's nothing."

"You look like you've been crying," I said. "Your face is all stained up."

He rubbed his hands in a circle motion over both cheeks and wiped the stains off. "It's nothing, Shayla," he said. "The trees make my eyes water."

"My mom has bad allergies too. She takes some little pills for them."

"Lots of people do. But I do not like taking pills myself," he said in his proper voice.

"Why not?" I asked.

"I'm not sure," he said. "I would rather just do without them."

"Me, too," I said. "My mom always has to make me take my medicine when I get sick."

"I wish I had a mother that could do that. I think I wouldn't mind taking the pills after all."

"I guess you wouldn't," I said. "I'm sorry, I didn't mean to bring your mom up."

"It's okay," he said. "My mother never really goes away. I really don't mind it at all when you bring her up."

I nodded. "I guess I really didn't think that you would. Since you told me and Kambia about her plants and all. My grandma Augustine says that the best way to never forget about somebody or something is to keep talking about them. She talks about my grandfather a lot sometimes. She says that he would be pretty mad at her if she stopped talking about him just because he's dead."

"How did he die?" he asked.

"It happened when I was really little. He was a metalworker at a machine shop on the west side of town. I don't really know what actually went on." I shrugged my shoulders. "He went to work one day and the watercooler at his job had sprung a leak. There was water all over the floor, and some of it seeped under the machine that he was working on. The machine had a bad cord or something. He got electrocuted. It was an accident. Grandma's minister told her that it was just his time to go. He said that none of us really know when or how we'll meet up with death."

"I do," Lemm said. "I know just how."

"What?" I asked. "What do you mean by that?"

He just blinked his swollen eyes at me and looked away.

"What do you mean by that?" I asked again.

"Nothing. I was just trying to make some polite conversation," he said with a fake grin. "The first rule of any social gathering, engage your host in pleasant conversation."

"Oh, brother," I said, smiling. "Where did you learn that corny foolishness from?"

He broke into laughter, but I could tell that it wasn't the real thing. It was hollow, like the phony laughs Mama used to give Mr. Anderson Fox to try and get him to pay child support. I remembered again what I first figured out about Lemm, that he used his words to try and hide what was going on with him. He was trying to do the same thing with laughter, trying to use it like Superman uses his suit and glasses.

I sighed. "What did you mean about meeting death?" I asked.

He stopped laughing and started walking away from the tree. "I spoke to your sister," he said. "She told me that you were going to see Lady Kambia. She said that you might be walking. That's how I knew that you were probably on this path. It's hot out here though. Maybe you should take the bus. I'll walk you to it."

"Hold up, Lemm," I said. He stopped walking and faced me. "What did you mean by the death thing?" I asked again.

"It's hot out here," he repeated. "Let's hurry to the bus stop. There's shade there."

"I didn't say that I wanted to catch the bus, Lemm," I said.

He seized my hand and started pulling me down the trail. "Of course you do," he said. "Taking the bus is the intelligent thing to do, and you always do the smart thing."

"No, I don't," I said, snatching my hand out of his before I got that firefly feeling again. "My mom says that I do really half-witted things sometimes, and so does my sister, Tia. She says that sometimes me and Tia take turns seeing who will do the stupidest stuff."

"Mothers always say that, don't they? They are very good at seeing when you do dumb things, but not so good at seeing when they do stupid things themselves. I hate that about them. I hate it when they can't see the things that they do," he spat. His sudden anger startled me the way it had the day that he was really mean to me and Kambia in his room. It was almost as if it were coming from another Lemm, a Lemm that I didn't want to hang around with. I felt bad for him, but I had to go see Kambia.

"I gotta go, Lemm," I said. "I'm just gonna walk. I'll see you later." I started walking off, but he fell into step beside me.

"I want to see Lady Kambia too," he said. "She's my friend also. You know that I wasn't very kind to her the last time I saw her. I would like to try and correct that."

"Okay," I said.

We started up the trail, but he had taken only a few wobbly steps when he pulled a small bottle of caramel-colored liquor out of his pocket and started to drink it. I stopped.

"You can't go see Kambia like this, Lemm. Her mom and dad

won't like it. Just go home," I said. "I'll tell Kambia that you said hi. She'll like that."

He shook his head and brought the bottle from his lips. "I don't want to go home, Shayla," he said. "My dad's there."

"So what," I said. "He seems okay to me. He was pretty cool to me and Kambia the first time that we met him."

"He's not cool to me," Lemm said. "He looks at me funny."

"What do you mean by that?"

He took another drink. "Nothing," he said. "He just does."

"But why?" I asked. I stopped walking and grabbed him by the wrist so he would stop too. "Why does he look at you funny? What do you mean by that?"

"Nothing. It ain't nothing worth talking about," he said, slipping into his street language. "He just looks at me funny sometimes, that's all."

"But why?" I asked. "I don't get it. Is it because you're drinking like him? He probably just wants you to stop. I'll bet he just doesn't want you to do what he did."

"My dad didn't do anything, Shayla!" he shouted at me. "I told you before, you don't know what you're talking about!"

"Yes, I do," I said. "Everybody knows. Everybody knows what he did to your sisters."

"Nobody knows anything, Shayla!" he shouted. "Nobody knows what goes on in my house!"

"Yes, they do, Lemm," I said. "My mom told me. She never gets anything wrong. I can always trust what she says to me."

"Can you trust what she does?" he asked, focusing his swollen eyes on me intently.

"I don't know what you mean, Lemm," I said.

"I trusted my mom," he said. "I always trusted her, but she had to leave."

"She ran off," I said.

He shook his head. Tears started to drop out of his eyes worse than Kambia's. Huge drops of water squeezed out of the slits of his eyes and ran down the tearstains that were already on his face. "My mother didn't run off, Shayla," he said. "My father ran her off. She drank a lot. She drank all the time—forties, wine coolers, beer, malt liquor—my mom drank it all. My dad said that it started a few years after they got married. He would work the late nights driving a cab, and while he was out, she would be out kicking back with her girl-friends and her big sister, my aunt Liza. He said he thought that things would get better when I came along, but she would just pour some wine in my bottle and head out to the club anyway. He said that he came home a few times and found me alone in the baby bed and she was nowhere to be found."

"Man," I said. "I can't imagine a mother doing that."

"She did," he said. "She told him that all her girlfriends were doing it and that the alcohol wouldn't harm me. It was just a way to get me to sleep through the night—that way she didn't even need to hire a sitter. She told my dad he ought to be okay with it because she was saving him some cash that way."

"Man, Jada would never do that to Gift," I said. "She sometimes gets a little crazy about leaving her with my grandma. She would never leave her by herself, and she sure wouldn't give her a drink."

"My mom would," he said. "I think if she had her way, she would give the whole world a drink." He sat down on the side of the trail and I sat down next to him.

"My mother promised," he said. "After she had the twins, she said that she would clean up. My dad took a loan out from his job and put her in a program, but she didn't stay. He came home one day and found her sprawled out on the kitchen floor with a fifth of rum. I was with her, but I don't remember because I was as drunk as she was."

"Is that when your dad tossed her out?" I asked.

"Yeah, he told her that she had to be someplace else when he got home. He took me and the twins to a cousin's house for a few days. When we got back, she had already taken off. It bothered me a lot," he said. "I didn't like her for what she was doing to all of us, but she was still my mom."

"Where did she go?" I asked.

"I don't know," he said. "We ain't heard from her, but I don't think that she stopped drinking. I know I didn't. My dad wanted to place me in some type of program too, but he couldn't afford another loan, so he tried to find another way to make me stop drinking. He sent me to live with my aunt Joyce Ann up north. She was into Bible learning. She didn't keep no liquor in the house, and she had seven kids and none of them had ever braced up to her," he said, wiping his face with the back of his hand. "She was major strict."

"Me and Tia have different dads," I said. "Her dad has a sister like that. Tia went to visit her once when I was around six. She said that all of her kids were afraid of her."

"I was afraid of my aunt for a while too, but I soon found out that I could fool her. Her kids were good, but they were dumb. They didn't know jack, and I was really smart. I started proper-talking around her, using big words, and telling her and her bridge-playing friends how nice they looked. She started taking me everywhere with her. She was a big woman in her community. She owned two dry cleaners' and a company that found jobs for black folks. Because of who she was, she was always getting invited to some party. I would go with her. 'This is my nephew from Texas. He talks real fine, and he's real good with his schoolwork,' she would say to everyone. 'Tell them something that you learned, Lemm.' I was always happy to. I would give them an excellent show, saying lots of clever things, and repeating all kinds of famous quotes. I would put on a play for them, mesmerize them, looking around the whole time for something good to drink. There was always bunches of stuff. I would get hold of all kinds of brew. Drink and put on a show for people, that's all I did. I was always good with my words and keeping things together. Nobody could tell when I was torn up, especially not my aunt."

"It took me a while to figure it out too," I said. "And I'm usually pretty good at figuring out when somebody is putting a scam on."

"My dad isn't," he said. "After I came back home, he couldn't even tell that I was still drinking. When he noticed that my eyes were red, I told him that I had eye strain, so he bought me reading glasses. When he noticed that I was stumbling around, I told him that I was dizzy. He took me to the doctor for an ear infection. He was proud of me 'cause I was doing real good in school, making all A's on my tests. He didn't know that I was doing it all juiced up, drinking the stuff he couldn't smell on my breath, covering up the rest with strong mints, mouthwash, and stuff like that." He paused and stared down at his lap for a long time, while I sat quietly, not knowing what I could possibly say to make him feel better. After a while he looked back at me. His face and the front of his khakis were all wet.

"What's wrong, Lemm?" I asked. "Just say what's bothering you."

"I can't tell you, Shayla. You won't like me anymore. You won't want to be my friend."

"Yes, I will," I said. "Don't be ridiculous."

"I'm not being ridiculous. What I have to say is very bad."

"How bad?" I asked.

He paused for a moment and settled himself. "Shayla, my dad didn't pick the twins up that afternoon," he said with labored speech, as if it was taking everything in him to get his words out. "I picked them up. The school called and said that they had some kind of problem. My dad was tired from work. He had been driving all night long. It was right after school, and I had just walked in the door. He told them I would come and that the twins would be all right with me because it was only a few blocks."

"Oh, no."

"I picked them up, Shayla. The ladies at the . . . the center turned them right over to me. They were busy trying to get the rest of the kids out. We lived in a really small town. They all knew me. They just didn't know that I was drunk. I picked them up, Shayla. Shayla, I'm the one who thought I saw my mom and stepped out in front of the truck. I didn't even know that I did it," he said. "When . . . when I woke up in the hospital, I couldn't believe that they were gone. I only got hurt a little bit. The truck wasn't going all that fast. It hit me first and threw me, but I landed in some bushes and only got a couple of broken ribs, a twisted ankle, and some cuts here and there. I don't even remember getting hit. I certainly don't remember the girls getting hurt."

"Oh, my God," I said.

"My dad thought I had gone straight," he said. "He didn't know. He told my lawyer that he thought I was all through with drinking and that he never would have told me to get the twins if he had known that I wasn't.

"That's why he looks at me funny. He really loved my little sisters. It was hard on him when he had to kick my mom out, but he had the girls and they reminded him of her. He loves me, Shayla. He worked real hard to keep me from going to jail. He blamed it all on him and my mom. I was good with my words and extra smart in school," he said. "They let me off. They said that the day care was irresponsible in giving the twins to me and that living with what I had done to them would be enough punishment, but the folks in town didn't think that it was. They were rough on me. They gave me all kinds of trouble because of it. I got really depressed. My school grades started slipping, so my dad moved us to another town, but people found out about it there, too. My dad came up with a solution. He told everyone that he had done it."

"He did?" I asked.

"Yes, but the town that we moved to was even smaller than the first town that we were in. When his boss got a whiff of the rumor, he let him go. He said that he had five children of his own, and no man who did what my father had done to his children deserved to have a good job. My dad lost everything. The whole thing started to get to him. He got so he couldn't even hold down a job. We been living on the state for years now." He took a final swig from the bottle and tossed it away. "I screwed up major. My dad counted on me, and I just screwed everything up. That's why he looks at me so funny. He doesn't even hug me anymore. He just mostly stays away from me, like he does my mom's plants." He tried to get to his feet. I stood up and helped him. "I like you, Shayla. You're like me, always struggling to figure things out. I just wanted you to know what was up." He wiped his face with the tail of his shirt. "I'm going," he said. "I can't go see Kambia like this. Anyway, I actually told my dad that I was going to the barbershop, so I guess it would be a good idea for me to go there instead. He'll probably give the shop a call. He likes to know where I'm at since I got in trouble with the law the other day. I'll see you later."

Lemm headed down the trail. I wanted to run after him, but

how could I? I didn't know what to say to make him feel better. I cared for him, but what did you say to someone who had just told you that he had killed his own blood? "There is nothing more important than blood," Grandma Augustine keeps telling me. "Most friends are like stray cats," she says. "They show up at your back door when they want something to eat or need cuddling, but when you want something from them, they ain't nowhere around. Blood is always there. When you ain't got nobody else, you got the folks who was born into the same family as you." Grandma was right. Through all the bad times I always had her, Mama, Tia—and now Kambia, who was my blood in another way. But who did Lemm have? He had only his father, whom he had seriously let down; the memory of a mom who had given him Jack Daniel's instead of milk; and the nightmare of his two sisters, whom he had accidentally pushed in front of a truck. It wasn't fair. He didn't mean to do what he did to the twins. I watched him walking unsteadily back up the path with regret riding his back and wished that I knew how to pull it off, but how could I? He wasn't Kambia. With Kambia I really believed that somehow I could help her out if I just found out who was hurting her. I couldn't do that for Lemm. I couldn't bring his sisters back. There was really only one thing I could do. I ran after him and caught his hand. As I took it I remembered once again what Grandma Augustine had said, that I had to figure out what kind of woman I wanted to become. I still didn't know. What I did know was that I was a girl who could hold hands with a boy whose own father didn't want to touch him. That didn't make me a woman, it just made me a friend.

Lemm and I walked back up the trail without talking or even exchanging glances. We made it to the barbershop, and I left him standing all droopy shouldered next to the old-fashioned red-and-white barber pole beside the door. I told him that if it wasn't too late, I would drop by his house later to see if he was okay. He told me that he would like that, and I hit the trail again on my way to see my other friend. While I walked, the comment that I had made to Mrs. Brooklynn trotted into my thoughts again. There certainly were worse things in the world than a badly written poem, things that even a great poet wouldn't want to write about, and I knew it for a fact because I knew what had happened, and was still happening, to Lemm.

# Chapter 7

**The Woman-Thing**
*by Shayla Dubois*
*(Draft One)*

It seemed like from the moment Terra got the "I just got my period" call from her best friend, Zari, Zari was already different. She used to be a tomboy, spent most of her time in ragged jeans and a baseball cap. She was a tough girl who didn't take crap off of anybody. She was always fist-fighting with her four older brothers, making them regret it whenever they were stupid enough to try and push her around. "You guys are gonna be really sorry you got in my face," she would yell at them before she started swinging. That's what Terra liked about Zari. Zari didn't care one bit about acting all frilly and girlie-girl. She didn't like lilac-scented shampoo or silk hair ribbons, and neither did Terra.

Terra was most comfortable in one of her father's old faded work shirts and a pair of her brother's khaki pants. She could put a serious beat-down on any boy that even looked at her crossways, and she hated those hideous lacy pink sweaters that her grandma sent her each birthday. "I'll throw myself in the bayou if you make me wear them!" she would yell at her mother.

Lately, throwing herself into the bayou was just what Terra felt like doing, especially when she was around her so-called friend Zari. They used to spend time together in her backyard, shooting hoops and talking about their favorite sports teams. Now all they talked about was Zari's boyfriend, Marquis.

With Zari, everything was "Marquis this" and "Marquis that." He had shown up around the same time as Zari's full hips and bumpy chest, and now he was the only thing in Zari's world. She could go on forever about the things that Marquis did or said. She told Terra about the love notes that he scrawled on toilet paper and wrapped around the handle of her gym locker, and the Chicken McNuggets that he spelled her name with at a McDonald's somewhere near the Katy Freeway. To Zari, the boy with the royal name was a king. If Marquis liked Star Wars, Zari liked Star Wars; if Marquis's favorite food was fried Spam, Zari's favorite food was fried Spam. He even got her to wearing those flimsy floral dresses, because he said that those were what real girls wore. Terra couldn't stand it. To her, Marquis was just a smooth-talking knucklehead who played the drums really badly in their high school band. How could he have turned her best homegirl into Zombie Girlfriend? Well, if that was what becoming a woman did to you, Terra wanted nothing to do with it. She had no choice. She was going to have to stop Mother Nature before she messed her up too—and she knew just how.

One of the older girls at her cousin Rosemary's sleepover last month had let Terra in on the girl-to-woman secret. She said the change usually took place on a girl's thirteenth birthday. Around midnight Mother Nature herself crept into a girl's bedroom and touched her magical fingers to the unfortunate child's abdomen. While she slept, everything in her became woman. Her organs, her emotions—no trace of girlhood was left. When she woke the next morning, she had completely crossed over to the other side, and she would soon get a visit from her monthly friend to confirm that she had made the leap. "After that it's all over," the senior girl said. "You can forget about doing any fun stuff. You're not going to want to play kick-ball or shoot hoops when those cramps are kicking your butt."

Cramps. The thought of being all crunched up in bed with a hot-water bottle and aspirin, like Zari sometimes was, didn't appeal to Terra at all. She wasn't down with pain. There was no way around it, she was going to have to stop Mother Nature from touching her. She wasn't ready to turn in her Buster Browns for high heels, and God knows she would die of embarrassment if she had to purchase a box of Kotex at the store.

It was the eve of her thirteenth birthday and she would spend it lying awake, waiting for Mother Nature so that she could get her straight. She would let her know that she didn't intend to spend the rest of her life wiggling in and out of panty hose, tell her that she could just go touch someone else. If those ridiculous preteen books that Mama liked to buy her were right, there was a whole world of silly little girls out there who wanted to be women.

Terra pulled her bedspread up to her chin and listened to the bells at Saint Paul's Cathedral chime 10:00. It wouldn't be long now, she thought. She laughed and patted herself on the back for her cleverness. Her plan was so simple—if only Zari had thought of it, she wouldn't be stuck with stupid ole Marquis. She yawned and stretched, trying to keep her drowsy body awake—then she felt it, a trickle, a strange dampness between her legs. She pulled the bedspread back, looked down below, and started to cry.

### The End


I had the dream again last night, and it was even more bizarre. There were five ladies in the tree as usual. They were dancing and swaying in their pastel gowns. I still wanted to join them, but each time I got close, they disappeared into the butterfly clouds. I tried and tried to catch them. Then, on one of the tries, something odd happened. When I reached the trunk of the tree, there appeared right beside me a little girl that even Mama and Grandma would have thought was me. She was my complete double, except she looked like she could have been a winter or so younger. The little girl was dressed in my gown and fluffy slippers.

She started to climb the tree before I could even get my hands on it, and this time all the ladies disappeared except one. One of the ladies drifted up into the air, but she remained just above the tree. She was hovering there in the air, looking down at the little girl with a smirk on her face. The girl shook her fist at her and threw as many mean names at her as she could, but the woman just smiled. This made the girl even madder. She started looking on the ground for a rock or something to chuck at the woman, but as she was searching underneath the tree my alarm went off and I sat up in bed.

I didn't know what to make of the dream this time either, so I got dressed as quickly as I could and joined Grandma for breakfast so that I could talk it over with her. She told me that there was a battle going on inside me. It was a fight between my womanhood and girlhood, and one of them was certainly trying to knock the other one out. "Do you remember what I told you about finding out what kind of woman you want to be?" she asked, pouring half-and-half on her steaming oatmeal.

"Yes, ma'am," I said, slicing a green banana into my Froot Loops.

"Well, before you can figure out what kind of woman you want to be, you have to first figure out if you're actually a woman at all. You're on the edge," she said. "You're standing in the middle of the road trying to decide what wagon to catch. You don't know if you want to wear lipstick like a lady or leave your face bare like a little girl. It's common at your age. It's common for you to want to fight your womanhood off. Let me tell you something, baby. If I were you, I'd stay a little girl until Mother Nature gave me no choice. Remember, once you put on a brassiere, you can't take it back off."

"She wouldn't want to. If you go around with no bra all the time, your boobs will drop to your belly," Tia said, coming into the kitchen in her new ruffled baby dolls.

"Boobs," Grandma Augustine said, shaking her head. "Where did you get a word like that? When I was young, a girl wouldn't dare even come up with a name to call her chest. You just had them, that's all. Some gals had bigger ones, some had smaller ones. Nobody talked about what they were, and nobody sho wouldn't hang a name on 'em. The world sho has turned into something strange. It used to be a time when what a woman had on her was kept private and respected."

"Grandma, how are you going to keep your chest private?" Tia said, walking over to Grandma Augustine. "Your breasts are right out there for the world to see. It ain't no shame in talking about what everybody already knows."

"Everybody already knows about going to the bathroom, too," Grandma said. "But I ain't never seen nobody just dying to share that kinda personal information with you. Ain't nothing wrong with folks being modest about some things. You don't need to set all your furniture on the front porch and call your neighbors to look it over."

"People do that every day, Grandma," Tia said, reaching over and grabbing a slice of banana off the top of my cereal. "Most folks just call it a garage sale."

Grandma broke into laughter. "Go on and get away from here,

smart mouth," she said, whacking Tia on the behind. "You too much of a mess for me to deal with."

Tia grabbed her and hugged her, then she sat down next to me and started eating out of the open box of Froot Loops, tossing them one after the other into her mouth.

"Lord, gal, ain't you got no home training?" Grandma asked. Tia just started crunching the cereal loudly, making exaggerated movements with her mouth.

"I thought you were sixteen, gal, not two," Grandma Augustine said, laughing. Tia laughed too. "You worst than Gift," Grandma said. She looked at the round wall clock over the refrigerator. "Lord, it's getting late. I better hurry up and finish. Jada will be over here soon with the baby. She's off today, but she got some errands to run. I told her that I would keep Gift busy so that she wouldn't have to pack her around. I gotta have my hands free so I can give Gift a bottle when she get here. She sho don't like to wait to eat."

"No, she doesn't. Maybe Mr. Anderson Fox and Jada should start feeding her at their own home," I said.

"They don't always have time to do that before they have to leave, and you know that," Grandma snapped. She poured more half-and-half into her oatmeal and stirred it up again. A thin haze of steam wound its way up to the ceiling. "I wish you would change your mind about that baby. She's your little sister, and ain't nobody but God can change that."

"How can he change it?" I asked.

"I don't know," she said. "I guess he can take the moment she was created and wipe it away. But trust me, little girl. You would be in for a world of sorrow if he did. It's gon' come a time when you'll be glad that baby got the same blood as you."

I scooped up a spoonful of Loops. "I don't think so, Grandma,"

I muttered, staring down at my bowl. "But you can believe in a happy ending if you like."

I got up from the table with my bowl of cereal and left. I was going to go and sit on the side of the front porch and finish my breakfast. It was the one place I knew of that nobody would take Gift. There were some pretty thorny rosebushes on the side of the porch, and everybody was afraid that Gift might accidentally get pricked, so they kept her away from them. As for me, I didn't mind the thorns as much as Mr. Anderson Fox's baby. It was worth a few pricks to avoid seeing Grandma and Jada playing with her. "Ain't she cute?" they would say as she tossed her legs about. "She's just the sweetest thing in the world. If you put her in a candy shop, nobody would be able to pick her out."

I ate my breakfast lickety-split, but I continued sitting on the porch with my feet dangling between the thorns. I thought about what Grandma had said about my womanhood fighting with my girlhood and tried to figure out what she was talking about. There was no part of me that felt anywhere near like a woman, and I certainly didn't look like one. I was thirteen, but my body was still refusing to say anything but eleven or twelve, and my face was covered with baby fat. I didn't play with dolls anymore, but I still kind of liked stuffed animals. Just this year Grandma gave me a stuffed tiger for my birthday. I stuck it in one of my dresser drawers, but sometimes I pull it out and sleep with it when Tia is spending the night at her girlfriend Maxi's place. It's not because I'm scared or anything, I just like to have something to roll over on. Though having the tiger sometimes makes me feel like a baby or a little kid. Those are the two things that I often feel like, certainly never a woman. I still don't even like boys, unless you count Lemm. I like Lemm a lot, but not the way that Tia likes Doo-witty or the way that Mama used to like Mr. Anderson Fox. It's something different. I don't want to get all kissy-faced with Lemm or put on pretty dresses that I think he might like. There's just something about him. It's the something that makes me feel like I got those fireflies flying around in me when he touches my hand. It doesn't make me feel any older, just really perplexed, like finding out that my favorite uncle has died and left me a priceless collection of antiques and bubble-gum trading cards.

When I told Tia about my feelings, she said that girls always feel that way around guys that they like. They feel like they've been asked to a really live party, but all of a sudden they break out in a contagious rash on the day that they're supposed to go. "You're just like every other girl in the world, Shayla," she told me. "You're noticing for the first time that it's okay to go to the record store by yourself, but it's so much better if you can take somebody else along. The feelings will pass, just as soon as you realize that it's better when it takes two to make a peanut-butter sandwich."

I didn't know exactly what Tia meant by the sandwich thing, but I had no intentions of making anything with Lemm. I didn't even care all that much for peanut butter. I cared for Lemm. There was just something about him that made me want to hang with him even when he did and told me stuff that would make the average girl not even think about wanting to be his friend.

I finished my breakfast and took the cereal bowl back to the kitchen. After that I sat down a few moments in the living room and let Tia brush my hair, then I said good-bye to everyone and took off.

I was going to take a trip over to Kambia's house. Kambia's mother had called me from the Dreyfuses' the night before and asked me to do her a favor. She said that Mrs. Dreyfus and her daughters had left town for a couple of days to go college shopping for Mrs. Dreyfus's middle daughter, Anita, and that she was going to be keeping an eye on Kambia by herself. She told me that Kambia was fine, but it had just occurred to her that Kambia might feel more at home if I could bring her her favorite Sophie Bear. She said that she would have asked Mr. Major to fetch it, but he was out of town again, visiting the same sick relative that he had visited before. "The key is underneath a large gray stone near the door, and the bear should be in the closet," she told me. "Thanks so much, sweetie, for helping me out."

"You're welcome, ma'am," I said, and hung up the phone.

When I got to Kambia's house, I nearly ran through the gate. I loved being there. It was so much nicer than my home. There were few like it in our neighborhood. It was an enormous white house with cherry-wood shutters on the windows, a lavish front porch that was supported by two grand columns, a walkway made of cut red bricks, and an ivory trellis that went from the manicured lawn up to Kambia's room. Grandma Augustine said that it looked like the house had been built around the turn of the century and then mod-erned up later with things like electric lights and indoor bathrooms. It was fairly run-down when the Majors got it. The last man who owned it had bought it as a gift for his daughter on her wedding day, but she ran off with her husband's best man just an hour before the wedding was to take place. The house remained boarded up for nearly twenty-five years before he sold it to the Majors for what they called "the cost of a few throw rugs."

I opened the front door of the house and trotted to Kambia's room, nearly tripping over Old MacDonald, a friendly, blue-eyed half-Siamese kitten that the Majors had bought only a week ago to give to Kambia when and if she came home. I picked him up and took him into Kambia's room with me.

When I entered her room, I set Old MacDonald down in the middle of Kambia's canopy bed so that I could search for the bear without his being underfoot. The second his paws hit the mattress, he looked down at the floor and howled like a caged tiger, so I picked him back up and placed him on the ground next to my feet. He purred and started walking in and out of the space between my legs. I had to keep looking down to stop myself from tripping over him.

With Old MacDonald on my heels, I walked over to Kambia's closet and opened the sliding door. The closet was just as she had left it, incredibly neat. Kambia's dresses were starched and hanging on silk hangers, and her shoes and sandals were polished and lined up in three perfect rows. Everything was so crisp and new looking that you would think that her clothes had never been worn. There were only a few loose lace trims on the dresses and scuff marks on the shoes to let you know any different.

I avoided moving her belongings out of place as much as I could as I searched in the back of the closet for Kambia's cedar toy chest. It was a nifty box, homemade by Mr. Major himself, with brass handles on the sides and a brass knob with a scowling gargoyle. Mr. Major said that the gargoyle was supposed to keep all of Kambia's evil spirits away, but obviously it had fallen down on the job. I scowled back at it as I pushed open the lock.

Toys spilled from every corner of the box when I pulled back the lid. Kambia had enough dolls, stuffed animals, yo-yos, and tea sets to fill Santa Claus's sled. Since the first day that the Majors met her, they had been buying her toys like they had just heard that Toys R Us was going out of business. They said that they wanted to give her all the things she didn't get at her old place, and that a child as wonderful as she was deserved to have a whole universe of toys to play with.

I didn't know if Kambia had a whole universe of toys, but she had more than enough for me. I tossed toy after toy out of the box onto the plush carpet, until I finally got to the bottom of the chest and discovered that the bear was the only thing that wasn't in it. A bit annoyed, I threw everything back inside and closed the lid.

I stood up and glanced around the room with my hands on my hips. Where could Sophie Bear be? It popped into my head that Honeysuckle Peach had said that the bear was in the closet. She didn't say that it was in Kambia's closet. I left Kambia's room, with Old MacDonald on my heels, and walked to the Majors' bedroom, where Kambia had spent her nights before she had to move out.

I opened the door to the Majors' room without any hesitation and went inside. I walked over to the closet and tugged open the door. The closet looked a lot like Kambia's. On one side of it Honeysuckle's dresses, nylons, cottons, rayons, and linens were all hung very neatly on the top metal rack of the closet, and her skirts and slacks were tucked in perfectly on a second rack underneath. On the other side of the closet Mr. Major's suit jackets and shirts dangled from the top rack in a straight line, and his starched slacks were flawlessly folded across plastic hangers on the rack just below. The closet floor on both sides was covered with polished shoes. I giggled to myself and started looking.

The first place I looked was at the bottom of the closet. There was nothing there but the shoes—not even a dropped cuff link, safety pin, or even a crumpled grocery store coupon that might have fallen out of a dress or jacket pocket. I got up from the floor where I was crawling around and jumped so that I could see the contents of the top shelf. To my surprise it wasn't as neat as the rest of the closet. It was as packed as the shelves at Diamond's. Every inch of it was taken up with either a cardboard box, a shopping bag, or a stack of paperback books, but I was still able to catch a glimpse of what I thought was a fuzzy brown bear in a sweater and poodle skirt.

I jumped up again and got a better look. When I hit the floor the second time, I was sure that it was Sophie Bear. I stood on my tiptoes and reached my hand up to the shelf to see if I could feel her. I just kept hitting either the boxes or the bags. I walked backward to try and see what the bear was wedged in between. It was in the middle of a pile of hatboxes and a stack of old magazines. The hatboxes stretched clear up to the ceiling. I decided not to touch them. I could see them tumbling down on Old MacDonald and giving him another reason to pitch a fit. It just made more sense to move the smaller stack of magazines out of the way. I stood on my tiptoes again, grasped the front of the stack, and gave the magazines a tug. A bunch of them fell to the floor, barely missing Old MacDonald, who took no time pouncing on them for a sniff. I moved him out of the way and started to pick them up.

Most of the magazines landed facedown. I flipped them over one by one as I retrieved them so that I could see what they were about. Many of them were cooking magazines with photos of decorated cakes and mouthwatering dishes on the front covers, but some were about fishing and had grinning men holding up hooks with oversize trout or bass on them. There were even a couple of lingerie magazines with skinny women on the covers posing in old-fashioned Playtex bras and long-line girdles. I recognized the kind of girdle that Grandma Augustine liked to wear.

There had to be at least thirty or so magazines on the floor, and since most of them didn't really interest me, I just glanced at the covers and stacked them in a pile on the floor to put back later after I got the bear. But as I was retrieving the last few I picked up one that caught my attention. It wasn't a magazine at all. It was an activity and coloring book. On the front was a cartoon drawing of a clown in billowy pants balancing on a high wire with a handful of colorfully decorated balloons.

I loved activity books, and so did Kambia. She was really good with the crosswords, word searches, and anagrams. I opened the book and thumbed through it, eager to see how hard the puzzles were. As I expected, the first few puzzles were the easy ones, baby word searches with words that even a five-year-old wouldn't have a hard time picking out. But as I continued flipping through the puzzles tucked in between the coloring and project pages, they got harder and harder, until I found some that both me and Kambia would have a hard time working. I tried to figure out a few of the answers in my head. They were too hard. I decided to do the lazy thing and flip to the solutions in the back of the book. I carefully turned the pages hunting for them. Then right before I reached the answer section, I opened up a page and something slid out. I bent down to pick it up, and my mouth must have fallen clear through the earth to the other side of the world.

It was wrapping paper, glittery gold paper, the same paper that the present Kambia received on her graduation had been wrapped in. I recognized the raised silver roses and carnations on it. I dropped it back to the floor and turned to the place where I was certain it had fallen from. There was another piece just like it folded between the pages. I took it out and looked at it, hoping to find the jagged edges where Kambia had torn it from the box. There *were* no edges. The paper was as new as the book, sharply creased the way it had come out of the package. I didn't know what to think.

I slipped it out and held it up so that I could be sure that I was seeing what I was seeing. Only, once it came out, I ended up wishing that I had left it where it was. There they were, right on the page underneath it, the paper dolls! The ones that I had tucked away in my drawer. There was a whole page of them—girl paper dolls dressed in frilly dresses, sailor suits, sweaters and plaid skirts. They were the exact dolls that had come crumpled in Kambia's box, only their hair hadn't been colored red and nobody had filled their eyes in with green.

I dropped the entire book on the floor and just stood there staring down at it while Old MacDonald crawled over it, meowing. A thousand thoughts crowded into my head. What did it mean that the Majors had an activity book with the same paper dolls in it that had wigged Kambia out? Nothing, I told myself. You could buy books with those kinds of dolls in them anywhere. And didn't all activity books pretty much have the same things? I imagined that there were paper dolls like them in books all over America, and even some foreign countries, too. I bet there were books filled with dolls like them wherever there was a little girl that liked to color in stuff like Kambia still did. But what about the wrapping paper? I had seen the pieces that Kambia gave to Honeysuckle when she eagerly tore them off the present. She was careful with them, but they were still torn, with jagged edges. That couldn't be the paper I had seen in the book. The whole thing didn't make sense. Even Linda James would have a hard time with what I had seen. I bent down to get the book again. As I did Old MacDonald jumped over the pile of magazines and raced out of the closet. A moment later I heard a faint voice yelling my name. I picked up all the magazines I could and threw them back on the shelf.

"Shayla, baby, where you at?" I heard Grandma's voice yell.

"I'm in here, Grandma," I yelled back. I hurriedly pushed everything back into place and ran out of the room. I opened the front door and closed it behind me real fast before Old MacDonald could make his way out too.

When I got outside, Grandma was leaning against a porch column, and I could tell right away that her lame leg wasn't the only bad thing that she had brought with her. She was clothed in sorrow from head to toe, and her face looked like she had washed it in gloominess instead of her usual peppermint soap.

"What's wrong, Grandma?"

"Did you find Kambia's bear?"

"Not yet," I said.

"You will, and it'll make her happy," she said. "And your grandma really needs to see some happiness in somebody else today, 'cause it ain't none in her."

"What's wrong, Grandma?"

She shifted her weight on her cane and sighed. "I got Doo-witty and his mama, Miss Earlene, to give me a ride down here," she said. "They was up at the house with Tia, and I mentioned that I needed to go this way."

"Doo-witty has a car?" I asked with disbelief.

"Yeah, he done sold another couple of his paintings. He made enough money to get his mama a used car. It ain't much," she said, "but it will get you where you got to go, and that's all anybody really got to have."

"I guess so," I said.

"Shayla, do you know what the word *trust* means?"

"Yes, ma'am," I said. "It means that you can count on someone, like Kambia does with me, and I do with you, Mama, and Tia."

"In a way, baby, but it means more than that. It means that if I ain't got but one can of sardines in my cabinet and you haven't eaten, I would open the can and give it to you before I even thought about fixing me a plate. It means that if you got in a car wreck and they needed my heart to make you well, I would cut it out of my chest myself and give it to them to place in you, and so would your mama and Tia. That's what trust is. It means that you can always expect that person's hand to be reaching for your hand even in the worst storms. It's like your bones inside you," she said. "You ain't got to ask them to do it—when you get to your feet, they know it's they job to hold you up."

"Yes, ma'am. I know, Grandma," I said.

"I know you do, baby. Anyhow, sometimes when trust gets broken, you can mend it. You can weave it back together just like you would loose yarn in a rug, but other times it gets so frayed and worn that all you can do is throw the rug out."

"Yes, ma'am. Grandma, what is this about?"

She took a deep breath and let it out. "I'm sorry I gotta tell you this, baby. But your mama and I decided that you needed to know what was going on, and she was way too mad to give you the news. I think I'm too upset to give it to you too. That's why I decided to do it right away. You know that I ain't no good with letting something heavy rest on my mind. They say the longer you let potato salad sit out in the sun, the worse it gets."

"What's going on, Grandma? What news? I just left the house a little while ago. What could be up so soon?"

"Jada done kicked out your daddy," she said. "She told him that he had to get his little stuff and leave their house for good."

"How come? Grandma, are you serious?" Her news was definitely not what I was expecting to hear.

"It's a mess," she said. "It's just a darn big, fat mess." She started wringing her arthritic hands. "I don't know, baby. I just gotta tell you. Jada come home last night from working an extra shift at her job and caught him doing something he wasn't supposed to be doing with some other gal right in the middle of her kitchen, next to her brand-new deep freezer. She caught him with some young gal that her restaurant had hired to pass out flyers and other types of promotions for their new dinner specials. She said that the gal had seemed real kind. She was from New Orleans, didn't know a lot of folks, so about a month ago she had her over along with two of Anderson's single male friends to play some cards and have some fun. She said they all had a great time, and when it was all over, the gal asked her if she could help clean up, so she left her in the kitchen washing dishes with Anderson while she put Gift in bed. She didn't know at the time that the hussy was in the kitchen offering your daddy a lot more than two-for-one coupons."

"That's awful, Grandma," I said.

"It ain't nothing nice, baby—and that's the truth," she said. "Lord knows it ain't nothing nice at all." She sighed again. "Jada told me that when she saw that little mare in her kitchen, she just lost it. She hauled off and slapped that gal into the middle of next year, then she picked up a metal spatula and applied it to her backside until she broke and run out of the house. After that she came back in the kitchen and told Anderson to get out of her house too."

"She did?"

"Yes, she told me that she didn't want to, but she didn't have no choice. She said that while your daddy was doing the wrong thing with that hussy, poor Gift was lying in her playpen just a little ways away in the dining room. 'I could have forgiven him for what he did to me,' she told me while I was making her a pot of coffee just a little while ago. 'But I trusted him to do right by Gift. Before I married him, I told him that he could make all the mistakes that he wanted with me, but he couldn't make even one with my baby. That's why I threw him out, Grandma Augustine,' she said, crying. 'I didn't care if he screwed me over, but he promised me to always do right by whatever children we had. I just wanted him to act correctly when it came to Gift. I don't understand, Grandma Augustine. I know that he loves Gift just as much as I do. I don't understand how he could choose that little trashy girl over his own child.'

"And you know what? I don't either," Grandma said. "I just don't know what in the world could have gotten into that man." She shifted her weight again. "I sho wished that I hadn't had to tell you that story, baby, but your mama and I didn't want you to hear it out in the streets. Folks can say really cruel things sometimes. You know how it is when folks start to talk."

"I know, Grandma."

"Yes, it's a shame before God, but most folks let they tongue loose before they even think about what's coming out of they mouth." She steadied herself on her cane. "When Jada come by to drop Gift off, she told me she didn't know where your daddy was at, but she was only there a little bit when I heard him rapping on the door. I went and answered it, and got a chance to bless him out some, but before I could tell him anything good, he pushed this letter into my hand and ran off the porch. Here," she said, pulling a white envelope out of her pocket and pressing it into my hand. "He left this for you. I hope it's got some answers to why he would do such an unchristian and ugly thing. You let me know if it do."

"I will, Grandma."

"Okay," she said. "You go on off and do what you have to do. I'm just gon' wait here until my ride comes back and gets me."

"I'll see ya later, Grandma," I said.

I left Grandma on the porch and walked back in the house. I flopped down in the middle of the living-room floor and turned the envelope over in my hand. There was nothing special about it. It was just a plain white note. On the front of it, scribbled in a really light pencil, were the words FROM YOUR FATHER.

I wanted to take the note and ball it up, but the word *father* kept me from doing it. Mr. Anderson Fox had never even tried to be a father to me, but he did try and was a father to Gift. He loved her, I was sure of that, as sure as I was about Mama and Grandma loving me and Tia. I had seen the tender way he held her in the hospital and had heard him humming a song to her underneath the tree. She meant everything to him that I didn't. How could he finally figure out what it meant to be a father and forget it in just one stupid night? I didn't get it. I couldn't think of any other way to answer the question, so I opened the letter and started reading it.

*I'm a player, baby girl. I can't really tell you how I got to be that way, but anybody that knows me can tell you that your daddy been this way most of his life. When I was a little dude, my mama and daddy used to send me to school and I would figure out how to work the girls out of their soda-pop money. I would tell them that they had on a fly dress or was really cute, some jive crap like that, and before you know it, I had a whole pocket full of change. I had so much cash that I would buy me and my friends all kinds of candy on the way home. My mama and daddy knew what I was doing, and they didn't like it at all. They would drag me to all kinds of church services trying to straighten me out. I must have stayed on my knees in front of somebody's congregation my whole teen years.*

*I never did want no kids. I just got involved with a chick and soon as I looked around, here one come. Then I had to figure out what I was gonna do about it. Most of the time I figured that it was easy for me to just put my feet in the streets.*

I know you done heard it around the hood somewhere, so I guess I might as well tell you that if you put them all together, I would have to say that I got round about eight children, including you and your sister Gift, but y'all the only two that I ever put any kind of claim on. It was always "Mama's baby, Papa's maybe" with the rest.

Your grandma told me this morning that I ain't never been no real kind of father to you, that I wasn't there to see the first time that you cornrowed your own hair or bought your first pair of stockings. She's right about that, but not everything. I'll tell you the truth. I came to hear one of your stories once. You was about ten or so, and you was reading at your school's library. I found out by accident. I came into town and stopped by the house to see your mama, but she wasn't home. Your grandma was there by herself. She was laid up with the flu. She told me about the reading, so I walked on over to the school. I didn't go into the library though. It was packed with folks that I didn't know, and to tell you the truth, I didn't want your mama to know that I was there. I didn't want her to get it into her head that I was open to doing that kind of thing. I stood in the hallway out of sight.

I didn't catch all of your story, but I could tell that you was good. I heard folks clapping like wild and saying how great they thought you were. "She got real talent," I heard one old lady say. "Her mama got something to be proud of. I wish some of my grandbabies were good with reading and writing. Lord, yes, her mama sho do have something to be proud of," that old lady said. I felt kinda proud myself when I heard that, and I just wanted you to know that. I just wanted you to know that I was out there standing in the hallway when you read your story.

*I imagine that when Gift get to be your age, she's gonna feel the same way about me that you do, but I want you to try and convince her of something different. I want you to tell her that I loved her and that I tried real hard to do right by her, but that I was a player, and no matter how hard I tried, I couldn't stay with her mama. I ain't asking you to lie. You can tell her the truth. You can tell her that I ain't never been good with just one chick. Baby girl, you know Jada is a good woman, but she mad, so she gonna tell Gift all kinds of bad things about me. A lot of them will be right, I can't lie about that, either. But you can let her know that you saw me loving her, and about that time I came down to the library to listen to you read your story, and how proud it made me. When you tell her that, she'll know that I ain't all that bad. Can you let her know for me, baby girl? Can you let her know that just for a little bit I was some kind of dad? Just do that for me, and I won't never ask you or your mama for anything else.*

I closed the letter and returned it to the envelope. There it was, what Mr. Anderson Fox really thought about himself and his kids. He had been honest, at least as honest as Mr. Anderson Fox could be. He had filled me in on things that I know he would never have told me with his own voice.

But I wasn't surprised by much in the letter. I knew that he never wanted children. We just kept coming like gas pains—all the Shaylas before me, Gift, myself—we all just showed up without being asked for. He wanted me to tell Gift that for just one evening he had been good at playing daddy, my daddy, and that he was actually proud of my writing.

I closed my eyes and tried to remember that evening so many

nights ago. I remembered being nervous and being upset because Grandma wasn't there. I had gripped the podium so hard when I read my story that my knuckles hurt. It would have made a difference if I could have seen Mr. Anderson Fox's face. It would have helped if I had actually known that he was there. I could have seen his face in place of Grandma's and maybe not felt so lost. Could I tell Gift that for just that one evening of my life I truly believed that he was my father? How could I? He was there, but like the Invisible Man. I wasn't sure that I would, but I *could* tell her that he loved her—of that I was certain, and nothing more.

I stuck the letter in my pocket and placed my feelings about it and Mr. Anderson Fox on hold. I couldn't deal with any of it. I could handle only one thing at a time. My mind belonged to Kambia. I had to make sense of what I had seen in the Majors' bedroom. I got up and peeked through the screen door. Grandma was already gone. I locked the door and went back to the closet, trying really hard not to step on Old MacDonald. I stood on my tiptoes and groped around in the pile until I felt the hard edge of the activity book. I brought it out and looked at it again. They were still in there—the wrapping paper and the paper dolls that looked just like the crumpled ones that I had tucked away in my drawer. I tried to reason everything out. You could buy an activity book with those kinds of dolls in it anywhere. They were as common as fur on a hamster, but the wrapping paper I wasn't so sure about. It was unique, special. I couldn't imagine the Majors finding another piece just like that anywhere around where we lived, and why would they even want to if they knew that it was the same paper that had been wrapped around a present that freaked Kambia out? I thumbed through the book and tried to get my mind around it, but it kept getting jumbled up with Mr. Anderson Fox's letter. He had come to hear me read one of my stories and had been proud when he heard it. No, I tossed the image of him standing out in the hallway out of my mind like an old newspaper. It meant no more than the cheap, emotionless greeting cards that he had sent me over the years. No, it meant nothing to me at all.

# Chapter 8

The sandman took a lunch break, and I woke early last night to find Jada and Gift lying next to me instead of Tia. They were conked out. Gift was wearing only a diaper, and she was curled up comfortably in the crook of Jada's arm, and Jada was sleeping peacefully with her knees pressed into my back. She was dressed in one of Tia's old rhinestone-studded T-shirts, and her short, curly hair was tied up with one of Mama's nylon handkerchiefs. She looked like she could have been on an old *Soul Train* episode.

Both Jada and Gift sounded like they could sleep until the next time Old Man Winter came knocking on our door. They were sawing logs even worse than Tia. I got up from the bed as quietly as I could. I crossed the room and sat down in a wooden folding chair next to the window so that I could enjoy the breeze blowing from the whirling blades of the window fan. I glanced over at the dresser and checked out a new Winnie the Pooh clock that Doo-witty had purchased for Gift. According to Pooh's honey-coated hands, it was 1:30 in the morning, thirty minutes after Jada gets off her job.

Ever since she tossed Mr. Anderson Fox out, Jada's been working all nights at the restaurant because the night shift pays extra. She's also been hanging out at our house with Gift. She says that she doesn't have much family and that she's closer to all of us than any of her girlfriends. She comes over right after she gets off at Spring Greens Eatery and crashes at our place until the next evening. When she's here, Jada mostly spends her time at the dining-room table drinking lemon tea and eating gingersnaps with Mama and Grandma Augustine.

While they snack, the ladies talk about all the things that they wish Mr. Anderson Fox could have been. "I wish he had been more dependable," Mama says, dipping her cookie in her teacup. "It would have been nice if I could have counted on him to go get Shayla a box of diapers on Monday and show up with them before Wednesday night."

"I wish he had been faithful," Jada says, selecting a lump of sugar from Grandma's antique porcelain sugar jar. "I wish that I could have counted on him to stay away from other women, the same way that he counted on me to stay away from other men."

"It would have been a blessing if he had understood responsibility," Grandma Augustine says, dropping a sprig of fresh mint into her steaming tea. "Jesus knows it would have been great if he had understood that he wasn't supposed to just make a baby, he was supposed to take care of it too."

They go on like that for hours until Mama has to go to work, then after she leaves, Grandma and Jada keep it up until it's time for Jada to leave.

Jada says that she doesn't really miss Mr. Anderson Fox. She says that she is just disappointed in him because of Gift. When she tossed him out, she assumed that he would at least try and come back for Gift's sake, but so far the only guy that has knocked on her door has been a door-to-door salesman wanting to know if she wanted to buy some fresh pork out of the back of his truck. "He asked me if I would like to purchase some oxtails," Jada said, laughing. "I told him I wasn't at all interested in tail, but if my husband showed up, he would take as much tail as he could get."

"Yes, he would," Mama and Grandma said, laughing. "Especially if it had a big butt and a really tight skirt," Mama added.

Snickering about Mr. Anderson Fox stops Mama and Grandma

from being so angry at him. It helps them forget that once again Mr. Anderson Fox has tracked sadness into our house on the sole of his shiny leather shoes.

Gift is miserable. She cries all the time now, even when Grandma Augustine holds her and tries to rock her to sleep. While Grandma's singing to her, she screams and throws her hands around. She doesn't giggle at all anymore, and even I miss the spit bubbles. I still don't love Gift, but just a tiny bit if me is starting to feel sorry for her. It's terrible what Mr. Anderson Fox did to her. He promised her the earth, but all he gave her was a handful of dirt.

Grandma Augustine says that when Mr. Anderson Fox packed his bag that night, he packed up Gift's essence and took it with him, as if it were an undershirt or a necktie. She says that while Jada was in the kitchen crying her troubles out, Mr. Anderson Fox took her Gift away. "He just picked her soul right up and stuck it in his wallet," she said. "When he walked out of that door, he took that child with him."

Personally, I don't believe that Mr. Anderson Fox took off with Gift's soul. It's still there. It's just baffled, the way mine was when he left. Her soul knows that it's missing something, but it doesn't know what, and neither does mine. Before I left the Majors' house that afternoon, I tore his letter up and threw it away. I didn't want Jada to know that it looked like he was out of Gift's life for good. I wanted her to have some hope. Grandma Augustine says that hope is like food. Having a little is much better than having none at all.

I pulled my chair closer to the window and thought about something else—Lemm and Kambia. I wanted to help them both, but I still didn't know what I could do.

Helping Lemm should be the easier of the two. He drinks too much. It should be easy to tell him just to cut it out—if it wasn't for his sisters. They wait for him each morning when he rises out of bed, and follow him around all day until he collapses in it again at night. Lemm says that there is just no way that he can get away from them. He says that when he isn't thinking about them, he's seeing them. He sees them whenever he passes a group of toddlers playing in a school yard. They are always there, little Lamonica and Lindy, sitting side by side in their two-seater stroller, sucking noisily on their bottles as some little boy, with a face that he can never quite make out, pushes them all over the yard. They look happy, and he imagines that the boy is happy too. Then suddenly the boy pushes the stroller out of the school yard into the street. A truck comes out of nowhere and plows into the three of them. Lemm closes his eyes to make the scene go away, but when he opens them, it starts all over again. He hurries home and hides out in his room. That's why he drinks so much. He says that when he drinks, he can't see the toddlers, the boy, or the truck. Everything becomes a blur. The more he drinks, the more blurry it all gets, until he passes out completely and he can't see anything at all. "The whole thing is like a video, Shayla," he told me. "Except I can't figure out how to eject the tape, so I have to find a way to make the whole screen go blank."

I told Lemm that I, too, thought that he should get some real help, but he said that as soon as his dad's sister found out how he had fooled her, she sent money for him to go talk to a doctor in a bigger nearby town. He said that the doctor was a brother, a sharp-looking dude with designer suits, thick gold rings, and a BMW with vanity plates. Lemm said that in the three months that he had appointments with the doctor, he showed up for every appointment really eager to talk about his sisters and why he drank, but during every other session the dude doctor got paged by some important client and had to rush off. He would leave him sitting on the leather sofa by himself, drinking an orange soda and wondering how he could get his aunt's money back. When the three months were over, all the dude doctor could tell him was that he had to stop blaming himself for what happened to his sisters, because it was just an accident.

"I already knew that," Lemm said. "What I needed to know was how."

Yesterday morning I thought we had it all figured out how. I picked Lemm up at his house, and together we went to the day care down the street. We stood at the fence for nearly two hours watching class after class of screaming toddlers chase one another and race Tonka trucks in a fun-looking sandbox. Every time Lemm swore that he saw his sisters, I squeezed his hand and asked him to tell me about some of his favorite things. Tia said that Mama used to do it to her when she thought she saw monsters in the room at night. I thought that it would help Lemm get rid of his monsters too. Whenever he thought he saw his sisters, I asked him to tell me about something he liked. I asked him all sorts of questions. He told me that his favorite ice cream was butter pecan, and that he liked to eat it in a huge bowl with vanilla wafers on top. He told me that he really liked basketball, football, and even tennis, but he just couldn't get into golf, because he didn't understand why anyone would want to stand out in the hot sun all day hitting a tiny ball into a hole with a metal stick. His favorite singer was Janet Jackson; his favorite song was any song by her. If he were banished to an island and could take only three things with him, he would take one of his dad's best fishing poles, a stack of Incredible Hulk comic books, and a lifetime supply of oatmeal cookies. I told him that I would probably take a pen and my blue notebook, but I would trade the cookies for several crates of Moon Pies.

When Lemm and I left the day care, it looked like he was going to be okay. We took a shortcut home down the old Negro Union tracks, and he even tried to belt out a Janet Jackson song. However, as we neared the end of the track we ran into a group of day campers out on a nature hike, and Lemm swore that he thought he saw the boy pushing the twins in their stroller right in the middle of them.

"Can't you see them, Shayla?" he asked. "Don't you see him pushing them around?"

"I don't see anything, Lemm," I said, pulling him on down the tracks. "It's just your imagination. Who's you favorite singer again?"

"I don't know," he said. "Are you sure you didn't see the boy?"

When we got back to his house, he pulled a bottle of Southern Comfort out of his chest and drank it until there was no more in the bottle. After that, his speech was so bad that I couldn't begin to know what he was telling me. I helped him crawl into his bed and watched him drift into sleep. While he slept, I glanced around the room and noticed for the first time that it was totally filled with remorse. Regret covered the walls, the floor, the plants, everything, like a sticky film that you couldn't wash off. There was no way that Lemm could get out of the room each day without tracking it out with him. I didn't think there was anything anybody could do to help him get away from his sisters, not even Mrs. Dreyfus. She had tried on a couple of occasions. Once she even showed up while I was there. Lemm was going through one of his mood swings, but it didn't bother her. She sat down on his bed and pleaded with him to let her help him. She told him that there were a lot of other teenagers going through what he was going through. "It's no shame to need help, son," she said, taking a bottle of gin out of Lemm's hand. "It's only a shame if you don't take it. I know you're hurting, but there are ways to take the pain away."

"There's isn't anything to take away, ma'am," Lemm said.

"There's nothing at all left. Ask my dad, he'll tell you. He'll tell you that I took everything away. There's nothing left."

"I don't understand, Lemm," Mrs. Dreyfus said.

"It's cool, lady," Lemm said, slipping into his street talk. "It's cool. Don't sweat it. I knew you wouldn't get it anyway. Just get out of my room. I'll be okay with Shayla. I don't need no tired counselor messing with my head."

Mrs. Dreyfus left, but only after she vowed to have a word with Lemm's father. Through the door I heard her tell him that Lemm needed serious help. "I know that it's none of my business," she said. "You seem like a good man, but I don't think you're doing the right thing for your son."

"Thank you, ma'am, but I know all about my son," Lemm's dad said to her in a very sad voice. "I've walked through the fire with him before. Nobody cares more about what happens to him than I do—I'm his papa. But he's right. There isn't anything to take away from him—from me. There's nothing at all left. It's all gone."

I don't think that Mrs. Dreyfus knew quite what to make of what Lemm and his dad said. I *do* know, but it doesn't help either one of us. Knowing why Lemm is standing on the train track doesn't mean that I've figured out how to get him off.

If I can't help Lemm with his problems, I certainly can't help Kambia with hers. I can't do anything about the hurtful packages that she got in the mail, because I still didn't know where they came from, and I refuse to believe that the Majors had anything to do with them. I didn't tell anybody about the wrapping paper and the paper dolls that I found in their closet. There was no way that the Majors could be hurting Kambia.

When I first met the Majors that day in Kambia's hospital room, I wasn't certain that they would take Kambia shopping for Linda

James novels, help her with her homework, or dance around her room with her, but I was certain that they would love her, and everything that I had seen so far told me that they did. Kambia meant everything to the Majors. They would never cause her harm by sending her mean presents. The paper dolls and the wrapping paper were just a coincidence, like two best girlfriends buying the same prom dress. They were as innocent as that. I wouldn't believe anything different. When I went to visit Kambia the other afternoon, both her father and her mother were there. They were sitting in chairs next to her bed taking turns reading her a fairy tale and trying to get her to talk to them.

"Do you want to hear another one, Daughter?" Ten Fingers asked, stroking her gently on the arm. "Me and your mama can read anything that you want to hear. We got all afternoon to spend just on what you want to do."

"Just tell us what story you would like, Kambia," Honeysuckle Peach told her. "I'll turn right to it and read in those funny voices that you like."

Kambia wouldn't answer them. They just opened the book to something anyway, something that they thought she might like, and Honeysuckle Peach started reading it in all kinds of embarrassing voices. It was the kind of thing that only a parent would do for a child. The Majors would never hurt Kambia.

As I sat hugging my knees and looking out on the sleeping world, I realized that they were probably doing exactly what I was doing, sitting in a chair at 1:30 in the morning, wondering how in the world to help her. I didn't have a clue. It was just something that I purely didn't know—but I did know that I was hungry. Grandma had fixed turnip greens and liver for dinner. I would rather take a whipping than eat either one of them. I felt real bad about wasting the food, but I threw them in the trash as soon as Grandma went to check on Gift. But now my stomach was telling me that maybe I should have made myself choke them down.

I left the window, walked as quietly as I could out of the bedroom, and headed for the kitchen. Tia had baked a big batch of oatmeal raisin cookies for Doo-witty this afternoon when she got home from her summer job at the Little Pig Toy Store. Doo-witty had gobbled up most of them, along with a huge hunk of cheddar cheese, but there were a few left, and I knew where Tia had hidden them out so that Doo-witty could finish them off the next time he came over. I was sure that he wouldn't mind if I snatched a couple.

I entered the living room cautiously. If Tia wasn't in the bed with me, she had to be stretched out on the living-room floor. It was the only other place where she would rest her head. She didn't like sleeping on our old lumpy sofa because in some places the rusty springs poked out, and she didn't like crawling in with Mama because she says that Mama sleeps worse than she does. As I went through the living room I listened for the sound of her snoring and carefully stepped over her head.

The kitchen was black as crude oil when I stepped into it. I snapped on the light, startling a mouse that was busy trying to find his own late-night snack underneath the kitchen table. He skittered off, tail flying, before I could let out a peep.

Without even a hint of guilt I found Tia's cookies, wrapped in plastic and stuck behind a stale loaf of wheat bread in the bread box. I pulled them out, opened the package, and took out three of the smallest ones. I was replacing the rest of the cookies when I heard the sound of rushing water. I looked up. It was Mama. She was standing at the sink running water into a jelly-jar glass that she kept on the nightstand next to her bed. It was a funny coincidence. She was wearing her cotton mouse-print pajamas and mouse slippers. They were a birthday present from me and Tia. They weren't really anything that she would buy for herself, but since they were from us, she decided to wear them anyway. They drive Grandma Augustine's cat, Nat King Cole, crazy whenever she brings him over. He races after Mama's feet, trying to catch the mice's plastic whiskers with his paws.

Mama got her drink and sat down across from me at the table. She couldn't have been in bed more than a couple of hours, but there was already a crusty layer of sleep in the corners of her eyes. She rubbed her fists in them to clean them out.

"What are you doing up, Shayla?" she asked when she was finished.

"I was hungry," I said with a full mouth.

Mama shook her head. "I see you figured out where Tia hid those cookies," she said tiredly. "I was thinking about looking for them myself."

"They're in the bread box behind the bread," I said. "You want one? I'll get it for you."

"Nah, I was just teasing. I can't handle all that madness on my stomach this time of night. You couldn't sleep?" she asked. "You didn't just get up 'cause you were hungry, did you?"

"No, ma'am," I said. "Jada and Gift are in my bed. They're making too much noise. I had to get up."

"Jada is over here again tonight?" Mama asked. "That child is gonna have to go on home sometimes. She can't stay holed up here because of Mr. Anderson Fox. He ain't worth half of the fretting that she doing over him. Good grief, I could have told her not to hang that chain around her neck. You can put a dog in water for ten years, but that still ain't gonna make him a fish. Anderson is just Anderson, that's all. I could have told her that."

"Me, too," I said, sliding a cookie over to her.

"I told you I didn't want one, little hardheaded girl," she said, taking a bite anyway. "I'm gonna wish I hadn't done this," she said, dropping crumbs all over the table. "My belly gon' be throwing a fit on me until it's time to get up."

"Mine too, Mama," I said.

I got up from the table. I was going to walk over to the sink and get myself a drink of water too. I had pushed my chair aside when Jada came running into the room.

"Vera, come quick!" she said to Mama. "I think somebody is trying to break into the house next door."

"What?" Mama said.

We went back into the living room, carefully stepping over Tia again. Once inside, Jada motioned for us to follow her to the window. "I got up to get Gift a bottle, 'cause you know she ain't been sleeping through the night since Anderson left," she said, pulling back the curtain on the side of the window. "I heard a noise, so I peeked out. It looks like somebody is trying to mess around with the lock or something."

"Why would anybody be doing that? It ain't even nobody there. The landlord can't get nobody to move in there, 'cause he won't fix the house up. Let me see what in the heck is going on," she said, peeping out.

I tried to look too, but there wasn't enough room. I did hear a noise, just like Jada said. It sounded like a rusty knob being turned back and forth.

"You right," Mama said, pulling her head back. "There is definitely somebody on the porch, but it's too dark for me to make out anything with my tired eyes. It's probably just one of them teenage crack dealers. They like to take up in the houses. I don't want that kind of nonsense next door to me. That house done set enough trash in my front yard. Jada, go call the police. We might as well stop this foolishness before it gets started. Before you know it, they'll be having all kinds of drug addicts parked right in front of my gate."

"All right," Jada said. She walked to Mama's room to get the phone. As soon as she left, Mama moved out of the way, and I looked out. There was definitely somebody on the porch, and my eyes were obviously not as tired as Mama's and Jada's, because in the bright moonlight I could see right away that it *wasn't* some teenage crack dealer. I pulled away from the window in a panic.

"Mama, wait!" I said. "Tell Jada to stop. It's not a drug dealer. It's Kambia."

"Let me see, girl," Mama said. She pushed me aside and looked out through the curtains. A couple of seconds later her shocked face emerged from the window. You would have thought that she had actually seen a drug dealer.

"That *is* Kambia," she said. "What in the world is that child doing at that old house this time of the night?"

"I don't know," I said. "I'm gonna go see." I ran for the front door.

"Wait a minute, Shayla," Mama said, stopping me. "You ain't going outside this time of night by yourself. I'm going to go get my robe and tell Jada to stop. You wait right here until I get back."

Mama dashed off to her room, and I ran back to the window and looked out. It was Kambia. There was no mistaking her thin figure and bony legs. She was twisting and turning the knob as if a bolt of lightning were going to shoot out of the sky and strike her if she didn't get the door open. I tried to pry the window up so that I could call out, but it was superglue stuck, wedged tightly from old age, dust, and rainwater. I banged on it instead, but I don't even think she heard the noise. A moment later Mama came hurrying back out in her terry robe, carrying a flashlight. "I'm not running outside without being able to see where I'm going," she said, yanking the belt of her robe tight. "That's how Bobby's daughter Zuri broke her ankle. Let's go see what's going on in this child's head."

Mama took her time getting down the steps, but I bounded down them. I opened the gate and rushed toward Kambia, with Mama calling, "Hold up, Shayla," behind me. When I reached the fence, I didn't bother walking up to the gate. I climbed up it, dropped to the ground like a criminal in a TV police chase, and raced up the steps.

Kambia wasn't on the porch anymore when I got there. The door was standing wide open, and I knew that she had gone inside, but I just couldn't make myself follow. I stood on the porch listening to the sound of Mama's slippers scraping our concrete walkway. I had never been in Kambia's old house before, not even when she still lived in it, and I wasn't sure if I wanted to go into it now. I thought about the wolves that she said were hanging on her walls, the ones that did all the horrible things to her. I knew that it wasn't wolves that hurt her, but when I looked into the blackness, I could imagine all sorts of scary things hiding just beyond the door. "Kambia," I called.

"Shayla, don't you go in that door fooling around without me," Mama called out from the gate.

"I'm not, Mama. Kambia, are you in there?" I asked, pulling the torn screen back and poking my head inside. All I got was more blackness for a reply. "Mama, hurry up," I said, turning back around.

"I'm coming, Shayla," she said, starting up the steps. She made it up to the porch, pulled back the screen, and turned on her flashlight. The batteries were pretty low. The beam lit up only a couple of feet. "It's better than nothing," she told me.

When we got into the house, Mama shook the light a few times to see if jiggling the batteries would make the beam brighter. No luck. We could see only a little ways in front of us, but it was still enough for us to see that the small hallway and living room were completely empty, except for some well-worn shag carpet that had a wet-dog smell and wall after wall of tattered, peeling wallpaper that looked to me like it had been ripped by animal claws. The sight of the wallpaper made me want to turn back. I kept going, though, calling out for Kambia in a voice that was loud enough for her to hear but not loud enough to wake the entire neighborhood. The neighborhood had been through enough drama because of Kambia and what happened to her in the house. I was certain that they wouldn't want any more, and I guess Mama must have felt the same way. She was calling out to Kambia in an even softer tone than I was. "Kambia, honey, are you in here?" she asked in a low voice. If Kambia heard her, she sure didn't let her know.

"Hey, where are you?" I called out.

We walked to the other rooms in the house, trying not to bump into the part of the wall that Mama's light couldn't light up. We checked out the next three rooms of the house—the dining room, the bathroom, and the kitchen. In the dining room all we found was more smelly carpet and peeling wallpaper; in the kitchen all there was was a plastic garbage pail overflowing with Budweiser beer cans and faded newspapers, and an old, cruddy one-door refrigerator that looked like it could have been placed in the house when it was first built. In the bathroom there was just a grimy cast-iron tub and a broken-down toilet that was leaning to one side.

"Lord, I don't know who that landlord thought he was gon' rent this place to," Mama said as we left the room.

There was only one place left in the house to look, the bedroom, and when I reached it, I paused just like I had done on the front porch. It was as if I could feel the pain seeping out from underneath the closed door. It was the place where Kambia had been hurt, where the men that she called her wolves hurt her so bad that she had to go to the hospital. I didn't want to go in there; just looking at the doorway made me feel something that I couldn't even describe. It was a sick uneasiness that started in my stomach and spread up to my heart. Ghastly things had been done to Kambia in that room. Things that she couldn't even tell me about, the kinds of things that made her not able to live in the real world.

I placed my hand on the knob, but I couldn't turn it. I stepped back and let Mama open the door for me. Mama opened it and shone the light in the room, but the batteries were almost gone, so we could hardly make anything out.

"Kambia, you in here?" I called. A noise came from somewhere in the room. *Scrape-thump, scrape-thump,* like something being moved around. Mama shone the light in the direction that it was coming from.

It was Kambia. She was making the noise. She was dressed in only her nightclothes, like me, and she was kneeling in a corner of the room. She had pried the rug up and was messing with something underneath.

"Kambia, what are you doing?" I asked, walking over to her and kneeling down too. She didn't look up at me. She kept her eyes to the ground, her bony fingers pushing and pulling whatever she was fooling with under the rug. The light in our living room snapped on, sending brightness through Kambia's bedroom window. Mama snapped her flashlight off, and came and knelt down beside me.

"Kambia," she said. "It's still nighttime, honey, it's time to sleep. You should be at home in bed."

"That's right, Kambia," I said. "What are you doing running around in the dark? Did you remember something that you wanted to get from here?"

She still didn't answer me, and I couldn't see her face to tell if she was even listening. I reached over, grabbed her chin, and tilted her head up. I gasped.

"What is it?" Mama asked, then she saw what I saw and gasped too. Nothing, there was nothing on Kambia's face, and nothing in her eyes. She had slipped into her own world again, there was no mistaking it. In her eyes was the same odd blankness that was in them the day that Mrs. Dreyfus called me about the dress.

"Shayla, how is she?" Mama asked.

"I don't know. Kambia, Kambia, can you hear me?" I asked. She looked right through me. I turned to Mama. "How did she get all the way over here by herself?"

"Beats me," Mama said. "Shayla, is she sleepwalking or something?"

"No, ma'am. She's awake. I've seen her go all blank before, but she usually just gets still. Kambia, are you okay?" I shook her shoulder lightly, but I still got no reply. It was like all the other times, except she was moving around. She wasn't going to answer me, but Mama didn't get it. She kept trying.

"Kambia, honey, say something. It's Ms. Dubois and Shayla. Honey, what are you doing here?"

Kambia's mouth didn't move, but her hands did. They kept searching for whatever it was she was looking for.

"She's looking for something. She must have left something here that she really wants to get. Let me see," Mama said. She pulled the rug back and snapped her light on again. She shined what little light there was over Kambia's hands.

At first it was hard to make out exactly what we were seeing, but when our eyes adjusted to the light, it was easy to see that Kambia had her hands stuck into a hole. There was a hole underneath the carpet where the floorboards had rotted away. It wasn't a deep hole. It didn't look like it went through the layers of two-by-fours, but it was wide enough to stick a few things into.

"Kambia, what's in there?" I asked, sticking my hand in beside hers. I touched a piece of cloth and pulled it out, but I dropped it as soon as I saw what it was.

"What's wrong, what is that?" Mama asked. She reached over and picked the cloth up and dropped it even quicker than I did. It was underwear. Kambia's ragged, stained underwear, the kind that we had buried that day down by the bayou because she said that having them around made her feel bad inside.

"Oh, my Lord, why would she want these?" Mama asked. This time I didn't answer. I was dumbstruck. I stuck my hand in the hole again. I touched something. It was balled-up paper. I brought it out and unfolded it. I was even more dumbstruck. It was a paper doll, a lady paper doll with red hair and green eyes, just like the ones that were tucked in my drawer.

"Mama, look," I said, holding it out to her. I stuck my hand in again and touched another piece of paper. This one was flat, with little ridges or something on the surface of it. I pulled it out. This time I wasn't dumbstruck at all. I knew exactly what it was before I saw it. It was the wrapping paper that the dolls had been wrapped in. I dropped it on the floor and stared at it the way I had done when I found it in the Majors' closet. Suddenly, Awareness came running into my head. She ran all over my brain, throwing open all the windows and doors in my mind. My head flooded with brightness, more light than a hundred of Mama's flashlights could produce. I looked over at Mama to see if she had had an explosion of her own, and I could tell that Awareness had been opening windows and doors in her head too. She had that look on her face, the one that you get after you tear your house up looking for your keys and suddenly see them dangling from the lock. They were there the whole time, you just couldn't see them.

Mama stood up. "Baby, I'm gonna go get Honeysuckle Peach and Mr. Major on the phone. You stay here and make sure that Kambia is okay. I'll be right back. I just have to go and let them know what's going on. Oh, God, what in the world am I going to tell them?" she said, walking out of the door, shining her flashlight in front of her.

I looked back at Kambia. I was glad that Mama hadn't told me to go and call the Majors. I didn't want to be the one to tell them what she was going to say. She was going to tell them something that they wouldn't believe on the phone, something they still wouldn't believe even after they saw it for themselves. She was going to tell them that for the past few months we had all been trying to figure out how to protect Kambia from Kambia. The dolls, the raggedy shoes, the stained underwear: They were all from Kambia. She was sending them to herself, and I didn't know why. As I watched her hands rooting around in the hole that was filled with things that only she could have known about or put there, I couldn't deny it. I was wrong about all the stuff going down with Jada and Mr. Anderson Fox—this was the one thing that I wouldn't have expected.

I went back to the dress day again and remembered how Kambia had bolted from the room. Both me and Mrs. Dreyfus thought that she had come back to herself and run out of the door, but maybe she hadn't. I stuck my hand down in the hole to see what else she was hiding. My hand struck paper again. It was smooth and glossy this time. I brought it up. It was a photograph of something, but it was so dim in the room without Mama's flashlight that I could barely see what it was. I got up from my knees and walked to a window. It *was* a photograph. I leaned toward the light coming from my house so that I could see it. It was a picture of a baby, a little girl about one or so in some kind of frilly little dress with a big white collar and rickrack around the hem. It was too dark for me to make out the exact facial features of the little girl, but I could tell that she had light eyes and fair skin, and that the little tufts of fuzzy hair on her head were light too.

I leaned toward the light a little more and turned the photo over. On the back was a group of letters. They were in really tiny handwriting. "Myababuo," I pronounced slowly, hoping that I was getting it right. What did it mean? I couldn't even guess. I brought the photo back over to where Kambia was and placed it back in the hole. I sat down next to her and put my arms around her shoulders. I remembered the first time that I had sat with her in the dark. It was under the house, the night when she first told me the scary story about her wolves. I remembered that when I left her, I had thought that if Tia would just come back home, she could make everything okay. Tia could make whoever was hurting Kambia run away, but I knew that it wouldn't work this time, because no matter what Tia did, she couldn't make Kambia run away from herself.

# Chapter 9

$W$hen I was in the fifth grade, I saw a play about a little boy in a wheelchair who desperately wanted to play football. Each afternoon he would sit in his driveway watching the other boys tackling one another in the field across from his house. One day, while he was watching, an old bum walked into the driveway and asked the boy if he could have a drink of water. The boy immediately wheeled into the house and fetched the bum a cool drink. The bum drank the water down quickly. He then repaid the boy for his kindness with the only thing that he had of value, an old gold ring with the face of a cat etched into it. The boy put on the ring. Suddenly his eyes went all cloudy. He closed them for a moment and opened them back up. To his amazement he was no longer in the driveway. He was standing in the field with the other boys, standing on his own two feet. The boy felt his legs. They were real. He wasn't having a daydream. He shouted with delight and looked back at his house. His mouth fell all the way to China. He was still there in his drive-way, sitting in his wheelchair. Somehow the ring had made it pos-sible for him to be in the driveway and out of it at the same time.

In many ways what happened to the boy in the play is the same thing that happened to Kambia. Mrs. Dreyfus says that somehow Kambia figured out how to be in two places at one time. One Kambia went to live with the Majors and had a good life being their daughter, while the other Kambia stayed behind at Jasmine Joiner's old house and was miserable. It was *that* Kambia who was sending the packages. She either couldn't or wouldn't leave her old house, because it was all that she knew, but she didn't want to suffer alone, so she found a way to make the other Kambia suffer too. Mrs. Dreyfus says that once she and Kambia's psychiatrist looked at all the evidence, it was easy to figure out what me and Mama had already discovered—that it really was Kambia hurting Kambia, and you could tell that she was struggling with her old and new life because of the types of packages that were sent. The stained underwear, the raggedy dress with the ugly threat on it, the cruddy shoes, they were all meant to remind Kambia of where she had come from. However, it was the paper dolls that actually gave things away. Mrs. Dreyfus says that with the dolls you could plainly see that Kambia was having a hard time making the switch. With them she was creating and then destroying herself over and over.

Mrs. Dreyfus says that Kambia's case is extreme, but what she is going through isn't unusual for girls who have suffered what she's suffered. She says that girls who have gone through what Kambia went through sometimes get very mixed up. They want to start over badly, but they're afraid to trust all the new things in their life. They have a hard time believing that they won't get hurt again. Does Kambia know that she was the one doing it? Mrs. Dreyfus says that you just can't know for sure. It's too hard to tell, because it looks like she was sending the packages while she was in one of her trances, but the packages were the things that were seemingly causing the trances in the first place. "It is confusing," Mrs. Dreyfus said. "I must admit that I'm completely baffled by it, but Kambia's psychiatrist seems to think that it is possible that there are several levels to what we've been calling Kambia's blanking out. What I mean by that is that she could be in several different kinds of states, even though all of them look the same to us. However, it doesn't matter. What matters is that she is powerless to stop herself from going into them in the first place."

Mrs. Dreyfus now thinks that Kambia *should* go to a special hospital where they can better help pull her mind back together and keep an eye on her at the same time. She says that she is confident now that no matter how much the Majors love Kambia, they can't help her. She says that both she and Kambia's psychiatrist feel that Kambia needs a special kind of help, so she got some of the patrons at her school who had paid Kambia's tuition when she started there to donate money for Kambia to stay at a private hospital in New Mexico. She also got them to agree to help the Majors rent an apartment close by so that they could be there if she needed them. When Mrs. Dreyfus told me the news this morning as we sat outside on Kambia's back porch, I wanted to scream at her and tell her that Kambia wasn't going anywhere, but I was too mixed up about Kambia. I didn't think that what Mrs. Dreyfus said made complete sense. I sat there with my hands folded in my lap, staring at her like she had just swooped down out of the sky like a big vulture and landed on the step next to me, until it finally popped in her head that I wasn't getting it, and she started to explain it to me.

"Do you understand me, Shayla?" she asked me. "Do you understand why Kambia was the one who was scaring herself? Do you know why she would have wanted to return to the place that she was at before?"

"No, ma'am, I don't," I said. "We both saw how she was the day that we went with her to pick up her stuff from the old house. She said that she hoped no other little girl would come to live there. That's what she said when she left the house. She was very happy to get away from there."

"I know what she said, Shayla. I know exactly what she told you, but the truth is, when she left the house that day, she didn't carry anything out with her because she had left most of her personal belongings behind to get them later. She left them there so that she would have to go back, Shayla," she said. "And honey, I don't think that she did it on purpose. She just couldn't help herself."

"But why? Why would she want to go back to some place where she got hurt?"

"I'm not really sure, Shayla," Mrs. Dreyfus said. "Do you know what the word *unconscious* means?"

"Yes, it means something you aren't aware of."

"Exactly," she said. "It's just what I told you. Kambia wasn't aware of what she was doing. She was sending herself the packages to tell herself that her old place was where she belonged, but she didn't have any idea that she was doing it. It's hard for me to explain to you, but here is something that might help."

She pulled a book out of her jacket pocket and handed it to me. On the cover was a girl about my age with a mushroom haircut, dimples, and a really, really sad face. The name of the book was *The Things That Barbara Couldn't Tell*. I opened it and thumbed through it. There was page after page of essays with girls' names at the top of them.

"I want you to turn to the fifth essay in that book and read it, Shayla," she said. "You read it, then you come in the house and say good-bye to Kambia. She's leaving this afternoon. She's got a long way to go, and it will be much easier for her if you are the one that will see her off. She needs to know that you are okay with her leaving to get better."

"I'm not okay with her leaving," I said. "I don't want her to go."

"You will, Shayla. Read the essay and you'll understand why it's good for Kambia to go."

Mrs. Dreyfus left the steps and walked through the back door.

She was wrong. Nothing could make me understand why Kambia had to leave. Mrs. Dreyfus might have been sure, but I still wasn't confident that Kambia needed to go. I had talked to her the day after we found her at the house, at least I had tried to talk to her. When her parents came to fetch her that night, they were so stunned that they didn't even know what to say to her. They saw the hole in the floor with all her old things hidden in it, but they were too shocked to say anything about it. They gathered Kambia in their arms and took her home with them, and I went too. While the Majors went to the kitchen and discussed what to do about Kambia, I curled up next to her and slept. I got up before her the next morning, and when she opened her eyes, I quizzed her. I asked her why she had been at the old house, and what she had been looking for. She just stared at me. It was no use. I left the bedroom and went to the kitchen to say good morning to her mom and dad. They were standing next to the kitchen sink looking like they had been walking with despair all night. Their bodies were all stooped over, and you could see a trail of hopelessness worn into the floor where they had walked back and forth. They turned to me with tired smiles when I walked over to them.

"Baby, do you want some cereal or something?" Ten Fingers asked me.

"No, sir, I don't want anything," I said.

"I don't either, child. I don't believe that I can eat anything at all today." He sighed and sat down at the kitchen table. I walked over and joined him. "You know what, baby?" he said, running his hands over his hair. "My mama had seven boys, and we were all flat dumb about girls. The only thing that we knew about them was that they sometimes smelled of rose or lemon water, and they didn't like you to put your dirty hands on they pretty dresses. We knew this because we had two girl cousins that lived one or two houses over from us and sometimes came over. When they came, it wasn't an hour before one of us boys had said the wrong thing to them and the tears went to falling. It happened every time they stepped foot in the house, until my mama and daddy finally got tired of it and sent us to an afternoon etiquette class that taught us how to act around young ladies. They told us how to treat them in a gentlemanly way and how to say the right things to them. They taught us how to have conversations with girls too, but nobody ever taught us what to say when a girl wouldn't talk to us at all. My sweet daughter won't even talk to me," he said with a really gloomy face. "What kind of man can't even talk to his own daughter? I just wanted to make things better for that girl. But it don't look like being here with me and Honeysuckle has done much good."

It took forever for me and Kambia's mom to convince her dad that he hadn't done anything wrong. She knew that he loved her. It had nothing to do with him being a man. When we said that, some of the glum rolled away from Ten Fingers' face.

"What are we gonna do about our daughter?" he asked Honeysuckle Peach.

"I don't know," she said. "I honestly don't know what to do."

Now Mrs. Dreyfus said that she did, but I didn't agree with her, and no story written by a girl with an ugly haircut could make me change my mind. Only, books were like hot blueberry turnovers to me; I couldn't resist them. I opened the book and started reading it.

The first essay was by an eleven-year-old girl named Pinky, which I thought was a really dumb name until I read that it was an affectionate nickname given to her by her mother, because when she was born, she was really plump and all cuddly pink with apple-blossom cheeks.

Pinky was her mom's only daughter, and they were really close until Pinky's mom and dad went through a really bad divorce, and her dad moved on with his life. Her dad got married again. He married some young, shapely girl that was only half the age of Pinky's mom. Pinky said that after her dad's wedding her mom just kind of freaked. She was sipping-straw thin, but for some reason she started spending all of her time at the gym. She wouldn't go to work or anything. All she did was exercise. The bills started piling up, and Pinky's grandma decided to help out the best way that she knew how. She owned the house that they were living in, so she decided to rent out one of the rooms to help get some cash to pay their bills.

That's when he moved in, Mr. Lipstick Candy. His real name was Mr. Harding, but Pinky called him Mr. Lipstick Candy because that was what he used to buy her a lot of. He bought her bag after bag of the fuchsia treat because she told him that she wanted to wear makeup, but her mom said that she was still too young to wear it. "Here's some makeup that your mom can't get mad about," he would say.

At first Pinky thought that Mr. Lipstick Candy was cool. He paid attention to her when her mom was too involved with her workouts. He bought her new clothes and toys, and even picked her up after school. She said that she would have kept thinking that he was the best guy she had ever met if he hadn't started touching her.

Mr. Lipstick Candy started out just putting his hands in the places that guys aren't even supposed to see. Pinky didn't like it at all, but she had had boys try to touch her in those places before, especially since she had begun to fill out some. She told herself that it wasn't a big deal, at least it wasn't worth losing his friendship. She kept her mouth shut and let it slide. That was a majorly bad idea. Soon touching wasn't enough. He started hurting her real bad, making her do things that made her feel foul inside and left her lying in bed alone in pain.

She wanted to tell her grandmother, but he told her that her grandmother wouldn't do anything, because he was the only one in the house paying rent. She tried to tell her mother, but her mom was too busy with her aerobics classes. Pinky didn't know what else to do, so she let him keep hurting her. She said that while he was doing it, things would get all screwy in her head. She wouldn't be there in the bed with him anymore. She would see herself standing outside the door watching him hurt someone that looked a lot like her. It was the only way that she could deal with him doing that to her, the best way that she could control all of the bad things that she was feeling. There had to be two of her—one Pinky who left home and went to school each day and even managed to have some fun at lunch with her friends, and one Pinky who spent the night curled up in her bed crying.

Then on a cool fall afternoon something awful happened. She was standing at her locker at school when she saw the nighttime Pinky come into the hallway. She walked down the hall, past the girls' bathroom, and up the steps to the fourth-floor landing. She tugged open the window and jumped. There wasn't even enough time for any of the kids around her to scream or run for help.

Fortunately for her, the nighttime Pinky didn't get hurt too bad. On the way down she got tangled up in a gigantic banner the Speech Club had put up to announce a debate on cheating and ended up in a tree. The custodians had to get a ladder and help her down. It was when she was climbing down from the ladder with bruises all over her that she realized she was the one who had jumped out of the window. She learned that everything that was happening, was happening to her. In the end it took five years of therapy for her to start getting better. Today she still doesn't remember walking to the window. She just remembers how her mother wept and told her that she was sorry when she came to the psych ward of the hospital to see her.

I closed the book and sat listening to the sound of Mrs. Abbot's shaggy mutt three doors down, barking at a wad of paper that was carelessly blowing across his backyard. Could what happened to Pinky have happened to Kambia? Could she do something really frightful to herself while she was being her old self? She already had, in a way. She had been wigging herself out for months with the packages and didn't even know that she was the one who had sent them. The first time I saw her on the bayou, I was sure that she was going to throw herself into the muddy water. It was the old Kambia that did that. What if she did it again? Maybe Mrs. Dreyfus was right about her needing special help, but she wasn't right about her needing it so far away. I didn't know what to think. All this time I had been worried about all the Shaylas in my life. I was so concerned about them that I couldn't even see that there were two Kambias. I had blundered badly, totally failed her as a friend. I had to make it up to her, but I couldn't if she was miles away. How could I let her know how sorry I was? I wouldn't say good-bye to her. It wasn't fair. There had to be a way to get her some help here.

I sat on the step for the rest of the morning, refusing to go in and see Kambia. I didn't want to see her mother packing up her flowered sundresses and favorite toys and selecting some of her best Linda James books. I wanted her to get help, but not so far away. She was my best friend, and I had promised that I would always be there for her. She would be all alone in New Mexico, and I would be all alone here, except for Lemm. He was good to be around when he wasn't drinking, but that wasn't often.

By midafternoon I still hadn't moved from the steps, even though Kambia's parents, Mrs. Dreyfus, and Mama had come out to try and persuade me to come say my good-byes. I told them all the same thing—that I didn't think it was fair for Kambia to be going away, and that I would never ever say good-bye to her—and just when I thought everybody had given up on me, I looked up and saw someone new standing at the back door. I nearly fell off the step when I saw who it was. It was Frog, Doo-witty's mother. She opened the back door and squeezed her huge bulk out onto the narrow top step.

"It ain't a lot of room out here, is it, girl?" she asked me.

"No, ma'am," I said, getting up to make space for her. "Are Tia and Doo-witty with you?"

"Naw," she said, pulling her skirt up over her rumply thighs to sit down on the step. "Doo-witty and Tia already went back to your house. I dropped them over here, but they decided to walk back."

"Oh," I said.

"They came over to say good-bye to your little friend. I was talking to your grandma about that," she said, staring at me with her popped eyes. "She told me that your little friend is going to go away to some kind of special hospital."

"Yes, ma'am," I said, wondering why she would even care.

"That's probably good," she said. "I don't know her or her parents too well, but it sounds like being at a hospital would be the best thing for her. Your grandma told me about some of the troubles she been having lately. It's a shame what happened to her in the first place. It's good that they got places to try and help her get better. Even when I was a girl, folks wouldn't talk about stuff like that. If a girl was being made to do something like that, she had to keep it to herself, 'cause nobody wanted to know nothing about it. You'd be surprised that it wasn't that long ago that life was still pretty cruel for children."

"I didn't know that," I said.

"Well, it don't matter," she said, tugging the hem of her dress down until it was stretched over her flabby knees. "At your age you don't need to know too much."

"Yes, ma'am," I said.

She cleared her throat, rattling what sounded like a gallon of phlegm. "I'm sorry. I been hit pretty hard with the allergies this year. It's a lot of that ragweed and cedar in the air. Anyway," she said, "your grandma told me that you been sitting out here on the step all day long and wouldn't come in, so I asked her if it was okay if I shared a few things with you."

"What kinds of things?" I asked, sitting down on the last step, next to her legs.

"You been seeing me all your life, ain't you, girl?" she asked.

"I have," I said.

"Yeah, I know. I've seen you grow up. Do you think I'm mean?" she asked.

"No, ma'am," I fibbed, not knowing what she would do if I said yes.

"Yes, you do," she said. "The whole neighborhood do, 'cause it's mostly true."

"Yes, ma'am," I said.

"Thirteen. That was a bad age for me," she blurted out. "I wasn't nothing at all to look at, and I wasn't like you. I wasn't just plain. I was downright ugly, and fat, too. The kids teased me something terrible! They called me Frog Face and let me know every time I turned around that I didn't look as nice as them. I was too big, my eyes was too popped, and my chin was too droopy. 'Hey, Frog Face! You belong in a zoo,' they would say."

"I'm sorry, Miss Earlene," I said, understanding how cruel kids could sometimes be.

"They were nasty to me," she said. "So I was even nastier back. I felt like, if nasty was the game they were gonna play, I was gonna best them in it. I was downright evil to be around. None of the other girls would play with me, until Bertie came."

"Who was Bertie?" I asked.

"She was a girl my age whose family had come down from South Carolina. Her daddy was some kind of architect, but he couldn't get no work, so he came down here to look for some. Bertie was sweet, and I was sweet back to her. She was the kindest girl I ever did meet. You see, because she wasn't from around the neighborhood, she didn't know that she wasn't supposed to like me just because of the way I looked."

"That's good."

"It was," she said. "She would share her snack money with me and everything, and we would hang out after school playing volleyball on the playground and slurping snow cones. We did everything that we could together. I ain't never had a friend like her, not even since I been grown."

"I'll bet she thought so too," I said.

"She did," she said. "She loved me more than she loved chocolate syrup. She even called me her sister and asked her mother could I move in with them."

"Did you move in?"

"Naw," she said in a voice thick with melancholy. "I didn't get a chance to. Five months after she moved here, her daddy got called back to South Carolina for a big job."

"That wasn't fair," I said.

"I didn't think so either," she said. "It wasn't fair at all. She was my only friend in the world, and she was leaving me because her daddy got some little old job. I was swelled up with anger and unhappiness. I cried for a week straight and broke all kinds of stuff in the house, and it didn't make no difference, she was going."

"Just like Kambia."

"Just like her, and I had no intention of saying good-bye. See, I thought if I wasn't there to say it, she just wouldn't go. She said that she loved me, and I knew that she wouldn't take off without seeing me face-to-face, so on the day that she was supposed to go away, I stayed at home in my bed listening to seventy-eights on my record player. And she left. That's right. She took off. Her family left, moved back to South Carolina, and I didn't hear from her no more, 'cause she was sweet as cinnamon bread, but she wasn't all that good at reading and writing. After she left, I tried to play with the other kids again, but they still kept teasing me. It made me mad. I'm still mad. I'm mean to most everybody except my son, and your grandma is starting to grow on me. Deep down she's a gentle soul. She always treats Doo-witty with love and respect. I like that, that's why I asked her if I could share my story with you. That's all," she said. "It was just something that I thought I would share with you, girl. You take it to mean whatever you want."

She started struggling to get up. I tried to help, but she brushed my hand away and, groaning, did it herself. I opened the door for her, and she squeezed her big frame back inside. I studied what she said. I had heard stories like hers before, but it was different coming from her. Like she said, she was generally flat-out mean. It had to take a lot for her to share that story with me. Besides, if she looked like she did now way back then, she didn't have any friends. I knew what that was like. Until Kambia showed up, none of the other girls would even look my way. Mama gave me a party for my eleventh birthday. It wasn't a big party, just a few balloons, a cake, and some hot dogs. I was hoping that some of the girls in my class would come, but only a couple of the boys showed up. They came because they had heard through the neighborhood grapevine that Tia was my sister. I remembered how bad that felt, like I had been in school for years, but all the kids saw when they looked at my seat was air. I bet that was the way Frog felt until her friend came along. Kambia was like my own sister. I didn't want to lose her, but not saying good-bye to her wouldn't keep her from going.

I left the step and went to find her. I waited outside Kambia's room until Mama and Grandma said good-bye to her. They gave her a quilt that Grandma had made a long time ago. She called it the holding hands quilt. On it was kids of all colors standing in a circle in a grassy field holding hands underneath a sea of puffy white clouds. The quilt was at least fifteen years old, so it had been in our family since even before I was born. It made me feel good that they cared enough about Kambia to give it to her. I watched through the open door as her mother tucked it away in one of her suitcases. "It sho is nice of y'all, ain't it, Kambia?" she asked her. Nobody expected a reply.

After Mama and Grandma hugged Kambia good-bye, they did the same to Honeysuckle Peach, and all three of them left the room. I waited in the hallway until they were long gone from it, then walked into the room.

Kambia was standing at the window. She was dressed finer than I had ever seen her dressed before, in a midlength white eyelet dress with a full skirt and a huge bow in the back. Around her neck was an elegant string of white faux pearls, and her hair sported a mass of big, fluffy curls. She looked like she was going to a cotillion or something.

"You got another new dress," I said, walking over to her. "It's pretty. You look like you're ready to take a picture."

She walked closer to the window and pulled the curtains back.

"Hey, what's out there to see?" I asked, peeping out next to her. "Is there a squirrel or something out in the tree?"

She pulled the curtains back a little more.

I put my arm around her shoulder. "Mrs. Dreyfus says you're going," I said, fighting back the bad tears. "She says that you're going to go live in a place with a lot of other girls. I'll bet that'll be fun. I'll bet the other girls will be nice, just like the ones at the center, and I know you'll have your own room. You can even take Sophie Bear. Won't that be fun?"

She pressed her face to the frame.

"Are you sure there's nothing out there?" I asked. "I saw a possum in one of our trees last week. It was really fat. Grandma said that she thought it was gonna have some babies. I wish I could have seen 'em. I've never seen little baby possums before. Have you?"

She left the window and walked over to her bed and sat down. I went and sat beside her. I looked up at the canopy.

"I wonder if you'll have one of those?" I said, pointing to it. "It would be really cool if you did. It's neat. I wish my mom had enough money to buy me one. Your mom's real nice, isn't she?"

She picked her pillow up and held it to her stomach. I took a deep breath and blinked real hard to hold the bad tears back. They spilled out anyway, flowing down my face onto my yellow smiley-face T-shirt, leaving big, wet stains.

"Kambia, why won't you talk to me?" I cried. "You're my best friend and you're going away for a really long time. Why won't you say good-bye to me? It's not fair. I love you, and you won't even talk to me. I'm sorry that I didn't notice what was up with you, but I don't get it. Why can't you just say what's wrong. If you say what's wrong with you, I'll bet they'll let you stay. Mrs. Dreyfus says that you have to go away because you're all mixed up about your old and new life. Just tell them that you won't go to Jasmine's anymore, and I'll bet they won't make you go to any old hospital. I don't want you to go. I want you to stay here with me!"

"You're being selfish, baby," Grandma Augustine's voice came from the door. I turned around and looked at her.

"It's not fair, Grandma," I said. "She didn't do anything wrong, and now she has to go away."

"Baby, she's not going away because she did anything wrong," she said. "She's going away because she did something right."

"I don't understand what you mean by that, Grandma," I whined.

She limped over to the bed and squeezed in between me and Kambia. She took Kambia's hand in one of her hands and mine in the other. "She's going away because she needs to get better, and we all know that," she said, looking at Kambia. "We wouldn't have known it if she hadn't sent herself all those packages. So it may have been scary, but it was still a good thing, baby. She found a way to tell us that she needed some other kind of help. So she ain't going away because she did something bad, but because she did something good. You wouldn't want to see her in any pain, would you?"

I shook my head vigorously.

"And I know that she wouldn't want to see you hurt either," she said, squeezing Kambia's hand. "She loves you and you love her. Love ain't suppose to hurt, baby. It ain't suppose to tear you to pieces inside. If you love her, you show her that you do and let her go do what she needs to do. New Mexico ain't all that far away. It ain't the other side of the world. You can do it. She trusts you to do right by her."

Grandma used her cane to hoist herself up from the bed, and I reached out and grabbed Kambia. I hugged her tighter than I had ever hugged anybody, so tight that even I couldn't breathe. Then I let her go and got up too, but as I was leaving she reached out and caught my hand and stuck something in it. It was the photograph that I had seen the night we found her in the other house. I held it up to try and see it again, but my eyes were so cloudy with tears that I couldn't make it out.

I bent down and hugged her again. "Bye, Kambia. Please come back soon," I said. After that I ran crying from the room. I returned to the back-porch step and sat down again. I was destroyed. It felt like I was all burned up inside, reduced to ash, like I had felt when Gift was born, only worse. I thought up a journal entry, one that I would write days from now, when it didn't hurt so much to put down my feelings. *My soul is scorched like Grandma's sausage patties*, I would write. *Kambia is leaving for New Mexico today, but to me it might as well be Neptune.*

# Chapter 10

**A letter to my mother—somewhere in the U.S.A.**

Dear Mama,

Did you know that last week was my birthday? Grandma
Fatima gave me a satin pouch filled with fifteen decorated
combs. She said that there was one comb for each time that my
world had revolved around the Sun. I wore two of the combs to
school yesterday, along with a cashmere sweater and poodle
skirt that Grandma found tucked away in the attic. I won
second place in the Halloween costume contest. I lost to goofy
Neville Newton. He dressed up like a summer squash. From
head to toe he was all in yellow.

Yellow is still my favorite color, Mama—yellow like the petals
of the elegant black-eyed Susans that you painted on the wall
over my bed, yellow like the squeaky rubber duck you placed in
the tub one evening while I was taking a bath. Remember how I
played and played with it? I splashed warm suds all over your
strapless party dress—but you never got angry. You just
laughed and laughed, until it seemed like there was nothing in
the room but your laughter, and I wished that sound was
something solid that I could grasp in my tiny hands and place
in my treasure box for ever and ever. . . .

unfinished

*    *    *

I went to church with Grandma Augustine today. I didn't want to go, but Grandma Augustine said that it would do me good to get out of the house and stop thinking about Kambia. She said that I should be grateful that I hadn't heard any news since Kambia left, because even if it meant that she wasn't any better, it probably also meant that she wasn't any worse. "You got to get out of this house and do something besides write," she said. "Kambia's in the Lord's hands now. He'll make her good as new. He's a compassionate god. He ain't never meant for little children to suffer." I wasn't so sure about that. Kambia had already suffered, and I didn't see where he or anybody else had tried to stop it.

I went to church with her anyway, though, because I was bored, and because I wanted to get away from Gift. She's crying even more lately, waking up *and* going to bed fussy. She's driving most folks in the house a little crazy—even Grandma Augustine is getting a little out of whack lately because of her. She told Jada last week when Gift was squalling that she had thought about going to the store and getting herself a pack of cigarettes to calm her nerves. "I thought about getting me a pack of Winstons," she said, "and I ain't smoked a cigarette in forty years. That baby needs her daddy. I wish I had him right here, I would give *him* something to cry about."

Grandma Augustine's church is a modest one. There are only about a hundred people who come on a regular basis, but they are serious Bible folks, and the service was filled with enough prayers, hymns, and testimonies to make even the worst sinner want to go take a dunk in the river. I wished that I felt the way that the other people did. I wasn't moved by most of what I saw and heard, especially the sermon. The minister strutted up and down the sanctuary in his black robe, saying how we should always make the right choices. He said that when we are confronted with a couple of choices, we should make sure that we take our time and think about them so that we choose the right one. "Don't step into a dark alley unless you think about what might be in it," he said. "There might be a mugger hiding there in the dark."

It was a message I had heard more times than my favorite dance album, usually during homeroom when my teacher gave us the monthly never-take-drugs speech, because, she said, you have no idea what you might actually be taking. A seemingly harmless little feel-good pill might end up being something that will make you feel very bad. It didn't seem worth the two hours I spent sitting next to Grandma on the bare wooden bench listening to an old man in a row behind me shout amens. It was a totally pointless sermon, and as soon as I walked out of the church, I wiped it out of my mind, like shaking clean an Etch A Sketch, but later that day I came to realize that there might have been a lot of sense in it.

After I exited the church, I waited patiently for Grandma Augustine by a small concrete birdbath with an angel on top of it. She was in an after-service meeting with her Monday prayer group. They were making plans to hold a prayer session on the steps of Diamond's because they had heard that he had ordered some videos for grown-ups that were going to be on display in the devil-water aisle. The ladies said that it was bad enough that he was already ruining the community with spirits, now he was going to cast all of the poor men in the community straight into the pit of fire by letting them get hold of them nasty picture shows.

Grandma's meeting went on longer than I expected. My stomach started to rumble. I had had only a slice of raisin toast and a glass of grape juice for breakfast, and my body was telling me that it was major time for me to get something else. I ran into the deacon's Sunday-school room, where Grandma was having her meeting, and told her that I was going to head on home and make me a biscuit and ham sandwich from biscuits that Mama had made before we left the house. She told me to be careful on my way back and not to eat all the food up before she got there. I said okay and ran out of the door. I raced down the steps of the church and ran into Lemm. He was standing on the sidewalk. He was dressed good, better than I had seen him dress in a long time. He had a starched, short-sleeved navy shirt and matching navy slacks, and a pair of brushed suede loafers, but the rest of him didn't look so good. His eyes weren't red, but they were sickly looking, sallow with dull pupils, and his skin was dry and ashy, like he hadn't had a drink of water since Texas freed itself from Mexico. But he didn't look drunk, and he was smiling—and not the fake smile that he used to hide himself from the rest of the world. This was the real thing. I couldn't wait to see what he wanted.

"Hey, what's up?" I asked, walking up to him. He grabbed me and gave me a kiss on the cheek that made those fireflies that I usually felt when he held my hand go wild, like they had just drunk a lot of caffeine. They were lightening me up everywhere. I wriggled loose from him and hoped that my cheeks weren't as scarlet as the dress I had on.

"I have good news. News that you couldn't even imagine," he said in his perfect proper voice. "It is the best news in the world, Shayla."

"What is it?" I asked excitedly.

He reached into his pocket, pulled out a piece of paper, and handed it to me. "Look at it, Shayla," he said. I took a glance. It had an address on it for some place in Florida, and there was a phone number scribbled underneath it. I shrugged my shoulders.

"What's the big deal?" I said, handing the paper back to him. "Who do you know in Florida?"

"I'm not completely sure," he said. "I'm not all the way certain, but I'm pretty sure that this is the address for my mother."

"What?"

"I think it's the address for my mother," he repeated. "I think that Florida is the place where she lives."

I took the paper from him again, looked at it, and handed it back. "How?" I said. "Where did you get it?"

"It was an accident. My father's sister sent him a letter the other day. When I was walking through the living room, I saw him reading it. My father's a mouth reader. He reads everything aloud to himself. He always has. I was out of it," he said, "but I distinctly heard the name Lillian, my mother's name. I couldn't make out anything else—the words were there, but I just wasn't alert enough to hear them, so I got alert. I didn't drink anything but tea the rest of the night, and when my father went to bed, I sneaked back into the living room and opened the drawer underneath the end table, where he keeps his correspondence. I read the letter. In it my father's sister said that she was down in Florida for a black sorority gathering, and she saw a woman that looked just like my mother working at the front desk of a classy hotel when she went to pick up her traveling companion. She said that the woman was my mother's twin and that she would give her favorite fur coat if it wasn't her, but that my father would have to be the one to find out if it was. She said that she and her friend passed back by the front desk, but the woman was gone and there was a chatty brunette in her place. She gave the brunette a little cash, and the girl gave her some information on the woman. 'I know that you aren't looking to take her back after the things that she did,' she wrote my father. 'But you may want to at least know where she's at, and that she's all right.' My mother, Shayla," Lemm said. "Shayla, I know where my mom is at. Isn't that great?"

"It sure is!" I said aloud, but in my head I thought something else. Lemm was excited because he thought he knew where his mother was. The same mother that had poured wine into his baby bottle and left him home alone while she went partying, the one that had made him so torn up that he pushed his own little sisters in front of a truck—that was the mother that he wanted to get in touch with. It seemed almost as cracked as Kambia going back to her old house. It was like wanting to go swimming with an alligator. "It's fantastic, Lemm," I said. "Have you called her yet?"

He shook his head, and doubt gathered on his brow. "No, I haven't tried to contact her yet. I'm just getting used to knowing that she might be somewhere that I could reach her. I didn't think she would ever turn up again after my father threw her out. I'm not sure if I even know what to say to her, but you know what?"

"What?" I said.

"I'm staying sober. I'm going to make sure that whenever I get around to talking to her, I can do it with a clear head. I want her to know that what she did left no permanent marks on me."

*But it did, Lemm,* I said to myself, but outside I said, "That's good."

"I thought you would say that, Shayla," he said. "That's why I came looking for you. I thought we should go to the park and celebrate. We can get some hot dogs or something like we did the last time and have an afternoon picnic. Maybe we can go back to that park. It was a pleasant place to be before I got into my little trouble. What do you think? I haven't seen you in a long time."

I thought it was an awful idea, considering what happened to him the last time we were at that park, but he wasn't lying. I hadn't seen him since Kambia left. Since she went to the hospital, I had mostly spent my days sitting in my room when Gift wasn't in it, writing in my blue notebook. I had written four whole stories since Kambia left. I had wanted to see Lemm, but I knew that he would be drunk, and needy, and I couldn't even do anything for myself, so I stayed away. A couple of times he had called me. I picked up the phone and pretended to be Tia. I knew that he couldn't pick out my voice from hers when he was full of Wild Turkey. It wasn't a cool thing to do, and it certainly wasn't a Shayla thing, but I couldn't help it. I was wrapped in grief from head to toe like a mummy. I made a decision that Lemm's problem would have to wait. It wasn't the first time that I had chosen Kambia over Lemm, but it was the first time that I had done it when she wasn't even around. I guess I did owe him a picnic for that. I think I owed myself one too.

"Okay," I said. "But I don't think we should go back to that park."

"Why?" he said. "I've dealt with the consequences of my actions. It's a wonderful park. Let's go have some fun."

"No, Lemm. I think we should go somewhere else. Let's just get some food and go to the park down the street. You got any money? I only have two dollars that my grandma gave me for putting flea powder on Nat King Cole. She shoulda gave me more. Nat King Cole doesn't like being powdered at all. He bites and scratches."

"I would too," he said, laughing. He reached into his pocket and pulled out a handful of crumpled-up dollars. "I got four," he said. "If we put them together, we'll have enough."

"Cool," I said. "We can stop at that hamburger stand next to the park and get some burgers."

"That is perfectly all right with me," he said.

We started down the street, with Lemm babbling on about his mother and what he would say to her when he finally did call her. The way he talked about her, you would have thought that he was going to make a call to a movie star. She had made him into a drunk, but he still wanted her. How could he not blame her for being kicked out of school, spending every night with his head over a toilet, and not having any friends? Did she get credit for every time that he woke up all hung over and didn't remember the things that he said to people the night before? She was the reason that he saw his dead sisters each time he passed a nursery-school yard. How could he talk about her like she was a queen? He really adored her, that was the only answer that I could come up with. He could overlook every fault that she had, just like Tia did with Doo-witty, and Jada did when she married Mr. Anderson Fox. It was that love that made him say that he was going to stop drinking. He said it was because he wanted to be sober enough to call her when he got ready. He didn't want her to know how screwed up he was. He was washing her blame away, like washing chalk drawings from a sidewalk. It would be her homecoming present. She would come home to a perfectly normal kid.

It was nice of him to do it, and as I watched him nearly floating down the sidewalk, giddy with just the thought of seeing her again, it occurred to me that that was the thing that gave me the fireflies whenever he touched my hand—his genuine sweetness. It was a sweetness that lay deep inside him, underneath his dead sisters, alcoholic mother, and grieving dad. That's what I felt whenever he held my hand. I felt what Frog said she had felt coming from her friend, Bertie. I was wrong the morning that we all walked home from Diamond's. I had told myself that he was good for Kambia because he was the only guy that she had ever met who was good to her without wanting anything in return, but the truth is, it was me who I was talking about. I didn't know all of Kambia's past, but I knew mine. There had been a few nice guys in my life, but all of them had wanted something. They were all Mama's friends, and they were nice to me because they wanted to get close to her, even Mr. Anderson Fox. He was nice to me all last year while he was playing Mama. Lemm was the first guy who ever liked me just because I was me. What did he want from me? Friendship was all that I could think of. It made me feel good knowing that. It was like thinking you had eaten the last cherry Jolly Rancher out of the bag and then opening it up and finding two more.

As we approached the hamburger stand, which was only a small whitewashed shack with a grill, counter, and sink inside, we ran into four kids going the same way. I recognized one of them right away. It was my ex-homegirl Maya, the D-Girl that I had gotten into a tussle with on Kambia's school grounds. She had shaved her shoulder-length hair down to a short buzz cut that rose barely an inch off of her head. If it hadn't been for the curvy figure, Daisy Duke shorts, and halter top, I probably wouldn't have known who she was.

"What's up, Lemm?" she asked, stopping next to us with her gang, which included Sheila, the pint-size D-Girl who had shown up after the fight was all over. She was wearing another butt shower, a clinging minidress with no straps. Grandma Augustine would die if she ever spotted me or Tia in anything like it.

"I suppose not a lot," Lemm said to Maya.

She broke out in a girlie giggle. "You so crazy, Lemm. You always talking proper. I swear you the only boy I know that uses all them funny words. Ain't he funny, Sheila?" she asked.

"Yeah, he is. He oughta be a news announcer or something with that kinda talk. Hey, where you learn to talk like that?" she asked, batting her eyes at Lemm. Lemm just smiled.

"Hey, Lemm," she said. "I ain't seen you around in a while. Maya told me you got into some kinda trouble with Five-O. What was that all about?"

Lemm hesitated for a moment. "Nothing at all. You know how policemen are with black males. They thought I was somebody else."

"Somebody who?" Maya asked.

"He doesn't know," I answered. "They were looking for another young dude like him."

"Aw, man, they do that crap all the time," said a bald-headed, buff boy in a muscle shirt and nylon wind shorts and sporting a wide silver chain around his thick neck. "They always going after a brother for something. You can't even walk the street no more without some cop pulling you over."

"That's right, straight up, homey," said another short, built-up brother with a shaved head and a fly black-and-red Nike short set. "They stopped me last week one night when I was walking to my place after work. It was just a little before midnight, and they asked me did I know that the neighborhood had a curfew for teenagers. I told them that I didn't know nothing about that and showed them my ID card from the rubber plant that I work at sometimes. I thought they would go on after that, man, but they followed me in they ride for another four blocks. I hate that crap, man. I know how you feel, little brother." Lemm nodded.

"Hey, these are some of my friends, Lemm," Maya said. "You already know my best homegirl, Sheila—and that's David and Breed," she said, pointing to the boys. "I told you about them before."

"Yes, I think I remember," Lemm said. "Who is Breed?"

"That's me, homey," said the boy with the Nike suit. "They call me that 'cause I like to breed dogs. I got three pits and a Doberman, and when I get my next paycheck, I'm gonna get me one of them rottweiler pups."

"Oh," Lemm said. "I hear those are kind of expensive."

"They can be, and I don't make nothing but enough to go hungry on, but I got my ways. I know how to hook myself up. Don't I, Sheila?" he asked, pinching her hip. She laughed and pretended to slap his hand.

"Leave my best friend alone," Maya said.

"I thought Debbie was your best friend," I said.

"What do you care? Shayla, don't make me go off on you," Maya said.

"I don't care. I just can't see anything coming between you and Debbie," I said.

"Well, stuff gets between folks. You would know that if you came up outta that library sometimes, Shayla," Maya said. "Anyway, Debbie, that cow, borrowed my dress and didn't want to give it back. When I asked her for it, she said that it was hers, and she know that I don't play that. I'm through with her sorry behind. She makes me sick. By the way, how's your little kooky friend? I heard that she went completely off or something, and they had to lock her up."

"She's not kooky!" I yelled. "And don't you worry about how she is."

"I worry about whatever I wanna worry about!" Maya yelled back. "Don't think 'cause we used to be girlfriends, you can tell me what to do. That was a long time ago."

"Not long enough!" I said.

"All right, all right, ladies," David said. "We ain't got to have all that drama, do we? Let's just all try to be cool with each other.

"Hey, man, what y'all gonna do after you get your burgers?" he asked Lemm. "Y'all wanna hang with us? We gonna go down to Joe Lima Bean's place and listen to some tunes and stuff. Y'all can come if you want. It'll be a lot cooler than hanging out in this boring old park. Is that okay with you, Miss Thing?"

"Fine," Maya said. "Lemm's cool. I already told you that. I wanted him to come and hang with us at the party that time, but he told me that he was feeling sick. And I guess Shayla's all right as long as she ain't hanging out with that loony friend." I rolled my eyes at her.

"So, what you say, little man? You and your lady want to go or not?" David asked.

"I'm not his lady," I blurted out. "And we were going to the park."

"Aw, Shayla," Maya said. "I just said that it was cool. What's wrong with you? You afraid to chill out with some sane kids? I'm not gonna beg. I don't have to. Everybody wants to hang out with me and my girl Sheila. We don't have to beg nobody to be our friend. Shoot, I was just trying to be nice to your butt. You can stay here and be a big ole nothing as usual, or you can come with us. It's up to you, girlfriend." She looked at her friends. "I don't know about y'all, but I'm fixin' to go get me something to eat."

"Maya, don't be like that," David said. She ignored him and sashayed off to the stand with Sheila right after her, but the boys stayed behind.

"Well, y'all gonna hang or what?" they asked. "What's the answer?"

The answer was no. I said it flat out, and not in my head like I sometimes did. I explained to Lemm I didn't need to go anywhere with Maya and Sheila, and that neither one of us knew Breed and David. I told him that I had heard Breed's and David's names around some, and that from what I knew, they were all that, but they still weren't the kind of kids that we should be chilling with.

Lemm said that he understood how I felt, but he thought that I was big enough to work out my problems with Maya. He told me that he had talked to her and Sheila a few times when he met them on the streets, and that except for the way that Maya spoke about Kambia, they seemed like fairly decent young ladies. He said that he didn't know about Breed and David, but he liked to make up his own mind about people. "Shayla, I really don't think that it would hurt us to spend a couple of hours with Maya and her friends," he told me. "It might just help me get my mind off my sisters for a while. Come on, Shayla. I know you love Kambia, but what are you going to do if she doesn't come back? Are you just going to hang out with me? I think you're going to be pretty lonely if you do that. Don't you think it would be better if we each had more than one friend?" It was a good argument, a sober one. I went along with him, though I didn't even want to think about Kambia not coming back. I walked to the stand and got a burger with no mustard and a grape soda. I sipped on the soda while Lemm and Maya's friends got their food. After that we all headed off to Joe Lima Bean's place, except for Breed, who said that he would join us there after he ran an errand.

Joe Lima Bean's place was where all the It kids and their popular pals hung out. It was a huge house down by the old Negro Union tracks. The house was once owned by Joe Rupert, whom everybody called Joe Lima Bean. He was a large, jovial man with a disposition as sweet as an angel food cake and with a gift for history trivia.

Nobody remembers where Joe actually came from. He just showed up one day in the Bottom, right around the time that the Aldriches were trying to start the old Negro Union Railroad. He built the house and told everybody that he was going to make a living growing lima beans. He borrowed a loan from the bank and planted twelve acres of them in the area behind his house because he'd heard that they were going to be bigger than sweet-potato pie.

He said that folks in the Deep South were eating them like popcorn. They were deep-frying them, sprinkling them on their salads like croutons, stuffing baked potatoes with them, toasting them like pumpkin seeds for snacks, even making them into desserts, like lima bean pudding. He said that people could do absolutely anything with lima beans, and he wanted to make sure that they had enough beans to do them.

Apparently they had more than enough. Except for an occasional pot, sometimes during the year nobody in the neighborhood was that hyped up on using the beans, especially not to make pudding with. Joe Lima Bean soon found himself stuck with a lot of beans, and when he tried to sell his crop to some of the small-time farmers who lived on the outskirts of town, all they could offer him were more beans. He ended up not being able to repay his loan. He was broke and helpless. He stood in one of his back windows and watched every day until the bean stalks dried up, and the bank came and foreclosed on his house. They tossed him out and put the house up for sale, thinking that it would bring in big bucks when the railroad was put in, but the railroad never came, so the bank just rented the house out, and kept renting it out until it got too run-down to live in.

I walked by myself to Joe Lima Bean's place, while Lemm and David strolled ahead of me, rapping about basketball and football scores, and Maya and her gal pal hung behind me, exchanging fingernail polishing tips and talking about how many miniskirts they had. Maya had almost ten, if you counted the one that she still had to lose five pounds to fit into, and Sheila had seven, if you counted the one that she had borrowed from her skinny cousin, the one that wanted more than anything to be an actress on a daytime soap.

As I listened to the girls' conversation I realized how ridiculous and shallow they really were. They were like those giant balls of bubble gum that you got out of the candy machines—attractive on the outside, but if you broke them open, you would see that there was nothing at all in the center. They were completely snared in a net of pointlessness. I was glad that I wasn't one of them, and even gladder that I preferred spending my playtime with Kambia.

As soon as I stepped foot on the walkway of Joe Lima Bean's place, dread surrounded me like a fog. It enveloped me, making it nearly impossible for me to follow Lemm and David up to the concrete porch. It was an intense apprehension, almost as if I thought one of Grandma Augustine's demons might be hiding somewhere beyond the decaying boards and sagging roof. I took a deep breath and willed it away. It lifted as I watched Lemm and David slide back some of the loose boards from the window and crawl in. I climbed in after them, telling myself that the feeling was nothing more than my just being uncomfortable around a strange group of kids.

It was much more pleasant inside the house than I expected it to be. Most of it was just bare walls and empty space, but the It kids had fixed the living room up. There was a shabby but comfy-looking matching velour love seat and sofa pushed up against one of the walls, complemented by a square smoked-glass coffee table that had only a small chip on one of the sides. Two painted crates were turned upside down to make a pair of nifty end tables, and there was even an old laminated wooden plant stand that held a clay vase of silk carnations. The place looked like home, made livable by the discarded furniture that the kids had hauled up from the banks of the bayou before they floated away.

Maya and her friends flopped down on the sofa, while Lemm and I took the love seat. We all opened up our brown paper bags and began chowing down on our greasy burgers and salty fries. As we were eating, David reached under the sofa and pulled out a massive boom box.

"Some of them band majorettes from Matthew Henderson Junior High brought this here and left it for everybody to listen to," he said, pushing in a round button on top. The room filled with a Diana Ross and the Supremes tune. "Man, I love this kinda music. Folks really knew how to jam back then. My mom got all the CDs from the old Motown era. She always puts them on when she doing housework. I caught her trying to dance to them once. Man, she was hopping around like she had a sticker or something stuck in her foot, and when I asked her if she wanted me to take it out, she got all pissed at me and told me to go to my room. Moms are crazy like that, ain't they, little man?" he asked Lemm. "My mom is always doing some stupid stuff. What about yours?"

Lemm stopped nibbling on his burger. "I don't know," he said. "I have not seen my mother in a while."

"I heard she ran off," Maya said, playing with the plastic straw in her Coke. "I heard that she just took off one day and left your daddy. That's sorry, I never heard of a mother doing something as sorry as that."

"It happens," Lemm said. "She's not the first woman to do it. And unless all the females on this earth suddenly take off for Pluto, she definitely will not be the last. Can we change the subject? There really isn't very much I would like to tell you about my mother."

"Boy, you sho do like that uptown talk," David said, shaking his head. "I'll bet you can get anything you want talking proper like that. I wish I knew how to talk like that."

"Sometimes," Lemm said, "but most of the time I get things that I don't want, just like everybody else."

"I hear ya, homey," David said. "Man, that's just the way crap goes. Don't nobody ever get what they want. If I could, I would have me all kinds of Mercedeses and live in a big-ass house. But shoot, man, that's just talk. It takes a miracle for a brother to live large these days."

"A sister, too," Sheila said. "We can't get nothing either."

The conversation went on like that for an hour, while David and the girls told us all the things that they would have if they ever got any real cash. It was no surprise at all to me that Sheila and Maya both said that they would have a whole new wardrobe, their own hairstylist, and all the makeup that they could fit onto their bathroom counter. They wouldn't be just D-Girls, they would be the bomb, the girls that all the other girls in the world wanted to be like. "Forget Janet and Mariah Carey," they said. "Nobody would think those tired chicks were sexy when they got a good look at us."

"That's right," David said. "Y'all girls would have it going on!"

Maybe Sheila and Maya would have it going on, but I knew one thing—I didn't care. In fact, I didn't care about anything either they or David had to say. It was funny. A while back I would have given up everything but my blue notebook to have Maya as a friend again, to be sitting across from her and her crew listening to their wants and desires, but now all I wanted to do was go. I wanted to grab Lemm and go back to the park, where we had decided to go in the first place. We could sit under the oak trees and talk about his mother or Kambia. I didn't want to know that Maya's favorite eye shadow was English Pea Green or that Sheila liked to polish her toes with a polish called Ice Blue Glitter, and neither did Lemm. The conversation was seriously boring him. His head was leaned against the back of the love seat, and he looked like he was about to conk out. I pushed his thigh with my hand to try and get him to see that I was also ready to go, but before I could get his attention, we heard a rap on the window. David got up to see who was making it. He walked over to the window and slid the boards back. Breed stuck his head in between the slats.

"Say, homey, gimme a hand," he said. "I got some big-ass bags here. Help me get 'em in."

"All right, man, what you got?" David asked.

David leaned his torso out of the window and a second later came back in with two large paper grocery bags in his hands. He lugged them over to the coffee table and set them down, then he returned to the window, emerged with two more bags, and did the same with them. After that he went back once more and slid the boards apart as wide as he could for Breed to climb in. Breed flung his muscular legs over the window and hopped down, smacking the wooden floor with his expensive leather sneakers. He placed his arm around David's shoulder, and the two of them returned to the sofa and sat down.

"Man, them bags was heavy as hell," Breed said. "I had to pay some little dude at the store to help me pack 'em down here, but it was worth it. I ain't gonna fuss, 'cause you know how a brother got to have his stuff."

"What stuff is that?" Maya asked, peeking into one of the bags. "You got some chips and candy, or some soda?"

"Just hold up, girl, don't be so dang nosy," Breed said, gently pushing her head out of the way. "Cain't you give a brother a chance to answer a question?"

"Well, answer it, then," Maya said. "Ain't nobody got all day to be playing around with you."

"Okay, okay, just get up off me, girl. I'll show what I got," Breed said, reaching for one of the bags. The minute he did, that dread fog that I thought I had left on the front porch floated underneath the padlocked front door and settled over the table. My entire body tensed up so rigid that I felt like someone had just opened my head and poured concrete into my body. I watched through the haze as Breed pulled out of the bag a sweaty six-pack with a brown label that read, VICK'S MALT LIQUOR.

"See, girl? All right, dang," Breed said to Maya. "Now, don't ask me no more questions."

"Where did you get that from?" Maya asked. Then, without waiting for an answer, she reached over and snatched a can from the plastic ring, wrestled it loose, and pulled the tab off. I glanced over at Lemm. He was now sitting straight up in his seat, his eyes fixated on the remaining five cans of the liquor, as if they were hundred-dollar bills.

"Hey, little dude, you want one?" Breed asked.

"Yeah, have one, Lemm," Maya said, turning the can up to her mouth. "It's real good."

"It ought to be," Breed said. "It cost me enough. I had to pay some older dudes to go in there and get it for me, then I had to pay that other dude to help me bring it back. Man, I'm broke. I didn't even have enough cash to get me something to eat. Anybody got any cash?"

"Naw," everybody said at once.

"Damn," Breed said. "Y'all sho is some poor-ass Negroes. I gotta start hanging out with folks that have some money."

"Me, too. You let me know if you find some," Sheila said, reaching for one of the liquors. "I'm tired of chillin' with people that ain't got no cash too." Lemm watched as she picked up the can, and followed her hand with his eyes.

"Say, homey, get you one," Breed said to Lemm. "I got five more packs where that one came from. Go on and grab one, little brother."

"No, that's okay," Lemm said. "I don't think it's a good idea. I'm already too full from the soda."

Breed looked at Lemm and laughed. He grabbed one of the cans, pulled back the top, and guzzled down a swig, spilling some of the liquid out the sides of his full lips and onto his T-shirt. "Damn," he said. "Not my Nike shirt. I just got this thing."

"Where'd you get it?" David asked.

"Aw, man—hell, I don't know," Breed said. "Me and my cousin Moses drove some dudes down to a store out south last Saturday night after it closed. Them dudes went in there and came out with all kinds of stuff. I got some sneaks, too. I just ain't had a chance to wear them yet."

"Really, man?" David said.

"Straight up, homey. I ain't even took 'em out of the box. Hey, little dude," he said to Lemm. "Man, don't nobody get full on no soda. Get you one of them cans. You ain't no punk, are you?"

Lemm cleared his throat. "Of course not," he said. "I just don't want one right now."

"Aw, man, this boy is sweet. He don't want his mommy to smell no juice on his breath. I thought you said the little brother was down," Breed said, slapping Maya's thigh. "I thought you said that you heard the only thing he wouldn't drink was pee. What's up with your man? Why he acting like a little punk?"

"Be quiet, Breed," Maya laughed.

"Hey, Lemm, if you don't want that, maybe you want some of this," Breed said, pulling a plastic dime bag of weed out of one of the sacks. He held it up. "Anybody got any papers?"

"Naw," everybody shouted.

"Damn," Breed said. "I can't depend on y'all for nothing."

"Not if it cost money, homey," David said, grabbing a can from the ring. He pointed it at Lemm. "Hey, Lemm. Why you drinking that soda? I thought you was a player, been brought down by the law and everything. You need to be drinking a man's drink. That fizzy junk is for girls."

"Excuse me," Maya said, slapping him playfully on the side of the cheek. He slapped her back.

"Ouch," she said, bringing her hand up to her cheek, "you hit too hard."

"I'm sorry, baby," he said, pulling her to him for a hug.

"You should be. I told you that sometimes you play too much," she said, batting her eyes at him. He leaned over and kissed her, and it wasn't the kind of kiss that Lemm had given me. It was all lips and tongue, lingering, the kind of kisses that Tia gave Doo-witty.

"Hey, y'all cut that out in front of company," Sheila said, tugging Maya by the back of her shirt. "Ain't y'all got no home training?"

"Hell, naw," Maya said, giggling.

"Aw, man, forget them," Breed said to Lemm. "Hey, little man, you gonna be down or what? I thought you was cool. Y'all want to join the party or what? You ain't gonna punk out like a little gal, are you? Are you?"

"No," Lemm said. "I'm not going to 'punk out,' as you put it. I just don't want a drink. Like I said before. I'm full."

"Aw, man, come on," Breed said, snapping a can loose and holding it out to Lemm. "You know you want it. Go on and get it while it's still cold."

"Go on and take it, Lemm," David said.

Lemm's hand didn't move toward the can, but I knew that he wanted it to. He kept both of them resting at his sides on the love seat, but I could see them moving slightly up and down, clenching and unclenching the fabric.

"Let's go, Lemm," I said, grabbing his wrist. "I didn't tell my grandma where I was going, and she's gonna be mad when she finds out that I took off in my church dress. Let's go home."

"Aw, man, look at that," Breed said. "You gonna let your little lady tell you what to do. Hey, little sister," he said, holding the can out to me. "You want one? Sheila and Maya got one. Don't you want a drink too?"

I shook my head. "No, thanks. I have to go."

"You do," he said, winking at the other kids. They broke into laughter. "You gotta go right now. Or your grandma is gonna give you a spanking?"

"That's not what I said. She just likes to know where I'm at."

"Well, you can tell her that you was having a drink with the big boys." The other kids laughed at that, too, big belly laughs that made me wish I was back home in my room. Breed shoved the drink at me again. "Here," he said in a severe tone. "One of y'all is gonna drink up, 'cause I know I didn't buy all this junk just to drink it myself. Your boyfriend is punking out. You can have his drink. Go on and drink up, little sister. One of y'all about to seriously piss me off."

Maya cut her eyes at Breed and looked back at me. "Breed always got to have some drama, Shayla," she said. "Look, homegirl. Do yourself a favor and drink it. You don't want to see him act no fool."

I didn't know what Maya meant by act a fool, but I had a pretty good idea. In the hood "act a fool" could mean plenty of things, and none of them were good. I reached out and took the drink from him. I yanked off the top, and the smell of the alcohol nearly made me gag. I swallowed hard and brought it up to my mouth, but Lemm snatched it from me before my lips got wet. He took a long drink and set it on the table.

"You satisfied, homey?" he said, going into his street accent.

"Yeah, I'm satisfied," Breed said with a sly smile.

"Lemm, let's go," I said. "I gotta go home."

"Why don't you go then, girl," Sheila said. "You ain't doing nothing but ruining things for everybody."

"That's right. Go home, Shayla," Lemm said.

"What?" I said, turning back to him. He didn't even look my way. He just picked up the can again, took a long swig, and set it back down.

"I said go home, girlfriend," he said, wiping his lips. "Aw, man, that's some good stuff."

"The best. Ain't none better in the whole store. You heard him, little sister," Breed said to me. "If you ain't joining the party, you might as well go on and get out."

"I'm not going anywhere."

"Go home, Shayla," Lemm repeated.

"No, come on, Lemm, you know you shouldn't be doing that," I told him. "Let's go. You told me that you weren't going to do that anymore."

"I guess I lied. Why you always got to be nagging me about stuff? Don't be such a baby. Go on and get out."

I couldn't believe what he was saying. He had had only a couple of gulps, so I knew he wasn't drunk. There was no way I could believe that he meant what he said. "Come on, Lemm," I said again. "My grandma is gonna be upset."

"Not as upset as me. I'm sorry, but you working my last nerves, little sister," Breed said, jumping up from his place on the sofa and roughly dragging my arm. He dragged me over to the window and pushed me against it. "It's time for you to get on up outta here, girl!" he shouted angrily. I was so scared that I couldn't even open my mouth. I slid the boards aside and climbed out.

"See ya never," Breed said, and slid the boards back into place.

I walked down the steps rubbing my arm where he had grabbed me. I wanted to go back in and ask Lemm what was going on with him, but fear blocked my way. I was too scared. I left the yard and started down the tracks, baffled about what I could have done to make Breed so mad, and once again wondering why I hadn't insisted on going to the park. I hadn't gone far when I heard Lemm's voice behind me.

"Hey, Shayla! Wait up, please. Hey, wait up!"

I stopped and waited for him to catch up. He ran up to me, out of breath, and caught me by the arms. "Are you okay?" he asked, pushing my sleeve up to get a good look at where Breed had grabbed me. Four red finger marks were beginning to emerge on my arm.

"I'm fine," I said. "It's no big deal. My mom had a boyfriend that used to push me and Tia around some when he got upset, until Grandma Augustine ran him off one night with her cast-iron skillet. My arm's just a little red. I'll get over it. Let's just go home."

"Are you sure you're okay?" he asked. "I didn't expect him to do anything like that. I would have said something if I knew he was going to do that."

"You did say something. You told me to get out."

"I didn't mean it. I'm sorry, I just wanted him to quit giving you trouble about the drink. You forgive me, don't you?" he asked with a kitten-cute look on his face.

I grinned. "Like I said, it was nothing. Let's just go, Lemm. My grandma *really* is gonna freak out when she can't find me."

I started up the tracks again, but I noticed that he wasn't following, so I stopped and walked back. "What's up?" I asked.

"I'm not going."

"What?"

"I'm not going, Shayla. I'm gonna go back and hang for a little while."

"With them? You're gonna go back and hang with them?"

"Just for a while. I'll come over to your place in a little bit."

"Why?"

"I can't explain it. It's a guy thing, Shayla. You wouldn't understand it. It's just something that I have to do."

"Yeah, drink," I said.

"Come on, Shayla. I'll come by later."

"You won't make it over to my place, Lemm," I said. "You'll be too drunk. You're always drunk. All you ever do is get drunk. I thought you wanted to be clean so that you could call your mom. You won't be if you go back and hang with Maya and her friends. Please don't go back."

"It's okay, Shayla," he said in a confident voice. "Trust me, regardless of what Mrs. Dreyfus or anyone else thinks, I can handle my own affairs. I'll just finish the one drink that I started. It would be rude if I didn't. Besides, I don't want Maya and Sheila to think that I'm angry with them because their friend has a short temper."

"You're going back because of Maya?" I asked, hurt.

"Not exactly. I just have to go back. I'll be okay. I'll just finish my one drink and leave. I'll see you later, Miss Shayla," he said, laughing. He leaned over and kissed me again quickly, and this time it wasn't on the cheek. He kissed me on the lips, then he ran back to Joe Lima Bean's house. I touched my lips for a second and ran off too.

Guilt was stuck to my lips like lip gloss when I walked back to the house. I could feel it spread all over me from one corner of my mouth to the other, telling everyone that Lemm's lips had been on mine. I was really worried about him, but I was even more worried about Mama and Grandma seeing his kiss on my face. I decided that it was best to get his kiss off before anyone else saw it. I crept into the house as quiet as a silent prayer and went to the bathroom. I closed the door and turned on the faucet over the sink. I watched in a panic as the warm water flowed into the basin. When it was almost to the brim, I snatched my washcloth off a wooden rack next to the sink and started washing my lips with some of Tia's fish-shaped strawberry-scented soap. I rubbed the soap between my palms until I got a handful of rich pink lather, smoothed it over my mouth, and scrubbed again and again. I washed my mouth until my lips stung and I didn't feel like I was wearing the kiss anymore.

After that I replaced the towel and went into my room, content that the only thing left on my lips was very clean skin. But as I walked over to my drawer to get my blue notebook and write down how I was feeling, I noticed that I could still feel a sensation. It was slight, like the feel of your finger when you press it to your lips to tell someone to be quiet. That's when I noticed that what I was feeling wasn't outside my mouth, it was in it. Lemm's kiss had gone deeper than just where our lips met. It was still there even after I had tried to destroy it with soap. What did it mean? It meant that Mama and Grandma were going to be very unhappy with me. I hurried to the dresser, got my notebook and my pencil, and opened to a new page. *Shame is flowing through my veins like blood,* I scribbled, *and when Mama and Grandma get through with me, I'm going to need a transfusion.*

I finished writing my entry and went to the kitchen. If Mama and Grandma were going to go off on me, I wanted it done and over, like the shot in my arm that I got whenever Mama took me to the doctor. I couldn't explain why Lemm had kissed me, or why I had let him, or why for some real strange reason I could still feel it lingering on my lips. It had happened so fast that I didn't even have a chance to tell him that I wasn't sure that he should be doing it. "The whole thing took place in just about a second," I would tell them. "The only person who could stop something from happening that fast is Grandma Augustine's God."

When I got to the kitchen, I discovered to my delight that I was actually the only one in my house. There was a piece of loose-leaf notebook paper pinned to the refrigerator to tell me where everyone was. The note was in Jada's handwriting, and I didn't have to see her name signed underneath to know that she had written it. I knew because she always drew little circles over her *i*'s.

The note said that Tia was with Doo-witty at some art show. Grandma was worried about me, but she was at her own house now, and she wanted me to give her a call when I got my behind in. Mama had been called into work unexpectedly because one of the store stockers had something called shingles, and Jada and Gift had gone looking for Mr. Anderson Fox. *Somebody told me that they saw him down at that new pool hall over on Theodora Street,* Jada's handwriting said. *He was shooting games with some hot, flashy chick with one of them painted-on dresses. I'm going to go down there and ask him if he's lost his mind. I'm going to tell him that he knows that I never meant for him to walk away from his daughter.*

I called Grandma and let her know that I was okay. She started to fuss at me a bit, but I told her that I had just walked in the door and had to go to the bathroom really bad. I hung the phone up and went back to my room and crashed on the bed. I was nearly giddy with relief. It would probably be a long time until anyone came home; by then the only thing that would be on my lips was my lips. The kiss would be completely gone. I wouldn't have to feel guilty or confused about it anymore. It would be like when I lost my first baby tooth, just something that happened that I couldn't control.

I stayed in bed until it was late. I was tired. I hadn't slept hardly any at night since Kambia left and Gift took to squalling. I was spending more and more time awake, staring out of the window, praying for Kambia to come back.

I drifted off into a deep sleep, and when I did, the dream returned. It had changed again. There were now only three dancing ladies in the tree, and when I got close to it, instead of climbing straight up, I waved at them and they waved back. They stopped dancing and beckoned for me to come and join them, so I started up the trunk as usual. Only this time the ladies didn't disappear into the clouds. Something else happened. The trunk of the tree got longer. It kept growing and growing as I climbed, the bark on it cracking loudly with each stretch, so I hopped down from the tree as quickly as I could before the ground was too far for me to get back to without injuring myself. I shook my fist at the ladies. "Hey, Shayla, wake up!" I heard one of the ladies shout down to me.

"Hey, wake up, wake up!" Everything faded away. My eyes popped open and I found myself staring at Lemm. I sat up, wiping my eyes.

"Hey, you showed up," I said, cleaning out the gunk. When they were clear, I noticed that he wasn't alone. Maya was with him, and she looked awful. Her face looked like she had just spent the night in a haunted house, and she was wet. Her whole body was glistening with sweat. The top of her halter was drenched, and large beads of sweat were gathered all over her forehead, but that wasn't the thing that made my eyes bug. She had her hand over one of her forearms, holding it tightly. She was bleeding. You could see it dripping from between her fingers.

"Oh, my God. What happened to you?!" I asked, running over to her.

"I think I got shot, Shayla!" she cried hysterically, starting to sob like tears were worth gold. "I got shot, but the bullet, it just scraped me or something, I think! There's a lot of blood, though. I think I'm going to throw up!"

"Got shot where? Lemm, what is she talking about?" I asked, looking back at him. That's when I noticed that he didn't look any better than she did. "What's going on, Lemm? What is Maya talking about?"

"Something stupid, Shayla," he said with a slight slur. "She's talking about something really dumb."

"You're drunk again, Lemm. What are you talking about?"

"I'm going to throw up or something," Maya repeated. "I really feel like hurling." I ran over to the corner of my room, got our plastic wastebasket, and brought it back to her. She bent over it and gagged a few times but nothing came out, so she just sat down in the middle of the floor, still holding her arm. The sight of it was making me kind of queasy too. I snatched my pillow slip off of my pillow and handed it to her. She wrapped it around her arm, but the blood started seeping through, so I gave her my other pillow slip to wrap around it too.

"What happened?" I asked.

"Something real bad, Shayla!" Maya answered.

"What did you guys do?" I thought about that day at the park when Lemm got arrested. "You didn't go back to that store again, Lemm, did you?"

"No, Shayla, I promise I didn't," Lemm said.

"Then what happened?"

"That fool Breed," Maya said, starting to sob again. "He got us all into a bunch of trouble."

"What kind of trouble? What the heck is wrong with you guys?"

"We went to buy a dog," Maya said. "Breed said that he would get us some more to drink if we went with him to buy this dog, so we all said yeah, then he borrowed his cousin Moses' car to do it. We were all going to go and buy a rottweiler from some brother that he knew over on Cole Street. The guy was some kin to the guy who runs the butcher counter at Diamond's store."

"King Red," I said.

"Yeah, he was a big ole fat red guy just like him, except he was a lot younger. When we got there, he had something like five puppies running around the yard," she said. "There was dog stuff everywhere. You had to be real careful where you stepped. Sheila wasn't. She got poop all over her new sandals. Breed, he picked out the one that he wanted, and then all he had to do was pay the guy. 'This is the one I want, homey,' Breed said to him. 'How much you gonna charge a brother to get him a dog? How much I got to pay?'"

"How could he pay? With what?" I asked. "I thought he said earlier that he didn't have any cash."

"He didn't," Maya said. "He borrowed three or four twenties from his cousin."

"I don't remember that," Lemm said, rubbing his temples.

"That's 'cause you was drunk," Maya yelled. "You was so drunk you could barely even get out of the car.

"Breed picked out the one that he wanted. It was cute. He had a yellow spot on his head. The dude told Breed that he wanted three hundred for it, and Breed lied and told him that was what he had. He had cut some paper the same size as his cousin's twenties and wrapped the bills around it. He gave the money to the red dude, and the red dude handed him the dog, then we were all just supposed to run as fast as we could and get in the car, but before we could, the dude opened up the bills and found out that Breed was trying to rip him off."

"Oh, Lord," I said.

"'Hey, man, what you think you trying to pull?' he asked Breed. 'You better give me my damn dog or I'm gonna kick your ass!' That's when Breed pulled out a gun."

"Breed had a gun?"

"We didn't know, Shayla," she said, talking quickly, almost at a ramble. "I swear we didn't. I know I didn't. He's crazy and all, but I didn't know he was packing. He just pulled a gun out and pointed it at the dude, but the other dude, he had a gun too. He came out with it and started shooting at everybody. We all tried to get out of the way. We ran in all kinds of directions. I ran as far as I could, but I musta got hit anyway. I just heard the bullet brush past me. Then I looked down and saw the blood. Breed was still shooting. He didn't even know that any of us got hit. Oh, God. The dude's lady was on the porch with his little boy! Breed smoked him! He didn't look like he could be no more than three, and Breed smoked him. I saw it all. His mama was trying to get him out of the way. She had him by the arm, and all of a sudden there was blood all over him. It was everywhere. His mama started screaming for somebody to call an ambulance. It was horrible! I got real scared. I tried to get to the car, but David got in it and he didn't even wait for us. He drove off. I couldn't even see Sheila," she said. "I didn't know where she was at, but Lemm was right next to me, so I just grabbed him and took off. At first we went back to Joe Lima Bean's, but we thought they was gonna come looking for us there, so we came here and your door was open."

"I left it unlocked for Tia."

"What are we gonna do?!" Maya asked, shaking her head wildly. "I don't wanna go to jail! My mom is gonna kill me. Shayla, you know how my mom is. She don't even like none of my friends anyway. What am I gonna do?"

"I don't know," I said. "A little boy got shot? Breed shot somebody's little boy? Why would he do that! Why would he do something so mean?"

"He's crazy!" she shrieked. "He's crazy, and we gonna go to jail for him. What are we gonna do?"

"Breed shot somebody's little boy?" I repeated. I felt like hurling too. How could somebody do something like that? We lived in the hood. Things happened. I had heard about folks getting shot before. Sometimes guys got into it over drugs or chicks, and bullets started flying, but I had never heard of anybody shooting a baby before. You played with babies and gave them bottles, you didn't shoot them. I couldn't picture anyone doing that to Gift.

"Lemm," I said. "How could you end up in something like this? I don't get it."

"I don't even remember going over there, Shayla," he said.

"We're gonna go to jail, I just know it!" Maya cried. "We're gonna go to prison."

"Why would you go to jail? You guys didn't do anything wrong. You were just there. It was Breed that did the shooting. Lemm, tell her that you guys won't go to jail," I said, trying to convince myself that what I was saying was true.

"You don't understand, Shayla," Maya answered for him again. "Breed, he been in all kinds of trouble before. He's gonna tell them that we was with him. I know he is. He's gonna tell them that it was our idea too. My mom is gonna kill me! My mom is gonna get me good. What are we gonna do? What are we gonna do?" She grabbed her knees and started rocking back and forth, hugging herself. "What are we gonna do, Lemm?"

"I don't know," Lemm said, placing his face in his hands.

My head started to swim. I sat down on the bed to try and sort things out. Lemm had really screwed up bad this time, all because he wanted something to drink. How could I have believed him when he told me that he would just finish his beer and come over? Now he and Maya and the rest of them were in big trouble.

I had to do something. He had asked me to lie for him before, and I had been so angry with him that I let him down. I would do it this time. I felt horrible about the little boy, but I couldn't let Lemm go to jail for killing him. He was already suffering enough because of what he done to his sisters. I couldn't let him suffer any more. When the policemen asked, I would tell them that he and Maya had been with me. Then he could go home and start not drinking again like he promised.

"I'll tell them that y'all was here with me," I said. "I'll tell them that you guys were here playing a game or something, or we went to the library. I can do that."

"Sure you can," Maya immediately said. "You can tell them that me and Lemm was here the whole time." She stopped sobbing and stood up, wiping her face. "They'll believe you. You never get into trouble." She walked over and hugged me, throwing her arms around me like I was *still* her best friend. I squirmed out of her grip, but it didn't phase her.

"Thanks, Shayla. Lemm said that you would know what to do. I knew he was right. You were always good at figuring things out," she said, retying the pillow slips around her forearm tightly after noticing a small dab of blood forming on top. "I'm gonna go home and get one of my sister's long-sleeved shirts and put it on. It'll hide anything. I guess I'll see you around, girlfriend."

"I guess you will," I said.

She walked over to Lemm and ran her hand over his head. "Hey, Lemm, you can take your head out of your hands," she said.

"Shayla is gonna fix things up for us. We ain't gonna be in no trouble."

Lemm just moaned.

She sashayed over to the doorway. "Man, I'm glad you were here, Shayla," she said. "I didn't know what I was gonna do. That dude Breed is a fool. I shoulda known better than to be hanging out with that brother. I didn't know he was gonna do no stupid junk like that. I can't believe he smoked that kid just like that. Man, I gotta start hanging out with somebody else. I'm gonna call my homegirl Debbie when I get home. She ain't gonna believe what I just went through. Check y'all later," she said.

The front door creaked and slammed. "Hey, is anybody home?" Jada asked. Maya and I both turned into statues, but Lemm didn't even seem to notice. He didn't look up or anything.

"Hey, anybody home?" Jada repeated.

"Don't tell on me, please, Shayla," Maya whispered. "Just be cool like you said."

"I told you I would, Maya," my mouth assured her, but that little voice inside me started saying, *You are making a big mistake.*

Jada walked to the back of the house, calling out to see if anyone was home. "Hey, y'all home?" she asked. I heard her open the refrigerator like she always did and place Gift's bottle in it. A little bit later she walked into the room carrying Gift. They were mirror images of each other, in hot pink overalls, cloth sneakers, and shoe-string braids that were parted into two ponytails on either side of their heads. I would have laughed at them if I weren't still feeling ill.

"Hey, Shayla," Jada said, hurrying into the room. "Did you get my note? I was down at the pool hall, but I figured it was time to come back. The police were down there. They were asking folks all kinds of weird questions. They said something about some children running around with guns. They said that they tried to rip some-body off for a cat or something, and when the guy didn't go along with it, they shot his little boy. Can you believe that? Can you imag-ine somebody shooting at child over a cat? Anyway, I knew that there wasn't anyone home but you, so I came back to make sure that you were okay. Are you all right?" she asked, but her eyes fell on Lemm.

"Hey, Lemm, I haven't seen you in a while. What's wrong with you? You have a headache?" she asked. She spotted Maya standing near the door. "Who is this, Shayla? Did you make a new friend?"

"Her name's—," I started to say, but she didn't wait for me to answer the question.

"I'm Jada," she said, shifting Gift on her shoulder and sticking out her hand to Maya.

Maya tried to cover her arm with her hand, but she wasn't quick enough.

"Hey, what happened to your arm?" Jada asked, noticing the bloody pillow slips.

"Nothing," Maya said calmly. "I ran into something and cut myself."

"Into what? Let me see," she said, reaching for Maya. "You might need to go to the doctor. What did you run into, a rusty nail?"

"Yeah," Maya said. "It was one sticking out from the side of y'all's house. We was playing a game and I ran into it. It's okay. My mom will look at it when she gets home. She works in a hospital. She knows what to do."

"Are you sure?" Jada asked. "Where was the nail sticking out, anyway? I better get a hammer and turn it down or pull it out."

"I don't remember where it was. I have to go. I better get home and let my mom put something on it." She headed for the door again. "Remember what you said you would do, Shayla," she said. "I'll check you later."

She hurried out of the room and I heard the screen door slam. Jada walked over and placed Gift on the bed. She immediately started to squall. Jada turned her on her stomach. "Come on, baby, don't start crying again. You've been bawling all day. Everything is going to be just fine." She pushed the bed against the wall. "You wanna sleep for a little?" she asked, rubbing Gift's back gently. Gift stretched her tiny legs and feet and closed her eyes. "That's mama's good girl. You just go on and get some sleep."

Jada turned the spread over Gift's back and walked over to me. "This is the first time she's been quiet today," she said. "She fussed all morning and afternoon." She looked over at Lemm, who was still sitting with his face in his hands, and back at me. She scrunched her brows up, and suspicion gathered on her face.

"Shayla, what's going on here?" she asked, placing her hands on her hips. "Something isn't right here. What have y'all been up to?"

I shrugged my shoulders. "Nothing," I said.

She walked over to Lemm and stood over him. Her hand flew up to her nose. "Whew! Whew! Lemm, have you been drinking? Look at me, little boy, when I'm asking you a question," she said in a tone that sounded so much like Mama that it blew me away. Lemm took his head out of his hands and looked at her. You could tell that he had been seriously crying. His eyes were almost swollen shut with puffiness, and his nose looked like Rudolph's.

"What's up with you, boy?" Jada asked.

"He doesn't feel well," I said quickly.

"No, I don't imagine he does. If I was as drunk as he was, I wouldn't feel too good either. Shayla, I'm gonna ask you again," she said. "What's going on here?"

"I told you, he doesn't feel well, that's all."

"I'm sure he doesn't," she repeated. "But that's not all that's going on here. What have y'all been up to?"

"Nothing, we haven't been doing anything, I swear," I said in a nervous voice. I took a deep breath and tried to calm myself before I lost it big time. I hadn't counted on Jada showing up. She was young, but in a way she still was my stepmother, and she was obviously pretty good at playing the part. It was like trying to lie to Mama or Grandma Augustine.

"Well, Shayla, what's the skinny? Would you like to tell me or your mother what's going on? I'll go and call her right now if you want me to, but I thought you would tell me the truth. I thought we were friends. Look, Shayla," she said quietly, "I'm not trying to get into your business, but I know your mother didn't give you permission to have any boys in her house when she wasn't here, especially not any drunk boys. Just tell me the truth, and I won't say anything to your mama or your grandma. Come on, Shayla, just give me the facts."

I went over and sat down on the bed next to Gift and folded my arms across my chest in a classic Tia move, but I felt bad the whole time I was doing it, because regardless of what I felt for Lemm, I really did want to tell her. I didn't want there to be anything bad between us, and I was also very tired. I liked the way it felt when Lemm held my hand. I liked the niceness that he passed on to me. I think I even liked the kiss that I could still feel on my lips, but I didn't like the drinking, the dead sisters, or the fact that once again there was something going on with the law. I was thirteen. I just wanted to read books, listen to hip-hop CDs, write stories, and have a body like my sister Tia's. That was all I wanted, that and my best friend, Kambia. I cared for Lemm a lot, but with him everything was so confusing and complex, like the hard puzzles in the back of Kambia's activity books.

"Well?" Jada said. "Have you been drinking too, Shayla? Is that why you don't want to answer my question? Please don't make me have to call your mother and tell her that. Just tell me what's up."

I responded only with silence.

"Shayla?" Jada said.

A loud knock sounded from the front door, a pounding, as if someone were desperate to get in. We looked toward the bedroom door, but it was the window that really caught our attention. A light was flashing in it, alternating red and white.

"Anybody home? It's the police," a male voice yelled through the screen door.

"Oh, my goodness," Jada said, glancing from Lemm to me. "What did y'all do?"

I didn't answer, but this time it wasn't deliberately. I was too scared to say anything. The pounding came from the door again. This time harder, more insistent.

"Anybody home?" a male voice called out again. It was followed by the creak of the screen door. "It's open," the voice said.

Jada hurried to the door. "What is it, Officers?" we heard her ask a second later in a really nervous voice.

"Can we come in, ma'am?" a female officer's voice asked.

"Oh, of course," Jada said. The screen door creaked again. Lemm took his head out of his hands and sat up straight.

"What can I do for you, Officers?" Jada asked.

"We're looking for a couple of teenagers," the female officer's voice said. "We're looking for a little boy and a little girl, about twelve or thirteen. Somebody told us that they might be here."

"There's a boy and a girl here," Jada said. "My stepdaughter and her little friend."

"We need to talk to them, ma'am," the male voice said.

"About what?" Jada asked. "Look, this isn't even my house, and my stepdaughter's mother isn't even home."

"It doesn't matter," the male policeman said. "There's been a shooting. We need to talk to them."

"That thing that happened with the little boy, the one that got shot?" Jada asked. "Is that what y'all are here about? Oh, my Lord! Oh, my Lord!"

"Where are they?" the female cop asked.

"Shayla is in here, but I know that she won't know what you're talking about," Jada said. "She's a good girl. She never gets into any trouble."

I closed my eyes and said one of Grandma's prayers. Reality was sinking in. To pull Lemm off of the tracks, I was going to have to get in front of the train too. I was terrified, really terrified. I had thought that it would be easy to get Lemm out of trouble, but it had sunk in that this wasn't like the first time. The police were looking for two teens who had helped Breed shoot a kid. It wasn't the same as getting in trouble over stealing a couple of wine coolers. I should have known that. I thought about Mrs. Dreyfus. Even though Lemm didn't want her in his business, I should have called her. She would have known what to do. It was too late now. Everything was too late.

I really did feel like throwing up. I opened my eyes. The two police officers were in the room. I had been wrong. They were both women. One looked like a cover girl—Barbie-doll figure, sexy hazel eyes, perfect lips, good cheekbones, and bouncy blond hair that looked like it belonged in a shampoo commercial. The other one was kind of guy looking, straight up and down, with GI Joe shoulders, a square jaw, and a boyish haircut. I assumed that it was her that had the deep male voice, but I was wrong about that, too. She walked over to the bed where I was sitting. "What is your name, young lady?" she asked in the female voice.

"I'm Shayla," I said, standing up. Lemm stumbled up too.

"Have you been here all evening?" she asked.

"Yes, ma'am," I squeaked in a high-pitched voice that sounded like I had swallowed a bird.

"What about you, son?" the blond cop asked Lemm in the deep male voice. She walked over to him. "Whew, you've been drinking."

"No. No, ma'am," Lemm lied.

"Yes, you have," she said. "What's your name, son?"

"Lemm."

"Lemm, were you and Shayla over on Cole Street this afternoon?" she asked. "There was an incident over there with some teenagers about your age. One of them looked a lot like you."

Lemm waved his hand. "Nooo. No, ma'am. Shayla and I have been here all afternoon."

"Is that right?" the blond cop asked.

"Yeah, ma'am," Lemm said.

"Is that right, Shayla?" the GI Joe cop asked me.

I nodded.

"Answer the question."

"That's right," I squeaked.

"Who else was here?"

"Nobody," I said, completely forgetting my promise to Maya. "It was just me and Lemm. We were watching TV."

She looked around the room. "I don't see any TV," she said.

"We . . . we were watching in my mom . . . mom's room," I stuttered.

"You know what," she said in a familiar tone, "I don't believe that you were watching TV at all. You weren't watching any TV, were you? Come on, tell me the truth."

"We were," I mumbled weakly.

"No, I don't think you were. It doesn't matter anyway. I can smell alcohol on your friend's breath, and you're both minors." Then she asked Jada, "Where's her mother at?"

"Why?" Jada responded.

"They're both coming with us," she said. "We got a report that there were three boys and two girls involved in the shooting. Your stepdaughter's friend fits the description that we've been given of one of the boys. I'm not sure about her, but there are members of the victim's family who saw what happened. We're going to take her down with us too so that they can get a look at her."

"Look at her for what?" Jada said. "She just told you that she was here all afternoon."

"Were you with her?" the GI Joe cop asked.

"No, I had something to do. But I know better than this. This child was not involved in a shooting. She wouldn't do anything like that. Tell her that you wouldn't be involved in something like that, Shayla," she said. "Oh, goodness! I better go call her mother."

"You do that. In the meantime, we're just going to take her for a ride with us. You call her mother and tell her that she went with us. My name is Sergeant Lisa Bowry, and you can also write down my badge number," she said, turning so that Jada could see the silver badge on her shoulder. "Come over here, young lady," she said to me.

I started walking toward her, my feet moving like they were buried in three-hundred-pound concrete blocks.

"Turn around," she said.

"Don't," Lemm spoke up, looking at her. "Shayla didn't do anything; I did. I made a mistake, a really stupid one, and I just showed up here to get her to help me out. That's all. It was me and another girl, Maya. She left just before you came."

"He's right," Jada said. "I just got so flustered that I forgot that. He's right. There was another girl here about their age. She was bleeding. She said that she hurt her arm."

"Which arm?" Sergeant Bowry asked.

"The right one, I think," Jada said. "She said that she ran into a nail on the porch."

Sergeant Bowry took a large black walkie-talkie from her belt and pushed a button on it. "John, did one of the girl suspects get shot?" she asked. "I know you already have one in custody. What about the other one?"

"Confirm on that," a scratchy voice came through. "One of the girls is believed to have been wounded in her arm. A few of the witnesses said that they thought they saw blood on her arm."

"Thanks," Sergeant Bowry said, and replaced the walkie-talkie. "Okay, go over and take a seat, young lady," she said to me. She pointed to Lemm. "You, young man, you tell me what's going on here."

"I made a mistake," Lemm repeated. "It wasn't Shayla. I'm the one that went with Breed."

"He's too inebriated," the blond cop said. "We can sort it out at the station." She pulled Lemm over to her and started searching his pockets. "Do you have any weapons or needles or anything like that on you, young man?"

Lemm shook his head. "Just this," he said, pulling out the paper with his mother's name and address on it.

"What's this?" the police officer asked, taking the paper from him and unfolding it.

"It's Shayla's," Lemm said. "I just want to make sure that it doesn't get lost or thrown away."

The blond police officer took the paper and looked it over. "It's some girl's phone number or something in Florida," she said.

"It's my pen pal," I said quickly. "My teacher at school told us that we had to write someone we didn't know a letter."

"What school?" Sergeant Bowry asked. "You go to summer school?"

"Yes, ma'am," I said. "It's a program for bright kids. I flunk my class if I don't write the letter."

"Here, you better come get it, then," the blond cop said. "And you two better not be lying to me. This goes against my better judgment. You'll both be in big trouble if I catch you fibbing."

I got up from the bed and took the paper from her. I walked back by Lemm.

"What are you doing, Lemm?" I whispered, feeling some courage slip into me. "You don't have to tell them. I can keep backing you up."

"What did you say to him?" the blond cop asked me.

"Nothing, ma'am," I said.

"Put your hands against that wall over there," she said to Lemm. She motioned my way. "You, little girl, you go take a seat again."

Lemm leaned against my bedroom wall, and the policewoman searched him just like the policeman had done in the park. Only Lemm didn't struggle or protest at all this time. He didn't call out for me to help him or anything.

"He's clean," the blond policewoman said. She turned Lemm around and cuffed him, and I wished that I could run over and take the cuffs off.

"He's not telling the truth," I blurted out. "He was here the whole afternoon. We watched TV."

"No," Lemm said. "I was with Breed. I don't remember all of it, but I know that I was there, and she wasn't."

"That's not true," I said. "You just don't remember because you were drinking. Tell them, Lemm."

"Shayla, I was drinking when my sisters died too," he said, "but I know I was there. I'm sorry. I don't want you lying for me. You're going to end up in jail. I don't want that. Just let me do what I have to do, what I need to do."

"That's good advice," Sergeant Bowry said. "You sit quietly over there and shut your mouth, little girl, before I take you down too. I don't usually say this to people, but I got a little nephew that I look after about his age," she said to Jada. "This young man could be in a lot of trouble. We'll call after we can get some of this mess figured out, but you should give his parents a ring and let them know what's going on. If he were my child, I'd want to be at the station as soon as he got there."

"I'll call them," Jada said. "I'm sure his number is around here somewhere."

"Good," Sergeant Bowry said. She tossed her head in my direction. "I'd call her mom too, if I were you. She needs to know what she's been up to."

"Don't worry, I will," Jada said, giving me a look of disappointment that made me wish that my head were turned to the wall like Gift's. I felt the bad tears welling up in me again, but I wouldn't cry. I wasn't going to. Tia was the crier in the family. I was tired of shedding tears. I was tired of it all.

The blond policewoman pulled Lemm by his arm. "Let's go, young man," she said. "You can tell us about the other girl when you get in the car."

"Yes, ma'am," Lemm said. "I'll try and tell you what I remember."

"I'm sorry," the sergeant said to Jada. "This type of thing is never easy to do or to see."

"I'm sure it isn't," Jada said, walking the group to the doorway.

Sergeant Bowry turned back to me. "You consider yourself lucky this time, little girl. Lying to the police can get you into serious trouble." She walked out of the room, followed by Lemm and the blond cop. Jada finished escorting the trio out of the house. I heard her go into Mama's room and call Lemm's father using the number that was scratched down next to the phone in what we all called the family little black book. I heard her tell Lemm's father what was going on, and that he needed to contact the police right away. She hung the phone up and returned to the room without placing another call to Mama. She came over and sat down next to me on the bed.

"I'm not going to tell your mother," she said. "That's your responsibility. I don't even know what I'd say. How long has Lemm been drinking?"

"A long time," I said. "Since he was really little. His mom started him on it."

"Oh, my goodness, sometimes I think the world is pure mad. You know that you seriously did the wrong thing, right?"

"I guess so."

"Do you know why? You're a fixer. You try to make everything all right. I figured that out from watching you with your little friend Kambia, how you tried to make sure that things turned out okay for her. That's what fixers do. I know," she said. "I'm one myself. I saw your dad and I saw that something was missing in him. That's the main reason why I had Gift. I knew that deep down your dad wanted to be a good father, so I thought I would give him that chance. You know women don't have to keep babies that they don't want these days, but I'm a fixer. I have to try and fix everything I touch. So I gave your father a child that he wasn't ready for and didn't even deserve. He was good with her for a little while, so I was foolish enough to think that it meant he would be good with her forever. That's what fixers do. We fool ourselves and others into believing that we can solve problems. I think that deep down that's why your mother and grandma grew to like me so much. They thought that I could do something to help Mr. Anderson Fox. They thought I could make him into the kind of person that they wanted him to be. I wish I could have, but I didn't know how, and you don't know how to fix Lemm. He's way beyond what you can do for him. Sometimes just being a friend is the best thing that you can do. I wish I had done that with Anderson. There's a price to pay for being a fixer. When something isn't fixed right, you're still stuck with it. You always get your heart broken."

I looked over at Gift. "Do you think she'll be a fixer too?" I asked.

"She just might. She got some of my blood and some of your blood in her, but I'm gonna try to teach her better. I'm gonna teach her that if she wants to change a life, she should start with her own. Don't you think that makes sense?"

"I don't know. I guess so," I said.

I sat and talked with Jada for nearly two hours. We talked about Lemm's drinking and Mr. Anderson Fox and her. I realized for the first time that if I had kept Mr. Anderson Fox's letter to go over again when I wasn't worried about Kambia, I probably could have figured out that Gift could never be a replacement for me. Regardless of how many sappy letters Mr. Anderson Fox wrote, she was a child that he'd never wanted, just like me. I was wrong for not liking her. When you broke it down, we were both on the same ship when it came to Mr. Anderson Fox. The next time Jada and Gift went down to the pool hall to look for him, maybe I would go with them. Maybe I would wait by one of the tables with Gift, and when he turned up, I would stick her in his arms and tell him that if he wanted to tell her about the time he came to hear one of my stories, he could tell her himself. It wasn't my job to fix what he had done to his daughter. I couldn't even fix what he had done to me. I uncrumpled the paper that Lemm had given me with his mom's address and phone number. Tomorrow morning, after I ate break-fast, I would go into Mama's bedroom and call the number. It was true what Jada said. I couldn't fix Lemm, and I should never have tried to. It wasn't my job to solve the problem that his mother had created. She was going to have to solve it herself.

# Chapter 11

$A$ bad cold visited Doo-witty this morning, so Tia and I spent some sister time together. We went to an art exhibit at a small gallery in River Oaks. We walked through room after room of a lavishly renovated old house, until we came to a section called *Modern-Day African-American Art*. The section was filled with beautiful paintings done with watercolors, and one of them caught our eyes. It was called simply *The Children*. It was a painting of two lovely, chubby-cheeked little girls in summer playsuits and thong sandals chasing an ice-cream truck down a busy urban street with dollar bills waving in their small hands. Tia said that the picture reminded her of me and Kambia, if we were about six years younger. I looked at the painting too. I didn't see me and Kambia at all. I saw Lemm's sisters and how they might have looked if they had grown up. Tia asked me how I could even be sure of what the girls would look like. I told her that I couldn't be, but that I had seen at least one female member of Lemm's family, and I thought that the girls might have grown up to look something like her.

I had seen one of the women in Lemm's family the day that he, Maya, and Sheila appeared in court. It was a small hearing, with Lemm and the girls, their parents, the lawyers on both sides, me and Grandma Augustine, a very attractive Asian woman with lovely ivory skin who was typing something on a funny-looking machine, and a plump, matronly judge who reminded me of Weezy from *The Jeffersons*. The only people that weren't present were the parents of the little boy who had gotten shot, because Lemm's lawyer said that they had declined to come. They said that they had already attended Breed and David's trial and that was enough. They couldn't take sitting in a courtroom and hearing again about what had happened to their child.

Maya and Sheila had the same lawyer, and he didn't say much. He just told the court that the girls were very young and hadn't done anything like that before. He said that the real culprits that day were the two seventeen-year-olds, Nicholas More, a.k.a. Breed, and David Norris. "The girls were just innocents. They were well brought up young ladies who happened to find themselves in an incredibly bad situation that day." The judge agreed with him, and she gave Maya and Sheila only five years of juvenile detention. She said that anything less and the neighborhood would be outraged. "The death of a child tends to unite even the most crime-ridden of communities," she said to Maya and Sheila's lawyer. "There isn't a person in this neighborhood who doesn't think that your girls should pay for their part in this crime. But they are only thirteen, and they don't have any priors. I'm going to let them slide some with a lighter sentence, one that will set well with me *and* with the community."

Choosing a sentence that would set well with the community was a good idea. When the neighborhood found out about the shooting, they were stunned and outraged, which is why the kids' hearings took place so quickly. They couldn't believe that a kid in our neighborhood would kill a baby while trying to do something as ridiculous as steal a dog. They were completely put out by the news. Mr. Anger ran from street to street, leaving his calling card at even the most mild-tempered folks' houses. Led by King Red, members of the community huddled together at Diamond's one afternoon, demanded swift justice, and discussed what they thought the court should do. Some people thought that the kids should be locked up until they needed canes and Poli-Grip to make it through the world and until they had spent the best of their years looking out through prison bars, while others were even more severe in their choice of punishment. They thought that the kids ought to receive the same sentence as the young boy who died. They wanted them to be taken out and shot. "One life for another," Bobby from Bobby's Rib Shack said, passing out free hot samples of his new lamb and pork sausage. "Let them use that tired excuse that they were only teenagers when they meet their maker. I'm sick of the way young folks rob and murder, then get away with it 'cause they ain't hit that magic eighteen. A crime is a crime, and that's what I tell my own children. Let them be judged like any man should be judged—by what he says and what he does."

"That's right. There ain't no innocence in evil," Old Man Courtland from Courtland Vaughn's Autos said, wagging his greasy finger at the rest of us to make a point. "I've been ripped off three times in the past two months by some of these teenage thugs. Last time they took everything out of my cash drawer. One life for another is what I say too."

"Ain't no way them kids should get off," Skinny Sandra from the Superfine Beauty Shop said, tacking a price list of her fancy hairstyles to a corkboard hanging on a nearby wall. "Some young girl come in my shop last week and got her hair cornrowed for three hours. When I asked her to pay, she said she didn't like the direction that her braids were braided in. I told her that she was the one who chose the hairstyle. It pissed her off so bad she pushed my cabinet full of hair products down and run off. Glass and shampoo was everywhere. I slipped down and cut my leg all up. That one life thing sounds okay to me."

It didn't to me. I agreed that it was a horrible crime. A little boy by the name of Marion Macomb was never going to grow up, play with Tonka trucks, shoot hoops, or have other kids tease him about his first name. When I thought about it, the unfairness and sadness of it made me wish that I had never agreed to go with Lemm that day. I don't think that he would have gone by himself. I made the wrong decision. Maybe if I had said no, Maya and Sheila would have changed their mind too. They liked Lemm. They probably would have followed him to the park and had a picnic with us. More than likely, they would still have been ugly to me, but at least the little boy would still be alive.

"Straighten up, girls, and stay out of trouble," the judge told Maya and Sheila, "otherwise you'll find yourselves right back in a court."

"Yes, ma'am," they both replied.

The judge pointed to Lemm's lawyer, a tall, handsome Hispanic brother with wavy black hair, thin eyebrows, and a sharp-looking charcoal suit that made him look like some ritzy rich folks' attorney instead of a state guy that was simply assigned to Lemm's case. "What do you have to say for your client?" the judge asked him, browsing through a brown folder that was filled with crinkled pastel papers.

Lemm's lawyer got up and said mostly the same thing about Lemm that the girls' lawyer had said about them. He said that Lemm wasn't the one who had shot the little boy, that he was still very young, and that he hadn't really known what was going on because he had had too much to drink. But you could tell that although the judge was listening, she wasn't buying the "very young" story. When the lawyer got through speaking, the judge said that she had read Lemm's file and was extremely annoyed that his defense was going to be that he had been drunk. She pointed out how many deadly and dangerous things teens do because of alcohol. She said she could see from his file that he had already had at least four other incidents with the law, and she had been informed just that morning that there was a recent incident in which he was arrested and turned loose because he had snowed his officers into believing he hadn't committed any offenses before. "Perhaps a hearing to see whether or not he should be tried as an adult is more in order," she pondered. "He's a young man with a lot of problems and a history of walking away from them. I just can't believe that they will get any better if I turn him loose too early on the street. He needs to know that alcohol or no alcohol, there are consequences for one's actions. What do you have to say for yourself, young man?" she asked Lemm.

Lemm told the judge that he was sorry for what he had done. He told her that, just like the girls, he wasn't thinking clearly that day. "I know that I used poor judgment," he said. "I am not making excuses for my actions. I am simply saying that I wasn't able to prevent myself from doing them. I am sorry that a child died. I didn't know that Nicholas had a gun. I only went there because he promised to get some more beer. I take full responsibility for being there. I know what it means to take a life. I would never go anywhere with someone if I knew there was even the smallest chance that they would hurt someone else. If I had been sober enough to know what was going on that day, I would have been somewhere else."

The judge told Lemm that she believed him, but no matter how eloquently he put it, he had made a huge error being there, and she could see by his file that he had made errors like it before. She stressed again that it didn't really matter that those errors were made while he was under the influence of alcohol. She said that perhaps it was time for Lemm to start living a more error-free life, and even though he was still quite young, she thought that perhaps a year or two in a real prison facility would shake him up, because she could see that his few brief stays in a juvenile detention unit hadn't really done him much good. She was about to render her decision, when Lemm's lawyer's assistant, a perky sister with soft brown eyes and really full hips, walked into the courtroom. She was followed by a slim, fortyish woman wearing a colorful tie-dyed pantsuit and thick, bushy dreadlocks that looked like she had been growing them out for years. She looked a lot like Lemm. She had the same chestnut eyes and slight overbite, but where Lemm's skin was a warm caramel brown, hers was dark chocolate.

"Excuse me, Your Honor," the assistant said. "This woman has firsthand information that might affect your final decision on my client's punishment. Would Your Honor please allow her to be heard by the court?"

"What kind of information?" the judge asked, looking over at the woman curiously.

"I could explain it, Your Honor, but I think that it's best that you hear it from her yourself," the assistant said. "Will you please allow her to speak?"

"I will allow it," the judge said. "But please be aware that I have already received quite a few written testimonies on Mr. Turley's behalf from his former teachers and a professional counselor by the name of Mrs. Dreyfus. They haven't swayed my choice of punishment for him, so I am earnestly doubting that this woman will."

The woman introduced herself as Lemm's aunt Elizabeth on his mother's side, better known as Aunt Liza, the sister that Lemm said his mother used to go out partying with. She said that she used to stay right down the street from them in the town that they came from. "We practically lived with each other," she said. "I was over to their house all the time, and I can tell you that this child ain't hardly responsible for his troubles."

"How is that?" the judge asked. "Please explain what you mean to the court."

"Don't worry, I will, Your Honor," Aunt Liza said, glancing over at Lemm's father. "Because I know that my sister's husband is a proud man, and there are just some stories that he feels shouldn't be told outside of the family."

"What stories? There isn't much of a family history for your nephew down in his file," the judge said, thumbing through the folder again. "I would welcome anything that you could tell me about his rearing that I don't already know."

"Yes, ma'am," Aunt Liza said.

We all grew silent as we listened to the stories that Aunt Liza had to tell. She talked about the liquor that Lemm's mom put into his baby bottle and about her sitting up with him all night drinking when he was only eight. She talked about the parties that Lemm's mother gave when Lemm's dad was at work, and how Lemm would get into beer-drinking contests with the men. When his mom was low on cash, there were shoplifting trips to the store to rip off any kind of alcohol that they could sneak into their clothing and her handbag and evenings when they went from bar to bar trying to find a doorman that his mother could sweet-talk into letting Lemm in.

"Your Honor, my sister was happy when Lemm's father tossed her out. She told me that all it meant was that she could finally drink without him being on her back about it all the time. When I called her and told her about the accident that Lemm had, and that the twins were gone, she was so drunk that she couldn't even write down the funeral details. We buried those babies without their mother," she said, sniffling. "She was the only one out of the entire family who wasn't there."

"Nor is she here today," the judge said. "Where is she?"

"She's in the hospital down in Florida, where I live at," Lemm's aunt said. "She came down to stay with me a little while ago. She told me that she wanted to start her life over, so I got her a job at the hotel where I work. She told me that she was through drinking. I didn't discover that it wasn't true until she ended up in the hospital with her liver nearly gone. She's in an intensive care unit. She wanted to be here, but she couldn't, so she asked me to come in her place." She turned and looked at Lemm. "Your mother is sorry. She wants you to know that she loved you from the very moment that you took her breast, and that she would have done right by you if she had ever been sure what right was. She wants you to know that she is the one responsible for how you turned out. She's the one that led you to the wrong door years ago, opened it, and pushed you in. I'm sorry, Lemm. Our mother passed alcoholism down to us like other mothers pass down their favorite recipes." Aunt Liza focused on the judge again. "Lemm is a boozer because my sister was a boozer. He had no more control over it than he had control over the balloon-shaped birthmark on the back of one of his knees or his first name, Lemm. His mother wanted to give him love, but she ended up giving him wine instead.

"I've been off the sauce for nearly six years, so I know that even the most lost of souls can find their way back. There's nothing anybody can do for my sister, but I think that it's still a whole lot that you can do for Lemm. He's a great kid. When he goes to school, he does very well. Don't punish him for what my sister did. Reward him for the things that he was able to do for himself despite what she did. That's all I came here to say. I don't have nothing else to add."

"Thank you, ma'am," the judge said. "Lemm, I can definitely see how your aunt could be related to you. She has the same gift for speech. Do you agree with her?" she asked, raising her eyebrows at Lemm. "Lemm, do you agree with what your aunt has to say? Do you think that your mother is totally responsible for how you turned out?"

"No, ma'am," Lemm said. "I have to take the blame for a lot of what I did myself."

"That's a good answer, Lemm. I'm glad that you and I are still in agreement that you need to do just that. Ms. Turley, did you say that the boy's mother is in critical condition?" she asked.

"Yes, ma'am, her liver is failing her. She's not doing too well at all."

"Thank you, ma'am. You may have a seat," the judge said.

Lemm's aunt took a seat next to Lemm's father.

"Lemm, I'm impressed with your honesty," the judge said, closing Lemm's folder. "A great deal of this is your fault—and you know it. But I can't just disregard the information that your aunt has shared with the court about your upbringing. How a child is reared does affect who and what he will become in life. I know that as a judge and as a mother. Based on that knowledge, and on your willingness to accept responsibility for your actions, I'm going to give you what I think is a fair and appropriate punishment. I'm going to give you the exact amount of time in a juvenile detention center that I gave the two young ladies, but I'm going to add a bit to it," the judge said. "I'm going to add to your sentence a period of no less than ninety days in an alcohol and counseling rehabilitation center for juveniles. This period will begin immediately after your return from Florida to see your mother. Regardless of what happened many years ago, she is very ill and you should go see her before things get any worse. One more thing—I saw in your file that at one time you were in therapy for your problems and that it didn't work out. Just let me tell you that this time it will work out, Mr. Turley. You'll either get cleaned up and straightened out, or the next time you appear in court you'll be looking at a prison term."

She sighed, and her voice took on a very motherly tone. "Mr. Turley, I'm cutting you perhaps more slack than I've ever cut a juvenile in my court with your history," she said. "Don't make me sorry that I let my guard down."

"I won't. I'm ready to get straightened up," Lemm said.

"I pray that you will," the judge told him. She beckoned to Lemm's lawyer. "Will you please join me in chambers, Mr. Munoz, so that we can work out the details of your client's sentence. This court is dismissed."

Except for Lemm getting to go free, the judge's sentence was the best one that he could have gotten, and when the guard led him back down the aisle, you could see relief walking beside him. He smiled at me. "I'll see ya when I get out, Miss Shayla," he said.

"Just 'Shayla,' no 'Miss,'" I said, grinning. "I'll see ya later too."

I got up from my seat to leave as well, but I was cut off by Lemm's aunt Liza. "You're Shayla, aren't you?" she asked, sticking out her hand.

"Yes, ma'am," I said, sticking out my hand too. She grasped it and shook it as hard as she could.

"Thank you, child," she said with a face crawling with happiness, then followed Lemm's father out of the side courtroom door. The thank-you was something that I was really hoping wouldn't happen, and to be honest, I had been trying to get out of the courtroom before it did. I knew that it wouldn't set well with Grandma Augustine. She wouldn't be happy about it at all. I tried my best to make it out of the bench before she got hold of me, but she was quicker than a lizard's tongue when she wanted to be. She caught me by the elbow and made me sit down before I could even step a foot into the courtroom aisle. I folded my arms across my chest. I knew what was coming and why.

I hadn't told Grandma Augustine and Mama about Lemm getting arrested until Grandma saw the incident on TV the night that they took Lemm to the station. It came on just as Mama was getting home from work, and the two of them gave me a really good workover before Mama had even changed out of her grocery stocker's uniform. They both yelled at me for old and new mistakes, but when they got through hollering, Mama had something unexpected to say.

Mama said that she had suspected all along that something was up with Lemm, something that even his charm couldn't hide. She said that she had been pretty sure that he was drinking, but that he was really good at concealing it from grown folks. "He always remembered to drink the stuff that didn't smell, and he covered up the rest with superstrong mints, but I still knew," she told me. "I knew that boy was drinking way more than soft drinks."

When Grandma heard what Mama said, she nearly lost her religion. She shook her cane at Mama and insisted that Mama explain her actions to her, and for just a moment it was Mama's time to be the fly in the hot soup.

"Why didn't you say something, Vera?" Grandma yelled. "Why didn't you tell that girl to leave that boy alone? Why didn't you stop her from getting into all that mess?"

"Mu'dear, I can't hide my kids in a box," Mama calmly told her, slipping her tired feet out of her leather work loafers. "I can't lock 'em up in a cage and keep the rest of the world out. I tried that last year with Tia, and things just went from bad to worse. Nothing is good that way. It doesn't work."

"Well, what does work?" Grandma snapped.

"I don't know. I didn't know when I told Tia that she couldn't see Doo-witty, and I still don't have a clue," Mama said. "Look, Mu'dear, there was a lot going on with Shayla this summer, all that stuff with Kambia and Anderson's new little girl. It was a long time before I actually figured out what that boy was doing. In fact, I didn't really know for sure until I heard that he got kicked out of school. It was only then that I was certain something was really up."

"You knew he got kicked out of school?" I asked.

"Yes. I went to see Kambia's counselor about it. I figured that I would tell her what I had heard and ask her for some advice, but she already knew what was going on. She told me that as far as she could tell, Lemm was just lying around in his bedroom getting drunk. She said that his daddy was aware of the problem and he was doing the best that he could with the situation. 'I don't think that Shayla is in any danger from Lemm,' she told me. 'To be honest with you, she's a positive influence on him, and right now he needs that more than anything. She's a levelheaded girl. I doubt that Lemm can get her involved in anything that she doesn't want to be involved in.'"

"Well, he did. He all but got this child put in jail," Grandma said, jabbing me in the shoulder.

"I know, and I take responsibility for that, as I do every bad decision that I make," Mama said. "But Mu'dear, I only heard that the boy had been kicked out of school for drinking. I didn't know that he had gotten mixed up with the law. I know that I should have gone to his daddy myself, but I didn't. I just figured that the man already had enough groceries to put away. I wasn't gonna throw any more in his sack. I know how it feels to be overwhelmed as a parent.

Besides, I had a professional woman telling me that my child was gonna be okay. I messed up. I'll admit that, but it ain't the first time, and heaven knows it won't be the last."

Mama walked up and stood in front of me. I thought about staring down at the floor, but I had a feeling that she would jerk my head back up so hard it would yank clean off of my shoulders. "Shayla," she said. "You are my youngest. I love you and I trust you, but you got no more times to get involved with a mess like this. You got that? I can't watch you from sunrise to sunset, and I wouldn't even if I could. You're a smart girl; quit acting like you don't know it."

"Yes, ma'am," I answered softly.

"Good. Now, I don't have any more to say about any of this," she said, heading for her room. "I'm done with it."

"Vera, is that all you got to say?" Grandma asked, bewildered.

"Mu'dear, I'm the one who asked the child to be friends with that boy in the first place. Now I've told her how I intend for her to conduct herself," Mama said. "There's no more to say, but you can do whatever you want to do. If you ain't got nothing better to do, you can wear your voice out hollering at her." And Grandma did.

Grandma kept yelling at me because she said that I had majorly disappointed her. She said that I had betrayed her trust by not telling her I knew it was Lemm drinking out of that bottle that day at Diamond's. She told me that I should have let her in on the truth before things went too far. "I thought you were getting close to womanhood," she said to me. "But your actions let me know that you are still nothing but a little have-to-be-watched-all-the-time girl. You knew that I liked Lemm a lot, but you also knew that he was like a brown moth sitting on a brown tree trunk. I couldn't spot him for what he was. Maybe it was because I'm an old woman, or maybe it was because I was just seeing in him what I wanted to see.

Anyway, it don't really make no difference. When you sit down to dinner with a chameleon, you become a chameleon. It changes you, too. You start wearing a different face for every occasion. I'm not proud of you for that, Shayla," she said. "I'm an elderly woman. I expect you to point out to me the things that I'm getting too broke down to see."

"I'm sorry, Grandma," I said, but it didn't help. No matter what I or anyone else said to her, Grandma was still mad at me for not giving her the 411 on Lemm. She had come with me to court only because Mama had to work and couldn't come, but she had let me have it all the way on the bus ride over. I just assumed that now that she knew I had called one of Lemm's relatives without telling her, she was going to let me have it again.

I crossed my legs and counted the curvy lines of grain in the wooden bench ahead of me.

"It's hot outside, ain't it today?" she said, shifting uncomfortably in her seat. "The bus pole burned my hand when I touched it."

"Mine, too."

She tapped her walking cane on the floor a few times and cleared her throat. "I was wrong," she said. "Did you call that boy's aunt?"

"No, ma'am, I called what I thought was his mom, and I guess she got the message. Lemm gave me his mother's number to keep for him."

"And you called her?"

"Yes, ma'am," I answered. "I'm sorry. I just thought that it was the right thing to do."

"Why?" she asked. "You knew all that stuff his mother was supposed to have done to him."

I looked at her and shrugged my shoulders. "I don't know. I

called her because he wanted to call her himself, but he couldn't."

"What if she had showed up drunk? Do you think that he would have felt better if that had happened? What could she have done for him then? What can she do for him now? Do you know what it means when your liver's failing?"

"No, ma'am, not really," I said. "I guess it means that you might die."

"And you think that he feels better now that he knows that? Is that why you asked his aunt to come here anyway, knowing that she was gonna bring some really bad news with her?"

"I didn't talk to her," I said. "I only spoke to an answering machine. I just didn't want him to go to jail for a long, long time. I just wanted people to know that everything wasn't his fault. He didn't mean to hurt his sisters, and he didn't mean to get involved with what Breed did. I just didn't want him to be blamed for everything."

"You like that boy, don't you?"

"He's my friend."

"That's not what I meant," she said. "I meant the way that Tia likes Doo-witty."

"I don't know. I don't think so. He confuses me some, though, when he touches my hand and stuff, but he's just a friend. He makes me feel good like Kambia does, but in a very different way. Anyway, he likes hanging around with me."

"I see. You think that's why he gave that number to you? I think that's why he gave it to you," she said.

"What do you mean by that?"

"Just let me say this. When I was a little girl, my daddy used to take me walking with him through the woods all the time. We would go on what folks today call nature walks. On some sunny afternoon we would go out and try to see what kinds of God's creatures we could spot. My father was much better at it than I was. We would come upon a cluster of trees or bushes, and he would say, 'Look at that, sugar plum. Can't you see that squirrel or that beaver? Didn't you see that coon or that armadillo? Look over yonder, there's a baby deer. Did you see him trotting around in them bushes?' Sometimes I did, but a lot of the time I didn't. I would tell him that he was making it up, and he would take me by the hand and sure enough we would spot either the animal or its tracks. See, he knew where and how to look, and I didn't."

"I don't get it, Grandma," I said.

"I do now," she told me. She patted me on the knee. "I see it in you."

"See what?"

"Shayla, baby, you got a great spirit in you that I never seen before in any child your age."

"Aw, Grandma, is this gonna be some Bible talk?"

"No, this ain't about the Bible, this is about you. There's something in you that ain't in Tia or your mama or even me. I didn't see it before, but Kambia did and so did Lemm. It's that something that drew them to you like an insect to a porch light. Shayla, I never met a child that tries to bury her feelings more than you do, but you feel more deeply than any child I've ever met. I was wrong for getting mad at you for being a true friend to Lemm. I don't think that you could have been anything else. When I told you about that dream you been having, I told you that you had to decide what kind of woman you would be, but honey, that's already been decided for you. You're gonna be that kind of woman that people always know they can go to for help. That's a good thing. It's more important than being beautiful or being popular or all of those things that gals your age worry about. You don't have to worry about finding a way to get all them ladies out of the tree. When it's time for them to come down, they'll come down all by themselves." She opened her straw handbag and pulled out a small tape recorder. "I want you to listen to this," she said, handing it to me. "I'm gonna go down to the ladies' room and fix my hair. I can feel some of my bobby pins slipping. You come on down there and get me when you finished."

"Aw, what is this, Grandma?" I asked, holding up the recorder. "Is this one of those Christian lesson tapes you like to listen to? I don't wanna listen to something like this. I thought we were cool."

"You just listen to it anyway, and don't give me no back talk," she said. "Now, let me out before my bobby pins fall clean to the floor."

I stood up so that Grandma could go past me. I turned the recorder over a few times, frowned at it, and pushed the blue button on the side.

"Hi, Shayla," Kambia's voice burst out. "I hope you miss me as much as I miss you. I was going to record you a letter about how cute my room is and tell you how kind everybody is to me, but this is the letter that my doctor told me that I had to send to you, so here it is."

I turned the volume up. "I was born in a place called Hope Blossom, right outside of Kansas. My real name is Ababuo. Shayla, it's the name that was on the back of the photo of me that I gave you before I left, only you thought that 'my' was part of it. It is pronounced 'ah-bah-BOO-oh.' My sister, Katrina, told me that it is an African name and that it means 'a child that keeps coming back.' She told me that my mom named me that because she lost a baby right before I was born. I barely remember my mom and dad. They both went to heaven in a fire when I was four. My sister, Katrina, and me were in the fire too, but some of the neighbors pulled us out. I didn't get hurt at all, but Katrina got an ugly burn on her neck. She didn't feel good about it at all, so she always wore some kind of scarf. But Shayla, I thought that she was still really pretty, and I loved her a lot because she always made me laugh. She used to tell me all kinds of jokes.

"Katrina tried to take care of me after my parents died, but she was only eighteen and worked at a hardware store. She worked all the time, but she still never made much money. She could never get the rent paid on time, but our landlady was really sweet. She let her pay whatever she could for almost three years before she finally told her that she had to pay all of the rent on time each month or we were going to have to find some place else to live. My sister didn't want that, so she started spending time after work with some of the guys at her job. They would give her some money and she would go into her room with them. I didn't know what they were doing, but it always sounded like they were hurting her, and it made me really sad. I told her that I wanted her to stop letting them in her room, but she said that if she didn't, we were going to end up living outside on the street because we didn't have anybody that would take both of us in. She said that she could probably find a man that would take her, but none of the guys that she knew wanted a little girl, too. I got even sadder when she told me that, and I kept getting sadder and sadder each time one of those guys came by. I wouldn't even go out of the house and play with the other children in our town. I didn't want to be friendly with anybody. I just wanted my sister to stop letting those men do things to her. I cried a lot, and everybody in our town blamed her for it. They all said that it was her fault because she was doing something bad, and that just made me cry more. My sister didn't know what to do to stop me from crying.

"One day some lady who I had never seen before and her husband came by after my sister got off work. They were friendly looking and they were dressed really good, in Sunday-school clothes. My sister talked to them in the kitchen for a long time, while I sat in the living room playing with my yo-yo. Then after a while she called me in and told me that I was going to live with them. She said that they were friends of my mom and dad's and that they were from Atlanta. She told me that they didn't have much money, but that they had more than she did and she wanted me to go live with them. She said that I wasn't happy with her, but she just knew that I would be happy with them. She packed my suitcase and told me that they would be really neat to me.

"They weren't neat to me, Shayla. They were mean, very mean. They made me do all kinds of horrible things with them and their friends, and they took pictures of it too. Sometimes I had to look at the pictures, so I got sad there, too. I just wanted to be somewhere else. I started making up other places that I wanted to be and going to them in my head. They told me to stop it, but I couldn't. I was always somewhere else. They got really angry about it and they hit me, but I still couldn't stop it, so they tried locking me up, but that didn't work either.

"One night they just came home with another girl younger than me. She told me that she was eight, and I had just turned ten. She was really cute, and she had three front teeth missing. She told me that two of them fell out, but she had lost the other one in a fall. She told me that the couple said that she was going to live with them now, and that I was leaving.

"Shayla, I thought they were going to do something bad to me, but they just drove me a long, long way in their car that night and threw me out. That's how I met my old mom. I was walking the street of some town that I didn't even know anything about, except that it was really big, and even though I kept running into people, they all acted like they didn't even notice me. It was winter, and my hands and feet were really cold. I stopped in some eating place to see if I could use the bathroom.

"That's when I ran into my old mom. She was in the bathroom, and she saw me and asked me whose little girl I was. I told her that I didn't belong to anybody, because I hadn't heard from my sister since I left Hope Blossom, and the people I was staying with weren't even my parents. I told her all the things that they did to me, and she told me that she was just passing through town, but that I could go with her and she would keep me safe. 'I'll make sure that nobody does any of that bad stuff to you again,' she told me. She seemed real nice and I trusted her. We went to Texas because she said that she had gotten some big check for an accident and all we had to do was go down there and spend it, but when we got down there, she didn't have any money at all. She just wanted me to do the same thing that the other people wanted me to do.

"It hurt, Shayla. The men hurt me a whole lot. It wasn't as bad as the last place that I was at, because nobody took pictures, but it still hurt. So I imagined that I was in all kinds of places and that I was all kinds of things, but Jasmine didn't care. Everything was okay with her as long as I still let the men hurt me.

"I was glad when I went in the hospital and the men finally had to stop. I still don't remember some things, like names of people, and I don't know why I was going back to my old place. My doctor says that I will figure everything out in time, but he told me that I had to tell you the part of it that I started to remember, because talking about it will only help me get better. He said I have to release my past so that I can get back to my present. I don't know what that means, Shayla. I just want you to know that I miss you, and that you are my best friend and I love you.

"Guess what? My name is officially Kambia Elaine Major. Mrs.

Dreyfus and my social worker went down to the state and begged them to let my parents go ahead and adopt me. I have a real mom and dad now, Shayla, just like you. I'll be coming home soon, and they say that we can all have a big party. I love you, and so do Sophie Bear and Old MacDonald. Bye, Shayla. I'll be home soon!"

I shut off the tape recorder and stuck it in my straw bag. I left the bench and walked out of the courtroom into the hallway, where to my surprise I found Grandma Augustine standing next to a huge potted plant, holding Gift and talking to Tia and Jada. Both Tia and Jada had on V-necked T-shirts and cotton shorts, while poor Gift was all decked out in one of my old baby outfits, a peppermint-striped dress with a matching bonnet. She looked like a candy cane. I walked over and made a funny face at her. She broke into baby giggles.

"Doo-witty and his mama drove them down here to pick us up," Grandma Augustine said, handing Gift back to Jada. "Ain't that nice of them?"

"It is. Where are they?" I asked.

"They went on down to Lane Bryant," Tia said. "Doo-witty's mom said that they were having a sale on slips and she was tired of folks being able to see straight through her dresses."

"I'll bet they tired of seeing straight through them too," I said, not able to help myself. Tia and Grandma laughed.

"Anyway," Jada said, trying to keep a serious face. "We told them that we would just come on in and wait, because we weren't exactly sure when y'all was gonna get out. We was worried that we might have a long time to wait."

"Naw, it's over," I said.

"Good, let's go get something to eat," Tia said. "I didn't eat breakfast. I'm hungry enough for two folks."

Jada and Tia started off down the hall, while Grandma Augustine and I fell into step behind them. As we passed a long row of rectangular windows and the sun poked its bright head in, my thoughts slipped back to what Grandma had said earlier. I realized that she was wrong. It wasn't me who had the great spirit—it was Kambia. Her mother had named her Ababuo. It meant "a child that keeps coming back," and I was elated that it was so very true. I hoped it was true for Lemm as well. I would miss them both when the school term started. I would be all alone. My heart was flooded with sadness just thinking about it.

"Shayla, you're too quiet. What are you fretting about?" Grandma asked. "I thought Kambia's little tape would make you happy. It's a tragic tale, but she's getting better, so there's some good in it."

"There's lots of good in it. It did make me happy. I can't tell you how much. I was just thinking, that's all. I was wondering how I was going to make it through school next term without her—and Lemm."

"How you gonna make it through?" Grandma said. "Is that what you all down-faced about? Look, baby, ain't no sense in worrying about how many miles you gonna walk tomorrow, when you ain't even finished up the trail you started today. Do you get my meaning?"

"I get it," I said. "I get it." I put my arm around Grandma and wiped everything out of my mind but the joy that I felt from listening to Kambia's letter.